BLOOD
DEBTS

BLOOD
DEBTS

TERRY J. BENTON-WALKER

TOR PUBLISHING GROUP

NEW YORK

BLOOD DEBTS

Copyright © 2023 by Terry J. Benton-Walker

A Tor Teen Book
Published by Tom Doherty Associates/Tor Publishing Group
120 Broadway
New York, NY 10271

www.tor-forge.com

Tor® is a registered trademark of Macmillan Publishing Group, LLC.

The Library of Congress Cataloging-in-Publication Data is available upon request.

ISBN 978-1-250-82592-6 (hardcover)
ISBN 978-1-250-82593-3 (ebook)

Our books may be purchased in bulk for promotional, educational, or business use. Please contact your local bookseller or the Macmillan Corporate and Premium Sales Department at 1-800-221-7945, extension 5442, or by email at MacmillanSpecialMarkets@macmillan.com.

First Edition: 2023

Printed in the United States of America

0 9 8 7 6 5 4 3 2 1

*For every child of color
who was denied the justice they deserved.
You always matter.*

AUTHOR'S NOTE

When terrible things happen to us, we must choose how to move forward in the aftermath; but it's not always clear which paths are the "right" ones, because morality is almost always gray. Countless people of color have had and continue to have to find a way to push forward in the wake of blatant and consistent denial of our right to exist in peace and equality. Some folks advise us to "go high" when others "go low," some urge us to fight back by any means, and more than I'm sure would care to admit are satisfied to sit back and wait for someone else to act for them. But who's right?

Several years ago, I found myself in a dark place, stripped of my autonomy and forced to try and find a way to move forward in the face of injustice—both in my personal life and the world at large. Writing *Blood Debts* allowed me to explore my complex feelings about justice and probe the nuances of morality, the effects of intergenerational trauma, and the cycle of violence.

My hope is that this story will leave you with the following questions: How far are you willing to go for justice? And how far is too far?

Happy reading.

Royal regards,
Terry J. Benton-Walker

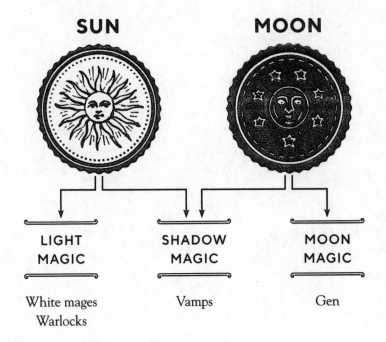

SUN   MOON

LIGHT
MAGIC

SHADOW
MAGIC

MOON
MAGIC

White mages
Warlocks

Vamps

Gen

DUPART–TRUDEAU FAMILY

Rinalt Montaigne
1960–

m

Justin Montaigne
Gen Council Root Doctor
1990–

Vanessa (Glapion) Montaigne
1958–2010

Cristine (Glapion) Dupart
1960–1989

m

Baptiste Dupart
1960–1989

David Trudeau
1982–2018

m

Marie (Dupart) Trudeau
1983–

Ursula Dupart
1984–

Desiree Dupart
1985–

Jacquelyn Dupart
1987–

Rosalie Dupart
1988–

Cristina "Cris" Trudeau
2003–

Clement "Clem" Trudeau
2003–

SAVANT FAMILY

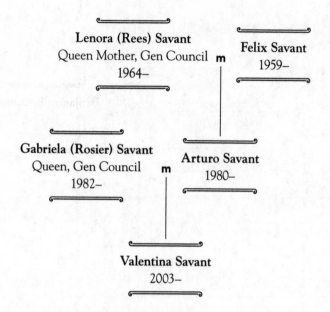

Lenora (Rees) Savant
Queen Mother, Gen Council
1964–

m

Felix Savant
1959–

Gabriela (Rosier) Savant
Queen, Gen Council
1982–

m

Arturo Savant
1980–

Valentina Savant
2003–

DELACORTE-STRAYER FAMILY

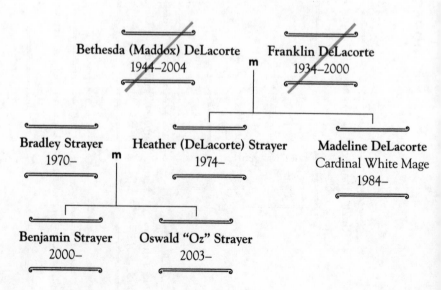

Bethesda (Maddox) DeLacorte
1944–2004

m

Franklin DeLacorte
1934–2000

Bradley Strayer
1970–

m

Heather (DeLacorte) Strayer
1974–

Madeline DeLacorte
Cardinal White Mage
1984–

Benjamin Strayer
2000–

Oswald "Oz" Strayer
2003–

BEAUMONT FAMILY

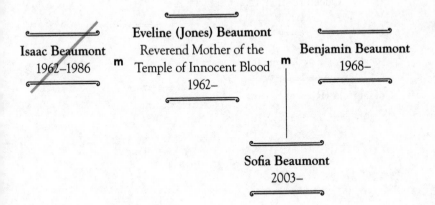

Isaac Beaumont
1962–1986

m

Eveline (Jones) Beaumont
Reverend Mother of the
Temple of Innocent Blood
1962–

m

Benjamin Beaumont
1968–

Sofia Beaumont
2003–

VINCENT FAMILY

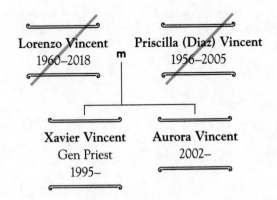

Lorenzo Vincent
1960–2018

m

Priscilla (Diaz) Vincent
1956–2005

Xavier Vincent
Gen Priest
1995–

Aurora Vincent
2002–

PART I

We know the road to freedom has always been stalked by death.

—ANGELA DAVIS

Honoring the Victims of Magical Malpractice: The Dupart Estate Massacre, Thirty Years Later

By Sharita L. Green
Academic Fellow

June marks thirty years since the most brutal magical massacre in recent New Orleans history, and this blood-soaked anniversary has reignited calls for local magical regulation.

A deadly power struggle for influence over the magical and nonmagical communities came to a head on the morning of June 19, 1989, when police discovered the mutilated body of Alexis Lancaster, eldest daughter of then-mayor Gerald Lancaster. Evidence and witness testimony collected at the time suggested that Cristine Dupart, Queen of the Generational Magic Council of New Orleans, murdered Alexis in a brutal magical ritual the previous night. That evening, Gerald Lancaster and others confronted Cristine at her estate, which set off a night of terror culminating in the violent deaths of eleven people, including Gerald and his wife, Deborah Lancaster—whose bodies were all riddled with what authorities believed to be snake bites. No further information was released to the public regarding the origins of those fatal wounds. Baptiste Dupart, Cristine's husband, was bludgeoned to death, but Cristine's body was never recovered, and she was presumed missing and decades later was declared dead. Investigators would close Alexis Lancaster's murder case, the instigation of the massacre and Cristine's disappearance with few satisfactory answers, no remaining leads and no one left to formally charge.

On the anniversary of her family's murder, Elouise Lancaster (now 48), surviving daughter of Gerald and Deborah and sister of Alexis, plans to march on the New Orleans Mayor's Office alongside the Redeemers in a call for magical regulation, a major hot-button issue in this year's mayoral election.

A 2017 study by the Center for Magical Data Analysis & Reporting estimates that "more than 20 percent of New Orleans' population practices or has practiced some form of magic

from p.1

within the past five years." As the U.S. capital for Generational Magic, New Orleans boasts "the most magical supply stores per capita in the southern region of the United States. Baton Rouge, headquarters of the white mages, comes in a distant second." With more than one-fifth of eligible voters involved in the practice of some branch of magic, government regulation has become an increasingly important issue that neither candidate can ignore.

"I stand with the Redeemer movement," says Benjamin Beaumont, Republican candidate and front-runner. "Anyone who claims to support gun regulation but not magical regulation is a blatant hypocrite. We owe it to the legacy of the Lancaster family to do the right thing and implement legislation that will bring perpetrators of magical malpractice to swift justice."

Democratic hopeful Michael Prince has an outlook very different from that of his conservative opponent. "Magic is rooted in the history of this city, whether people want to acknowledge it or not," Prince says. "Magical regulation is far more complex a matter than I think anyone has taken the proper time or respect to consider. In the present judicial system, magic users of color would be more likely to be penalized and receive harsher sentences than their white counterparts. Ben Beaumont and his conservative colleagues have communicated no plans to address that issue. But I vow to do proper due diligence to define a solution that benefits our entire society, not just a single, select group."

ONE

CLEMENT

Everyone I love either dies or deserts me, and not even magic can do a gotdamned thing about it.

Magic also can't get rid of the strikingly beautiful boy lying next to me, who turned me *all* the way off late last night with his "hot take" that magic is a tool created by white people to enslave and distract Black folks. For weeks, I nearly went broke and developed a caffeine addiction, trying to get Nate's attention at the Bean. Now I wish I'd just drunk my lattes and minded my business.

Nate rolls over and grins at me. "Good morning, my Black king."

"Morning." I give him the smile he's expecting. Maybe it's best he turned out like all the others. Otherwise, I'd just lose him, too.

He props up on one elbow, eyes bright like he's been awake for hours. "Our talk last night sent my mind racing, you know? And then I had this dream—"

"I'm so sorry, Nate, but I have a really important appointment this morning, and I'm already super late. I forgot to tell you last night, and I felt bad waking you early, so, umm . . ."

His face falls, and he sits up. "Oh, okay then. Sorry."

Kicking him out makes me feel like a royal ass, but today's the day we find out if fate's going to take its foot off our family's neck or if I'm going to lose Mama, too. Nate will be okay. I might not.

He slides out of bed and bends over to pick up his shorts. He catches me watching his perfectly peach-shaped butt and grins. "If you, uh, change your mind—"

"Sorry, but no." I get out of bed and pull on a pair of basketball shorts.

He shrugs one shoulder and throws open the curtains. Blazing sunlight bounds through the window, and he throws his arms back dramatically like it revitalizes him.

Mama said the people who first owned our estate loved sunrises, so they built all the bedrooms facing east. I fucking hate sunrises. I also pity people who're afraid of the dark. The magical quiet of night has always been my sanctuary. Besides, my monsters tend to prowl in broad daylight.

"No worries," Nate says. "I don't want to leave you, my king, but absence makes the heart grow fonder," he recites as he clears the space between us, arms out for an embrace.

I flinch out of his reach and laugh as I throw on a shirt. "Do you have any idea who you just quoted?"

Before he can answer, someone knocks hard on my door. I'm glad for the interruption, but not the person behind it. She bangs again.

"Clem!"

I yank the door open and lean against the jamb, crossing my arms over my chest. "And to what do I owe the displeasure of this early-morning intrusion, my good sister?"

Cris peers past me at Nate, who's collecting his things—very slowly—and frowns when I slide into her line of vision. It's barely eight o'clock, and already her dark curls are brushed back into a ponytail and she's dressed in some cutoff jeans and a tank. And she's done her full-on skin-care routine, judging by the way her tawny skin glows in the morning light. My sister, ever the overachiever, even on summer break.

"What do you want?" We both know what today is, and I'm in no mood for her shit this morning. At times, I resent her for being able to hold on to hope when it slips through my fingers.

Hope is for white people and idiots—like you.

I squeeze my eyes closed. I've wondered more than once if the gods cursed me with anxiety, which turned my subconscious into an internal frenemy who loves to remind me I deserve this pain.

"You missed breakfast," Cris says.

I roll my eyes. "Y'all wake up before God."

"You know Mama needs to eat before her doctor's appointment; but I see, as usual, you have other priorities." She cuts her eyes at Nate, who's fallen still behind me.

Before I can rebut, her bedroom door opens and her boyfriend, Oz, saunters into the hallway, grinning at her like some corny white guy from a low-budget romance movie.

I cut my eyes back to her. "You usually shoo him out before you show up at my door to cast stones. You're getting sloppy, sis."

Cris glowers like she wants to cross me. It's the same look she gave her ex-bestie before crossing her in front of the entire school last spring. I narrow my eyes, daring her. But we both know she'd never do it. And I don't care if that's "mean." Nothing I've done compares to how she hurt me. And what's even more fucked up is she's my twin sister, the only person I thought never would.

"Morning, Clem," Oz says, hugging Cris from behind.

"I told you I'd be right back," she says under her breath, which he kisses away.

Watching that redheaded jerk press his lips onto the side of my sister's face makes me want to vomit on them both.

Oz, clinging to Cris's waist, nods at Nate behind me. "Who's this?"

"None of your damn business," I say.

Cris huffs. "Clem, really?"

I turn to Nate. "You ready?"

He shakes his head at Oz and dips between us. "Text you later."

Oz steps from behind Cris and leans one hand on the wall, like we're old friends or some shit. And I wish he'd stop putting his hands all over everything and everyone as if it all belongs to him. His hazel eyes are level with mine and his face has reddened, camouflaging some of the freckles draped across his nose and upper cheeks.

"Listen, my guy," he says, "I really don't understand why you don't like m—"

"I'll be down in a second," I tell Cris before closing the door on whatever fucked-up tête-à-tête her clown of a boyfriend thought we were about to have.

I'm sick of trying to get Cris to wisen up about him. She thinks I hate Oz because he's white, but I actually hate him because he's an opportunistic sleaze who just so happens to be white. Mama told me to always trust my gut with magic and people—and Oz is walking ipecac.

I wait a moment and press my ear to the door, catching the tail end of Cris whisper-shouting something inaudible at him followed by the thumps of their footfalls headed downstairs.

I pull down a large plastic container from the top shelf of my closet and set it on my desk. I remove the lid and get smacked by the powerful and comforting aroma of cinnamon coming from the mixture of luck oil inside, which I made from bayou water, cinnamon, and patchouli. Submerged in the luck oil is a brand-new midnight-blue candle. It's been soaking for thirteen days, in preparation for a conjuring ritual I want to perform for Mama this morning.

Despite my dwindling hope, I still pray to Papa Eshu every day to ask him not to take her away from us. I'm not sure if my prayers have made it outside of this bedroom, much less to the spiritual realm, but I can't give up. I can't lose anyone else.

I'm trying a luck spell because healing spells are too hard. Normally, I'd ask Cris for help, but since she's given up magic for whatever ridiculous reason, I'm on my own. The last (and only) time I tried healing magic was three years ago. I attempted to mend a small bruise on my cheek I'd gotten from running into a door, but instead, I ended up conjuring a black eye and the bubble guts like I'd never experienced before. Cris mixed some healing powders with blessed water for my eye but said I'd have to let the stomach thing pass on its own and prescribed ginger ale and saltines in the interim.

And since I'm not trying to accidentally murder Mama (or give her the shits), I'll stick with what I'm sure I can do, which is this "fast luck" spell. I've never conjured one before, but the instructions seemed easy enough. Make the luck oil, soak a blue candle in it for thirteen days, and on the thirteenth day, carve your intent on the side of the candle with a blessed blade. Light the candle and say a prayer to Mami Karu, the gen goddess of fortune. Maybe if I do all that, she'll bless our family with good news from Mama's test results today.

It's been nearly three weeks since her last appointment. Her doctor had drawn so many vials of her blood, I was worried she was gonna prune. Today we might find out what's making her so sick.

Last weekend, I blessed Dad's old pocketknife—the one with the initials of Dad's dad, who I never got to meet.

The blessing was an easy ritual, only requiring blessed water and a sincere prayer to the ancestors under the light of the Moon. I remember tossing the knife onto the mess on my desk afterward. I sift through the books, papers, and random shit there now, but the knife's gone. I check the drawers, under the bed, the pockets of the clothes strewn across the floor, and everywhere else it could possibly be. But it's nowhere to be found.

I take a deep breath and go down the hall to Mama's bedroom. My heartbeat reverberates all the way to my feet. I can't have lost Dad's knife. Not today.

When I knock on the door, Mama calls softly for me to come inside. She lies in the middle of the four-poster, sunken into the plush bedding that seems as if it's devouring her whole. I wish I could take her hands and pull her out, drag her safely back to who she used to be before she got sick.

Her hair hides beneath a scarf, tied into a knot on the side of her head, and her tired eyes glisten when they fall on me. "Morning, baby."

"Hey, Mama," I mutter, nearly choking on the words. "How are you feeling?"

She pushes herself up and smiles. "As best as can be expected.

Every day I get is a blessing." She reaches for me, and I sit on the bed and lean in so she can plant a kiss on the bridge of my nose.

Her sickness was sudden. One day she was fine, and the next, Death lingered at her bedside. Even now, the thickest shadows in the farthest corners of her room seem to harbor dark omens.

"Did I leave Dad's knife in here when we were reading yesterday?"

That's always been our thing—reading in bed together, her with her romance or thriller, and me with whatever interests me, genre be damned. It's one of the few things that hasn't changed since Dad died and she got sick. I cherish those times with her, though when each comes to a close, I remember that's one less from so few we have left. Making more memories with her is only investing in my inevitable loss.

She frowns and takes a quick glance around the room. "Not that I've seen. I'm sure it's around here somewhere, unless you took it outside of this house, which would mean you and I are going to have a very serious issue—"

"I haven't. I swear." Lying is easier than upsetting Mama right now.

Dad's knife is the last part of him I have left. I do what I need to do to be okay.

She purses her lips and narrows her eyes at me for a moment before her expression softens. "Ask your sister. She's like Kathy Bates in *Misery*, so she probably can tell you its last whereabouts."

We share a small laugh that ends on a sting in the pit of my stomach.

I stand up to go, but Mama grabs my hand.

"Hey," she says gently. "Don't worry about me."

I hate when people say "don't worry," like worry is some trinket I can leave home.

"My heart is already heavy with the burden this has put on you and your sister," she says. "No matter what those test results say today, everything is going to be okay—I promise."

I don't hide my grimace. "Please don't promise things you have no control over."

She doesn't say anything to stop me when I turn to leave or when I close the door gingerly behind me.

I find Cris downstairs in the kitchen, glowering at the brewing coffeepot on the counter like she wants to uppercut it.

"You seen Dad's knife?" I try to steady my voice, but my chest tightens. Dr. Thomas will be here soon. I'm running out of time.

She shakes her head. "Where'd you last have it?"

"My room—where it always is."

She turns back to the coffeepot. "Maybe one of the randos you let sleep over stole it."

"Or how about I ask your skeez of a boyfriend?"

I don't understand why Cris is so judgmental. Not everyone can catch every single curveball life throws like she can. The rest of us are very, very far from perfect.

"I'm not arguing with you today," she says coldly.

"I don't want to fight either. I just need to find Dad's knife. It's important."

She spins around, scowling. "Why, Clem? Why do you need that knife *right* this particular moment when we have other, more important, stuff to worry about?"

"I'm conjuring a luck spell for Mama."

She shakes her head at me. "Why are you still bothering with the gods and magic when you pray to Papa Eshu every day and he still hasn't bothered to answer?"

I try to ignore the dark feeling that rears up inside me. I've often wondered the same.

"Just because magic is meaningless to you all of a sudden doesn't mean I have to feel the same way," I tell her.

She throws her hands up with a flourish that infuriates me like only she knows how to do. "Gods above, don't start that again."

"Why?" I lean on the island counter separating us. "You love pointing out all my shortcomings, so let's talk about yours for a change. Magic was *all* you talked about for *years*. You were the one who first got me into it even when I was criminally bad at it. But you spent day and night teaching me and loved every second.

"Then after Dad died, you acted like even mentioning the word 'magic' was the same as holding you upside down over a vat of acid." I straighten up and steel my stare. She hugs herself but narrows her eyes right back at me. "But you didn't even trust me enough to talk to me—your twin. You have no idea how much that shit hurts."

I've tried to have this conversation with Cris before, but never this direct. My patience for her mess today is as short as the time I have left to conjure my luck spell before Mama's doctor gets here. Cris's hands fall to her sides. "Clem . . ." She stares at her feet and shakes her head. "I can't—"

"Save it. Just call me when Dr. Thomas gets here."

I'm storming past the foyer when the silhouettes of two people behind the frosted glass of the front door stops me. I peer out the window, and my stomach turns over like the engine of an old car.

Oz stands outside, deep in conversation with Dr. Thomas. Shit. I'm out of time.

They both keep glancing back at the door awkwardly, until Dr. Thomas puts a hand on Oz's shoulder and gives it a hard pat and a squeeze—the condescending way white men love to "congratulate" you on a job well done. Oz smiles and jogs lightheartedly from the porch to his car next to Dr. Thomas's white Mercedes in our driveway.

I open the door just as Dr. Thomas reaches for the doorbell. He's a white man with short auburn hair and a sterile, unreadable face I've always found difficult to trust. The pits of his light blue button-up are already drenched thanks to the merciless Louisiana heat that barrels into the considerably cooler foyer. The air ripples behind him, the high humidity creating floating translucent waves.

"Oh!" His pasty face flushes and splits into a grin. "Hello!"

"Morning." I step aside and gesture for him to come in.

"Is your mother ready for me?" He sweeps past me, blue leather medical bag in hand.

I shut the door and round on him. "I didn't know you and Oz were friends."

His brows furrow, and he presses his thin lips together for a silent moment before laughing too loud for something that wasn't a joke. "You mean the Strayer boy? Oswald?"

"Yeah, the one you were just patting on the back on the front porch."

"His mom and aunt are family acquaintances. He's always been a good kid. I was actually just commending him on making the honor society again this year." He gives me that same look all adults give teenagers when they're bullshitting. "And how are your grades? Top of the class, dare I hope?"

"Cris!" I shout over my shoulder, startling him.

"What?" she snarls as she whisks into the foyer, then stops on the spot. "Oh, Dr. Thomas, hey!" She checks her phone and frowns. "Time got away from me, I'm so sorry."

"No problem," he says, flashing a smile that shows too many teeth.

"I'll take you up."

I follow them upstairs, and Cris knocks on Mama's bedroom door and announces Dr. Thomas, who heads inside after Mama's tired voice invites him. The moment he closes the door, a chill rips down my back.

I fucked up. I lost Dad's knife, and now I can't finish conjuring my fast luck spell. If Mama's appointment goes left today, it'll be all my fault.

Cris takes my hands in hers to stop me wringing them. "Hey," she says, just above a whisper. "It's going to be okay. I'm sorry about what I said before. You've been praying nonstop. I'm sure Eshu heard you. Part of being gen is having faith, in your connection to the gods—and in yourself."

I pull my hands away, and she huffs, looking offended. She has some nerve trying to preach to me in the middle of her asinine magic boycott. But it does make me feel a little less like an unmitigated fuckup.

I sigh and lean on the wall outside Mama's room, and Cris does the same beside me.

"What do you think of him?" I whisper. When she looks up, I nod toward Mama's door.

"Dr. Thomas?" She shrugs. "I don't know. He seems nice enough."

The good doctor's willingness to do home visits at a discounted rate never sat well with me. He claimed it was because he was a fan of our family's bourbon, but people only do favors if it somehow benefits them, and I have no idea what he's getting out of this. Not to mention, he doesn't seem to be a very good doctor. He's been treating Mama since she first got sick, and she's only gotten worse.

"Did you know he knew Oz?" I ask.

She frowns. "He's a doctor, Clem. I'm sure he knows a lot of people."

"Well, those two seemed really chummy on the front porch just now."

She heaves an exaggerated sigh. "So what?"

"He said he was congratulating Oz on making honor society, but you and I both know Oz is closer to homelessness than scholarship."

"I'm not debating with you right now about how much you hate my boyfriend," she snaps. "Don't you think we have enough to worry about?" She gestures at Mama's door.

"Are you really going to do this?"

"I said lay off Oz," she warns through her teeth, but then her expression shifts, softening until she's staring blankly at the floor as if stuck in some lovesick memory of that creep.

"Whatever."

A long stretch of silence passes in the cold space between us before my sister finally says something.

"I get that you're scared. I am, too." She slides closer. "We gotta stay strong for Mama. Today could be the day we find out she's going to be okay."

"But what if it's not?" My voice cracks, and I hate myself for it.

"But what if it is? If you constantly think negative, then that's the only energy you'll attract."

I sigh and look into eyes the same as mine, yet so very different. "Then why won't you pray with me?"

She folds her arms across her chest with a huff. "I wish you'd grow up."

"I wish you hadn't."

She grunts under her breath and moves to the other side of the hallway. Transference of frustration is mental guerrilla warfare, but whatever. It's like my twin sister is gradually evolving into a stranger.

Neither of us bothers saying another word, and eventually, after what seems like more than a couple of silent eternities, Dr. Thomas emerges. He deposits a container labeled with Mama's name, which holds several vials of her blood, into his bag.

"How is she today?" The innocent hope in Cris's voice, out there in the open for anyone to strangle to death, makes me cringe.

Dr. Thomas's eyes shift between Cris and me and Mama's door. "Can we chat in private?"

I exchange a nervous glance with Cris. The urge to grab her hand hits me, but instead, I shove mine into my pockets. *Please*, I plead with Eshu in my head. *Not yet. Not like this.*

Cris leads us to the sitting room off the foyer. The drapes have been drawn, so sunlight warms the quiet space, but my body shivers, though not from cold. I lower myself onto the couch, and Cris sits beside me. I don't realize I'm chewing my lip and fidgeting until she squeezes my hand. I fall still.

"As you know, we ran some tests after my last visit," Dr. Thomas says. "I'm sorry to report the results weren't good. Your mother's kidneys, liver, and lungs all show preliminary signs of failure. Her heart is working overtime as a result, which is taking an immense toll on her." He pauses to take a breath—Cris and I both hold ours. "I'm afraid your mother is not long for this world. Our goal moving forward should be managing her pain and keeping her comfortable. I do wish I had better news."

My insides turn to ice. This can't be happening.

"Is there nothing more you can do?" asks Cris. "Aren't there other specialists you could refer us to?"

Dr. Thomas shakes his head. "I'm very sorry, you two. We've done all we can. Whatever your mother is suffering from is unprecedented, and there's not much else modern medicine can do."

Cris swallows hard. Her voice is hoarse, strained when she speaks again. "How . . . much time?"

"Couple weeks at best—maybe longer if our luck doesn't run out."

My soul floats away, leaving the empty shell of my body behind.

"Please let me know if there's anything I can do for your family." Steel-faced, Dr. Thomas waits a moment, but when neither of us says anything, he heads for the door. "You two take care now."

He leaves, and the weight of the news sucks all the air from the space.

Cris's breath hitches and then she holds it in until her body quivers. I still feel weightless and slightly faint, as if I'm in a lucid dream. But I'm not. This is a fucking living nightmare.

One more person gone. Pretty soon you'll have no one left.

I clutch my head and grit my teeth so hard I'm afraid they'll crack. *That's not true,* I repeat over and over, but it does nothing to settle my thoughts. The voice doesn't say another word. There's no need. My stomach churns itself into a hurricane of distress, launching me from my seat.

Cris reaches for me, but I flinch away.

"How is everything gonna be okay now?" I ask, tears already blurring my vision. "You and Mama *both* lied to me today."

Her bottom lip quivers and her mouth opens, but nothing comes out. Of course, she has nothing to say. The people who hurt me most never do.

My lungs struggle. A bout of dizziness tilts my world, and I have to sit on the floor before I fall over.

Cris drops beside me and puts a hand on my back. "Did you take your anxiety meds today?"

"Those pills aren't going to change anything."

"No, but they'll help you deal with it better."

Anxiety surges my heart like jumper cables. I feel like it's going to crack my rib cage, and every breath becomes harder to draw. Cris gets up and disappears from the room. I lie back on the carpet and rest my hands on my chest. I close my eyes and count to ten slowly, feeling the measured rise and fall of my chest while attempting to steady my breathing like Mama taught me.

Cris is back before I reach ten. "You okay?" she asks.

I nod and count to eight in my head.

She sits on the floor beside me and waits quietly, my meds in one hand and an open bottle of water in the other.

I make it to ten and sit up with one last deep breath in and out. She hands me two pills, and I swallow them with some water. "Thanks," I say. "If I hadn't lost Dad's knife, I would've been able to cast the spell, and we would've gotten different news today. This is my fault."

She shakes her head. "None of this is your fault." I don't believe her, which I think she picks up on in the quiet moments that pass between us. "Besides, it's not too late. Until you find your knife, maybe you can do an easier spell, like a good luck gris. I know a simple one I can walk you through."

I sit back and raise one eyebrow. "You're going to conj—"

She raises a finger. "No, no. I'm going to coach, and you will do it yourself."

"But—"

"Take it or leave it, Clem."

"Fine," I say.

Cris is extraordinarily adept at annoying the shit out of me, but I'm glad to have her. Maybe she can help me save Mama—or "coach me through it."

She leads me to the kitchen and scribbles a list of items onto a notepad and hands it to me.

"Get everything on that list and bring it upstairs," she says. "I'll be in my room when you finish."

She's gone before I can say a word.

> Items for Cris
> 1. A dollar bill (one of yours, not mine)
> 2. 1-inch cinnamon stick
> 3. Peppermint oil
> 4. A blue sack
> 5. A stick of palo santo
> 6. Crossroads dirt
> 7. Hemp string
> 8. Matches
> 9. This notepad and pen

I have to improvise a bit to get everything on the list.

For starters, I only have a twenty-dollar bill, which I imagine is a fair alternative since twenty dollars is more valuable than one. We're out of peppermint oil, so I borrow a peppermint candy from the dish on the coffee table in the living room. I used all the cinnamon sticks we had for my luck oil, so I replace that with a stick of cinnamon gum. I have no idea where Cris imagined I would find a blue sack in this house, but I end up substituting one of the dozens of purple Crown Royal bags Dad was saving in a drawer of the basement bar for whatever reason. Close enough.

Once I've collected everything, I throw it in a reusable shopping bag and head upstairs. Cris hears me coming and meets me in the hallway.

"You got everything?" she asks.

I nod, and she follows me into my room.

I kick a pile of dirty clothes aside to make space for us on the floor. We sit across from each other, and I dump the contents of the shopping bag between us.

She picks through everything and sighs loudly. "This isn't what I asked for."

"I did the best I could. This stuff won't work?"

She sits back on her heels. "We'll see. Light the palo santo."

I strike the match and hold it to one end of the pale, twisty stick of wood that resembles a gnarled finger. It ignites, and I allow it to burn for a few seconds before blowing out the fire. Orange embers glow on the blackened tip, throwing a spicy, woody scent into the air amid thick, curling tendrils of white smoke. I hand it to Cris, who blows on the end, charging the embers.

She waves the palo santo over the conjuring supplies so heavy swatches of smoke hang in the air between us. "Draw a four-leaf clover on a sheet of paper and fold it up."

My pulse kicks up. I'm not good at drawing.

As if sensing my encroaching anxiety, she says, "It doesn't have to be perfect. Remember, magic is more about intent than skill."

"Right," I mumble as I draw a crude four-leaf clover that ends up looking like it'd been chewed on, but when I show it to Cris, she says it's good enough.

When I've folded the drawing into a neat square of paper, she says, "The four-leaf clover is an ancient and universal magical symbol for luck—and a good one to remember." She hands me the palo santo and rips out another piece of paper from the notebook. She folds it into a cute tiny envelope that she hands to me in exchange for her palo santo stick. "Now pour a little crossroads dirt in the envelope and fold the lid down."

As I'm following her instructions, I'm fighting the overwhelming urge to ask her for the hundredth time why she would turn her back on something she's so damn good at.

"Next, we're going to wash everything in the smoke and place it inside the sack—the talisman, the envelope with the crossroads dirt, the peppermint, the stick of gum, and the twenty," she says.

I pick up each item, swirl it back and forth in the thick smoke from the burning palo santo Cris waves between us, and drop it into the sack.

"Now, add a few breaths before you tie it closed with the hemp string," she says.

I blow gently over the collection of conjuring items sitting at the bottom of the bag, then tie it tightly closed with the small cord of hemp I cut from the roll inside Mama's conjuring cabinet.

"Last part," she says. "Make your intentions clear to the ancestors who wish you goodwill."

I nod and think for a couple of beats. The cloth sack is light in the palm of my hand. It's almost strange to think something seemingly so insignificant could have so much power.

"I'm asking the ancestors who wish us well to bring us good fortune—for Mama's health." I bite my bottom lip and glance at Cris, unsure what else to say.

"That's perfect," she says. "Let's give it to Mama. We should probably all talk anyway."

"Right," I say as I stand with her, clinging to the gris.

It'd be helpful if it got heavier or glowed or hummed with magical energy or something—anything to let me know the spell worked. But gen magic doesn't subscribe to instant gratification. That's why this branch of magic is so hard to master. Some spells can even take months or years to take effect. But I hope this gris works fast. We might not have much time left.

We find Mama's bedroom door open. She's inside, standing in the doorway of her en suite, her black silk nightgown bunched at her hips. Her eyes are bloodshot, and her face has paled, like she's been crying. The sight nearly pulls me to my knees. I know what it means.

But Mama can't give up. Not while I'm still trying.

She sniffs and wipes a fresh stream of tears from both cheeks. "What's this?" She points at the gris in my hand.

I stare down at the sack I'd almost forgotten about. "We, I, uh . . . I made this for you, because, um . . . I-I thought it might help—"

"Baby, that's so sweet of you," she says with a pained smile.

Watching her battle tears makes me feel like I'm sinking to the bottom of a swamp. What have we done to make the gods to punish us like this?

"Mama spends the most time in bed," Cris says. "Hide the gris anywhere around there for maximum effect."

I kneel at the foot of Mama's bed and lift her mattress. I set the gris on the box spring and try my best to spread out the items inside so the mattress will lie as flat as possible. I'm about to drop it back into place when something catches my eye.

Frayed threads hang from a slit about as wide as my hand in the mattress's bottom.

"What's this?" I mutter.

I reach inside and feel around. My fingers brush against something fuzzy and soft. My skin prickles, and I whimper softly, hoping it's not a giant spider. I pull it from the hole and let the mattress thump back in place.

Cris and Mama stand nearby, their grave eyes glued to the small black hex doll with red button eyes and scraggly black yarn for hair gaping up at me. The ugly thing is naked except for the miniature knapsack tied to its waist by a cord of hemp. Pinned to the side of its head is a small diamond earring—the same one Mama tore the house apart looking for on the day of Dad's funeral. Those earrings were the last gift he'd given her before he died.

Mama gasps, breaking the stark quiet of the room. My pulse flies. My breaths come faster. I open the doll's crude suede knapsack and pour its contents onto the bed.

Inside are some pieces of dried root of some sort, a vial of unidentifiable grains, a few other odd trinkets, and lastly, a neatly rolled strip of parchment. I unroll the faded paper to find a talisman drawn in bloodred ink—a scythe carving the moon in half above a coffin.

I'm pondering what these symbols might mean when Cris's earlier words replay in my head. *Magic is more about intent than skill.*

I'm no gen-magic expert, but the intentions of whoever drew these images seem pretty clear to me—and also to Cris, who stands back, nearly in the hallway, her eyes wide, one hand cupped over her mouth.

Mama picks up the hex doll and scrutinizes every inch.

"Is this what I think it is?" I ask her.

She looks at me, holding back the words she doesn't need to say.

Mama's not dying.

Someone's killing her.

TWO

CRISTINA

No matter how hard I try, I can't fucking escape magic. No matter where I hide, it always finds me.

Mama and Clem mutter to each other, eyes roving over the tiny hex doll that seems as if it's sneering at me from across the room.

For months, I slogged through day after day, barely holding back tears and failing mostly. But whenever I stumbled, my guilt shoved me forward so I could continue to care for our ailing mother. It was the least I could do. I suffered quietly, because that's what I deserved for bringing tragedy upon my family. But the gods have granted me a reprieve. This one isn't on me.

I resist the urge to double over and cry out with relief.

However, someone *did* try to murder our mother. I'm still trying to wrap my head around *that*.

Similar to gris, hex dolls are primitive magic. A collection of magical ingredients, relics, or talismans, combined with something personal, like Mama's lost earring, can turn the tides of someone's fortune for worse. And if the conjurer is willing to wait long enough, they can even summon Death.

But who would want to hurt Mama?

She removes her earring and flings the doll into the empty fireplace on the far side of the bedroom at the same time a firm hand on my shoulder makes me jump.

Odessa, our housekeeper, stands behind me. Her silver hair, pinned back and tied in a satin scarf, calls extra attention to the weathered lines along the warm chestnut skin of her face and deep-set eyes of the same color that study me before finding Mama and Clem beside the hearth. She's already dressed in the plain, paper-sack-brown dress she wears while she's working, even though Mama told her long ago she doesn't need to wear a uniform.

"I didn't mean to startle you, child." Her low, earthy voice cleaves through the thick air. "Is everything okay?"

I shake my head and stand aside. She sees the doll in the fireplace, which stares back with menacing, oversized button eyes. Her back stiffens and she wrangles the gasp I watch build in her chest as Mama explains what happened. Odessa practically raised Mama and our aunts after my grandparents died, and she's been like a surrogate grandmother for both me and Clem, especially since Mama fell ill.

She spreads her hands in front of her in disbelief. "How could that be? We turned this entire house upside down after you got sick."

"I don't know," answers Mama.

Odessa pulls me into a hug. I'm not sure how, but she always knows when I need one. For a moment, pressed into the soft warmth of her body, I can breathe again, revitalized by the soothing scents of shea butter on her skin and coconut oil in her hair. She's smelled the same since I was a kid.

"Someone must've planted it after," says Clem. "Someone who had access to our house—and Mama."

I step back from Odessa. "But who? And for what reason?"

Mama's the kind of person who makes a new friend every time she leaves the house. She doesn't have enemies—none I know about. Unlike her mother (and me), she's a good person. She broke our family's murderous cycle . . . then I accidentally restarted it.

I loved magic once—even more than I love Oz. But it wasn't until after the terrible thing we'd done together that I realized magic and I aren't good for each other.

Clem throws me a pointed stare. "I can think of someone."

I glower back. He better not dare drag Oz into this mess. I'm sick of him always coming down on Oz as if he doesn't have a plethora of his own faults.

I go over to the fireplace—despite the coldness that ripples through me more aggressively the closer I draw—and snap a picture of the doll. I've seen what magic can do, how far it can reach, how unrelenting it can be—it terrifies me.

I kneel to examine the small firefly branded onto the flap of the doll's pouch. It's the logo of Firefly Supplies, the chain of magical-supply stores owned by our cousin, Justin Montaigne.

"What are you doing?" asks Clem.

"Just thinking we could show this picture to your associates and see if any of them recognize it," I suggest, standing back up. "Do you remember the names and numbers of all the boys you invite into our home, or nah?"

He growls, but Mama interrupts his return fire.

"Cut it out." She wags her finger between the two of us, her other hand on her hip. Maybe I'm imagining things, but she already seems a little stronger—or maybe she's just fed up with our fighting. "I don't know what's going on between you two, but now is *not* the time to lay it all out."

Neither Clem nor I say another word, though he looks like he could spit bullets. I'm sure I share the same expression.

Just once, I wish he'd use his twin powers for good. Even worse, he's made me ponder more than I care to admit if maybe he's right about Oz, especially after the argument Oz and I had before he left this morning, which left me reeling emotionally and physically. But I won't give Clem the satisfaction of being able to say "I told you so."

Oz might be obsessed with generational magic, but there's no way he did this. After Mama first got sick, he suggested someone might've crossed her. I thought he was just being typical annoying Oz, which was why I told him if he didn't leave my family out of his fixation, we were done. The irony of him being right after all this time makes me feel like I've swallowed a swarm of stink bugs.

"I don't need anyone playing detective, so never mind all that." Mama adds a few fresh logs to the fireplace from the pile beside the hearth and douses the doll in lighter fluid. She strikes a match and tosses it in. Spectacular green and yellow flames devour the doll.

I brace for the inevitable sulfurous smell of evil—which doesn't come. Instead, the burning doll reeks of sweetness. Honeysuckle and chocolate. It hisses and pops as if the magic contained inside refuses to die peacefully. Suffocating heat barrels into the room, and I'm sweating already.

"We should start cleansing," says Odessa. "I'll fetch the supplies."

"You're right," Mama says. "And thank you."

Odessa nods and heads downstairs to the conjuring cabinet, where Mama keeps all her magical supplies. The same one Oz and I argued about this morning outside of Clem's room, because I refused, for what must've been the fiftieth time, to unlock it so he could ogle the contents. After he left, I wanted to set that damn cabinet on fire and dump it in the nearest swamp.

"We need protection," Clem says. "I'm thinking Wise John's Moon."

I shake my head. "That spell won't work."

"How would you know?" He screws up his face at me. "You're done conjuring, remember?"

Wise John's Moon is one of the most powerful protection spells, but it has stipulations, as do many gen spells. Mistaking the fine print already burned me once, and I'll die before that happens again.

That's how I know.

"Whatever, Clem," I say. "You know there's no way our aunts are coming back for that."

For Wise John's Moon to work, the closest living family of the central person in the protection circle must be present, which includes all siblings and children. But Mama's four estranged sisters won't come back here. The Dupart Five is finished. Mama said they'd gotten that nickname when they were kids, because they stuck so close to one another. I guess anyone would after surviving such a traumatic childhood together. Our home used to be alive with family—dinners around the gigantic dining table, Christmases spent eating Dad's bread pudding and opening presents in front of the fire, summers filled with backyard barbecues and seafood boils that lasted well after the fireflies came out. But their relationships with one another soured, and one by one, my aunts all left.

"None of them have even bothered to come visit since Dad's funeral," I add, which makes Mama hang her head, because she knows I'm right. I'd be surprised if she had all their current phone numbers saved.

Clem sighs and his shoulders slump. "We gotta try, Cris."

Mama sits on the edge of her bed and runs her hand across her forehead. "Your brother's right. Start with Ursula. I'm sure you'll find her at the Wishing Well. She can help wrangle the others. Odessa will help me with an Eshu cleanse while you two are out— make sure whatever this mess someone put on me is completely gone."

"Okay," I say.

Mama hugs Clem and gestures for me to join.

I wrap my arms around them both and close my eyes. Before a little while ago, my every waking hour felt like I was suffocating, close to my final breath, but now someone's clapped an oxygen mask onto my face and cranked it up to the max. Maybe the universe is giving me an opportunity to make up for how I've broken us. Helping Clem with the luck gris was a good start.

Damn. He was right—I *am* really good at this. But that's how magic sucks you in—right before it drives your life off the rails.

Mama plants a kiss on the tops of both our heads. "Okay, get going before it gets too late. We need to conjure Wise John's Moon as soon as we can. Call me if you have any trouble, and no fighting amongst each other."

"Yes, ma'am," Clem and I echo each other.

We exchange the stifling heat of Mama's room for the cool air of the hallway, and Clem frowns at his ratty basketball shorts and ashy knees. "Do I have time to change?"

I nod. "I need a mental minute anyway."

"Yeah." He tugs on his shirt and chews his lip. "This is just . . . almost too much."

"Are you sure you're good?"

He shrugs. "She almost died, Cris."

I hug my brother again. For a moment, we both forget how angry we were with each other not long ago. I feel his sharp intake of breath. I hold him tighter, and he exhales. I miss him.

I'd give up everything I own of value to go back to before, when our relationship wasn't cracked, when Dad was alive, and no one was trying to murder Mama.

"Mama's going to be okay now," I tell him, but worry still lingers on his face.

"Will she, though? Someone hurt her on purpose. If we hadn't—"

I shake my head. "Don't say that. Your gris saved her. Now it's my turn."

He stares at me curiously. "What do you mean?"

"I'm going to find out who did this—and I'm going to make them pay."

"How?"

I cross my arms. "Haven't gotten that far yet."

He rolls his eyes. "Well, the call might be coming from inside the house—"

"I already told you, it's not Oz—so drop it."

He throws up his hands and heads for his room. "Whatever," he says over his shoulder. "I'll be downstairs in a few."

Oz is far from perfect, but he loves me. The warm feeling that diffuses through me whenever I think about him confirms as much. He was a lighthouse when I almost drowned in my sea of guilt when I . . . when Dad died. I could mourn with Oz in a way I couldn't with my family, because I couldn't look them in their faces knowing I'm the one who blew the massive crater in our lives.

Oz wouldn't save me to sacrifice Mama. My gut tells me this goes way deeper.

I turn with an exasperated huff and crash into Odessa, who's balancing an armful of white peace candles. A few thump to the floor, but she manages to hold on to the rest.

"Sorry! Let me help you."

She purses her lips. "Your brother has good reason to be worried about that white boy, Cristina."

"Odessa, please—"

"Listen to me, child, and after I've said my piece, I promise I'll leave you to it."

I sigh, hoping this browbeating won't last too long. "Okay."

"It's been thirty long years since that lynch mob pulled your grandaddy from his porch"—she jerks her head in the direction of the front door—"and murdered him and your grandmother on their own front lawn. I had to hold your six-year-old mother down to keep her from running outside after them. And now every night, all these years later, when I lie in bed, I can still hear her screams, feel the phantom kicks of her little feet."

I stoop to collect all the spilled candles while she continues fussing quietly.

"And we weren't the only ones who suffered. New Orleans never recovered from the loss of your grandmother. Cristine wasn't just our Queen, she was the keystone of our magical community. And those pale devils took her away from us. They destroyed your future before you were even born."

Odessa doesn't know, but I'm agonizingly aware of the miserable state of my future. Back when we were friends, my ex-bestie, Valentina Savant, never passed on an opportunity to remind me of my place in the world thanks to my family's dark history. She casts blanket-thick shadows over anyone in her vicinity, smothering them so she can shine. Soon her lies took root in my mind, and I became complacent existing in the background of her story. Life is easy for everyone who accepts Valentina's mother as Queen of the Gen Council and Valentina as Queen of New Orleans International Magnet High. And while Valentina may be vile, she and her mom are both Afro-Latinas—so at the very least, power remained within the Black magical community after our family lost control thirty years ago.

"Not all white people are bad," I tell Odessa as I scoop the last candle from the floor.

"That is true," she says, "but I'm old now, Cristina. I do not have the strength left in me to hold down another screaming child."

"I honestly don't think we're in danger of Oz leading a homicidal mob to the house anytime soon," I say, returning the candles to her stack, one by one. "But it's not like Grandma was innocent either. Didn't she murder the mayor's daughter?"

Odessa's eyes go dark, and her arms tremble so hard she nearly drops the candles again. "That is a lie woven in the depths of the never-realm that you should never repeat. Have more respect for your grandmother—your namesake."

I suppose it's fitting I'm named after her since we've both disgraced this family. I wonder if Odessa would still love me, too, if she found out I'm the reason Dad died.

"If she was innocent, why'd no one try to clear her name?"

"Because five kids, no older than six, were orphaned in the most horrific way imaginable. Your great-aunt and great-uncle wanted the family to heal and focus on protecting the children. So, we did. Some of us still are. Now run along and be safe. I have to tend to your mother."

I place the last candle on her stack, and she whisks away.

In my room, I sit cross-legged on my bed and stare out the window, past the decorative iron lattice of my Juliet balcony at the majestic willows outside and the squirrels that play along branches that cut the sunlight into spears that pierce the ground below. The serenity outside makes me want to check out of life, enjoy these few moments of peace.

But before I can breathe a sigh of relief, my phone vibrates. It's Oz.

"Hey," I say.

"Hey, uh, you busy?"

"I have a few minutes," I admit, though reluctantly.

"I wanted to apologize about this morning. I shouldn't have pressed you about your mom's conjuring cabinet."

"I appreciate the apology," I say, "but I really don't understand your obsession with gen magic."

"Well, I'm sorry I think generational magic is cool," he retorts. "You know, you used to at one time, too."

I don't know what causes the fiery surge of adrenaline inside me. Maybe it's the complete upheaval of my world in only a matter of hours. Or maybe I'm just sick of dealing with Oz's bullshit after spending the majority of this hellish morning defending him.

"I'm glad you think Black folks' culture is cool. People actually died for the magic you've chosen as your latest hobby. Gen gods literally created our magic to survive colonization and slavery and lynching—all because of white people. Pokémon are cool. Generational magic is my heritage, Oz."

"Whoa, whoa, *whoa*"—I imagine him pumping his hands, as if I'm somehow overreacting, which ratchets up my rage—"I don't know where all this is coming from. I was calling to apologize, remember?"

"Your aunt is Cardinal of the white mages," I remind him. "You have top-level access to light magic, yet you insist on invading our space. I don't get it."

It isn't so much the fact that Oz is white that bothers me about him practicing gen magic as it is his obsession, which has transformed into a staggering sense of entitlement. There are two whole *other* branches of magic he can dabble in—light magic and shadow magic; and hell, I don't care if he creates his own as long as I don't have to deal with his bullshit anymore.

"*Your* space?" He scoffs. "No branch of magic belongs to any one group of people. The gods decide who to bless with magic, so if gen magic wasn't meant for white people, how can I conjure?"

"I don't know, Oz, maybe the same way white people steal our hairstyles and clothing and music and continents and anything else that isn't bolted down."

"Ha!" The shrill sound rings my ears.

I want to hang up on him, but I also want to curse him out. This call's already conjured a prickle of nausea in the pit of my stomach that grows the madder he makes me.

"Can't you see how reverse racist that is?" he continues—to my dismay. "I mean, come *on*. Am I not supposed to love you because you're Black? Don't you love me?"

"You've got to be fucking kid—" A sudden and sharp twinge of pain zips through my stomach, making me wince. I'm not sure what it's from, but I press on. "You're not even capable of grasping how everything coming out of your mouth right now is disrespectful as fuck."

"Look, I'm sorry," he says hastily. "I don't want to fight. I only wanted to apologize and check on you and your mom."

"She's fine."

"Huh?"

"I said, 'She's *fine*.'" After that infuriating debate, there's no way in the infinite realms of the magical universe I'm going to tell him what happened this morning.

"But how'd the doctor's visit go?" he presses. "Are you all okay?"

Oz usually asks about Mama, but today's line of questioning seems . . . odd. Anxiety drops Clem's earlier question onto the front porch of my mind.

My gut gives a sinking jerk.

"Clem told me you ran into Dr. Thomas this morning before you left," I say.

"Yeah, I did."

"What did you two talk about?"

He sighs hard. "Nothing. I just said good morning and went about my business."

"Dr. Thomas said he was congratulating you on making honor

society. I'm sure you can imagine my confusion, considering you had to enroll in summer school for geometry."

"I lied, okay," he snaps. "He's friends with my mom and aunt and always harassing me about school, so I just tell him what he wants to hear. Mom's head is so far up Benji's ass she's forgotten she left the rest of us on the outside. All that matters to her is making sure he gets into fucking Cambridge. She realized how much of a screwup I was a long time ago and went all-in on my brother. So, yeah, I tell little white lies to Dr. Thomas, because he's one of the extremely few people who make me feel good about myself. Why are you drilling me about this?"

Oz has always been jealous of his older brother. He'd been forced to live in Benji's shadow just as I'd existed in Valentina's. Maybe that's what drew him and me to each other. I'm familiar with feeling not quite good enough, stumbling through reality each day as best you can and gathering what scraps of affection you can from wherever you can and still feeling undeserving of that little bit.

But I have to know, or else my conscience won't let me be; and neither will Clem or Odessa, who are both intent on being Oz's judge and jury for whatever reason.

"Oz . . ." My voice trails, and I go over the words carefully in my head before I release them. "I'm going to ask you something, and I expect you to tell me the truth. No matter what."

"Umm . . . okay," he says tentatively.

"Remember when Mama first got sick, and you said someone might've crossed her?"

"Yes. . . . Where are you going with this?"

The words taste metallic on my tongue, yet I allow them to linger before spitting them out. It hurts me to ask this as much as I'm sure it'll hurt him to hear it, but I have to know.

"Did you have anything to do with Mama getting sick?"

"What exactly are you asking me, Cris?"

My stomach feels like it's being squeezed in a stone fist. I winch and push through because I have to know. "Did you cross her?"

The line goes silent so long, I check to make sure he hasn't hung up.

When he finally responds, hurt hangs on his words. "I can't believe you'd ask me that. You really think I'd cross your mom?"

"Don't play mind games with me! Just tell the truth."

"Cris, I love you more than anything in this stupid world—even magic. I might fuck up a lot, but I know how much family means to you, and I'd never do anything to hurt you. I thought at least I showed you that much, but I guess not."

He doesn't sound angry like I'd expect. Instead, disappointment radiates from him, which makes me feel even more shitty—a feat I thought impossible. Maybe I'm destined to ruin every single relationship I hold dear until my guilt drags my hopelessly damned soul to the never-realm. For all the pain I've caused, it's probably what I deserve.

"I'm sorry," I say. "Today's just been really hard for me." My stomach settles again, and I sigh with quiet relief.

"I understand," he says, though unconvincingly. "I'll give you some space."

"I love—"

He hangs up.

I toss the phone onto my bed and fall back onto my pillows.

Sometimes I wonder if loving Oz is worth the trouble. Before we'd first gotten together, my gut said to run far, far away from him, but the thrill of him pushed me further into his world. I can't explain it. It was like magic. But falling for him was the snowball that started the avalanche that buried my life, and now I have no idea how, or even if, I can dig myself out.

Valentina and Oz had dated for the better part of a year. But the meaner Valentina became, especially to me, the more Oz drifted into my orbit. At first, I begged him to leave me alone, not wanting to incur Valentina's wrath. Burying the feelings that had started to grow for him was a small price to pay to avoid social homicide. He honored my wish for a while; but one day, in a fit of extreme idiocy, he broke up with Valentina and admitted he'd fallen for me. Of course, she didn't believe I had no part in it and assumed we'd been sneaking around behind her back. She turned on me, soured our mutual friend, Sofia Beaumont, against me, and alienated me from most of the school.

I took it all in stride until a year ago, when she accosted me in front of a slew of other people on the last day of school. Before we fell out, she'd asked me to help her craft a spell she'd planned to use against her competition for cheer captain the following year. She had no idea I'd cracked the spell—until I used it on her. I thought a quarter of our peers witnessing her braids falling out and her shrieking to her car would've cooled her crusade to end me for a while.

But that same night, Valentina violated me in a way I'd never thought even *she* could. Once, when we were fifteen, Valentina, Sofia Beaumont, and I were over at Valentina's house, and Valentina had nicked some Irish whiskey from her parents' stash. We all got trashed and talked about all kinds of silly random stuff, like most normal people do in private with their best friends. Except I had no idea Valentina was recording the whole thing. I vomited when I saw Valentina's Instagram post the night after I crossed her. She'd shared a snippet of the video from that night, where I ran down the list of all the boys in our grade I'd ever fantasized about losing my virginity to. The caption read, "For anyone wondering why this loser and I aren't friends anymore. Just embarrassing."

There was no denying it—Valentina and I would *never* be cool again. What she did was a code-red friendship violation, and there's no coming back from that. It almost broke me, especially when I started getting unwanted attention from boys at school, but I wouldn't give that bitch the satisfaction.

Last year, only a few weeks into summer, I finally figured out how to hit her back—harder.

I found the Scales of Justice spell toward the back of my great-grandmother's old handwritten spell book. It was supposed to even the odds, make Valentina suffer the way she'd made me suffer. But instead, the spell took Dad, and my family and I have been suffering ever since.

I hate myself for what I did that night. If there was a spell that would allow me to trade fates with Dad, I'd conjure it without a second thought—but none exists. I've searched relentlessly. But magic is too cruel to let me unmake my mistake. Instead, it holds my eyes open, forcing me to watch the pained smiles on Mama's and Clem's faces nearly a year later as they're still trying to recoup what small fragments of happiness they can in our new fucked-up normal, courtesy of me.

And there's not a single person I can confide in who won't hate every fiber of my soul after I tell them what I did. I'm not even sure I can trust the gen gods anymore.

I haven't told Oz either. Only because I don't care to have magic as an active third party in our relationship; but of course, he would love that.

The Scales of Justice threw my life out of balance by taking Dad. But maybe I can even out my universe by protecting Mama. I need a plan first, though. I peel myself off the bed and check the drawers of my bedside table where I usually keep my journal, but it's not there. I search every nook and cranny of my desk, scour every shelf in my room, tear apart my closet, destroy my bathroom, and rifle through all my bags, but still come up empty-handed—which is perplexing.

I never lose stuff. My room is my only sanctuary. The peace and order of this space has been the only part of my life I've had control over lately.

I recall Clem's search for Dad's knife this morning, which I chalked up to him being his usual absentminded self. But now I'm wondering if someone *did* steal his knife—and my journal. Although I'm not sure why anyone would swipe my journal. There's nothing interesting—to anyone other than me—written inside. I only use it to capture random thoughts, like a recipe, poem, grocery list, anything.

My journal was the last thing Dad gave me before he died. It's bound in a sapphire cover with "fly boldly in the pursuit of your dreams" embossed on the front. Dad always pushed me and Clem to be the best versions of ourselves and still cheered even when we weren't. He made me feel like royalty.

My journal and Clem's knife hold significant sentimental value to both of us, as do Mama's diamond earrings for her.

I find my brother downstairs all groomed and moisturized, waiting by the garage door. He's wearing a graphic tee with a skull on the front and some cutoff jean shorts, and in classic Clem fashion, he has a book tucked under one arm for today's adventure.

"Have you seen my journal?" I ask him.

His eyes widen and he clutches his invisible pearls. "You mean the Muva of Responsibility actually *lost* something? We are truly in our last days."

"This is serious, Clem. Don't be a jerk."

"I didn't take your journal, and before you even go there, neither did any of my dates. We'd all rather tongue-kiss a hundred vaginas than read your boring diary—although a few might enjoy that."

"Real classy." I push him out of the way and head into the garage.

I hope to the gods I'm wrong, but if my suspicions are correct, our mission to get everyone home and conjure this protection spell just became even more dire.

Someone could be after me and Clem, too.

THREE

VALENTINA SAVANT

Valentina Savant would never forgive her mother if she destroyed Granny's legacy, which was why Valentina had to make sure that didn't happen. And was also why she currently followed close behind her mom and Granny, who were on their way to a meeting of the Generational Magic Council, which they ruled.

The ancient tunnels cutting through the underbelly of St. John's Cathedral were as musty as they were dank and riddled with cobwebs and dust, but Valentina luxuriated in every moment down there. Gen Queens had trekked through those same passages for hundreds of years to lead their council and the people of the generational-magic community. Valentina would become a part of that history, too. Only problem was, she wished she could catapult her mother from the throne that should be hers.

Gabriela Savant was barely a mother and no one's queen. She'd been a mouse before ascending the throne, and even with all that power, she'd only become a mouse with a crown. And what a fucking waste. But Valentina had next, and she would not squander her rule. She would be a viper in a crown.

That was—as long as her mother didn't fumble Valentina's future.

Mom leaned over and whispered angrily to Granny, "Bringing Val was a mistake."

Valentina's stomach sank. She hoped Granny would keep their secret—that Valentina's presence tonight had been entirely her own idea, that she'd pleaded with her granny for weeks to let her come. Valentina preferred her mother not know she'd already set her sights on the throne.

Granny stopped so abruptly Valentina nearly smashed into the back of her. The long skirt of Mom's dress rustled in the harsh quiet of the tunnel as she spun around. The gold embroidering on the hunter-green fabric shone in the glow of a nearby wall sconce whose torchlight fought desperately against the gangs of darkness on either side of them.

Granny tucked the cerulean snakeskin clutch that matched her dress under one arm and frowned up at Mom. "I'm confused." She cocked her head to one side, standing tall in the low light, despite being a full head shorter. She had a gentle, oval face and skin the color of taupe with bold copper undertones and was small in stature; but her five-foot-four frame was packed to the brim with the tenacity of a giant—one who wasn't afraid to stomp on anyone who stood in her way.

Mom heaved a deep, exasperated breath. "Not sure why you're confused, Lenora. It's a simple concept. Valentina is *my* child, not yours, which means I'm the one who decides what's appropriate for her. More importantly, we don't need any more trouble with the Council, especially after the chaos you caused last year."

Mom's words cinched Valentina's stomach like a Victorian murder corset. She had no idea what "chaos" her granny had been involved in last year, but what she *did* know was her mother's rule was not absolute, nor was her claim to the throne. The Council could vote to remove a queen's sovereignty (or any member) at any time and for any number of reasons.

Valentina could not—and would not—allow that to happen before her reign.

"That part, Gabriela." Granny wagged a finger at Mom's chest. "Are you Queen of the Generational Magic Council, or do you just enjoy dressing up in expensive gowns"—she angled her eyes up to Mom's silken crown, tied into knots with the points sticking up— "and poorly tied tignons?"

A few of the knots *did* look like they'd been tied in a rush, like whoever'd done it didn't care very much. And generally, Mom didn't. She never had, which was why she didn't deserve to be Queen.

And that worried the fuck out of Valentina.

A couple of years ago, Granny stepped aside and appointed herself Queen Mother. Valentina never understood why Granny would willingly abdicate her power. All Granny would tell her was it was time to move the Council forward.

Granny said she'd always dreamed of passing her throne to her son, but Daddy had refused. Arturo Savant only cared about two things (spoiler alert—neither was his wife or kid): his shitty real estate business and laying up at the House of Vans. He had less than zero interest in affairs of the magical kind.

Valentina had asked Daddy why he rejected Granny's offer, and he'd accused Granny of not being a "good person" (whatever the fuck that meant) and only wanting to control people, especially her family. He was so full of shit. He'd abandoned Granny just like he'd done her and Mom.

Desperate, Granny had reluctantly turned to Mom. Valentina wondered whether, if Mom had refused, too, Granny would have asked *her* to take the throne. It wasn't implausible. It was what Valentina deserved.

And she was the heiress Granny deserved.

Mom gathered her skirt again with a huff. "Next time, how about *ask* me before you invite my daughter to a meeting of *my* council."

Valentina wondered how long it would take Mom to grow tired of clinging to the hope that her loyalty would make Granny respect her and Daddy love her again. How many nights would Mom cry herself to sleep after a long day of ignoring Daddy's antics? Until that happened, Valentina had bought noise-canceling headphones to drown out her mother's pitiful sobs that seeped through the bedroom wall every night.

She had to be better than her parents. It wasn't like she had to try very hard.

Granny tutted under her breath. "No matter how high you may fly, little bird, don't forget the sky you enjoy so much, the one that makes you feel free and boundless, belongs to *me*. My granddaughter is sixteen, which means it's time we start preparing her to continue *my* legacy, whether you like it or not."

Rage simmered on Mom's fawn-colored cheeks, even in the soft candlelight, but a warm rush of pride radiated in Valentina's. She didn't just want to fly. She wanted to rule the sky, too. And make her granny proud.

Lenora Savant was an incredible grandmother and as good as a mother to Valentina—light-years better, actually. Before Valentina completely stopped giving a damn, she'd nearly driven herself mad trying to understand why her parents claimed they loved her but acted like they wanted nothing to do with her. She'd nearly fainted with excitement on her birthday when Daddy pulled into the driveway behind the wheel of her new car. Until Mom had said, "Now we don't have to chauffer you around anymore," and Daddy had groaned in agreement. Valentina never fought with her mom over a dress she wanted in the mall like her best friend, Sofia Beaumont, did every school year, because Valentina's mom didn't do those things with her. Instead, Valentina's parents gave her a credit card so she could buy whatever she needed, and they wouldn't have to bother. Once she bought an Xbox, expecting to get chewed out when the monthly statement came, but her parents just paid the bill and said nothing.

She couldn't even recall the last time her family ate dinner together. Daddy was rarely home in the evenings, and Mom spent the majority of her time depressed and aloof, so no one cooked. It was Granny who'd saved Valentina from a lifetime sentence of McDonald's by teaching her how to cook.

"I'm not fighting with you tonight," Mom announced. "Save your energy for when Eveline flips her shit once she sees we brought Valentina." She turned and marched off.

Valentina tensed. She loathed being talked about like she wasn't standing right there. Like her feelings didn't matter. Like she didn't matter.

Granny didn't respond. Instead, she lifted her arm, and Valentina instinctively tucked underneath with a grin. Granny had kept their secret. Valentina felt restored, like she only ever did when she was with her granny. She wondered if that's how kids with normal, healthy parents felt all the time.

Her grandmother held her close, and they walked like that the rest of the way to the chamber. Only once did Mom glance back; and she frowned when she saw them embracing. But Valentina didn't give a shit. In fact, she enjoyed watching Mom stew in the same anger and frustration she'd felt while having to deal with her and Daddy's bullshit on the daily.

Valentina often wondered why the gods cursed her with two parents who were absolutely nothing like her. But every day she thanked those same gods for her granny. Without her, Valentina would've never understood where she belonged. And that was right fucking here.

Their dramatic trek through the underground passage ended at a tall set of wooden doors, which Mom pushed open to lead them inside the Council Chamber. Granny took her arm from around Valentina and straightened the pleated front of her dress. The clicks of everyone's heels against the stone floor echoed in the cavernous space that reminded Valentina of a medieval throne room. Humongous columns stood back from either side of her path, stone-faced sentinels propping up the ceiling on their shoulders.

Valentina wore a royal blue sheath dress that perfectly complemented her granny's. She was happy she'd chosen her crystal-studded pumps and the sapphire earrings Granny had given her for her birthday, because she sparkled like a true heiress beneath the dozens of candelabra hanging from the ceiling by thick, gold-flecked ropes. She'd also swept her braids up into an intricate knotted bun, which would suffice until she had her own crown. But she still looked damn good strutting down the main aisle of heavily polished bloodred stone. It was a shame no one else saw since they were the first to arrive.

Valentina wondered how many times she'd have to witness the Council Chamber in person before it stopped enthralling her. This was only her second time, so the answer definitely wasn't *two*.

Granny had first brought her this past spring. She'd even let Valentina sit on the opulent throne—crafted from wood, emeralds, and stone—perched atop the highest tier of the stone dais. Valentina had traced her fingers along the grooves and indentations of the images of snakelike willow branches with gorgeous, jeweled leaves that coiled around moons carved from smooth stone that was cool to the touch. A tingling sensation had sparked to life at the tips of her fingers and jolted up her arm to the top of her head and back down to settle in her chest. She didn't know what it was, but she'd liked it and wanted to hold on to that feeling forever. After they'd left, Valentina finally convinced Granny it was time to start preparing her to ascend the throne.

She'd been born ready. She'd grabbed the extraordinary future before her by the throat and would never let go.

Valentina chased away the anger that'd begun to nibble at the edges of her mind as she watched Mom ascend the dais and lower herself onto the throne. But Granny, having already settled into her smaller throne to Mom's right, motioned for Valentina to come stand beside her.

"If you start attending meetings regularly, I suppose we'll have to get a throne for you, too." Granny smiled, and Valentina beamed—inside and out.

Her own throne.

"I'd love that," she told Granny, who gave her hand a loving squeeze.

Valentina made the mistake of looking up and meeting Mom's intense frown. She swallowed her happiness and shrank behind her granny, who was squinting at a notification on her phone and hadn't noticed Mom's glower of disapproval.

Valentina found herself wishing more and more that she could move in with her granny and leave her parents behind. But they'd never let her, because the only thing Gabriela and Arturo Savant agreed on was that they didn't want her, nor did they want Granny to have her. Valentina was trapped, like an abandoned animal in a cage.

A loud creak filled the room as the chamber doors opened.

Justin Montaigne, Council Root Doctor, entered. His flighty eyes quickly scanned the room and widened when he saw Valentina. Justin was a somewhat attractive, skinny, brown-skinned guy almost twice her age. Valentina took him for the kind of rat that would eat a hole in the bottom of your ship and be the first to bail.

A woman with radiant sepia skin walked in behind him and pulled the doors shut. The Reverend Mother of the Temple of Innocent Blood. Eveline Beaumont. She wore a skirt the color of rich, red wine and a matching jacket over a black lace blouse. When Eveline turned around, her eyes narrowed at Valentina in the shadow of the ridiculously wide-brimmed hat she wore. Granny's childhood friend was as sharp as the golden tip of the long black feather speared through the satin band of her hat. Knowing Eveline, that was probably a deadly weapon masquerading as a harmless feather—much like her.

Eveline gripped her gold leather handbag, veered around Justin, and stormed up to the dais. "Why is Valentina here?" she asked as she stepped onto the first tier, where her throne sat beside two others. "Meetings are for members only."

Eveline's ferocity frightened Valentina, but she admired it far more than her mother's timidity.

Granny cleared her throat, drawing the whole of Eveline's ire. "Our heiress has every right to attend meetings."

Valentina side-eyed her mother, who still sat silent. At least *someone* was standing up for her.

Eveline pursed her lips, and her eyes bored into Granny's for a moment before she glanced at her gold watch. "An heiress is not an official member of the Council, and be that as it may, I would appreciate, at a minimum, a heads-up before anyone outside this council is invited to a meeting. Sensitive matters discussed here are not for public ears." She glanced at Valentina and offered a pity smile. "Surely, you understand, sweetheart. We have policies for a reason."

Valentina hated the way Eveline sometimes talked down to her, like she was nothing more than an inept child, fumbling along the edge of understanding.

"The Council voted to add my seat as Queen Mother," suggested Granny, preventing Valentina from responding to Eveline, "so perhaps it's time we add one for the heiress."

"We've voted to remove seats as well," Eveline said, frowning down at her watch again.

Granny scooted to the edge of her seat, ready to lay into the Reverend Mother, but Valentina touched Granny's shoulder and shook her head when Granny looked back.

"I can just wait outside," Valentina whispered.

She'd always admired Granny's brash fearlessness but realized that was also Granny's fatal flaw. A little fear could be healthy at times, and, most importantly, could keep you in power—and alive.

If it meant that much to everyone, Valentina would retreat to the car. But the day would soon come when no one could kick her out of *her* Council Chamber—and she'd remember Eveline's slight.

"Have either of you heard from Xavier?" asked Eveline, thankfully changing the subject. "Ben's town hall debate is tomorrow morning, and I'd rather be home helping him prep as opposed to wasting time on the disrespectful and the tardy."

Valentina bit down on her lips to keep from shouting that she'd leave already if everyone promised to shut the fuck up about her crashing the meeting.

The doors creaked open again, and relief dawned on Eveline's face. "Finally," she said, turning on her heel to face the doors. "Let that be the last time you make a dollar wait on a dime—".

Eveline startled once she realized the person who'd just walked into the chamber was definitely not the Council's Gen Priest, Xavier Vincent.

A woman with skin like pearls and hair the color of the setting Sun approached, leaving the doors swung wide in her wake. She was dressed entirely in black—from her strappy heels to the fitted gown that halted at the knee in the front but kissed the floor in the back and even the tiny dramatic veil that draped across one eye, secured by a black hair clip. She looked like she was going to a famous fashion designer's funeral.

Granny tensed in her seat, and Eveline let a low growl slip out. Both Mom and Justin sat in a silent stupor. No one seemed happy to see the head of the white mages: Madeline DeLacorte.

White mages practiced light magic, fueled by the Sun, which granted them power over nature, the elements, and healing. Gen, like Valentina and her family, conjured their magic from the Moon—with a little help from concoctions, talismans, symbols, and spells. Their abilities were rooted in community for purposes such as protection, healing, fortune, divination—even revenge. But the Sun and Moon were simply conduits for magic, all of which originated in the spiritual realm. And the minor gods, extraordinary magic folk who were granted godhood in the afterlife, ruled over their respective branches of magic.

Madeline DeLacorte strode down the center aisle like a rich supermodel. Light reflected off what must have been thousands of obsidian stones that covered every inch of the dress that hugged her frame. She'd pinned her hair up in a deliberately messy bun with stray loose curls that outlined and softened her austere face. She had buried the generous splattering of freckles on both cheeks beneath a layer of makeup. Those freckles ran in Madeline's family. Valentina knew, because once upon a time, she'd dated Madeline's nephew, Oz Strayer. But that story had ended badly, and she was perfectly fine pretending it'd never been written.

"Now, now, Eveline . . ." Madeline's singsong voice and sweet

Southern accent reminded Valentina of pecan pie sweetened with arsenic. And Valentina fucking hated pecan pie. Madeline posed at the foot of the dais, one hand on her hip, showing off the luxurious jeweled cuff glittering on her wrist. "I'd wager you're worth a bit more than a dollar."

Valentina hoped no one could hear the pounding of her heart in the stifling quiet following Madeline's smartassery. Her gut told her an impromptu visit by the Cardinal of the white mages (sometimes referred to as white witches) was anything but innocent.

Granny flicked a hand at Madeline. "You have quite the nerve to come here dressed like that."

"What?" asked Madeline, feigning shock. "You don't like my outfit?"

Valentina looked closer and noticed that even the woman's veil was decorated with tiny gemstones. And her heart lurched at once. The same ensemble worn by anyone else would've been deemed high fashion, but for a white witch, it was lethal as fuck.

Light magic was strongest in daylight, so white mages often stored magical energy in crystals, jewels, or stones they called "enchantments," which they used for powerful casting at night, when their abilities were at their weakest. And Madeline DeLacorte's entire fit was dripping in enough enchantments to blow St. John's Cathedral and everything within the surrounding city block straight to the spiritual realm.

The Cardinal Mage's dress was no mere statement, it was a declaration of war.

"You may not remember," said Eveline, "but I wasn't a fan of your mother's theatrics either." She lifted her hand above her head and snapped three times.

The sound rang out, and a few short moments later, a door behind the dais Valentina hadn't noticed before creaked open.

She turned as a half-dozen people dressed in brown robes and frightening grimaces poured into the chamber from an anteroom. Council Security. Valentina knew about them, too (courtesy of her granny); and there were plenty more where those six came from. They split into two groups and lined up on either side of the dais, angled toward the Cardinal Mage, awaiting their command.

A few days ago, Valentina had collected a few crumbs from some of Granny's conversations about Council business and figured out that the white mages had beef with the Gen Council for some reason. But she'd had no idea things had gotten *this* bad.

Valentina gathered her nerves and stole a glance at her mother, planted on the throne and looking as nervous and useless as Justin, who stood beside his own seat like a child, waiting on someone to give him permission to be present. So much power and potential— all wasted on them.

Madeline gave the Council's foot soldiers a quick, unimpressed once-over and raised an impertinent eyebrow at Eveline.

"I'll also remind you this entire building is blessed by Baba Eshu himself," Eveline added in a voice Valentina guessed was to make it clear to Madeline that she was over her shit.

The tiny black stones stuck to the webbing of Madeline's veil glowed bright orange like dozens of miniature Suns, stealing the breath straight from Valentina's throat. Molten orange light oozed, nearly weightless, into the air and collected over Madeline's hand, held palm-up in front of her. But as quick as it was born, the light dimmed and fizzled into nothing. Madeline snapped her empty hand closed, and her smug grin melted into a grimace.

Valentina's nerves settled. She'd wanted to come to the Council meeting, but not to die.

"This cathedral is the only place in the entirety of this realm where no one can conjure, cast, or vamp," said Eveline, "no matter how special they might *think* they are." She tutted under her breath, sat on her throne, and crossed her legs.

Valentina felt herself standing a little taller beside Granny. Despite how she felt about her mother and Justin, every person on that dais was a member of the same magical community, and Madeline's intrusion was disrespectful as hell.

"Your oversized panic room isn't as safe as you think it is," Madeline said, her honey eyes offering the smile her lips did not. "But that's not what I've come to discuss."

"I already told you—while I might have to deal with your bullshit as you have a seat on the Magical and Spiritual Coalition, my husband is not beholden to you," replied Eveline. "Whether you like it or not, Benjamin is running for mayor of New Orleans, and gods willing, he's going to win."

Valentina remembered her best friend, Sofia Beaumont, revealing that her father was running for mayor before he'd officially announced. It'd always seemed odd that Eveline would support her husband going into politics as a conservative, especially considering they were fighting so hard for magical regulation right now. Anti-magic protests had also started cropping up again, which only worsened the overarching situation—not to mention pissing off Valentina, who hated watching willfully obtuse people debate her humanity in real time. But aside from all that, Eveline had everything to lose by putting Ben in office—and the irony of him being a white man was not lost on Valentina. She couldn't figure out what just yet, but there was something important she was missing in all this.

"Well then," said Madeline with a grimace, "this meeting will be shorter than I anticipated, but let me make myself quite clear: Before I allow a group of limp white dicks to lord over my gods-given right to wield magic, I will decimate the entirety of New Orleans and every one of your cute little thrones along with it."

Granny stepped up beside Eveline. "Now, see here—"

"Aht-aht!" interrupted Madeline. "You of all people should be on my side, Lenora. Gods know you don't need the government plundering through all the sordid details of your magical mischief—like how you came to power, for instance."

What was Madeline going on about? Granny had told Valentina she'd inherited the throne eons ago in 1989 after the last Queen, Cris's grandmother, murdered the mayor's daughter and disappeared.

Three whole decades later and Cris was still as messy as her ancestor. They all deserved what they got.

But Granny had no shortage of secrets—and that was what worried Valentina. It was only a matter of time before one lunged from
the darkness to choke the life out of her future.

"What do you want, Madeline?" Gabriela asked, startling Valentina, who'd forgotten her mother was even in the room.

"We mages have been upfront and unwavering in our stance regarding magic and politics," Madeline said. "I have mostly left you
all to your own devices"—she shot Lenora a mean side-eye—"but
I will not stand idle while you flag down the foxes and give them
a guided tour of the henhouse. This is my last time making this
request. Convince Ben to end his political endeavors."

"Or what?"

Valentina choked on her first anxious breath after the words
bounded from her lips. She didn't know what had made her speak
up, but she couldn't sit quiet like her mother and Justin. She had to
know—what were Eveline's plans going to cost the Council? What
would they cost *her*?

But Madeline didn't answer. She only raised an eyebrow at Valentina and turned to leave.

Valentina clenched her fists in the shadow of her granny's
throne.

Each rhythmic tap of the white witch's heels was like an acidic
prick to Valentina's gut. Madeline disappeared through the chamber doors, leaving them open. A chill wind blustered in from the
tunnels and bit at the bare skin of Valentina's arms. She hugged
herself.

Her future was fucked.

But she was going to do everything in her power to salvage it.

FOUR

CRISTINA

The late-afternoon air in the French Quarter smells like cigar smoke mingled with the scent of seafood frying in a nearby restaurant. Trolley bells ring a couple of streets over, the sound bounding across rooftops of the pastel-colored historic buildings. It feels sinister that the world outside continues trundling along while my universe was almost upended for a second time just this morning.

Despite the short walk from the car, my shirt sticks to my back with sweat by the time Clem and I arrive at Ursula's bar. It's an expansive corner unit with a plain brick front and an umbrella-lined balcony upstairs. A hand-painted sign that reads THE WISH-ING WELL hangs above the front door.

I try not to look, but my eyes stray to the place that birthed most of my guilt and pain. This July—next month—will be the first anniversary of Dad's death, which happened across the street at Spirits of Nola.

He'd gone out with friends and ended up at that bar. He usually frequented the Wishing Well, so it was always strange they chose to go somewhere else that night. The bartender said that after several drinks Dad had slumped in his seat, let out a muffled groan for help, and fallen to the floor. The coroner said Dad had died of a heart attack. But I'm the only one who knows what really happened.

The Scales of Justice took him.

When I first read the disclaimer scrawled across the top of the page in my great-grandma Angeline's elaborate script, I was certain it didn't apply to me. I went to bed confident I'd finally deflected some of Valentina's malice back at her. But instead, I woke the next morning to discover that Dad had died overnight while Valentina continued to thrive. There was only one explanation.

I must've scoured that entire spell a thousand times, searching for a loophole. Something. Anything that would remit me of the responsibility for Dad's death—and the guilt.

I will never forget those cryptic words that I wished to the gods I'd heeded.

> *Warning to the conjurer who seeks to tip the Scales of Justice:*
> *The fortunes of two individuals may ever be weighed.*
> *If the conjurer feels an enemy has unfairly shifted their fortune,*
>   *this spell will tip the Scales back into the conjurer's favor, thus*
>   *restoring justice.*
> *But woe be to the conjurer who misjudges their fortune, for this spell*
>   *will irrevocably tip the Scales <u>out</u> of their favor.*

I still have no idea how I could've possibly misjudged. I'd only made her braids fall out, but Valentina had humiliated me on a *massive* level. She threw my life into disarray simply because she could. I only wanted to even the score, but instead, I made things dreadfully worse.

I should've known better than to blindly trust that spell book. The last line of the Scales of Justice instructed me to dip a blank slip of parchment into a bath of moonbeams to know when the spell was finally complete. I lifted mine from a shallow pool of azure moonlight I'd made in a small glass bowl with a pair of my eyebrow tweezers, and glowing words emerged on it as if I were developing a photo in a darkroom. I'm not sure what I expected to appear on that little piece of paper, but it damn sure wasn't a riddle.

> *When the dead rise to claim the living,*
> *When fire dances over water,*
> *Silence will devour your enemy's pleas,*
> *and then you will know justice has been served.*

Dad is with the ancestors now; the dead have claimed the living.

The night of his funeral, we released lanterns over the Mississippi, and my heart sank into the depths when I saw the flickering light from our small troop of lanterns reflected on the dark river. After I said my final goodbye to Dad, I burned that piece of paper. The riddle had been solved.

Afterward, my secret smothered my voice. And me, too.

Dad was the heart of our family. The Scales of Justice ripped him from our lives. And now I must carry this burden for the rest of mine. I lost my power. And my love. I lost magic.

I'm not sure what Great-Grandma Angeline's deal was, but that's not my idea of justice.

Clem slips his hand into mine, tugging me from my reverie. We both stare at the gaudy neon SPIRITS OF NOLA sign, which seems to glow brighter, mocking us. I want to rip it down and fling it onto the highway.

"I fucking hate that place," he grumbles.

I drop my gaze. "Me, too."

"I miss Dad so much."

"I know," I tell him.

After Dad died, Clem shut down completely. He stopped reading, barely ate, hardly showered. Smiles became strangers. Every evening after sunset, I'd draw the curtains in his bedroom and open the windows for him, and he'd spend the night in bed gazing at the dark sky and sobbing.

If Clem ever found out I was the person who stole the Moon from his sky, he'd hate me. And I couldn't live with that. I can barely live with myself now.

"Hopefully, Aunt Ursula is in a cooperative mood today," I say.

Clem sighs and throws me a *yeah, right* look.

I peer through the front window of the Wishing Well, which just opened. The inside gives off a rustic executive vibe, reminding me of a miniature country club. It's a wide-open space with a long wooden bar toward the far end, set before a towering display of bottles on the wall. To one side is a small stage and empty floor space in front, which I assume is an impromptu dance floor when this place really gets jumping at night. Leather couches and wing chairs take up the rest of the floor space, the small cocktail tables between them already set with flickering electric tea lights in tiny blue globes that look like minute full Moons.

Aunt Ursula's perched behind the bar, deep in conversation with the guy standing on the other side. The place is empty otherwise. Mama says Ursula got her supermodel height from our granddad. The white dress Ursula wears complements her rich mahogany skin and hugs the curves she loves bragging about. She pushes her shoulder-length merlot-tinted hair behind her ears and puts her hands on her hips. She's a force, inside and out. I can see why Clem's so drawn to her. I love my aunt, but we were never as close as she and Clem were. I'd had my fill of "forceful" people bowling me over for a lifetime.

A man on the receiving end of her terrifying glare is slender and blond, dressed in distressed jeans and a wrinkled khaki blazer. He's one of those entitled white guys who thinks stubble and mousse makes him way more attractive than he has any right to be. He points a finger at her, his neck and ears burning electric red with what I bet is fury.

I'm not sure what we're interrupting, but I'm not fancying a taste of Ursula's wrath this afternoon. "Maybe we should wait."

Clem cuts his eyes at me and goes inside.

Ursula and the guy are so engrossed in their argument that neither of them notices us come in.

She leans on the bar and narrows her eyes. "I'm not gonna keep telling you to stop fucking with me, Jack. Keep threatening me and you'll have bigger problems than trying to keep that raggedy bar of yours open." She flicks her hand toward Spirits of Nola across the street without looking up.

Clem and I press into the shadows near one of the booths and watch quietly, still unnoticed.

This Jack guy must own the bar—the place where Dad died. But something else about Jack seems familiar . . . I can't recall exactly what, though.

He clenches his fists so hard they shake. "You're the one who's fucking with *me*! We announce live music one night a week, and then you suddenly decide to have music three goddamned nights? And not only that, but you somehow manage to book the Seers? I've been trying to get them for *months*. I even offered double their standard booking fee, but they couldn't even bother to return my calls." He shakes his head like he wants to spit on Ursula—which would be the worst decision he'd ever make in his life.

Ursula snickers. "Live music at a bar isn't revolutionary. Also, Black folks are no longer obligated to tap-dance for y'all, no matter how much money you throw at us. Face it, Jack, your business is mediocre because you are."

He lowers his voice. "You think I don't know how you've been doing it?" He takes a step closer, but Ursula doesn't flinch. "You might have magic, but I have plenty of friends in City Hall."

Magical and nonmagical folk have been at each other's necks since the first minor god was created. Many have speculated but none have determined what exactly makes it easier for some to access magic than others. There's no hard-and-fast rule. It all comes down to the will of the minor gods, who they choose to imbue with power and who they choose to shun. And it's been my experience that despite what they may say, the shunned are always *really* salty about it.

Ursula scoffs, but Jack barrels on. "When we're done with you, maybe you'll end up at the House of Vans like your sister. That's where all y'all belong anyway."

Clem knits his brows at me, but I shrug. I've never heard of the House of Vans, whatever that is.

"Let me make one thing very clear to you," Ursula says. "I'm not afraid of you or any of your little friends. I answer to higher powers." She pulls herself up even straighter. "You got some nerve coming in here accusing me of stealing from you as if you were capable of a truly original thought."

He kicks one of the barstools, and it clatters to the floor. Clem and I both jump, but Ursula stands unfazed. Her sisters nicknamed her "Bulldozer" for a reason. If you get in her way, she'll plow right over you and keep it moving.

"Get your sorry ass out of my bar before you set something in motion you can't stop," she warns.

Jack turns, muttering curses under his breath, and barely takes two steps before stopping abruptly. His stormy blue-green eyes shift between me and Clem, then settle on my brother. A shadow slinks across Jack's face, and his brows pinch for an awkward moment.

"I remember you," he tells Clem. "You're that little thug who attacked my son."

"Actually, your homophobic son had been bullying me for years," Clem says, one brow raised. "But now I see where he gets his crappy personality."

That's where I remember Jack from! He's Zachary Kingston's dad. Zac taunted Clem relentlessly all freshman and sophomore year, all the while catfishing him with a finsta of a guy named "Mauro." They chatted for *months* before they finally met up. Clem had asked me to drive him, just in case Mauro was an ax murderer. I was as stunned and pissed as Clem when Zac showed up instead.

They argued until Zac was red in the face. Clem got in the car with me and didn't say a single word the entire way home. After that, Zac turned up his contempt for Clem, which finally erupted into an all-out brawl between the two of them. He still won't tell me what Zac had said to push him over the edge, but Clem lost it, blacked out, and whooped Zac so bad that Zac had to be carried from the cafeteria. People still tease him. Sometimes they call him "Ambien" and mimic fainting when they pass him in the hall. I may or may not have had something to do with that.

Jack throws one last glower over his shoulder at Ursula and storms past us and outside.

"Hey, you two!" Ursula steps from behind the bar and, smiling, picks up the overturned stool and sets it upright. "Well, are you gonna come hug your favorite auntie, or what?"

We do, and she squeezes us so tight, I'm afraid she's going to break us in two.

"That guy's a real as—I mean jerk," Clem says.

She rolls her eyes. "Jack Kingston is nothing but a bag of stale air. Not even worth the time spent fretting about him. So, what brings you two to this side of town?"

"We need your help," Clem says.

Ursula's smile evaporates. "What's wrong?"

"It's Mama," he says.

"Is she okay? Has she gotten worse?"

He spreads his hands in front of him sarcastically. "Well, you'd know if you ever came to visit, or called, or texted, or sent a raven—anything that would've let us know you cared."

I touch Clem's elbow. He may be right, but we can't piss Aunt Ursula off—we need the Bulldozer to bring the rest of our aunts home.

Ursula sighs and massages her temple. "I'm not getting into that with you two right now."

"That's not why we're here," I interject. "We found a hex doll in Mama's bedroom this morning. We don't know who put it there or why, but it's what made her sick—and almost killed her."

Ursula's breath hitches. "Was it the only one?" The gravity of her tone makes the hair on my arms stand up.

I turn to Clem and we both share an *oh, shit* expression. "I—I don't know."

Ursula frowns at both of us, one hand on her hip. "I thought I taught you two better."

Clem opens his mouth, but I squeeze his wrist and he swallows whatever he was going to say, which I'm sure probably wouldn't have been helpful.

I say, "We need you and the rest of our aunts to come home tonight so we can—"

"Conjure Wise John's Moon." Ursula folds her arms over her chest and leans back against the bar. "Maybe I did teach you something after all."

"So, will you help us?" asks Clem.

She sits up with a sigh and smooths her dress over her thighs. "No."

"What?" Clem and I both exclaim as she heads back behind the bar and picks up a clipboard.

She glances up at us, as if we're now interrupting the important work she's pretending to do. "Did your mama send you here to summon me? Marie is more than capable of resolving this on her own since she knows every damn thing. And please deliver my exact words when y'all report back."

"What's going on between you two?" I had no idea things were *so* bad between Mama and Aunt Ursula. Whatever it is, I imagine it must be pretty awful. There's no disagreement between me and Clem serious enough to ever stop me from protecting him.

"It's not my place to tell," she says. "Nor do I think it's your place to know."

I see I'm not the only person harboring secrets. I wonder what Mama and Aunt Ursula are hiding. It's not unlike Mama to keep things from us. She tried to hide her illness for days.

Clem steps up to the bar, wringing his hands before sticking them in his pockets. "Aunt Ursula, please. We're just asking for a couple hours. She almost died. We already lost Dad. . . ." His voice trails.

"If you can't do it for Mama, then do it for us," I add. "Whoever planted that hex doll had Mama's earrings. Clem and I both had personal stuff go missing this morning. We might be next."

Clem blanches. "I hadn't thought about that."

Because you were too busy being an ass.

She sets the clipboard down. "What was taken?"

"My journal and Clem's knife," I say, "the one Dad gave him."

"And what did your mama say about all this?" she asks, studying my face.

I feel Clem's eyes on me, too.

"I didn't tell her."

Ursula cuts her eyes at me and scoffs. "Then you two need to go talk to your mama and let her handle this. I'm sorry, but I cannot get wrapped up—"

"Come on, Cris," interrupts Clem. "We're wasting our time. She doesn't give a damn about anyone but herself."

I'm so pissed I could toss a barstool, too. I really don't get "adults" sometimes. I'm not hopeful everyone else can contain their shit long enough for us to finish one simple conjuring.

Ursula's frown deepens. "If you don't watch your mouth, I'll smack you in it like we're not family."

Clem rounds on her, but this time the raw fury in his eyes prevents me from trying to calm him. My brother can be a bit of a hothead, but this is one time we're on the same wavelength.

"I used to look up to you," he tells her, "but I don't even know who you are anymore. You were right, though—you did teach me better. We don't need you. Not *this* you. The aunt I loved would never look the other way while someone attacked her family. Period." He grabs my hand and nearly pulls my arm from the socket, dragging me toward the exit. "We'll figure this out on our own," he tells me. "We're the only people who care anyway."

Before I can say anything to the contrary, he yanks open the door, and the humid Louisiana air slams into my face.

Aunt Ursula's voice stops us.

"Wait."

We turn to see she's come from behind the bar and gestures for us to come back inside.

She sighs and rests her hands on her hips. "I'll see what I can do."

FIVE

CLEMENT

"You okay?" My sister's voice is quiet, softly tiptoeing around the waning tension in Ursula's bar.

"I'm fine," I say.

I don't know what came over me earlier, but I don't regret anything I said to Aunt Ursula. There's no beef deep enough to let a sibling die over. Adults claim they gain wisdom and experience with age, but based on my family, it seems they only become more selfish and jaded.

Cris and I sit at the bar in silence, waiting on Aunt Ursula to come from the back office, where she went to call her sisters. I don't care if she needs to summon Obama and Michelle, as long as Mama will be okay. I drum my fingers on the cover of *The Color Purple* sitting on the bar in front of me. I haven't been able to focus enough to read a single page since Cris pulled out of the garage. Anxiety holds my mind hostage like that sometimes, and I've had to learn to deal with it.

She leans close and lowers her voice. "I was serious about finding out who crossed Mama."

"I'd like to know who's behind it, too."

Cris's resolution doesn't surprise me. My sister is the queen of problem-solving. I tell her often she's in denial of her calling to be a private investigator.

It still feels surreal Mama might be okay after all. It had to have been because of the gris Cris helped me make. Otherwise, I wouldn't have looked underneath her mattress and would've never found the hex doll. Mama's still here because of me—and my magic. My chest swells, and I feel a little more powerful, because I've managed to restore some control over my life.

But the moment my head comes down from the clouds, reality sets in and so does my anxiety. Someone tried to take Mama from us—and I'd also like to know who and for what fucking reason.

"Maybe we can work together," Cris suggests. "But only on two nonnegotiable conditions."

"Umm . . . okay."

She counts off the terms on her fingers. "First, this stays between the two of us. Second, leave Oz out of it."

I fake-retch when she says his name, and she rolls her eyes. For the sake of peace, I won't say anything else to her about her creepy-ass boyfriend, but that doesn't mean I trust him. More importantly, maybe her asking for my help is the beginning of the return of our relationship.

I miss my sister so much.

"Deal," I say.

Our heads shoot up when Ursula reemerges.

"Okay," she says. "I talked to Desiree and Jacquelyn, and they're going to meet us at the house later this evening. But in usual Rosalie fashion, she's not answering her phone or texts."

"Maybe she's at work," says Cris.

Ursula checks her watch. "Last I checked, she was still part of the acting company on Justin's riverboat. We'll go pay her a visit. It's four o'clock now, so I just need an hour or so to wrap up a few things here and hand the bar over to my assistant for the rest of the night." Cris and I exchange a worried look, but Ursula anticipates our concern before we can say it. "I also spoke to Odessa, and your mama's going to be all right. They already swept her room and bathroom thoroughly and haven't found any other hex dolls. She's taking an Eshu bath and is already feeling better. Stop worrying."

The tension in my chest unwinds a bit at the news that the ugly-ass hex doll didn't have any cousins hanging around in my mama's room. But I'm also sick of people telling me everything will be okay. I've never been able to trust fate to just smooth things out. Fate stole Dad and almost took Mama, too. But now I've got hold of her again, I won't allow blind hope to distract me so fate can snatch another person I love. Fuck fate.

Wise John's Moon will grant me some peace—if only temporarily. I can trust magic. It's reliable. Controllable. It's fate's lust for my pain that will forever haunt me.

"Do you want us to wait here?" I ask.

"With Jack breathing down my neck, it's not in my best interest to have two minors sitting in my bar this evening, family or not." She retrieves her purse from a shelf underneath the bar and fishes out some cash. "You two grab some food on me. I'll call you when I'm ready."

I pocket the money and lead the way outside. The streets bustle with people, mostly tourists, popping in and out of local restaurants, shops, and bars—all contained within aged buildings. I love New Orleans. There's no other place like it. My city has a rich history that lives in every column, every old sign, and every wrought-iron balcony overlooking the busy streets below. The myriad of colors and Gothic architecture practically hum with raw magic. It's like each building has its own treasure trove of secrets locked away behind the brightly painted doors and curtained windows. The city I love gives me hope the people I love will come together and do something right for a change.

"Wanna go to the Golden Key?" asks Cris.

I shrug. "Sure, I don't care."

We turn the corner and a three-story building with soaring, intricately carved columns catches my eye. Royal-purple velvet drapes hang inside each window, making the place look even more mysterious. A wooden sign hangs above a pair of gargantuan double doors in the front. The script on the sign is so small I have to squint to read it.

It's the place that assclown Jack mentioned earlier. The House of Vans looks like some sort of fancy hotel or lounge, but it has a flair of mystery that makes it feel like something more.

One of the doors opens and a boy emerges. He's about my height with a low haircut and bright bronze skin that beams in the sunlight. His eyes fall on me and he stops, suddenly frozen in place. His face holds an expression of conflicted interest and surprise.

I know him from school.

But I don't know much about Yves Bordeaux, except Cris claims he was the only person who was genuinely kind to her after Valentina turned everyone else against her. He and I have never had a class together and he's not a member of any clubs or student organizations. He's a social ghost. That always intrigued me about him—not to mention how unbelievably cute he is. But we've only ever said hello to each other in passing.

Shit. I'm staring.

He waves, but before Cris or I can wave back, he turns and hurries in the opposite direction.

"That was weird," she says.

"I thought y'all were friends?" I ask.

"We're cool, but the f-word might be a stretch."

The door to the House of Vans opens again and a man tentatively steps outside. He peers up and down the street, then hurries to the other side before strolling up the sidewalk. Nagging curiosity needles the back of my skull.

"I'm guessing you don't know what the House of Vans is or why he was in there?"

She points at me. "Bingo. Let's get going; I'm hungry, and I'm sure you're starving since you skipped breakfast."

My stomach betrays me, roaring in agreement. "I might be feeling a bit peckish."

Our former family restaurant, the Golden Key, isn't packed, which I'm grateful for, because if I have to wait any longer to eat, I might take a bite out of Cris. My stomach rumbles again the moment we walk inside and I catch a whiff of the delectable flair of Cajun spices wafting from the kitchen.

The restaurant owner, a tall bald man with stark, black eyes, approaches with a smile as wide as his belly, which looks weird protruding from his slender frame as if he's seven months pregnant.

"Ugh, I'm really not in the mood for him today," I whisper to Cris. She elbows me and smiles as he walks up. "Hi, Roger."

"Cristina! Clement!" He spreads his hands and pulls us into an unwelcome hug, smashing our faces into the muddled scent of grease and raw fish clinging to the fabric of his shirt. When he releases us, he claps me on the shoulder with one of his meaty hands, which buckles my knees. "It's so good to see you two here. What brings you over?"

"We came to see Aunt Ursula and decided to grab an early dinner," Cris answers quickly, as if trying to beat me to it—but joke's on her, I don't want to talk to Roger anyway.

Shortly after Dad died, Mama sold all the businesses, including our brewery and this restaurant. Roger appointed himself an honorary family member after buying it, even though no one wanted one.

He ushers us to a table next to a wall of doors, which are open to the patio, where a few people are already eating in the warm air beneath the spotty shade of the arbor covered in leafy green vines.

"How's Ursula doing?" he asks.

"She's good," Cris says. "How about you?"

I shoot her a look. I wish she'd shut up and let him go back to whatever he was doing before we came in. Naturally, she ignores me.

"I've been great—so has business." He slugs my shoulder and I have to bite my lips to keep from cursing. "I don't see Ursula around as much anymore, but your aunt Jacquelyn used to come in fairly regularly. She'd order takeout a few times a week." He leans closer and lowers his voice to add, "Couple times I saw her slipping into the House of Vans. Hate she got caught up in that sorta place."

I look up. "What sort of place is it?"

"Oh, uh . . ." His face turns a vivid shade of pink and he glances quickly over his shoulder at no one. "Looks like they need me in the kitchen. I'll fetch your server. You two have a good lunch and let me know if there's anything you need. Eat your fill, it's on the house."

Before either of us can thank him, we're watching his backside weave through the maze of tables and disappear into the kitchen. If I'd known that was all it took to get rid of him, I'd have brought up the House of Vans when we first walked in.

Cris sighs, grimacing at her phone.

"What's the matter?" I ask. "Lose some Instagram followers?"

She flips me off. "I did a search on the House of Vans, but nothing comes up."

Now I'm even more intrigued. But thinking about that place reminds me of Yves and the way he looked at me. I can't get him out of my head.

We order, and our food arrives shortly after—a po'boy sandwich for me and fried catfish for Cris. We haven't eaten here in a long time, but the food tastes as good as I remember.

"If Aunt Ursula isn't ready by the time we finish eating, we should go by there," I suggest. "Find out firsthand what that place is."

She frowns with annoyed disapproval that makes my skin crawl. "The House of Vans sounds sketch. We have enough to worry about without getting bogged down in unnecessary side quests."

I roll my eyes. "All due respect, sis, but I don't think you are the best judge of what or *who* is sketch."

Her fork clatters to her plate and she stares lasers at me. "You only found out that place existed five minutes ago. Why do you even care so much?" She leans back and crosses her arms. "Are you trying to add Yves to your roster?" I frown, and she raises an eyebrow. "What? You thought I wasn't smart enough to notice?"

"No, that's not it—"

"I hate that you lie to me, Clem, but I hate even more that you lie to yourself."

I clutch the tail of the tablecloth in my fist and almost snatch it off the table. "You're not exactly the best person to advise me in this area."

"What's that supposed to mean?"

"Your boyfriend is a straight-up clown. No matter how *nice* he was to you, he still kicked off all that shit with Valentina, knowing good and damn well she was evil—and then he didn't even try to get her to back off when she started bullying you. He's only interested in you because of all the rumors about our family. You're less of a girlfriend to him and more of a circus attraction he gets to explore all by himself. You honestly deserve better, and I have no idea why you can't see that."

She withers in her seat and her eyes water. "You're an ass." Her chair scrapes hard against the wood floor as she pushes back from the table and storms to the bathroom.

I almost call her back to apologize. *Almost.* I despise the way she scolds me like I'm her damn kid. I miss how things used to be between us before Dad died and Mama got sick. Now she thinks I'm some sort of irresponsible, scarlet gay. She has no idea I'm still a virgin.

I've done stuff, of course—who wouldn't with a hot naked guy in their bed and hormones raging? But I've never gone all the way before. I want to save that experience to share with someone I bond with on a level deeper than agreeing on which restaurant has the best salmon cakes or debating superhero matchups. Seems I might have better luck tracking down a unicorn. With wings.

Sick of thinking about my dysfunctional family, I settle into my book. When Cris finally returns, I don't bother speaking to her—although she seems not to care. The way she sinks into her seat without a word and turns her head toward the patio suggests she's still pissed.

Much to my relief, we don't have to broil in silence long before Aunt Ursula shows up to collect us, which means Cris must've texted her from the bathroom.

"You two ready to head out?" Ursula asks.

"Ecstatic," grumbles Cris, jumping up from her seat.

I purse my lips and tuck my book underneath one arm.

Ursula's eyes shift between me and Cris, who's already halfway to the front door. "What's the deal with you two?"

"You don't even want to know," I tell her.

I've been on riverboats before, but none like the *Montaigne Majestic*. Complete with a casino, a fully stocked magical supply store, too many bars to count, and a dine-in theater, it dwarfs the other boats lined up along the dock. Warm yellow light glows from the many windows tiled between the white columns and lattices, reminiscent of the historic buildings of the French Quarter.

The muddled sounds of jazz, laughter, and loud voices meet us as we cross the gangway onto the boat set against the backdrop of the Sun sinking behind the harbor. Smokestacks puff tufts of steam like gargantuan cigars, and the boat's horn bellows, drowning out everything else. The boat's about to depart, which means the evening show must start soon. The whole place feels magical, as if we're preparing to sail to a new world in the middle of the night.

It's been a few years since I've seen Aunt Rosalie. I wonder if she'll be as hard to convince as Ursula, but if we were able to persuade the most bullheaded of all Mama's sisters, anything is possible.

As soon as we board, we run into our cousin, Justin Montaigne, who pulls everyone in for a hug. I opt for a fist bump instead, which turns his bright smile into a frown. And I don't care. Justin is so flighty that I'd advise anyone close to him to hang a bell around his neck so they'll at least get a warning before he runs out on them.

Justin was the first person I came out to. He helped me find my way—at first. But then, like everyone else, he fucking disappeared—ironically, around the same time Ursula left. It's like they had a pact to ghost me together. He even moved off our estate, where he'd grown up in a smaller home near ours. He bought this boat and turned it into his home and business, where he also operates one of his Firefly Supplies stores.

He stands back, having found his smile again, with his hands on his slender hips. Despite my present feelings about Justin, he does look dapper in his tailored cream suit and cerulean button-up, which has several buttons undone around a thin patch of chest hair. His thin, pointy-featured face will forever remind me of a rodent, which ironically aligns dead center with his personality.

Ursula wastes no time. "I need to see my sister."

He glances at his watch and frowns. "No can do, Ursula. The show's about to start and Rosalie's my leading lady."

"We only need a few minutes," she says.

"Is something wrong?" he asks.

She hesitates a moment. "It's a family thing."

He raises his hands on either side of him. "And what am I?"

"Justin . . ." she sighs. "It's a long story that I can't get into right now, but it's very important that I talk to Rosalie immediately."

"I have a boat packed with folks here to see her tonight," he says, gesturing to the people piling through a wall of open French doors that lead into the radiantly lit main atrium. "Whatever drama you're dying to drop on her will have to wait until *after* the show." Ursula sighs louder this time, and he adds, "Look, I'll even set you three up in a VIP booth. Whatever you want is on me. The second the final curtain drops, I'll personally escort you to Rosalie's dressing room."

She glances at us. "That okay with you two?"

We both nod, and she tells us she'll let Mama and our other aunts know we'll be there promptly after Rosalie's show.

Justin leads us inside, and I can't help but stare up at what must be the biggest, grandest chandelier I've ever seen. As we pass underneath, it swallows most of the ceiling and practically glitters with gold and crystal adornments that compete with the warm light emanating from hundreds of decorative bulbs.

A poster sits on an easel tucked into one of the dark corners of the main atrium. That's a strange place to put an announcement. It's almost as if the person who placed it didn't think it was important enough to warrant a more prominent spot in the room. The top of the ad reads ONE NIGHT ONLY in gaudy, gold disco lettering. In the center is a picture of a light-skinned Black woman with an oval face, a duplicitous smile, and a tignon crown atop her head, the knots tied with meticulous precision. The bottom reads, "Celebrating 30 Years in POWER. Lenora Savant, Queen Mother of the Generational Magic Council of New Orleans. Coming this July!"

Bleh. On second thought, I think that poster got a way better spot than it deserved. I'd throw it in the dumpster where it belongs.

We ascend a grand, curved staircase up to the theater balcony where the VIP booths are located and find ours perched just off-center of the stage, overlooking the main floor and the sea of white-clothed candlelit tables. Guests already fill most of the seats below. It's not a very large room, but it gives off a vibe that's ten times as grand as its size. I take it all in, the leather wing chairs, the enchanting candlelight flickering against the tabletops, the old wooden floors beneath it all, and wonder how many stories this theater has seen—how many more it still has left to see and what they'll be.

I don't care for Justin much anymore, but I'm still impressed by what he's managed to create on the *Montaigne Majestic*.

I feel richer just standing in our booth. There are two tables clad in dark linens with four plush velvet armchairs at each. Orchids sit on the tables between sets of burning olive-green candles. Ursula curses and blows them all out before sitting down.

"Nice to see you haven't changed." Justin smiles and stops short just inside the door. "Oh, and sorry, but this won't be a private booth tonight. It's a short show, so I'm sure you'll manage."

"Who else will be here?" Ursula turns, but he's already vanished. She grumbles under her breath and shakes her head.

"Why'd you blow out the candles?" I ask.

She glares at them for a moment before turning to my sister. "I'm not the only master conjurer in this booth. Your sister should know well as me."

Cris shifts uncomfortably in her seat and tosses me an annoyed look. I bet she hasn't shared her aversion to magic with our aunt, which would make an interesting conversation starter. I consider lobbing the grenade to spite her but decide against it. Before she quit magic, I saw her do some really impressive shit with raw moonlight, one of the purest, and hardest to wield, catalysts of gen magic.

"We don't trust candles we don't bless ourselves," Cris says without emotion, as if she just got cold-called in chemistry class. "Green ones are supposed to bring luck and fortune, but I'm guessing these serve Justin, not his patrons."

"Right," adds Ursula. "I bet there are more than a handful of broke people in the casino right now who'll agree."

I huff under my breath and lean back in my seat. It doesn't surprise me that an opportunist like Justin would do something so deceitful. Maybe I'm a bit biased due to how our relationship soured, but I don't care. Dad used to tell me my feelings were always valid. And right now, I feel what I feel about Justin.

We sit in awkward silence for a while, before I reach the end of my mental tether. I announce I'm going to the bathroom, to which Ursula nods and Cris pretends not to hear.

The hall outside the booth is empty, as is the bathroom. After finishing up, I decide to explore a bit. There's still about fifteen minutes before the show starts, and I have no desire to spend any longer than necessary stuck in that booth with my aloof aunt and crabby sister.

The scene downstairs is completely different from upstairs. Up-tempo jazz plays from speakers hidden somewhere in the lush décor. People in expensive-looking suits and flashy cocktail dresses cling to glasses filled with champagne or cocktails and amble up and down the hallways and rooms, enjoying an evening of gambling and debauchery. It's like a scene from one of Gatsby's parties, except Black people are invited.

I'm not sure what kind of air fresheners Justin uses on this boat, but even the air smells fresher on here, like going for a walk in the woods after a short, hard rainfall. I stand in the crowded atrium with wide, grandiose archways leading into different sections of the boat, marveling at the pulsing energy of everything and everyone. Then I catch sight of Yves.

He's waving at two tall, burly bouncers who stand on either side of the entrance to the casino. They both dip their heads silently as he passes.

Curious, I try the same method, but one of the bouncers grabs me with his sausage-sized fingers and shoves me back.

"No one under twenty-one permitted in the casino," he growls.

"But you just let him through." I point at Yves, who takes his time approaching one of the blackjack tables where several people play.

He folds his arms. "No identification, no entry."

Checkmate, asshole.

I take my fake ID out of my wallet and hand it to him. I got it so I could party with a guy who preferred clubs to quiet evenings at home. That's never really been my scene, so it's good to know the hundred dollars I dropped on this ID won't go to waste. While the bouncer studies it, I peer around him.

Yves steps up to a woman whose loose auburn curls spill over the back of the bloodred dress she wears. She smiles and kisses both his cheeks. He gives her something that resembles a miniature version of one of those old-school perfume bottles. I don't think that's White Diamonds. She deposits it into her purse and hands him a small envelope, which he tucks into his back pocket. He turns to leave, and we make eye contact.

"This is fake," grumbles the bouncer.

"What?" I cry, turning my attention from Yves. "No, it's not."

"Arcade's in the lower deck," he says, still clutching my ID in his grubby fingers. "I'll hang on to this."

Yves walks up and touches the bouncer on the elbow. "He's cool, Steve."

Bouncer Steve frowns at him. "You know the rules. Don't make me call Fabiana."

Yves holds up his hands in mock surrender. "Understood." He motions for me to follow him to the other side of the atrium, as if I'm a friend he was expecting.

I snatch my ID out of Bouncer Steve's hand. "Fucker," I mumble as I trail Yves to the other side of the atrium.

"Are you stalking me?" Yves asks me.

Even the way he leans against the wall with his hands in his pockets and his head slightly tilted is unbelievably adorable. It sets me ablaze like a lighter to dry kindling. He's even more mesmerizing up close. His brown skin gleams in the subtle light of the corridor as if it's been infused with pearls bathed in moonlight. His dark eyes are like gateways to another time and space.

He grins. "Should I take your silence as a yes?"

I laugh nervously and shift my feet like a kid. I've never been this shy in front of a guy before. But this one makes me forget the simple art of speech.

"Of course not," I say. "I, uh, just saw you again and wanted to say hello properly. Sorry about earlier."

He chuckles. "No worries."

"What were you doing in there?" I jerk my head back toward the casino.

His smile falters, and he hesitates before saying, "Just running an errand for my sister."

"She must be pretty important to get you past those goons at the entrance."

"Everyone's important. So, uh, why are you here?"

"My aunt's in the show—Rosalie Dupart. I'm here to see her."

His eyes brighten. "You'll enjoy it. I've already seen it twice. The guy who owns this boat is the lead writer on all the productions."

"Yeah, I know," I admit, though I'm reluctant to bring up my connection to Justin. He's the last person I want to talk about right now. "Justin's my cousin."

"Cool. He's so talented. I love how he likes to twist the classics. Tonight, they're performing an Aladdin retelling with a sapphic love story."

A horde of butterflies takes flight in my stomach. "You're into theater?"

"Total theater geek, here." He pokes his chest with his thumb and grins. "It's the crossroads of every art form."

I smile. "I never thought about it like that."

"How do you think about it?"

"Like art is the most powerful magic in the world, and all artists are conjurers in their own right. I enjoy the theater, but I honestly prefer books."

Yves practically beams. "You're a reader, too?"

Everything around us evaporates as we allow the conversation to swallow us whole. I get the urge to lose myself in his world and never come back out. I hate to tear myself away from him, but I have to get back to the booth before Aunt Ursula launches a search party. But my feet refuse to budge.

"Give me your phone." He sticks out his hand and wriggles his fingers. "I want to give you my number."

I unlock my phone and hand it over. When he returns it, it's still warm from his touch.

"Text me sometime," he says. "Maybe we can see a show one night—or just hang out, y'know, and discuss the meaning of life and stuff. No pressure."

My heart beams. "I'd like that."

He dips his head and disappears down the hallway. Long after he's gone, I stand there, captive in the reverie of moments just passed. I rub my thumb across my phone and smile.

I navigate back upstairs to our booth and pause outside, staring at the blank message on my phone's screen. How soon is *too soon* to text him? I go back and forth about whether to send Yves a message until, eventually, I delete the blank draft, shut my eyes, and blow out a long breath. I don't know why I'm acting like this over a boy, who, until moments ago, I'd hardly ever spoken to.

I reach out to open the door to our booth and bump hands with someone else. Surprised, I yank mine back. "Sorry—"

"This is a VIP room," says a gangly Black man with bright golden-wheat skin and long gray hair pulled back in a ponytail. He's wearing a plain black tuxedo and an overwhelming number of gold rings like tiny bracelets around his spidery fingers. He stares down his crooked nose at me with beady, judgmental eyes.

I narrow mine. "I know that. My family's inside."

Next to him stands a familiar-looking Black woman with a similar light-skinned complexion. They both seem old enough to be my grandparents. Her jet-black hair's swooped dramatically into a high bun, and her oval face is heavily made-up. There's no telling what she looks like when she excavates herself from underneath all that at night. She's short and has what might appear to be a kind face, but I get the sneaking suspicion it's only to lure you to within the limited range of her stubby arms so she can slit your throat with ease. She wears a lavender gown and clutches a large purple and gold shawl draped around her shoulders.

The woman taps the man on the shoulder. "Don't be rude, Felix. You know we decided not to pay extra for the private booth tonight." She tucks the sequined clutch she carries under one arm and smiles, tilting her head in a gesture I presume she thinks is sweet but comes off as condescending as fuck. "I'm Lenora Savant, and this is my husband, Felix. What's your name, dear?"

The lady from the god-awful poster in the main atrium. *Dear gods, please tell me we don't have to sit in this cramped booth with her and Thin Man for the whole show.*

"Clement Trudeau," I answer, watching them both warily.

For a moment so brief that if I blinked I would've missed it, her smile disappears. "Would you happen to be Marie Trudeau's boy?" When I nod, she furrows her brow at the door. "Is she . . ."

"No," I say. "I'm here with my aunt and sister."

"Family outing?"

"Why do you care?"

She chuckles. "Just curious about the occasion."

"Do we need one?"

She humphs under her breath. "You're absolutely right." She studies my face a silent moment and whispers something in Felix's ear. He nods and hurries away. "Thirsty," she adds with a polite chuckle when she notices my eyes following him down the hallway.

"Aren't there servers for that?" I don't mask my skepticism. "That's kinda the point of VIP, no?"

She takes a measured step toward me, and another, until she's close enough for me to smell her floral perfume mingled with the scent of spearmint on her breath. She leans in so we're face-to-face, all hints of pleasantry in her expression long dead.

"You are most certainly your mother's seed." Her eyes rove over me, which feels like bugs crawling over my bare skin. She smiles and pulls the door open, then turns back. "Don't linger in the hallway too long, dear. You'll miss the show."

Then the creepy woman slips inside our booth.

SIX

CRISTINA

"What's going on between you two?" Aunt Ursula asks the moment Clem leaves the booth.

I cross my arms. "He's a jerk."

Regardless of if he thought he was being honest, what he said about me and Oz made me feel like shit. I wish he'd take an unbiased view of his own incredible ability to be irrational and selfish.

Ursula laughs. "Aren't all brothers jerks?"

"How would you know? You don't have any."

"No, but once I had friends who were as good as—" Her face falls, but as quick as the emotion comes, she chases it away. "I have four sisters, which can be a lot worse than a single brother."

"Why won't you say what happened between you and Mama?"

"Your mama made it very clear she didn't want you or your brother involved in the drama, and that's one of the few battles I'm not interested in fighting. Marie pretends she doesn't have teeth until she bites you—you got that from her, you know."

I almost chuckle aloud at the irony. Magic ripped out what teeth I thought I had. But Ursula's observation about Mama doesn't surprise me. I've only ever seen Mama *really* angry once, and it was a frightening sight to behold. I'd always respected Mama, but after she finished gathering one of my middle school teachers who'd said my braids weren't proper dress code, I learned not to fuck with her.

"Why'd you leave?" I ask. "You really hurt Clem when you left."

I stopped giving a shit a long time ago about why any of them left. And I don't want to see my brother go through anything like that ever again.

"That breaks my heart, but I had to leave for my own sanity. Things had gotten too toxic in that house. And I thought ripping off the bandage would help Clem heal faster."

She shoved my brother off a cliff to save herself. Duly noted.

Clem reeled after they all left, but Ursula dealt the heaviest blow to his psyche. He pleaded with her to stay, but all she told him was she *just couldn't,* and he *was too young to understand.*

Afterward, he sealed himself in his room for a month. I think he depression-read about a hundred books during that time. After the first week, I made frequent trips to Barnes & Noble to feed him new material. He refused to talk to me, so that was the only way I knew to help. I lost count of how many books I contributed to the massive hoard filling the built-in shelves above his desk.

I worry about Clem more than anyone. I see the cracks in his façade, and I'm terrified how all that raw pain is going to change him.

"That doesn't mean I don't care about my family," Ursula adds, a hint of sadness in her voice. "Not a day goes by that I don't think about all my sisters. Sometimes people grow apart, and that's okay. One day you'll see, too. You and Clem will soon travel down your own unique paths."

Clem and I give each other a fair amount of space, but I find comfort in knowing he's never too far away—even when we're fighting. I won't let our relationship crumble like our mama and aunts' has, no matter how much of an asshole he can be.

Ursula conveniently changes the subject to school and other less interesting things while we wait for the show to begin. Just as I start to wonder if Clem is going to make it back in time, the door opens.

"Where have you—" I swing around in my seat and am cut short by the sharp-eyed gaze of an older light-skinned woman whose lips prune instantly at the sight of me. The angle of her nose in the air and the elaborateness of her purple dress tell me she's well-to-do—or at least thinks she is.

Ursula stands up, and her face contorts when she sees the woman. "I'm going to murder Justin."

"You?" The woman scoffs. "He'll hear from me first. This booth was supposed to be *VIP.*"

"Then why are *you* here?" Ursula retorts.

Clem slips inside after the woman and his wide eyes find mine. *Who is she?* I mouth, and flick my eyes toward her.

He stands beside my seat. "I ran into her outside, and she's major stranger danger," he whispers. "She says her name is Lenora Savant."

Shit. I thought I knew her from somewhere.

I've only seen her in pictures or from afar, but Valentina idolizes her "granny," so much that at times I wondered if she subconsciously resented her mom for not being Lenora.

The door opens again, and a tall, spaghetti-thin man walks in and looms behind Lenora like a sleep-paralysis demon. "He confirmed—" he starts, but Lenora nearly smacks him on the lips with two fingers and makes a sound like an airlock sealing.

Valentina Savant enters next and slithers up beside her grandmother, who hugs her close.

Her eyes find mine. She tenses at the same time goose bumps rise on the back of my neck. We glower at each other. I can't believe we used to be best friends. When I first met her, I never imagined we'd hate each other one day. And here we are.

I hear the whimper that dies in the back of Clem's throat beside me.

Neither Valentina nor I speak.

Clem's eyes leap back and forth between us, but he's quiet, too. He knows better than to get in the middle.

I haven't been this close to Valentina since I hexed her bald. Unless her box braids, which are up in a ponytail tonight, are attached to a wig, it seems she found a way to regrow her hair. Good for her.

She's wearing a white puff-sleeved midi dress and nude mesh pumps with a matching handbag. It all looks really cute on her, but I'll choke on the compliment and die before I let her have it.

I stopped flattering Valentina shortly into our friendship because she's always been the kind of person who feels owed that attention and never bothers to reciprocate.

"We won't be staying long—" Lenora wrinkles her nose at me and my brother. "—it's a tad crowded in here."

Ursula steps in front of us and we have to lean to one side to peer around her. "Address my niece and nephew again and I will tie that cheap shawl around your neck and drag your ass to the never-realm by it."

Clem latches on to my shoulder. I grip the arm of my chair and slide out a bit in case I need to move quick to prevent my aunt from going to jail tonight.

Aunt Ursula has never been afraid to make an enemy. If she'd lived a few centuries sooner, I could totally see her hanging the severed ears of the people who dared wrong her over her mantel. However, this particular disagreement is quite intriguing, because I'm curious not only why she has a full-on feud with Valentina's granny, but also how neither Clem nor I knew about it.

Lenora turns to her husband. "I'm suddenly no longer feeling a show tonight, Felix."

His mouth melts into a cartoonish frown. "Agreed." The way he drawls when he talks reminds me of an evil sloth.

Valentina narrows her eyes like she wants to pounce on me. I bet she blames me for this, too. I wish I could take credit for ruining her evening, but I'm still trying to grasp exactly what the hell is going on here.

Lenora turns to Ursula, who shifts her weight from one foot to the other. "You can have the booth. Consider it a gift—for you and these sweet children. I do have a soft spot for kids. I truly believe every single one is a gift straight from the spiritual realm. Giving birth is like being chosen by the gods."

Ursula trembles like she's going to slug Lenora, and my stomach twists as I think of all the ways this situation could get much worse before it's over.

"I guess these moments are the closest you'll ever come to experiencing motherhood." Lenora ogles Ursula's midsection. "Celeste was a brutal and ruthless bitch, but by gods, did I admire the way she could turn a crossing." She takes her husband's arm and says, "Enjoy the rest of your evening."

Valentina scowls at me one last time before leaving the booth with her evil-ass grandparents.

Ursula stands rigid with her back to us. The door clicks shut, and silence rings in my ears. After several moments, I swear I hear her blood arrive at a rolling boil. I've *never* seen Aunt Ursula this angry before. Neither Clem nor I have the courage to break the quiet.

I have no idea who this Celeste woman is or what she could've done to Ursula, but now I understand why Valentina worships her granny. They're both unspeakably wicked. A person's worth is not tied to their ability to conceive, nor are they obligated to pop out children to serve the patriarchy. Lenora Savant is undeniably one of the Black people Harriet Tubman would've shot.

"Nah," mutters Ursula, so low I barely hear. She pushes her hair behind her ears and crosses her arms. Her foot taps an angry rhythm, and she shakes her head. "Nope. Not tonight."

She snatches the door open and stomps into the hallway.

My heart sinks through the bottom of the boat.

"Dear gods," murmurs Clem.

I shrug and get to my feet. "We can't stop her, so we may as well watch. Besides, I'm dying to know what all that's about."

I lead the way, trailing after Aunt Ursula, whose tall frame plowing through the crowd in pursuit of Lenora isn't hard to keep up with.

No one in the congested atrium regards Ursula barreling through, nearly tossing people in her wake, because the sound of glass shattering, followed by screams and shouts, erupts from the short hallway leading to the Firefly Supplies shop, which commands everyone else's attention.

"What's going on?" asks Clem.

"No idea," I say. "But it's been one hell of a day. Mercury must be in retrograde again."

We follow our aunt all the way down the gangway and the pier to the parking lot, where she finally catches up with Lenora. Neither party notices Clem or me as we perch in the background to watch.

"You—raggedy—old—uppity—bitch," Ursula snarls at Lenora.

The woman whirls around with a grimace and looks Ursula up and down. Valentina steps up, but her granny holds out an arm, stopping her. Surely, this girl doesn't think we're about to brawl in this parking lot. I'm glad to see her grandfather wrap his spindly arms around her like a freakishly tall praying mantis and drag her back from the action.

"No matter how far you've managed to claw your way up the social ladder in this city, you'll always be the gutter snake who sacrificed her best friend for power," says Ursula.

Lenora chuckles. "You keep telling me that, but you can't prove any of your ridiculous allegations. Your mother is the only person to blame for your family's fall from grace." She folds her hands in front of her and sighs. "Ursula, dear, there's no need for all this animosity between us. Cristine, rest her soul, wouldn't want that. Can we at least agree to be cordial?"

Wow. This woman is either a great actress or our aunt really is delusional.

"How about I beat your ass?" replies Ursula.

My breath vanishes at the same time Clem latches on to me. I'm not sure if I should intervene or stand back and let the Mess Express leave the station.

"Careful now." Lenora tuts quietly. "I think Celeste already taught you that your actions have consequences."

"You threatening me?" Ursula erases the distance between them, but Lenora doesn't flinch.

"These are facts, not threats, and I don't usually run down my résumé for people like you, but since you are Cristine's daughter, I'll do you a courtesy this one time." Lenora draws her shoulders back and lifts her stubby nose higher. "I am Queen Mother of the Council that governs the entirety of the generational magical community across the U.S. of A., and you, Ursula, dear, are the litter fumbling through the gutters that I overlook, because I have other, far more important things to concern myself with than trash. Perhaps it's a blessing the gods haven't allowed you to procreate."

Ursula slaps the woman so hard it makes me jump. Lenora grunts and falls against the windshield of her car with a dull *thunk*.

I throw myself in front of Ursula, who's ready to finish what she started. "Please, Aunt Ursula, *no*," I plead as I try to goad her back toward the boat.

Valentina lunges, but her grandfather yanks her back. She sneers and grits her teeth like a viper ready to strike.

Lenora pushes herself upright and snatches her dress and shawl straight. She jabs her gold sequined purse at Ursula and snarls, "Big mistake."

The corners of Ursula's lips curl downward. "One day, hopefully sooner rather than later, you're going to have to own your shit, and I pray to the gods every chance I get that I'll have a front-row seat when that happens."

Lenora grips her purse so tight it flashes in the moonlight like an angry disco ball. Felix herds her and Valentina back to the car and coaxes them both inside. Lenora doesn't stop glaring at Ursula until Felix drives away.

I wish I had some palo santo to spark up right now to dispel all of Valentina's negative energy. I can feel it on my skin like a thin film of toxic waste. That's one friendship I don't regret losing.

Once they're gone, Clem puts both hands on his hips and grins. "Wow! *Two* free shows in one night. We couldn't have gotten a better deal if we'd had a coupon."

"Shut up, Clem," says Ursula. "Let's get back inside and try to catch the rest of this show." She takes a deep breath and motions for us to follow her. "Although, I'm surprised the boat hasn't left the docks yet."

"So . . . you're just gonna gloss over what happened back there?" I point my thumb over my shoulder toward the parking lot as Clem and I walk on either side of our aunt.

She glances up at the dark sky and shakes her head. "I shouldn't have allowed Lenora to take me out of character, especially in front of you two. That woman and her ugly gall just gets under my skin like very few things in my life can."

Relatable. That's exactly how I feel about her granddaughter.

"What did you mean when you said she sacrificed her best friend?" I ask.

"Lenora and my mama grew up together, and once upon a time, were friends. But Lenora's testimony to the police made my mama a prime suspect in the murder of the mayor's daughter—and also brought that mob straight to our front lawn that awful night thirty years ago."

"You think Lenora set up Grandma?" asks Clem.

"I wish I knew the truth," Ursula says. "But it just seemed odd that Lenora was a key witness in the case when she stood to gain so much from Mama's downfall."

She's right. That entire family has the scruples of a cartel, so it's not far-fetched Lenora might set up Grandma to steal her throne. And my heart trips over itself when I realize what that could mean.

If my grandmother was framed, that means our family should've never been disgraced. And my grandparents' lives were thrown away because of a lie, cutting off those left and the rest of us to come from an entire generation of love and wisdom.

My grandparents should've lived. And my grandmother's throne should've passed to Mama—and then to me. Odessa was right. My future was stolen from me.

And that means everything Valentina's said to me over the course of our hellish friendship might've all been lies. She made me feel second to garbage, all while I might've been the true heiress to the Gen Council. A large part of me wonders if that's why she's been so nasty to me.

I've been cheated.

But the possibility of me being an heiress seems too good to be true; and given my luck lately, it probably is. Even if it were true, I'd have to prove my grandmother didn't murder the mayor's daughter to change anything, and that might be close to impossible since all this happened thirty years ago. Besides, I need to focus on unmasking whoever crossed Mama before they attempt to finish what they started. But first, we have to sit through the rest of the show so we can finally talk to Aunt Rosalie.

We board the *Majestic* again but must squeeze through the throng of tightly packed people who stand on either side of the atrium, parted around the scene unfolding in the center of the room.

Two security guards drag a handcuffed man toward the exit. Behind him, other guards also escort several more people, who all tussle and shout. I push to the front of the crowd for a better look.

The guy in the lead is a small-framed white man with dark hair and a scruffy, devil-may-care look. He's wearing a black tee, jeans, and Vans—his accomplices are dressed similarly. Bold white lettering on the front of his shirt reads THIS ISN'T THE WILD WEST. REDEEM NEW ORLEANS. REGULATE MAGIC.

"Fucking Redeemers," Ursula grumbles under her breath.

The radical right-wing religious group that cropped up out of nowhere earlier this year. A homely pastor's wife, with her pasty complexion, stringy hair, and duplicitous smile, leads the movement, which is based in her ignorant and outdated beliefs on how to "redeem" our world from the sins of magic. A prime example of what happens when old, racist white women choose to build an oppressive movement instead of a craft room, like anyone else with good sense. And I hate that she gets way more publicity than anyone like her deserves.

"They've been growing a huge following across all four major magical cities in the South," Ursula tells us. "They've set up shop and started wreaking havoc in Baton Rouge, Atlanta, and Miami."

"The commotion we passed through on the way out must've

been because of their shenanigans—and also why the boat never left the dock," I say.

Clem shakes his head, and Ursula's jaw tenses.

"They're getting bolder and bolder with these little 'protests,'" Clem says.

"More like they've given themselves license to vandalize our property and terrorize innocent members of our magical community," I say, and Ursula nods in agreement.

Last month, some Redeemer dude shot a gen man he'd accused of crossing him at a bar one night. The police did nothing about it, and neither did the Gen Council. But in all this, what I find most interesting is Redeemers favor harassing gen folks far more than the white ladies who practice light magic—and it doesn't take an aerospace engineer to understand why.

The lead guy stops right in front of me, nearly tripping up the officers who hold him. For that small moment, his eyes ensnare mine and narrow. His jaw tightens, and he hocks and spits a disgusting glob of phlegm onto the floor near where I stand. He raises his cuffed hands to show me the glaring red X's drawn on his wrists before the cops yank him off his feet and carry him toward the exit—and I see the back of his shirt.

It reads OR ELSE in bolder, dripping red font.

Redeemers may be trash, but I get why they fear magic so much. Magic made me feel powerful once—probably how guns make nonmagic folks feel. And that sets a dense chill curling through my chest, because giving up magic means I've effectively disarmed myself.

But even so, I don't regret my decision to end our toxic relationship. I've heard people say money is the root of evil, but I'm convinced those people never knew magic.

And that's why I'm going to set things right by my family—without it.

SEVEN

VALENTINA SAVANT

Granny and Grandpa were too busy fuming up front to notice Valentina turn off her phone and slide it into her handbag. Her hands trembled with rage. If Cris and her trash-ass family had nothing else, they'd have the audacity. And had it not been for Valentina's grandfather restraining her, she would've dragged Cris and her aunt up and down that parking lot.

She was willing to bet that despite also being angry about what'd happened at the pier, Grandpa didn't mind the silent car ride. Felix Savant treated conversation like an endangered resource. He was like an old willow: steadfast and frustratingly quiet. As such, Valentina wasn't as close with him as she was with her granny, but he was the nearest thing to a father she'd ever had. Although in her particular case, that wasn't saying much.

"Shit!" Valentina exclaimed, cutting through the quiet tension inside the car. "I mean, *shoot,*" she corrected when her granny spun around to glower at her.

"What?" asked Granny.

"I think I dropped my phone in the parking lot. I'm sorry."

Granny sighed and turned back around. "Take us back, Felix."

Grandpa grumbled under his breath and made a U-turn. He drove back to the pier and parked near where Ursula had attacked Granny earlier. Granny wasn't fond of Cris's family, particularly Ursula, but tonight, Valentina had learned just how deep that feud ran.

"Be quick," ordered Granny.

"Yes, ma'am."

Valentina got out and pretended to search the ground for her phone, gradually making her way to Ursula Dupart's black BMW with the "W5HGW3L" vanity license plate. She remembered it, because Granny had commented on not wanting to run into Ursula when they'd passed the car on the way to the dock. But little had they known, they'd be sharing a VIP booth with the woman— and Cris and Clem.

Valentina hadn't so much as stood in the same room with Cris since the day her ex-bestie had humiliated her in front of half the school. Granny had toiled through the night and even had to call in a few favors to find a spell that would regrow Valentina's hair. But Valentina had gotten Cris back with the Instagram post. It was a low blow, but Cris needed to be taught a lesson. Sometimes you had to bend the code to get results.

Valentina hadn't always hated Cris. It was nice having a friend who was also gen, especially since her other bestie, Sofia, had never been able to make magic work for her. But that was a secret Valentina had promised Sofia she'd take to the grave, and she intended to—for now.

Everything had been cool between Valentina and Cris—until Valentina realized Cris was no ordinary gen. Valentina wasn't jealous, but what troubled her was that Cris's grandmother was Queen before Granny—and that meant if Cris started feeling *too* superior, she might set her eyes on the throne, too. So, Valentina had had to humble her friend—and fast. It'd worked well, and the more Valentina whittled Cris down like hard water over a rough stone, the less remorse she felt for what she'd had to do to her friend.

But then Cris smothered the last wisp of Valentina's self-reproach when she ensnared Oz. Valentina and Oz had been together on and off since seventh grade. He'd professed to be madly in love with her, but she never felt the same about him. She'd enjoyed being with him, but that was about it. They'd never had sex. She wasn't interested in that either—with him, at least.

Valentina had always considered herself ruthless, and even took pride in it at times, because that was what a queen had to be if she wanted to hold on to her power. But Oz and Cris had both shown her they were also capable of ruthlessness.

Valentina checked that no one was watching and knelt beside the rear tire of Ursula's BMW 5 Series. She took out a small vial, half full of black jinx salt, from her purse and poured half of the contents into the palm of her hand. She slung it across the tire then went around and did the same to the rear wheel on the other side. She dropped the empty vial into her purse and fished out two more, one filled with water and the other with blessing salts she'd ground into a fine powder.

Lucky for her, the clear sky let the Moon shine bright tonight. She held up the vial of water until she could see moonlight reflected inside. With one hand, she popped the cap off the powdered blessing salts and sprinkled some inside, which she'd learned sealed the moonlight reflected in the water, making it easy to harvest its magical properties. She shook the vial until the solution inside glowed ghostly blue. This was trapped moonlight—or moon-glo, as Valentina had named it.

No matter how hard she'd tried, she'd never been able to conjure raw moonlight—not like Cris. Valentina had wondered more than once if Cris had lied about not being able to teach her because she feared Valentina would upstage her. But despite her ex-bestie, Valentina had found another way. Moon-glo wasn't quite as effective as the raw stuff harvested direct from the Moon, but it worked well enough.

Valentina dabbed the moon-glo on her thumb like parfum and swiped an X on the sidewalls of Ursula's rear tires. The marks glowed an icy blue, then shifted to burnt orange before evaporating into curling tendrils of white smoke. She clutched the vial of moon-glo in her hand, kissed the side of her knuckle, and held her fist toward the Moon. As she tucked the vial into her purse, she muttered thanks to the twins, Atta and Neki, gen gods of mischief and vengeance, respectively.

Enjoy your ride home, bitch.

Valentina turned her phone on as she walked back to the car. Grandpa donned a look of relief when she opened the door. Granny had been in midrant about something, but she cut it short right as Valentina slid into the backseat. Granny gave Grandpa a stern look that meant this conversation would continue later in private.

"Did you find your phone?" asked Granny.

"I did," Valentina lied. "It must've slipped out of my bag."

"Mhmm." Granny turned and stared out the window.

"Granny?" Valentina asked.

"Yes, baby?"

Valentina hated when her granny's voice sounded frayed at the edges from exhaustion. Granny had to shoulder too much on her own—she was strong, but she was still human.

"Since our evening was cut short, is it okay if I spend the night with you and Grandpa?" she asked, sweetening her voice the way she knew Granny liked, despite the dread smoldering in her gut.

She didn't want to go home tonight. Her parents were arguing more often, the fights intensifying by the round.

"Of course, my baby," Granny said. "Your room is always ready whenever you want a sleepover."

"Maybe I should just move in." Valentina waited for Granny to squee in agreement, but Granny didn't. Valentina chuckled (instead of crying like she wanted to) and said, "Kidding, of course."

Grandpa and Granny shared a look Valentina couldn't decode from the backseat, but still made her fold into herself and want to disappear. She was sick of feeling like a burden to everyone.

Granny turned on the oldies station on her satellite radio and sang terribly to Luther Vandross, Patti LaBelle, Diana Ross, and a bunch of other people Valentina only knew because of her. Grandpa scowled the rest of the way home, in a different hell than Valentina, but in hell all the same.

Valentina wasn't sure how, but Grandpa got them home in record time. Her grandparents' neighborhood was major goals. They drove by a string of gargantuan colonial-style homes, the majestic kind, wrapped in blankets of thick, gorgeous ivy, with long porches and tall, ornate columns. It was the kind of place a queen and her family would live. There was nothing wrong with Valentina's neighborhood—it was nice—but it wasn't *this*. Going home after a stay at Granny's always reminded Valentina she deserved better—which was depressing as fuck.

Her grandparents' home was a beautiful French château style with a set of heavy wooden front doors that reminded her of the ones leading into the Council Chamber in the basement of St. John's Cathedral. Her grandparents had lived in this home as long as Valentina could remember. Granny said the previous owner died unexpectedly, and the surviving family couldn't afford to keep it, so she'd bought it for next to nothing. Granny deserved it—it was a McCastle fit for the Queen.

Grandpa parked the car in the garage, and Valentina followed them both inside the house. He muttered something and vanished to the basement, probably to smoke cigars and listen to jazz until he fell asleep in his recliner. Granny gestured for Valentina to follow her to the kitchen, where she pulled down two teacups and saucers from the cabinet.

"Would you like some tea?" she asked.

"Yes, ma'am." Valentina sat on one of the stools at the counter and watched her granny set up the electric kettle and select two bags of lavender and chamomile tea from an old colorful tin.

Every square foot of Granny's home gushed stately opulence, each room resembling a page ripped straight from an interior-design magazine. It was . . . a lot. Plush, oversized furniture that felt as if it were custom built for a family of miniature giants. Rugs and tapestries that'd traveled through more countries than Valentina, her parents, and her grandparents combined. And the paintings hanging in every room looked like something on loan from the Louvre. That stuff was cool, but what mattered most to Valentina was this place was safe. It could've been a single-wide trailer with beanbag chairs and air mattresses for all she cared; as long as it was Granny's, it would feel the same.

Valentina's home wasn't as large or luxurious as her grandparents'. It wasn't awful either—if she ignored subtle imperfections like the fist-sized hole in her parents' bedroom wall courtesy of one of their arguments last month or Mom's abandoned craft room, where a layer of dust had settled on everything. If she could only see her room as a bedroom and not a cell.

"Join me in the sitting room?" Granny asked as she finished setting up their steaming cups of tea on a tray, complete with cute little ceramic containers for lumps of sugar and cream and even a mini tray for the biscuits. Valentina was fine grabbing a few cookies in one hand and her tea in the other, but Granny liked doing these things "the proper way," so Valentina let her.

She went to the sitting room and switched on a brass floor lamp in the corner. The room housed a small company of plants with all kinds of leaves, some wide and fanlike, others thin daggers, and even a genuine Venus flytrap, which Valentina thought was dope. She wanted one, too, one day, but she had her hands full taking care of herself right now.

Granny sat the tray on the coffee table, lowered herself onto the couch, and patted the space next to her. "You still take your tea with four lumps and a gallon of cream?"

"Ha ha," Valentina said as she sat on the couch. "I can do it." She reached for the cup, but Granny popped her hand gently.

"I said I got it." Granny grinned.

While she waited for her tea, Valentina's focus strayed to the floor—and the one extravagant thing in her grandparents' entire house that she adored more than she admired. The beautiful blue rug with stunning, elaborate designs in a palette of deep golds, reds, and blues that seemed to dance with Valentina's eyes.

Of all the hundreds of expensive things in Granny's house, that rug had always felt the most special. It had a quiet aura about it that captivated Valentina and was also why the sitting room was her favorite room in Granny's home. She imagined the gods crafting the gorgeous rug on an ancient golden loom and gifting it to Granny when she took the throne. Of course, that was complete bullshit, but it was nice to dream from time to time.

"That rug is genuine Mashahir, you know," Granny said when she caught Valentina staring. "A gift from Bethesda DeLacorte after I became Queen. She'd meant it as the first step toward peace between gen and white mages. Given how Madeline's been carrying on, Bethesda's probably rolling like a log on the Mississippi in her grave right now." She handed Valentina her tea.

Valentina took a sip. It was perfect. As usual. "Were the gen at war with the white witches or something?" she asked.

"Oh, no," said Granny. "My predecessor, Cristine Dupart, and Bethesda didn't have the best relationship. Diplomacy was never one of Cristine's strengths. But I'm not interested in dwelling in the past tonight." Leave it to Granny to dead the subject before Valentina could probe any further than Granny cared for her (or anyone) to go. "I'm concerned."

Valentina shifted uncomfortably. "About what?"

Granny sipped her tea and clinked her cup back onto its saucer. "I had no idea things would escalate the way they did tonight. I'll admit, Ursula's outburst caught me by surprise, but I'm more than capable of handling her; and I certainly don't want you worrying yourself and thinking you need to move in here to look after me."

Now Granny's response to Valentina's moving-in "joke" made sense. Granny was wrong, though. Valentina didn't worry about her, at least not like that. Granny had long since proven she could take care of herself; she just needn't do it alone anymore.

Valentina had her back from now on.

"Okay," she said, playing into her grandmother's assumption to avoid delving into her personal issues. But she wasn't ready to move on from this topic just yet. "What did Ursula mean when she said you sold out your friend?" she asked.

Granny took a deep breath in, and when she let it out, her shoulders sagged along with her expression. "Cristine Dupart was my best friend, but we grew apart. Once she became Queen, she became less of a friend to me. Power consumed her. After the mayor's daughter was murdered, the police questioned me, and I told the truth—simple as that. When Cristine died, Ursula was not long out of diapers, so there's no way she has a handle on the truth like she thinks she does."

Valentina knew Granny had been acquainted with Cris's grandmother and namesake, but tonight was the first she'd heard the term "best friend" thrown in the mix. The gods had a seriously fucked-up sense of humor to pair her and Cris together two generations later. Granny had been right to cut ties with Cristine, just as Valentina had done with Cris. *Three whole decades later, and nothing's changed about that family.*

"Then what's Ursula's deal?" asked Valentina.

Granny patted Valentina's knee in that patronizing way she did to signal that a particular subject was no longer available for discussion. "Let's shift back to the present, sweetheart. Since we're baring our souls in the tearoom tonight, there's something I've been wanting to ask you for a while."

Anything Granny had told Valentina up until then hardly qualified as a nip slip, much less "baring her soul." But she'd play along. It wasn't like she had a choice, although she wasn't fond of these questions, especially considering she could sense the one she didn't want to answer lurking somewhere at the edge of this conversation.

"Okay," she said, trying (and failing) to hide the reluctance in her voice.

"I've picked up on a bit of tense energy between your mom and dad lately. And I've noticed you've been asking to stay over more often—we love having you here, and you are more than welcome to come as often as you like, but I'd be less than a granny if I didn't ask if everything was okay at home."

Valentina gripped the edge of the couch cushion to prevent

herself from launching into her grandmother's embrace and confessing everything. She thought to throw open the floodgates, send up every flare within reach, so Granny could rescue her—consequences be damned. But she couldn't; not without starting a war between her parents and her grandparents. No one was coming to save her.

She would have to save herself—like always.

Valentina nodded. "I'm fine." She didn't look up despite feeling Granny's eyes on her, because it would've taken only one millisecond of eye contact for Granny to know Valentina was lying.

"Valentina . . ." pressed Granny.

"I . . . um . . ."

Why was this so hard? Why couldn't she either tell the truth or shut the conversation down? She could handle anything else life threw at her, but why the hell was this the thing that made her feel absolutely powerless? She took a deep breath to gather her nerves and blew it out slowly.

"It's okay, I swear. I just wish Daddy and Mom would get their shi—I mean, *stuff*—together." She finally looked up, tears blurring her granny's face. The pressure steadily built behind her eyes like water pressing against a creaking dam.

She sniffed and wiped her face with her hands. She hated herself for not being able to control her emotions, to hold back these damned tears. She needed to show Granny why she deserved the throne. How could she rule an entire magical community if she couldn't handle this shit?

"That's the thing about parents—none of us are perfect," Granny said, and produced a kerchief from somewhere close by that she handed to Valentina. "Not even me, which you may find hard to believe, but don't fret, because your granny's not far off." She winked, and Valentina laughed despite her tears. "Witnessing your parents' failures is a blessing if you can learn from their weaknesses and use that to chart a path to being better; and also a curse, because it can hurt like hell." She took both Valentina's hands in hers, which were as soft as they were strong. "No matter what, my baby, promise me you'll be better."

"I want to be like you." Valentina regretted the admission the moment Granny shook her head.

"No," Granny said. "Remember what I just said—be *better*."

"Yes, ma'am."

Granny held out her arms, and Valentina sank into them.

But she didn't cry again. There was nothing more to cry about.

She had to be better, no matter the cost. But there was still something lingering in the background, something that could uproot any possibility of "better" she might've had.

When she pulled back, Valentina asked, "What are you going to do about Madeline DeLacorte's threat?"

Granny grimaced and took a sip of her tea. "I'm still trying to figure that out. But don't worry—I'm going to handle her and anyone else who has the gall to threaten my position on the Gen Council."

Valentina forced a smile despite losing her appetite for tea. Not worrying wasn't an option when her future was on the line. And if Granny and Mom weren't going to make a move to neutralize the very real threat that Madeline's and Cris's families posed, then it was simply up to her—as usual.

Except she had no idea where to begin.

EIGHT

CLEMENT

I still can't believe Aunt Ursula slapped the shit out of an old lady.

I've always admired how she grabs life by the throat, while I can only dream of having even a modicum of that control.

We make it back to our booth to find we've missed the first half hour of the show. It's a bit hard to settle down and pay attention after the battle royale in the parking lot just now. However, Rosalie's performance makes short work of completely captivating me. She plays the part of Princess Jasmine, who falls in love with Aliyah, a female vagabond whose fortune is forever changed by an ancient lesbian genie trapped in an exquisite old wine bottle. When I think of talking to Yves about it later, my heart gives a small leap.

Aunt Rose is a different creature onstage from how I remember her when she lived with us. She's always been free-spirited and an intensely passionate person—it wasn't unusual to find her sprawled on a blanket on the lawn, bawling over some song or book she felt a strong connection with. When she's onstage, her brown skin shines with bright undertones, and her long, wavy black hair sways with every movement, as if she's a dancing siren, drawing every person in the audience under her spell.

When the final curtain falls and the lights come on again, I let out a deep breath and join in on the standing ovation. Cris smiles and claps beside me, and Aunt Ursula gives a few annoyed smacks of her hands before shouldering her purse and heading for the door.

Justin bursts through it before she can reach for the handle, and she almost slaps someone for the second time tonight.

He holds up both hands, narrowly avoiding the assault. "Whoa, what's the deal? And what happened to Lenora and Felix?"

"Why in the hell would you put me in this booth with that woman?" asks Ursula. "You *know* how I feel about her, so why would you do something so messy?"

His brows rise, and he looks among the three of us expectantly. "Did she say something to you?"

Cris nudges me with her elbow. His question does seem odd. I know Justin. He may be messy, but he's also deliberate. Everything he does has a purpose—even deserting his family.

"Ha! What *didn't* that rude bitch say?" Ursula pushes past him into the hallway. "Take me to my sister *now*. I'm done playing with you, Justin."

Dejection replaces the curiosity in his eyes, and he stands aside. We let him and Ursula lead the way to Aunt Rose's dressing room, where we'll hopefully convince her to come home with us tonight so we can conjure Wise John's Moon.

I fall in step with Cris. "I'm sorry about what I said at the Golden Key," I tell her. "I wasn't trying to be mean, I just—"

"It's okay," she says. "I get you want to look out for me, but I can take care of myself."

I'm not confident in that, but I nod anyway.

I lean close and whisper, "Was it just me, or did it seem like Justin purposely set up that argument between Aunt Ursula and Lenora?"

"Totally not just you. But why?"

I shrug. "He asked if she said anything almost as if he'd expected her to reveal something."

"I caught that, too. But all she did was insult Aunt Ursula."

"We'll never know the truth, because Justin is a selfish liar and Aunt Ursula protects secrets like a mob boss."

We cut through the theater and backstage to Aunt Rose's dressing room, where Justin raps on the closed door and leads us inside after she calls for him to come in.

Rosalie sits on a couch with one of the extras draped across her lap. The woman seems upset we interrupted her quality time with

Rosalie, who clutches a glass of bourbon in one hand and the woman's petite waist in the other.

Ursula steps around Justin and clears her throat loudly. Rosalie smirks and nudges the girl, who slides off and leaves the room, looking crestfallen.

"Well, I'll leave you all to it," Justin says, and leaves.

Rosalie beams at us. "Cristina! Clement! What a surprise to see you here. You've grown so much!" She's exchanged her costume for a satin robe, but she's still wearing her elaborate stage makeup. The shimmering gold paint on her eyelids and the dusting of rose blush on her cheeks still fails to detract focus from the rich browns and stark whites of her eyes.

"Hey," we both say.

"Did you all see all the commotion right before the show started?" She shakes her head and sips her drink. "Those damned Redeemers have been vandalizing all the Firefly stores for weeks now, and the police won't do jack shit about it."

"I don't care about those fools," says Ursula. "We came to get you."

"*Get* me?" Rosalie scoffs and leans back in her seat. "Did y'all enjoy the show? If I would've known you were coming, I could've hooked you up with the VIP experience."

Ursula gives an exaggerated sigh. "Never mind all that, Rosalie. We need you to come home for a couple hours—"

"Not gonna happen," says Rosalie. "I'm meeting someone in a few minutes."

An anxious fire lights in the bottom of my gut, and rage rears up from the flames like a molten dragon. I don't understand why everyone in this family is so fucking difficult. A part of me wonders why I miss them all so much. All they know how to do is hurt one another and run away.

Ursula spreads her hands. "Who is more important than your family?"

"I'm afraid that's none of your business." Rosalie refills her glass and takes a drink. "Is there anything else you want—other than me going back to that fucking crucible, which is definitely *not* happening?"

The dragon roars and breaks free inside me. "Someone tried to kill Mama, Aunt Rose!" I shout before I can stop myself.

I feel every eye in the room on me, but I don't give a shit. I wish there was another way to conjure this gotdamned spell. We're all going to die if survival depends on getting these people to release their claws from one another's necks for a couple of hours.

Cris's judgmental glare scalds the side of my face, but I don't look at her. I will not give her the satisfaction of an I-told-you-so. I'm trying the best I can. I don't think she understands how anxiety and depression make you feel like you're wearing weighted clothing, struggling to go about what everyone else considers a normal day.

"We found a hex doll in her mattress this morning," I say. "We don't know who put it there, or when, or why, but what we do know is everyone needs to stop fighting and get their asses to the house *now*, so we can conjure Wise John's Moon before someone murders us all."

Aunt Rose's face telegraphs her wall crumbling, and I heave a sigh of relief. Her smug expression fades and her voice softens. "I thought she was just . . . sick."

Ursula sits next to Rosalie and puts an arm around her. "Come on, Rose. Marie practically raised you after Mama and Daddy died. She deserves better from all of us—you, most of all."

Rosalie sets her glass down. "Okay. Let me change and get my things together. I'll be quick."

Aunt Ursula and I ride in stifling silence. I got the impression when I suggested riding with her instead of with Cris and Rosalie that she preferred I didn't but couldn't bring herself to say so.

That stings. And I feel dumb for trying, but, yet again, here I am. I just wish I could know my aunt again. I miss being in her space. I miss her energy. I miss *her*.

But the thought of slipping back into her world and possibly ending up gutted again makes me feel hollowed out. And yet, my curiosity won't let me be great.

Maybe I should just ask the question that's been picking at the Ursula-sized scab in my brain since the parking-lot confrontation. Anything would be better than this agonizing quiet.

"Who is Celeste? And what did she do to you?"

Ursula's grip on the steering wheel tightens. "Nothing. It's very classless of folks like Lenora to throw out damaging lies about other people."

"So, you *can* have kids?"

She tightens her stranglehold on the wheel. "I said *drop* it, Clem."

"I don't get it."

"Because there's nothing for you to get."

"I don't get *you*! I can't just switch people on and off at my convenience like you do. So, I apologize if me giving a damn about you is annoying." I turn to the window with a huff.

I wish it wasn't so easy for people to get a rise out of me. If only there was a spell to protect my emotions. I'd lock them all away without a second thought.

"What do you want from me?" she asks, as if me wanting to be loved is such a tremendous burden. How dare I demand such a thing?

"The truth!" I yell, resisting the urge to punch her dashboard. "You can't even be honest about what was *so* bad you had to bolt from the house like it was haunted. You just left . . . like I didn't matter."

"I cannot *wait* for the day you find out the world isn't always fucking black-and-white," she grumbles.

My world hasn't been anything but black for a long time, because people keep stealing the fucking light.

"You don't know the shit I've had to deal with over the course of my *entire* life," she continues. "After my best friend died and my relationship with my sisters went to shit, I needed to be on my own. And I don't have to justify that to anyone—especially you."

"I didn't know your best friend died," I say, calmer now. "Why didn't you tell me?"

Aunt Ursula has always been private. I knew she had some sort of life outside of what she displayed at home, but mostly, she kept family separate from personal.

"Because I don't have to tell you everything," she says. "I really wish you'd lay off me."

I throw my hands up. "Say less. You're not worth the headache. Please just help Mama and then you can go back to your wonderful life. I understand how incredibly important it is to you."

She reaches for my hand, but I snatch it away. "Clem, I—"

She chokes on the words at the same time an ear-bursting *POP* resounds. The interior of the car fills with the pungent stench of burnt rubber. Our sedan launches into the air, and the force clamps my mouth shut, trapping the scream now banging against the backs of my teeth.

A sound like a bomb exploding makes my ears ring. The airbags shoot out, smashing into the side of my face.

We turn upside down. Aunt Ursula reaches for me.

Her fingertips brush mine.

The car slams into the ground with a crunch like lightning splitting asphalt.

My head hits something hard.

A wave of black swallows me.

Cold water rushes around my head and down my back. I sit up, startled, spitting out salty water and clawing at the sandy ground. I crawl up away from the shore onto the beach and stop to take some slow, deep breaths.

What the fuck?

The sand shifting between my fingers is soft, cool, and black. I've never been to a black-sand beach before—nor did I think any were close to New Orleans. I stand up and look around.

The sky is bleak and empty, except for one large glowing orb. The Moon? No. Too solid and a thousand times brighter. I shield my eyes. To my left, sand stretches on forever, endless dark water to my right. The air is tepid and smells of salt water and nothing else. Where the hell am I? Where's Aunt Ursula?

I put my hands up to my mouth and call, "Hellooo!"

The silence stretches on, boundless like the beach. I'm alone. My heart plummets. Did I die? Is this the spiritual realm? I almost choke on the lump in my throat—or is this the never-realm . . .

A shadowy, humanoid figure appears on the horizon. They slink across the desolate canvas in the distance, as if they lost all hope long ago.

"Hello!" I shout again.

They freeze for a long while, then turn and begin to walk in my direction. Maybe they can tell me where the hell I am, or even better—help me get back home.

"Hey!" I wave my hands above my head and start toward them.

They pick up pace. Their speed-walk evolves into a jog, and then an all-out sprint.

I stop on the spot, nearly tripping over my own feet.

They keep running, closing the distance between us. Fast.

I can see now it's a man. Freakishly tall and imposing, ripping across the beach like an Olympic gold medalist.

Coming straight for me.

When he bellows my name, his voice ruptures the air like thunder.

"CLEMENT!"

I turn and run.

"CLEMENT! STAY WITH ME!"

I clasp my hands over my ears, but it does little to block out his screams. It's like he's inside my fucking head.

"Leave me alone!" My toes catch on a small hill of sand, pitching me forward. I fall on my hands and spring upright again, hardly slowing.

"CLEMENT! COME BACK!"

I glance over my shoulder and immediately wish I hadn't. My insides electrify. A frightened whimper dies in my throat.

He's almost caught up to me.

Up close, he seems eight or nine feet tall, at *least*. He's bald, naked, built like a god, and running barefoot across the sand as if it were flat grassland. His solid white eyes contrast with the midnight blackness of the rest of him like spotlights, locked on to me.

His icy fingers clamp onto my shoulder, and I shriek.

It feels like Death themself has me in their clutches. Cold radiates from his touch, as if he's slowly emptying all the life from me and replacing it with . . . something alive—like . . . essence of *him*.

I try to run, but my legs feel like cotton candy. My voice is gone.

I can only stare wide-eyed into the blank face of the being devouring me from the inside out.

And then the Moon, no, whatever the fuck that thing is in the sky, explodes in a blinding display of light. The force frees me from the being's grip, flinging me several feet through the air.

My back smacks hard against the sand.

The air rips from my lungs.

And my world goes dark. Again.

NINE

CRISTINA

The ambulance careens around a corner, nearly sending my stomach flying out of my mouth. I brace myself against the neon-yellow straps holding me against the rickety seat that jostles as much as the medical supplies and various tubes and things as the driver seems to be aiming for every pothole they can find. Aunt Rose follows in my car, and Aunt Ursula, who'd just begun to regain consciousness as they loaded her into a different ambulance, is ahead of ours.

I lean forward and squeeze my unconscious brother's hand tighter. The EMT calls Clem's name while attending to the bloody wound near Clem's temple.

My mind won't leave those terrible, hour-long seconds I stood outside the smashed car that had trapped my brother and aunt inside. My heart sank into my stomach until we pulled them both to safety. No matter how much Clem and I fight, I don't know how to survive a world without my brother in it.

Clem's entire body seizes. He yanks his hand out of mine to cover his face and lets out a shriek that makes my spine shiver.

"Clem—" I pull his hands down and look into his wide, flitting eyes, which seem lost in another world. "—you're okay. You were in an accident. We're on our way to the hospital."

"Uggh." He relaxes and exhales.

I fall back against my seat, wiping my wet eyes with the back of my hand. After the EMT confirms Clem's going to be fine, the rest of what she says to him bobs in and out of my mind like a buoy in choppy water.

I could've lost Clem. I don't want to feel that agonizing cinch of my heart ever again. And that's exactly why I can never tell him my secret. If he knew I conjured the spell that took away the most important person in his life, he'd hate me. And I'd lose him.

We arrive at the hospital, and Clem and Aunt Ursula are whisked inside, where they're met with nurses who take them to separate triage cubicles in the emergency wing. Rosalie follows Ursula, and I stay with my brother. By the time Clem's comfortable in a bed, he's completely come around, already bitching about possibly having a scar on his temple from the tiny gash the doctor stitches closed.

Our cubicle is tiny, only big enough for the patient bed Clem's currently reclining on. There's only standing room near the entrance where I wait, but my heart's racing too fast for me to sit still anyway.

The doctor laughs from where she hovers over Clem, tying each knot with delicate precision. "You might have a little scar, but I think it'll look badass."

I smile and nod when Clem glances at me for reassurance. Besides the minor head wound, he only has a couple of purpling bruises to the left side of his face, from the airbag, and some cuts and scrapes on his arms, from the broken glass. In a few days, I imagine he'll look almost normal again. Thank the gods.

Fast-approaching footsteps draw my attention and I turn to meet Mama's worried eyes as she rushes into the cubicle. She sweeps me into a crushing hug, which startles me into a stupor for a moment, but I wrap my arms around her and squeeze back. I take a slow, deep breath in and exhale as I lean into her—and the strength resonating from her. It's been ages since I could, and only this morning I was afraid I'd never get this chance again. But now it's like she was never sick.

"You're really okay," I say when we part, more stunned observation than question.

The heavy bags I'd grown accustomed to seeing darkening the skin beneath her eyes are gone. Her brown skin glows anew, like it's been revitalized from the inside out. She stands tall and resilient in front of me, fully renewed from the destructive magic meant to kill her.

She smiles and tugs on a stray strand of my ponytail. "Yes, baby, thank Papa Eshu." Even her voice sounds fiercer, smoother.

I'm not sure which of the gods, if any, deserves thanks considering the magic they govern nearly killed her, but I bite my tongue.

Mama swoops to Clem's bedside, and he stares up at her with an expression of surprised relief.

"You should be home resting," he tells her once the shock wears off. "I'm fine."

"As long as there is breath in my body, nothing will ever stop me from being there for my babies." She kisses his temple and looks to the doctor. "Will he be okay?"

"A mild concussion, but all his injuries appear superficial," she says. "We're going to run some tests to be certain."

Mama nods. "Of course. Thank you."

The doctor leaves, and Mama and I both get a moment to throw our arms around Clem and fuss over him before he's wheeled away for a barrage of scans and X-rays—all of which come back fine. The doctor prescribes Clem some narcotics for pain and sends us away with orders for him to rest.

Mama, Clem, and I step outside the cubicle at the same time Rosalie and Ursula emerge from theirs. Ursula has similar bruising on her face and arms as Clem, but got away with no stitches, though her tired expression makes her look as if she's been dragged through the never-realm.

"Would you believe that racist-ass cop gave me a tick—" Ursula stops in midrant when she sees us. "Oh, Clem! Are you hurt?"

He shakes his head, and she grapples him in a hug. He doesn't hug her back and steps closer to me when they part. I wonder what that's about.

Ursula locks eyes with Mama. "Marie . . ."

Mama hugs Ursula, who closes her eyes and clings to her sister. "I'm so glad you're okay," Mama says, rubbing Ursula's back.

Ursula steps back and smiles uncomfortably. "You seem fine, too."

Mama's face hardens for a moment, but she turns to smile at Rosalie. "Hey, Rose. You look good, sis."

Rosalie's stubborn grudges and love for her sister battle on her face, but she forces a smile. "Thanks."

We all leave for the parking garage, and Ursula follows quietly behind Mama, who speaks with Rosalie and ignores Ursula's brooding. The tension between them makes me uneasy. Whatever happened, it's obvious neither of them is over it; and curiosity about the reason won't stop poking the back of my mind.

Mama informs us Desiree and Jacquelyn are waiting back at the house. Clem gets into my car before anyone can say anything about driving arrangements, which leaves Ursula to grudgingly accept Mama's invitation to ride with her. Rosalie joins them.

Clem cracks the door and says in a quiet, anxious voice, "Do you mind just checking your tires real quick before we leave?"

"Of course," I tell him, and do a quick walk-around and give him the thumbs-up before getting into the driver's seat. "What do you think happened?" I ask, buckling my seat belt.

He shrugs. "Bad tires, maybe? I've heard of blowouts happening before, but I never thought it'd happen to me."

"I'm just glad you're okay."

Clem and I bask in the peaceful silence as I turn out of the parking garage and follow Mama's car through the nighttime streets back home. Today's lasted an entire year.

"Aunt Ursula and I were fighting before the accident." Clem's still staring out the window at the dark city, the streetlamps we pass strobing his face with a dim, otherworldly light.

"About what?" I'm hoping the answer won't be what I know full well it is.

He sinks lower in his seat, still facing the window. "I don't understand any of them—"

"Then stop trying."

He throws his hands up. "It's not that easy. My mind doesn't work the way yours does."

"I'm looking out for you, *because* I understand how your brain works, Clem. I don't want to see you get hurt again chasing behind selfish people. Please don't get sucked back into our aunt's drama."

He sighs and returns to silence. I wish I could protect my brother from himself. But I guess it's hard to let people go when you keep losing them. I don't push the issue further, because the guilt that sits at the edge of my conscience reminds me I've hurt him, too. He just doesn't know it yet.

"While I was out," he says, "I had this dream that didn't really feel like a dream."

"I'm listening." Even this topic is better than continuing the pointless discussion of our dysfunctional family.

"I woke up on a black-sand beach and there was something there with me—" He pauses and hugs himself. "—and it chased me. This giant, umber-skinned man or spirit or whatever it was, caught me . . . and it was like I could feel him . . . latching on to my soul." He shudders and falls quiet.

"That sounds scary as shit. But it was only a dream. You were unconscious for a while."

"Mhmm . . ." is all he says, gazing out the window.

I'm not sure I'm going to change his mind about anything to-night.

I pull into our estate and follow Mama's car up the road to our home.

"I can't believe we actually got them all to come back," Clem muses aloud.

"Don't celebrate too early. We still have to keep them all docile long enough to conjure Wise John's Moon."

And I'm worried as fuck. The Dupart-Trudeau family fails team-building fantastically—every single time.

"Is it foolish to think they might all move back someday?" he asks.

"Yes." I park behind Clem's car and throw my door open. "I'd advise you not to get your hopes up."

He rolls his eyes and gets out.

We file into the house behind Mama, Ursula, and Rosalie, and head to the kitchen, where Desiree sits at the island with her laptop and a glass of bourbon. Her fingers clack on her keyboard for a few moments longer before she looks up at us through her red-framed glasses and smiles. She's dressed in a white-and-black pantsuit and heels, which suggests she's come straight from work. She's Michael Prince's campaign manager, which I only know because I've seen her with him on the news talking about his campaign for mayor of New Orleans. She and I aren't exactly close, but Michael's a Democrat and pro-magic, so at least she's on the right side.

Desiree is my least favorite of my aunts, but she doesn't know that. Although I considered telling her when she wouldn't stop harassing me about enrolling in some program at Howard University up in D.C. this summer. Even if I did care, Mama was sick and my family needed me, but Desiree, for whatever reason, couldn't wrap her brilliant mind around that despite all those degrees in political science and law that she loves to flaunt. She's the kind of woman who will shove others out of her way to shatter the glass ceiling first and pretend not to notice when the shards she sends raining down slice everyone behind her to ribbons.

"Clement," Desiree says softly, and gets up to kiss him on the top of his head. "How're you feeling? I was here when your mama got the call that y'all had been in an accident. I stayed behind so someone would be here when your aunt Jacquelyn arrived."

"I'm fine, really," he announces and sidles closer to me, likely avoiding another hug onslaught.

I'd think after losing so many people, he'd try to soak up as much affection as he could get whenever he could get it. But then I remember that with him, it's all or nothing.

"Glad to see you're okay as well, Ursula," says Desiree.

Ursula offers a dry greeting, and the room falls into throttling silence.

Stewing in the tension, Rosalie says, "Hi, Desiree. Great to see you, too, sis."

Desiree grimaces, deeply wrinkling her flawless brown complexion, and says hello, but Rosalie's already plundering the liquor cabinet, unbothered now she's successfully needled her older sister.

"Make me one, too, please," Ursula tells Rosalie.

"If Desiree hasn't cleared out all the bourbon already," Rosalie mutters.

With an even deeper frown, Desiree returns to her seat and continues tapping the keys of her laptop, now with angry gusto.

Clem heaves a deep breath beside me, and I pass him an *I told you so* look.

"Where's Jackie?" asks Mama. "We should get started."

Desiree throws a furtive glance at Ursula and Rosalie, who huddle near the liquor cabinet with their backs to us. But Desiree doesn't have to answer, because at that moment Jacquelyn steps into the room. She's a short and curvy natural beauty with light gray eyes, the only one of my aunts who inherited them from my grandfather. Her fair skin flushes with color as she stands at the edge of the kitchen, dressed in sweats, her hair in a messy ponytail. She bounces a fussy baby, who looks no older than six or seven months, judging by the few tiny teeth I spot poking through their gums every time they wail.

Enigmatic Jacquelyn. It's very on-brand for her to show up with a surprise baby. Mama said when they were younger, Jacquelyn often got lost because she couldn't compete with the titans of personality that her sisters were. As a result, Jacquelyn grew to be secretive and withdrawn; however, tonight she just stepped onstage as the main character at the drama factory.

"Sorry," Jacquelyn announces. "Baptiste's a bit irritable because it's his bedtime."

Ursula whirls around. "Who?"

"Shit," Rosalie mumbles. "Here we go."

Here we go is right. We're supposed to be coming together to protect each other, and we're already on the cusp of a throwdown.

Ursula sets her drink on the counter and slowly approaches Jacquelyn. My eyes bounce between the two of them like a tennis ball at Wimbledon. She stares down at the whining baby, and Jacquelyn clutches him tighter. After what seems like ages, Ursula cracks a smile. A collective—albeit premature—sigh escapes everyone. I still hold my breath. We have a better chance of winning the lottery than everyone walking away from this unscathed.

"Lemme see that baby," Ursula says, arms outstretched. Jacquelyn hands him over, and Ursula rocks him, cooing softly. "His name's Baptiste?"

"Yes," Jacquelyn says, pride nudging her shoulders back. "After Daddy."

"That's sweet," says Ursula. "I think that fits him." He watches her with large, curious eyes and she stares back. "And who's his father?"

Jacquelyn looks away. "Ursula, don't start . . . please. I didn't come here for this."

It doesn't make sense that Aunt Jackie would hide her kid from us. Though Ursula's delivery isn't the greatest, I would like to know the true reason behind all the secrecy, too.

Ursula looks affronted. "It's only a question. I had no idea you were even dating again, and you show up here with a *whole* baby out the blue and I'm not supposed to be curious?"

"Give me back my baby," demands Jacquelyn.

Ursula returns baby Baptiste and glares at her sister. "Tell me the truth, Jackie. Is he a Van Kid?"

Clem knits his brows at me, and I shrug. I've never heard of a Van Kid before, but judging by how pissed Aunt Jackie's looking right now, it can't be anything good.

Jacquelyn shoves Ursula hard, and Ursula stumbles backward into the counter.

"Well, this certainly is low-class of us," Desiree mumbles.

Rosalie rolls her eyes. "We already know you think you're better than everyone, Desiree. You don't have to remind us every got-damn minute."

My entire body stiffens. Clem stares at me with wide eyes. I can't believe this shit either. We're a few seconds out from a full-on brawl right here in the kitchen. If someone really wants us dead, all they'd have to do is lock us all in a room for an hour and let us finish one another off.

Desiree slams her laptop closed and hops up from her seat at the same time Ursula starts for Jacquelyn.

"*Enough!*" shouts Mama. The room falls silent and still. "This is *un*believable. We haven't been together five minutes and y'all have gone berserk! Have you forgotten why we're here?"

Thank goodness for Mama. We need to cast this spell so everyone can just go. All this fighting is giving me a migraine.

"Fine," interjects Ursula. "Who's going to lead the conjuring?" She looks at me and I freeze. Of course she does. Last she remembers, I had *a fire inside me conjured by Eshu himself,* or so she thought. A lot has changed since then. That fire's long gone out, if it was ever there in the first place.

"I'd rather not," I say.

"Why?" Ursula's brow wrinkles with irritation.

Mama watches me curiously, though not with judgment like Ursula.

"It's been a long day, and I'm exhausted," I lie. "I don't want to muck it up."

"I'll do it." Clem throws his hands up. "I almost died today, but sure, let's all cling to our bullshit instead of trying to protect our family. Just meet me in the dining room in ten minutes so we can get this over with."

He snatches an empty mason jar from the pantry and storms out of the kitchen. Everyone but Mama either drops their head or looks away.

I catch up to Clem in the dining room, where he grabs the key from the top of Mama's conjuring cabinet. He unlocks it, and the hinges whine as he pulls the old cedar doors open. The inside overflows with all sorts of conjuring materials, the sight of which throws me into a warm reverie. Mama taking an indigo candle from the multicolored collection on the bottom shelf to burn for us when Clem and I were stressed about finals. Or the time she filled a cloth sack with grains of paradise from one of the many tinted apothecary jars, most with yellowed handwritten labels. She'd stitched a protection talisman on the side of the sack and she gave it to me after Valentina began her campaign to make my life hell. For so long, magic was a beloved partner. Until it betrayed me.

I start to say something, but my breath snags at the sight of him retrieving our great-grandmother's leather-bound spell book from the top shelf. He turns and startles when he notices me, but my eyes remain stuck on the book in his hands.

That book ruined my life. And yet, we must rely on it to protect what we have left.

Magic is such a mind-fuck, and I'm over it.

"What do you want?" He sets the book and mason jar on the dining table and flips to the page containing the spell for Wise John's Moon.

"What's the matter with you? One minute you're all doe-eyed about our family coming back together, and the next you're going off on everyone."

He looks up and raises a brow. "I can love someone and still be sick of their shit."

"Is that how you feel about me?"

He sighs and turns back to the book. "Why won't you conjure anymore?" He pauses until he realizes he's not getting an answer. "Does it have something to do with Dad dying, because I—"

"Clem. Don't."

"Whatever." He snatches up the book and jar, grabs a container of crossroads dirt, and brushes past me.

I follow him outside the front door, just as our aunts begin assembling in the dining room. Crickets sing a nighttime tune from the shelter of the shrubs and bushes near the porch as I lean on the railing to watch my brother do what I can't anymore.

He sets the empty jar on the top step and checks the spell book once more before placing it aside. We both turn our gaze upward at the same time. The Moon, nearly full, beams from where it sits amid the black sky, awash with Stars and very few clouds. It's a good night to capture raw moonlight.

Clem starts to speak the incantation, but when I raise a finger, he stops and glowers at me. "What?"

I point to the crossroads dirt. "You forgot the mark."

After Aunt Ursula left Clem flapping in the wind, I took up the charge of helping improve his conjuring. I learned a lot about him during that time. He's never been one to allow details to slow him down—and he almost always forgets the marks. I tried to teach Valentina how to do this once—back when we were still friends. I'm not sure why it never worked for her, and she'd gotten mad at me because I couldn't explain it. I hate how insidious magic is—how it seeps into every aspect of my life and warps everything into a mess of complexity.

But if my brother needs me, I'll be there for him. Besides, coaching him technically isn't conjuring. This at least feels less scary, which is all I have left to gauge if I'm doing what's right. I lost sight of "right" after I lost Dad.

Clem snatches the container and tips it, hastily spilling the dirt onto the porch to draw a large crescent moon fixed with a small cross attached to one of the corners. Once he's finished, he sets the empty mason jar in the center of the moon.

"Nope." I gesture for him to move it over. "Cradle."

He pinches the bridge of his nose and closes his eyes a beat before moving the empty jar inside the cradle of the moon. "Or you could just do the damn spell yourself."

I cross my arms. "You're welcome."

"Thanks," he mumbles.

I fight back my smile and nod.

Clem stares up at the Moon. "O Wise John, hear my plea," he intones. "From this realm to the next, send down your power unto me."

The Moon swells in the sky, blazing almost as bright as the Sun. Beams of light, like tiny shooting Stars, spiral across the sky and down to us, leaving corkscrew streaks behind.

I pick up the container of crossroads dirt. "Hold out your hand." He does, and I pour a bit onto his palm. "Rub your hands together. The friction from the grains will help with guiding the moonlight."

The beams draw nearer, and Clem holds out his hands. I show him the motion—mine cupped at chest level, moving in a circular motion like opposite cogs in a gear. He mimics me, collecting the thin streams of falling moonbeams and massaging them over his hands and into the empty mason jar. When it's full of glowing, blue luminescence, he kneels and drags one finger through the mark, breaking the lines. At once, the stream flows in reverse, as the Moon sucks back its light.

"Don't forget to thank your ancestors," I tell him.

"Oh, yeah," he says, clinging to the jar of raw moonlight. "Thank you, Wise John."

Today has been the closest I've come to doing magic in almost a year. I wonder if it's possible to miss something and fear it at the same time.

"Not too shabby," I say, holding the door open for him to go back inside.

He rolls his eyes as he steps past. "Moonlight is warm." He hugs the jar close to his chest like a steaming mug of coffee. "Did you know?"

"No," I lie. "Magic is full of surprises." I wish that part was a lie, too.

I'm relieved to find my aunts all in one piece, but not surprised. Mama's always been the only one who could keep them from killing one another. It's strange seeing her up and moving around as if she hadn't been on her deathbed only this morning, but it makes me smile all the same.

She and Jacquelyn stand at the head of the table. Mama holds Baptiste and giggles with him. Ursula and Rosalie talk in low voices to each other at the other end of the table, and Desiree's heads-down in her laptop (because of course she is). Someone's already helpfully cleared the table of the settings and linens, and now the naked, dark wood awaits Clem.

The peaceful energy in the dining room feels vastly different from the venomous vibes in the kitchen earlier. It reminds me of when I'm sitting in front of the fire on a cold night or when I'm wrapped in a weighted blanket. It's a magical feeling, but I hate it, because it's also familiar.

They're all going to leave. And I'd like very much to unsubscribe from disappointment and trauma for a while. I just want to finish this spell so I can get to work uncovering who tried to kill my mother.

After consulting the spell book again, Clem pours the crossroads dirt into a crescent moon at the center of the table and then eight concentric circles surrounding it, one for each person present. He places the jar of moonlight in the moon's cradle and looks to me. I nod. We're ready.

I turn off the light, and the jar throws an eerie glow under everyone's faces that makes the whites of their eyes shine. We all stand around the table, me across from Clem, who's at the helm, cradling Great-Grandma Angeline's spell book. I'm not sure why my heart sounds like it's beating between my ears, but I get that Clem feels the same when he lets out a shaky breath.

"I beseech thee . . . ancestors, uh . . . hear my plea from across realms." His incantation is choppy because he keeps pausing to check the spell book. But even so, as he speaks, the jarred moonlight pulses until it nearly bubbles over. "I seek to invoke, umm . . . the powerful shield of Wise John's Moon."

The light boils a bit longer, then simmers and dies to a dull pulse.

Clem's shoulders drop and he plunges back into the book. "I-I don't know what I did wrong."

"Here, I'll finish it." Ursula moves to take his spot, but Mama's voice stops her.

"No." She hands Baptiste back to Jacquelyn, steps behind Clem, and squeezes his shoulders. "You did good, baby. I'll take over from here." He nods and tries to hand her the spell book, but she waves it away. "I don't need it."

"Oh," mumbles Clem as he shuts the book and steps aside.

A chill trips down my back. Aunt Ursula had always hinted at Mama's magical prowess. I never doubted her, but I'd also never seen Mama really flex her conjuring muscles beyond the regular everyday spells for things like good fortune or health.

Mama lifts her hands on either side of her, and when she speaks, her voice erupts from her throat with such intensity, it's as if she's drawing power directly from the spiritual realm.

"Ancestors!" Even the walls seem to tremble under the power of her swelling presence. "Hear my plea! Papa Eshu, I beseech ye! Throw open the gates to the spiritual realm for your faithful servant, for I seek Wise John to invoke the powerful shield of his Moon.

"O Wise John! The eight familiar souls around this conjuring circle call upon your favor of protection. Safeguard these loved ones from those who would seek to curse us with magical affliction. Cloak our bodies and our spirits in the light of your Moon so we may continue our work in honoring the gods, our ancestors, our family."

When the final word bounds from her lips, she drops her hands, and the moonlight shoots from the jar like a geyser.

Electric blue light crashes into the ceiling, spreads to all four corners, and bleeds down the walls. Everyone turns to watch as the brightly pulsing light pools on the floor, engulfing our feet. Faint glimmers spark to life throughout the pool as it washes up my legs, dragging a sense of warmth and peace with it—like the feeling after turning in a final you pulled an all-nighter to study for and are pretty sure you didn't bomb. As it creeps up my body, spiraling in luminous tendrils, the color pales until it turns ghostly gray and the glimmers all fade. I look up to see everyone painted in the same pallid glow.

"Bless you, Baba Eshu. Thank you, Wise John." Mama places her hands on the table, which sucks the light from all of us like an industrial vacuum. The tabletop glows white and the mark erupts in turquoise flames that flicker and die as abruptly as they knew life. The crossroads dirt burns away, and the pool of white light atop the table transforms into dense fog, then drops through the table and to the floor, where it hangs thick at our ankles.

The lights flick back on, almost blinding me. When I open my eyes, Mama stands in the doorway, her hand on the switch. "It's done."

I'm breathless. She makes magic look effortless. I wonder if I could've ever achieved that kind of power. But it's my fault I'll never know.

"I need a refill," announces Ursula, already on her way back to the kitchen. Rosalie falls in line behind her. The others follow, leaving me and Clem alone, standing in the spent moonbeam fog.

He pulls a sack from his pocket. It's attached to a hemp string about as long as his forearm. He squats and twirls it in a counterclockwise circle just above the mist, chanting something under his breath. As he does so, the fog churns and flashes, forming a funnel cloud. It strobes and turns crimson before swirling up into a cyclone, which swells and lengthens as it sucks up all the mist from the floor. It twists up to the ceiling and bleeds into the walls, then disappears.

Clem stands and wraps the string around the sack, then pockets it again.

"What the hell was that?" I ask.

He scoffs. "You're not the only one allowed to have secrets."

TEN

CRISTINA

Clem dips his shady ass into the kitchen with Mama and our aunts before I can ask him anything else.

I've never seen that spell before. I wonder what he's up to, but he'll never tell me. He's just as stubborn as I am. I guess it runs in the family.

I join everyone in the kitchen, where they're already in the throes of an intense discussion. Clem clears the space, retreating to Mama's shadow on the other side of the room. Mama frowns at Ursula, who's going off near where I stand. I glare at Clem, but he just stares right back.

"I don't understand how, even now, after the old hag nearly killed you, you still can just shrug it off and move on." Ursula spreads her hands on either side of her and slaps them onto her hips. "And I'm extra agitated right now, because this is *exactly* why I didn't want to come back here. I knew you would drag me back into this mess."

"I didn't drag you into anything," Mama says. "I needed you for the spell, not your drama."

"Well, I'm not like you, Marie. I've lost too much to be forgiving."

Mama narrows her eyes at Ursula. "I really don't enjoy competing in the Trauma Olympics, but I think I have you beat when it comes to loss."

"Then you should be a lot angrier than me," Ursula says. "Because on top of that, you could've lost Clem *and* me tonight. You might be able to let her slide with that, but I cannot."

"Who?" My interruption earns me a scowl from Mama, but I don't care. I'm sick of all these damn secrets. "Do you know who planted the hex doll?"

"No, baby, your auntie is just delusional," says Desiree from behind her laptop.

"Shut—up, Desiree," shouts Rosalie, which is exactly what I was thinking.

Mama closes her eyes and massages her temples but doesn't intervene.

Ursula slaps her hand on the counter, and everyone quiets. "I don't have proof, but my gut tells me Lenora planted that hex doll and also screwed with my car tonight after our little altercation."

My stomach sinks. "But why would she—"

"Don't!" Mama points at Ursula. "I told you to leave my children out of this."

"Leave us out of what?" I ask.

Mama takes a sharp breath in and blows it out. "Cristina Serafine Trudeau, if you ask one—more—question, you will forget what outside looks like before you get off punishment."

My cheeks heat and I swallow back the rebuttal that'd been brewing since she interrupted me. Across the room, Clem shakes his head at me from where he stands behind Mama. I agree with Ursula that if Lenora's the one messing with our family, we cannot let her get away with it.

And it turns my stomach that Mama can.

"This needs to stop, Ursula." Mama's voice is soft but not short of authority. "I'm *not* losing anyone else."

My chest fills with a buzzing sensation like it's going to explode. I have to clench my jaw to keep from asking another question and suffering Mama's wrath. Even Clem stares at her curiously.

"We're done here," Mama continues. "Thank you all for your help with the spell. Wise John's protection lasts a full Moon cycle—which is thirty days. It's late now. You're all welcome to stay here tonight. Your old rooms are the same as you left them, and I'll get one of the kids' old bassinets from the attic for my precious little nephew."

This Mama seems realms different from the one who conjured

Wise John's Moon moments ago—enough to make me wonder if that hex doll curse changed her somehow.

Ursula shakes her head and finishes the rest of her bourbon.

"Ursula," says Mama, "I'd prefer if you stayed. I'll take you home first thing in the morning. It's late, and you should rest." Ursula frowns until Mama says, "Please."

"Fine." She slams her glass down and heads upstairs. Clem's eyes follow her until she disappears from view.

Desiree closes her laptop with an exaggerated huff. "This meeting could've been an email."

"You know what?" says Rosalie. "I find it tragic that you are not nearly as important as you think you are."

Desiree hugs her laptop. "I'm not going to apologize for having a career, which, might I add, is not playing dress-up and prancing around the land of make-believe. Some of us have real jobs that bring about *real* change in the world."

Rosalie cackles loudly.

Why the fuck is their beef so visceral? Clem and I can be mean to each other, but our aunts are downright cutthroat. I don't get how you could be so vicious with someone you claim to love.

"Come on, you two," says Jacquelyn, leaping into the line of fire. I wince, remembering how she'd been the target not long ago. "We've fought enough already."

Desiree fires back at Rosalie. "Oh, what a joy it must be not to have to use your brain, to get by in life purely on the merit of your looks. Sleeping late in the arms of beautiful folks after long nights of shucking and jiving to the tunes of Justin's twisted imagination."

I wonder if Wise John's Moon can protect our family from one another. If so, now would be a good time for it to kick into effect.

Rosalie lifts her freshly refilled glass to Desiree. "My dear sister. How much I've missed your unconditional love and respect."

"Rose . . ." Mama warns.

Rosalie ignores her, eyes still targeting Desiree. "You sit there all smug in your little pantsuit with your pixie power cut, thumbing your nose at anyone you disapprove of, because it makes you feel better about all the questionable shit you do that you think no one knows about. And you don't have to say it, Desiree, but I know you think I'm just some ditsy whore, flitting about the city on nothing but liquor and a whim, but I don't give one single fuck about your or anyone's opinion of me." Before trudging upstairs, she says over her shoulder, "Good night. I'm going to check on my sister."

Desiree shoulders her bag, kisses Mama on the cheek, says her goodbyes to the rest of us, and leaves. Mama and Clem go to their rooms, leaving me in the kitchen alone with Jacquelyn and baby Baptiste. I let out a sigh of relief now that disaster is finally over.

"I hate that they fight so hard with each other." Jacquelyn's expression bears the weight of our family's dysfunction, but it seems something more drags her down, too.

"Is that why you left?" I ask.

She shakes her head. "I was in love with a guy. His name was Carlisle." She stares longingly out the glass French doors leading to the patio as if Carlisle's going to suddenly appear on the other side to whisk her away. "He made me happy, made me feel like I mattered. But Ursula and Desiree hated him. I couldn't take the mental strain of the constant arguing and judgment, so I left."

I wilt a bit. "Why didn't they like him?"

"They accused him of being racist."

My heart clenches. I'm not sure what I'd do if I found out something so world-shattering about Oz. "Was he?"

"If you'd asked me back then, I'd give a much different answer than I would now."

"Oh . . ." I nod at the sleeping baby in her arms. "Is he Baptiste's dad?"

A darkness grips her. She hugs her baby tight enough to make him grunt in his sleep. "No."

"Why'd Aunt Ursula ask if he's a Van Kid? What's that?"

She stands and readjusts Baptiste in her arms. "Jealousy makes people say cruel things sometimes even if they don't mean it. At least that's what I tell myself so I can go on loving my sisters."

"But—"

"I need to put Baptiste down. Good night, Cris."

"Night," I say, but she's already gone.

I guess Clem was right. I'm apparently *not* the only one who can have secrets.

ELEVEN

CLEMENT

After a hurricane of a day, lying on my bed in the calm and quiet dark feels like lounging on a cloud in the spirit realm. Now I've finally stopped moving, my body reminds me I was in a car accident this evening. *Gee, thanks.* A dull, annoyingly consistent throb hammers my skull, and I glance at the bottle of prescription pain medicine on my bedside table.

The pills make me (more) anxious. I turn to my open window and the black sky beyond instead. I'm afraid those pills will give me an artificial escape from reality, and I don't need those problems. For now, Advil will have to suffice.

My phone sits in the middle of my chest, pressing down on my heart with the weight of an anvil. I still haven't texted Yves. With everything that's been going on, I'd forgotten to reach out. Though it's only been a couple of hours since he gave me his number; but I guess endless drama has a way of making time appear to hurtle.

I wish I could call my friend Isaiah and tell him every detail of my hellacious day. We became friends this past school year over a mutual hatred of our sophomore programming class. But his mom sent him to Chicago to spend the summer with his homophobic dad, who got him an internship at his job. Isaiah knows it's a poorly cloaked subterfuge for his dad to have an entire summer to polish the gay off him, like he's a fucking piece of tarnished silverware. Dread drove him into depression the last couple of months of school, and our budding friendship dwindled, too. He has enough problems without me dumping mine on him, too. I text I miss you instead.

He responds immediately.

Miss you more. Dad's been watching me like a
hawk.

Prolly scared I'll hook up with one of his male
coworkers and embarrass him.

His boss is cute af tho. I should suck him off outta
spite lol.

I chuckle at the string of tongue and eggplant emoji that Isaiah
sends next.

LMAO. That wud be hilarious, but he'd also kill u
and I'd have to find another friend.

Try to be good, pls.

No promises :')

Guess who I ran into in the Quarter today

???

Yves Bordeaux. <3<3<3

Oh! He's soo stinkin' cute. NOW who needs to
behave???

No promises.

Night, bitch. I love you.

Nite. Love you more.

Grinning, I set my phone aside at the same time a warm breeze
floats through the open window, painted by the clean scent of summer night amid subtle hints of the estate greenery.

We barely managed to pull off Wise John's Moon and everyone
still exploded into chaos moments after. Cris was right; our family's
going to be useless in helping figure out who crossed Mama. That's
why I tacked on the latent mod to Wise John's Moon. Since Cris
has given up magic, it's up to me alone to protect us. And no one
else is dying on my watch.

Fuck it.

I text Yves, because conquering the fear of first contact is far more appealing than wallowing in family drama. It's only What's up?, but my heart takes flight the moment I hit send. The seconds tick away after to the tune of my pulsing headache while I wait for my screen to light up with a response.

I'm obsessing over whether I should've said something else and whether I should send a follow-up message when the scent of impending rain drifts through my window—but it brings something else with it. Voices.

I ease up from the bed and sneak to the window to peer outside. Ursula stands beneath the willow at the corner of our house. She's not alone, but shadows conceal whoever she's with.

"I'm still your friend," pleads the calm voice of a man.

"That doesn't give you the right to spy on me," says Ursula. "Scrying is dark magic, Jean-Louise. When are you going to learn your lesson about that shit?"

"That's not why I'm here," he says. "I heard Marie was sick, and I figured for you to come back, things must've gotten pretty bad. How is she?"

"My sister is none of your concern."

The man, Jean-Louise, shifts in the shadows. "I just want to help."

"Tuh!" The chill sound of her voice cleaves through the warm air. "Oh, I definitely don't want *your* brand of help."

"How long are you going to punish me for something I didn't do?"

"Maybe until you're dead—like Auguste." Her voice cracks, and she hugs herself tighter against the brisk wind that kicks up from the encroaching storm.

"I hope you've been giving that same energy to your cousin, Justin," he says. "You know, he's latched on to Lenora Savant—"

"I don't give a damn what Justin is doing," says Ursula.

"Ursula, please—"

"A storm's coming. Leave, Jean-Louise. And don't come back here." She turns and disappears around the corner, leaving Jean-Louise alone beneath the tree, just as dark clouds strobe in the distance.

I bolt from my room, stumbling over shoes and clothes littering the floor, and nearly crash into the wall headfirst. The sound of thunder cracks and rumbles the walls as I race downstairs. I make it just as Ursula steps back inside. Panting, I lean on the banister and half smile.

"What do you want?" she asks, closing the door softly.

"Late-night visitor?" I reply, a single brow raised.

She rolls her eyes. "Mind your business, Clem."

"Why didn't you invite him in?"

She heads for the kitchen.

I follow. "Are you going to answer my question?"

"Trust me, you don't want the likes of that man in this house."

"Why not?"

"The less you know, the better," she says in a solemn voice.

"What did Jean-Louise do?"

She glowers at me. "If I catch you eavesdropping again, I'll hex you with nightmares for the rest of your life."

"You wouldn't do that to me." I only partly believe that. "Who is Auguste?"

Ursula goes rigid, immediately terrifying me, but she pinches the bridge of her nose and says, "Clem, go to bed."

"I'm not a kid anymore, Aunt Ursula. I don't have a bedtime—"

"Then go somewhere other than where I am and bother someone other than me!"

I hold up my hands. "Fine, fine." I back slowly out of the room. "Good night."

She shoos me with her back turned while she plunders the liquor cabinet.

I feel the familiar pull of my aunt's frustratingly enigmatic world, though I'm afraid to heed the call again. Then I remember she (or I or both of us) could've died tonight, and I wonder if that was like some divine signal or something—that maybe I should give it one more try.

I go back to my room and discover Yves texted back while I was downstairs.

Can I call you?

My heart somersaults. I have to retype Sure! three times because I keep misspelling it in my nerv-citement.

The phone rings a moment later. I clear my throat and answer, attempting to sound nonchalant, not like I just unwrapped a new PlayStation on Christmas, which is exactly how I feel.

"Hey," I say.

"How are you, Clem?" His upbeat voice sounds even more enticing than I remember. My cheeks start to ache, and I realize I've been smiling since I read his text.

"How'd you know it was me? I didn't give you my number."

He laughs. "A benefit of not sharing your number often is you always know who has it."

"Touché."

"I wondered if it took you so long to text me because you've been hard at work trying to solve our riddle without me."

"Huh?"

"The meaning of life," he says. "You figured it out yet?"

"Oh, no, sorry. I was, uh, in a car accident earlier."

He gasps. "Oh! I'm so sorry . . . I didn't mean . . ."

"It's okay, really. No one was seriously hurt."

"Who were you with?" he asks.

"My aunt, Ursula. She owns a bar in the Quarter."

"The Wishing Well, right?"

"Yeah," I say. "How'd you know?"

"You'd be surprised what all I know."

"Oh, really?" I ask.

"Yeah," he says with bravado. "Try me. Ask me anything."

"What's the House of Vans? And why were you there?" The line goes silent so long that I ask, "You still there?"

"Um, yeah, sorry," he says. "You're pretty forward."

"You said ask anything. Besides, conversations where people don't talk about what's really on their mind are a waste of time."

"It's a pleasure house, if you know what I mean," he says with a heavy breath. "A person's wildest dreams come true behind those doors."

"Aren't those illegal?"

"Eh, technically, but there are ways around that."

"And you went there to . . . uh . . ."

"No, no," he says quickly. "My sister owns it."

I pull the phone away to let out a sigh of relief. Yves frequenting a brothel crosses the line of how much weird I think I can handle at this point in my life. "Ooh . . . Sorry."

"It's okay. I usually don't share that with people so soon after meeting them for obvious reasons. I'll give you an out if you, uh, don't want to be friends anymore."

"No wonder you like Justin's plays. You're as dramatic as him."

He laughs. "I guess."

"So, you and your sister must know a lot of people."

"Fab has made it her business to acquaint herself with all the right folks. And I know a lot more than she thinks I do, just from hanging around her so much."

It's a shot in the dark, but worth a try. "Ursula was meeting with a guy named Jean-Louise tonight, but she won't tell me who he is. Does the name sound familiar?"

"Well, yeah. There are a lot of guys in New Orleans named Jean-Louise."

"Oh." I don't hide the dejection in my voice. I was really hoping for a lead.

"I can do some digging and get back to you tomorrow," he says, instantly lifting my spirits. "But I'll have to deliver any intel I find in person."

"Not that I mind, but why?"

"Gives me an excuse to see you again."

I can hear him smiling on the line, which practically sends my spirits into orbit. And then my stomach kills the vibe—right on cue—cinching anxiously at the thought of seeing Yves again.

"Well, I better let you get to work," I say. "Wanna meet at the Bean in the morning?"

"Sure. Good night, Clem."

"Night." I end the call and realize my cheeks are aching from grinning nonstop again.

But even better than securing another opportunity to see Yves, I might have a lead on finding out exactly what Aunt Ursula and Jean-Louise are hiding.

And maybe then I'll know how to find my way back to her.

TWELVE

CRISTINA

"Peace offering?" Clem stands in my bedroom doorway with two mugs of fresh coffee.

I can't help but smile. "Get in here." I take my cup and close the door after he sits on my bed.

"Yesterday was a lot," he says. "After watching everyone go at each other so hard, I don't want to fight with you anymore."

"I understand." I want to ask him again about the spell he added onto the end of Wise John's Moon, but I don't push my luck. I sit next to him instead.

"I brought tea, too." He leans in and drops his voice. "Last night, after everyone went to bed, I overheard Aunt Ursula talking with someone under the willow outside my window."

"So, you were eavesdropping?"

He clicks his tongue. "Do you want the tea or not?"

I hold up my hands and motion for him to go on.

"His name is Jean-Louise. He and Aunt Ursula used to be friends, but now she seems just shy of hating him. Before she ran him off, he told her Justin was tight with Lenora."

I sit up straighter. "If that's true, then why would Justin put us in Lenora's booth last night? He must know Aunt Ursula and Lenora hate each other."

"I don't know, but I'm going to help you find answers. I think you should look into Justin, and I'll start with Jean-Louise."

I groan and hang my head. "Seriously, Clem, for your own health, you have *got* to drop your fixation on Aunt Ursula. Did she really mess you up that bad?"

"I'm not messed up," he snaps, which I guess I deserve. "Contrary to your belief, I don't mind owning my shit. Yes, I am intrigued at the possibility of learning more about my aunt since she won't tell me why she iced me out, which I believe might have something to do with whatever happened between her and Jean-Louise. Maybe he'll also tell us what he knows about Justin and Leno—"

"Fine," I say with a defeated sigh. We can't afford to overlook any leads, but I wish he wasn't so willing to put his emotional well-being at risk. "Did you find out anything else?"

"Before the accident, Aunt Ursula told me a close friend of hers died a few years ago. She does not seem to have gotten over it. And last night, she mentioned someone named Auguste to Jean-Louise. So, later, when I was talking to Yves—"

"Whoa, wait a minute," I say. "Since when are you and Yves talking?"

"I ran into him on the *Montaigne Majestic*, and he gave me his number. Why do you care? You said you two weren't friends."

"I don't. I just think it's interesting that even though you claim to be helping me, you seem to find no shortage of ways to serve yourself."

"Yves is cute and single and so am I—" He shrugs, and his eyes light up in the early-morning sunlight bounding through my open window. "—I'll take a hefty serving of him any day."

I fake-retch, and he laughs.

"Thanks to my devilish good looks and irresistible charm, I've befriended someone who might actually be a lot of help figuring out who crossed Mama," he says. "Yves and his sister know a lot of people in this town, including their secrets. You're welcome."

"When I asked you to help me, I only requested you do two very simple things—"

"And I have! I haven't told Yves anything confidential, nor have I mentioned Oz since the Golden Key. I didn't even check under your bed to see if the carrot-headed creepazoid was hiding under there before I sat down." He makes a strained face and adds, "He's not under there, is he?"

I slug him in the arm, and he shrieks with laughter.

Sometimes I wish I could tell my brother that his insults feel like little drops of poison that sour my stomach whenever he rags on Oz. Maybe it's the added shock and stress of everything going on. I woke up with Oz on my mind this morning, pining for one of his vanilla-and-warm-spice-scented hugs.

"You're an ass," I tell him. "Look, Yves is nice and all, it's just that no one *else* can know what we're doing—especially Mama. If she finds out, she'll ground us until we have to cross her ourselves to break out of here."

He nods. "On that much, we agree."

"I never thought I'd see the day Mama would be so weak," I say in a hushed voice. "What if that curse changed her?"

He sits ramrod straight and frowns at me. "Mama is *not* weak. Cut her some slack—she literally came back from the brink of death a day ago. The curse didn't change her—Dad's death did—it changed all of us." His face falls, pulling my heart down with it. "And I understand how she feels. I don't know if I can survive losing someone I care about again."

I slide closer and put my arms around him. "You won't have to, because I'm not going to let anyone take another person from us."

Including myself.

Clem leaves to go on a coffee date with Yves after I—grudgingly—give him my blessing. My gut tells me we can trust Yves, although the thought of him and Clem growing closer hasn't quite settled with me yet. It worries me, seeing Clem so readily plunge back into the sharks' den of romance, but I can't hold him on the shore forever. Besides, it's nice to see some light returning to his eyes.

Thoughts of Justin and Lenora simmer in my mind the entire drive across town. It's hard for me to believe Justin would ally with Lenora and betray his family. Then again, no one would believe I'd do the things I've done either—yet here I am. At least I'm trying to make it right.

Sweat lines my forehead just from the short walk from the parking lot to the docks. If the start of June is already so blazing hot, fire will be raining from the sky by August. I used to love New Orleans, but now the heat isn't the only thing suffocating about this place. Ever since Dad died, I've been ignoring an itch to get far away from here. Maybe even leave the States altogether. I groan and wipe my forehead. And the heat isn't the only thing unbearable out here today.

I hear the Redeemers chanting long before I make it to the *Montaigne Majestic*'s gangway, which is roped off and guarded by a lone, brown-skinned man, who stands at the edge with arms crossed over his broad chest. He's dressed in all black and has a radio receiver attached to his shoulder. He watches the crowd with a fortified expression, which none of the protesters challenge.

Instead, they bellow "Pin the witches to the ground, regulate their magic now!" from where they collect around the entrance. I scan several hand-painted signs as I approach, each making my stomach churn a little harder in turn.

**Witches think they're <u>above the law</u>,
but they belong <u>beneath the ground</u>**

Protect PEOPLE, not MAGIC

Magic is MURDER

One corner of my mouth twitches downward in disgust, but I push through the crowd anyway. The brazenness of the mass of mostly white faces, every single one beet red with fury over the magic that, although I've given it up, is no less a part of my heritage—of all Black folks' heritage. My ancestors died to give us this power to fight back against our oppressors, the same gift the Redeemers disrespect to our faces. Maybe my feelings about magic are misplaced.

Maybe the problem is—and always has been—me.

So much has happened over the past day that I'm not sure how I should feel anymore. But I need to stay focused on uncovering who hexed Mama. That is the thing I can control right now.

The beefy security guard doesn't move a muscle when I step in front of him. "Boat's closed today," he grumbles.

"I'm here to see Justin. I'm his cousin, Cristina Trudeau. It's important." When he doesn't respond, I add, "I'm not with them," and flick my eyes over my shoulder at the protesters.

He sighs and pushes the button on the radio receiver at his shoulder, and it chirps in response. "Justin, you know a Cristina Trudeau?"

"Let her through, Steve," Justin replies over the comm.

The guard lifts the rope and allows me to duck under and pass onto the boat.

The *Majestic*'s interior is just as lavish in the daytime, though the ambience feels vastly different without the music and lights and dressed-up guests milling back and forth.

The boat's atrium has been transformed into a temporary base for a construction company, which I assume Justin hired to repair the damage done by the Redeemer anarchists last night. Most of the open floor space is taken up by tools and equipment, and I have to sidestep several people carrying armfuls of wooden boards and two men balancing a long pane of glass peppered with sawdust between them. The somewhat satisfying din of buzzing construction tools and shouting replaces the riling protest carrying on outside, which eases my thumping heart a little bit as I make my way down the short hallway toward the Firefly Supplies shop.

Two men work on replacing the glass front door of the shop. Several nearby display windows are without panes, and the shelves just beyond are charred and broken, the blackened remains of their contents strewn about the floor. The place smells of ash, fresh-cut wood, and paint. Justin stands inside the shop, broom in hand, sweeping his ruined merchandise into dusty piles.

Justin turns as I approach and leans on the broom with a pained smile, but his eyes can't seem to stray too long from the destruction. He's dressed far more laid-back today in sneakers, chino shorts with his radio clipped to the waistband, and a gray tank with the Firefly logo in the center.

"Morning, Cris," he says. "Pardon the mess." He looks around once more and shakes his head. "Racist Redeemer assholes. None of the white-owned magical businesses in New Orleans have been hit like this. I'd say I'm surprised, but after four hundred years of this shit, who of us is anymore?"

"Do you know why they're targeting gen all of a sudden?"

I've always wondered what we gen did to anger the nonmagical public so much, especially when white mages and vamps do *gods only know* what with light and shadow magic every day.

Justin cocks his head and raises a brow. "This all started with our family. I'm surprised you didn't know."

"If you're talking about what happened thirty years ago, yes, I've gotten a lecture about the whole ordeal from Odessa no less than a hundred times," I tell him.

"Don't be too hard on her. She just wants you to know your history. Power is built on the foundation of knowledge."

"Are you going to answer my question or not?" I'm really not up for another lesson today.

He chuckles under his breath. "After the mayor, his wife, and the rest of the mob were found dead on y'all's front lawn the next morning, the mayor's mother accused your grandmother of using magic to slaughter all those good Christian white folks who'd come to lynch her. The mayor's wife started the Redeemers shortly after; she wreaked havoc in our community for a few steady years before her movement tanked and stayed dead—until recently. This month is the thirtieth anniversary of Alexis Lancaster's murder, which kicked off this whole mess."

His words knock my mind off-balance. All of this because of Grandma Cristine?

"I had no idea," I mutter, shame curling in my chest.

Maybe I should've been more receptive to what Odessa's been trying to tell me. I just wish it didn't always feel like she was molly-whopping me with the information all the time.

Justin grips his broom harder. "Black folks have to watch police murder our people in the streets daily, but the Redeemers expect us all to avert our empathy to the death of an insufferable white woman that happened three damn decades ago. Talk about caucastic irony."

He clears his throat and says, "I'm sure you didn't come for a history lesson, and I'm running short on free time today, so what's up?"

"Oh, yeah"—I show him the picture of the hex doll on my phone—"do you recognize this?"

He leans in to get a better look. "It's one of ours, which I'm sure you know." He points to the Firefly brand, the same logo as on his T-shirt. "We sell hundreds of those things a month at this location alone."

I sigh and slip my phone back into my pocket. "We found that one hidden between Mama's mattresses. It's what made her sick."

Something dawns in his eyes, something more than surprise and concern. "Is she okay?"

"She is now, but she would've died if we hadn't discovered that hex doll when we did."

"Who could've done something like that to her?"

"That's what I'm trying to figure out."

He shrugs. "I wish I could help, but I have no way to find out who purchased that doll."

"Well, maybe there's something else you can help with," I tell him. "Why'd you stick us in that VIP booth with Lenora Savant and her family last night?"

"Did something happen?" he asks, donning a familiar expectant look.

My gut keeps telling me that Justin's acting real suspect right now. Maybe it's his peculiar line of questioning, or it could be his myriad of facial expressions that give me the impression he's masking all the secrets he's stashed away like a squirrel storing acorns for winter.

And I'm not sure he's going to want to share any of his stores with me. But I have to try.

I recount the abridged version of Ursula's scuffle with Lenora for him. "You had to have known they hated each other. Why put Aunt Ursula in that situation?"

An indescribable battle wages in his troubled expression. He's hiding something. "I shouldn't have . . . but I thought if those two got together . . . maybe some truths might . . . slip out."

My brows pinch together. "What *truths*?"

"I—I can't do this, Cris." He shakes his head. "I'm sorry about putting you all in that booth. I shouldn't have done that. I shouldn't have done a lot of shit."

If he doesn't stop speaking in riddles, I'm going to snatch his broom and whack him with it.

"What 'truths' were you hoping came out in that booth?" I ask again.

His phone alarms in his pocket, and he drops the broom when he checks it. "Shit! I have a meeting—like *now*." He dusts off his hands with a loud, frustrated sigh. "This month is also Lenora Savant's thirtieth anniversary on the Generational Council, and she's demanding I curate a special production to celebrate her like she's Diana Ross and this is *Dreamgirls*. She'll be here any minute to discuss the dress rehearsal in two weeks. Would you believe on premiere night she wants me to shut down my entire boat for her 'private event' and is also demanding a hefty cut of ticket sales?" Justin rolls his eyes. "You should go. I feel my blood pressure spiking."

"But wait, can you please just tell me—"

"Let it go, Cris." The gravity of his tone drops his voice an octave deeper. "I've helped all I can."

"But you haven't done anything." Frustration bubbles over in my chest. I want to scream. Justin's holding back, but I don't know what or why.

He narrows his eyes at me, and his nostrils flare. "You have no idea all I've done." He steps closer and lowers his voice. "Too many people have died already. I won't be next."

"What are you talking about? What did you do?"

"Go home, Cristina," he snaps. "I don't want to talk about that anymore."

"Talk about what exactly?"

Justin and I both spin around to find Lenora Savant perched just inside the shop entrance, dressed in a purple belted blouse, dark skirt, and heels. The brim of her hat casts an ominous shadow over the fair almond skin of her face. She gives a tight, cunning smile and drums her fingers along the side of the black leather purse she holds.

"Did you two hear me?" she says. "I asked what you were talking about."

"Nothing," answers Justin. "Cris was just leaving."

"Ah, I see." Lenora raises a thinly arched brow at me. "Did you get what you needed, sweetheart?"

I should bolt while I can, but my feet and heart betray logic. Lenora walks around New Orleans like she owns the city, much like how Valentina struts around school. Aunt Ursula is about as subtle as a freight train, but I don't think she's wrong about this woman.

"Did you do it?" I ask her.

She stares at me curiously. "Did I do what now?"

I clear my throat, buying time to consider retreating before it's too late. "Did you do something to my aunt's car last night to cause an accident?"

She laughs, startling me at first, and puts one hand on her chest, collecting herself.

"I don't see what's funny," I say. "My brother was in that car. He and my aunt could've died."

Justin reaches for me, likely to calm me down, but I shrug out of his reach. Lenora's grin fades and she steps closer, her dark eyes spearing mine.

"I'm so sorry to hear that," she says. "Ursula and I may have our differences, but I would never stoop to such an act. Family is everything to me—and yours has been through quite enough. Tragedy seems to follow you all like stray dogs."

"Then what was that whole 'big mistake' threat about?" I imitate the ominous tone she'd taken with Ursula.

Justin looks at Lenora inquisitively. "You didn't—"

She holds up two fingers, and Justin quiets. She treats him like her husband. It's as if she controls them both.

"That was a warning, not a threat," says Lenora. "Ursula has allowed misplaced anger to land her in situations with people who haven't been as gracious as me. If she's not careful, she'll fling herself into another difficult predicament."

Justin shifts uncomfortably next to me and looks away. Lenora doesn't seem to notice, but I don't miss it. Something's up between these two.

"What do you mean?" I ask.

"When your aunt was not much older than you," she says, "she had a best friend named Celeste Richard, who fell in love with a very fine warlock. The Richards were close friends of our family. I remember Ursula being quite jealous of Celeste's newfound love, probably because she hadn't been able to secure the same for herself, likely due to her difficult personality. Either way, on the day they were supposed to elope, Celeste's fiancé disappeared. Celeste rightfully thought Ursula was responsible, and, well . . ." She hugs her purse in front of her and sighs. "Your aunt should probably tell you the rest."

Ursula can be cruel and vindictive when provoked, but I don't believe she'd intentionally harm her friend. "Why are you telling me this?"

"Because it's a lesson worth learning, beloved. Don't bring bad fortune on your head like your aunt. The continued strife of your family brings me no benefit or pleasure." Her face lights up and she opens her purse and rifles through it. "In fact, I'd like to do something to show you how much I mean that." She hands me a business card for the general manager of Henri's, a restaurant in the French Quarter. "This is my absolute favorite restaurant. Call them after lunch and place a catering order for dinner for your family tonight. My treat. I'll call Henri and set everything up when I'm done here."

"Thanks," I say tentatively, and pocket the card. Justin watches me with what seems like pained detachment, as if he wants to say something but can't. "I should go."

I step over piles of ash and trash and head for the exit. The creepy sensation of Lenora watching me leave makes the back of my neck prickle.

"Take care, sweetheart," she calls after me. "And give your dear mother my regards."

My blood ices.

THIRTEEN

CLEMENT

Tucked into a lonely corner booth at the Bean, I sit with my arms folded on the cool surface of the table and check my messages again. Nothing.

The café's not too crowded today; a group of college students hover over laptops and textbooks at one of the larger tables, and one of the employees hangs up paintings for sale by a local artist on the display wall near the front door.

The tiny, invisible asshat of a demon inside my head whispers nasty things to me—like getting close to Yves is a waste of time, because he'll eventually leave, too, if he hasn't ghosted me already. I glance down at my phone again. But I'd like a friend right now, especially since Isaiah's gone for the rest of the summer. I'm terrified of being hurt again, but I'm tired of living with this anxiety. Life would be so much easier if I could be fearless like my sister.

"That's going to make for one awesome scar." The gentle, playful voice snaps me out of my torturous musing. Yves nods at the two tiny stitches on my forehead and smiles, quelling the firestorm blustering inside me.

"Heh, one can dream." I hide the smile that comes from realizing Yves didn't stand me up after all.

"What were you thinking about?" Across from me, he leans on the side of the booth, and his biceps flexes under his sleeve. "Don't tell me you've solved the meaning of life without me."

I give a small laugh. "Not hardly."

The meaning of life. What a fucking joke. I barely understand the shit that goes on in mine.

"Well, let's get some coffee and talk about it," he says.

A few minutes later, Yves and I settle back into my somewhat secluded booth.

"I can't believe you drink your coffee black." I scrunch my nose up at him.

He makes an exaggerated show of relishing his drink. "And I can't believe you drink yours with all that crap in it. You can't even taste the coffee."

I sip my caramel macchiato and roll my eyes. "Coffee is like life. Sometimes you have to dress it up to hide the bitter taste."

"Can't argue there," he says. "So, I talked to my sister and was able to pry some information out of her, but it was like squeezing water from an old stone, so you owe me!"

"If what you have for me is good enough, you can name your price."

He cuts his eyes at me devilishly, which makes me stiffen downstairs. I immediately feel embarrassed until I remember I'm sitting, so no one can see. "Don't be surprised if I hold you to that."

I swallow hard and smile. I've never been nervous to flirt with a cute boy before, but something about Yves is so disarming. He feels dangerous, but I might already be under his spell.

"My sister says the man you're interested in is Jean-Louise Petit, who happened to have a pretty epic falling-out with your aunt Ursula."

"Did she say why they fell out?"

"She didn't know details but said it had something to do with their friend Auguste Dupre. He died a few years ago from an opioid overdose. Word on the street is it was all Jean-Louise's fault."

Aunt Ursula's friend who died.

"What happened?"

"The only person alive who knows what really went down with Auguste is Jean-Louise, but he's gone into seclusion. He rarely leaves home nowadays, and when he does, he doesn't talk much." He shrugs one shoulder and says, "That's all I got."

"Thank you," I tell him. "It's way more than I had."

"Why do you want to know about Jean-Louise and Auguste?"

"It's a long story steeped in a lot of drama that I'm afraid will make you run away screaming into the night if I tell you, and I'm kinda enjoying our conversation so far."

Yves chuckles and stares down at the table. "I, uh . . . was surprised you still wanted to hang after our conversation last night." His eyes snap up to meet mine, which makes me feel like I'm bathing in a sea of fresh moonlight. "It's not easy making friends when your sister runs the most notorious pleasure house in New Orleans."

If anything, our talk endeared him even more to me. Something can be said about having a connection with someone who won't judge you or your messy family. Someone who understands and respects every part of you, even the ugliest. It makes me feel safe. Well, safer.

"Sex work is honest work," I tell him. "People need to get over themselves. Besides, I appreciate you looking out for my sister after the fallout from Valentina's stupid Instagram post."

I almost wish Cris and Valentina would just fight and get it out of their system before their feud goes too far; though it'd seemed to have stalled—until the incident on the *Majestic*. A bunch of the boys at school started harassing Cris, as if that video was some sort of fucked-up casting call. I stuck close to her as much as I could, but it was tough, because we had different schedules. I was relieved to know Yves had taken up my post whenever I couldn't be around. Though I didn't know much about him, he'd always seemed like a cool guy from afar.

He shrugs. "The benefit of staying in my own lane is I don't have to adhere to the whims of the popular jerks who think they run the school. The downside is that even though I chose it, that life is no less lonely. Maybe we both needed someone to be kind."

"I still think that was very sweet of you." I sip my drink, and Yves stares down into his cup. "What's on your mind?"

"That just got me thinking about my sister and her business . . . and me. I've never had anyone I've felt comfortable enough with to talk about it."

"What about it?"

"I work with her a lot. I guess you could say I'm like her left hand." When I raise a brow at him, he clarifies, "Because she's left-handed." Ah. Makes sense. He traces the rim of his mug with one finger. "I'm okay with it now, but I want out eventually."

"You should get to choose your own path."

"Therein lies my problem. I don't know what I want to do or where I want to go, I just know it's not *that*. Sometimes I feel like I'm being dragged through life." He stretches both hands across the table and flashes an embarrassed grin. "Sorry to be a downer. We can talk about happier things."

I put my hand on top of his without realizing what the hell I'm doing until it's too late. His fingers twitch beneath mine and relax. I give his hand a squeeze and then quickly hide both mine in my lap. "My dad used to tell me that people will try to make us think we have to have this life shit figured out by now, but that's a big, fat lie."

"Were you close with him . . . before . . . ?"

"Yeah." I sigh.

After Dad died at Spirits of Nola, it was all everyone talked about. Even at school. The fake sympathy was the worst. People used it as currency to gain access to gossip. I would've rather been miserably alone with my grief.

"I understand," Yves says. "I lost both my parents when I was eight."

"I'm sorry."

"It was a car accident the night of Fabiana's eighteenth birthday. We didn't have any other family, so she took care of me. Having to take on so much responsibility so young nearly broke her."

She reminds me of Cris.

Guilt reflects on the surface of the dark pools of Yves's eyes as he tells his story. Now I understand why he continues to work for his sister even though he doesn't seem to like it very much. Yves is painfully loyal, which draws me deeper into his world. I don't get the impression he's a flight risk—not like barista Nate, who only believes in committing to hotep conspiracy theories.

"She got suckered into becoming a sex worker by some sleaze," he says. "But she clawed her way up the ranks and now owns the House of Vans."

"Wow." I don't imagine many people, when thrown in Fabiana's particular predicament, end up in similar places of power.

We sip our coffees, and no one says anything for several agonizing moments. I fear our conversation is growing cold along with our drinks.

I snap my fingers, grinning at him. "Coffee."

He stares at me curiously. "What do you mean?"

"The meaning of life, duh. It's coffee."

He laughs, and it's the most beautiful thing I've ever seen. The way his entire body shows up for the emotion is like poetry—how his eyes crease at the corners when he squeezes them shut, or the way his nostrils flare with each heaving breath, or how his leg casually bumps mine under the table. And the way he holds it there, propped against mine, sending sheaths of heat up my thigh.

"Funny," he says. "But not exactly what I had in mind."

"All right then," I say with a playful sigh. "I guess I'll have to think a little harder."

Our conversation wanders well into the afternoon across a collection of topics that never seem to grow old. We talk about music, books, movies, and even have the great debate of tea vs. coffee. But as swept up into Yves's world as I am, there's still something attached to my ankle that gives a strong tug every time I feel myself slipping away.

I can't stop thinking about Aunt Ursula, Jean-Louise, and Auguste.

"Would you happen to have plans for the rest of the evening?" I hurl the words across the table before I can change my mind.

Yves shakes his head. "What's up?"

"Wanna help me with something?" A part of me feels selfish

for pulling him into this, but I really don't want our time together to end.

His face brightens. "Sure."

Yves and I sit in my car, which I've parked on the street of a sleepy neighborhood filled with old, paneled cottages. We both eye the sky-blue front door of one particular house, with its well-manicured flower beds that burst with fireworks of color. A few muddy puddles sully the pristine yard only a few feet from the street, a by-product of last night's rainstorm. Overall, the home appears inviting enough in the late-afternoon daylight, but something in the pit of my stomach refuses to settle with what we're about to do.

I spent the late hours of last night investigating Auguste Dupre's death, but all I was able to find were the names of his parents and a couple of brief news stories that accused him of overdosing on drugs. I have to know how Jean-Louise and Aunt Ursula were involved. That's why we're outside the home of Walter and Adeline Dupre. That's also why I feel like I'm about to scream or vomit or scream-vomit. But this is the best place to start my quest for answers.

"Are you sure this looks okay?" I tug on the old band T-shirt I'm wearing and glance at Yves in the passenger seat. I haven't worn this thing outside the house in years. I dropped out of band over summer break the same year I joined. I fell for one of the guys who played quads—a tall, dark-skinned demigod of a boy who immediately cast a spell on me. Unfortunately, he sprinkled his magic freely around school that year.

"It looks cute on you." Yves smiles. "I didn't know you were a band geek."

"I played snare in a past life." I haven't picked up a drumstick since I got my heart stomped on at band camp. I don't even know if I remember how to play.

"Maybe that's it," he says. "Art is the meaning of life."

"Expound."

"Art is how we express the best and worst parts of life, how we record and process our most sacred experiences." He ticks off each form on his fingers. "Music. Film. Painting. Writing—"

"Nah, I think it's way deeper than that. We don't live just to create. Art is only a small part of being alive." I tug on my shirt again. "You can wait here if you're not comfortable with this."

He chuckles, and his hand brushes against mine. A bolt of something akin to electricity shoots through my hand and the rest of my body. He draws back a moment after we touch.

Maybe he felt it, too?

He smiles. "Weird people are the best people in the world."

I laugh nervously. I hate the way he makes my brain all giggly and bubbly. No one has ever made me feel that way before.

"Well, let's go." I grab a clipboard from the backseat and make my way up to the blue front door of the cottage with Yves right behind me.

Clouds have rolled in, granting us a hiatus from the unrelenting Sun, though the humidity still makes outside feel like a convection oven. Even so, I still prefer the hottest day in New Orleans to the cold anywhere. Winter feels lonely and destitute, like death.

I ring the doorbell and rock back and forth on the balls of my feet, while my heart bangs against my sternum like a big-ass bass speaker. The door opens and I look into the dark, somewhat weary eyes of a woman I assume is Adeline Dupre. Her hair is pulled back into a poufy ponytail, and fine lines mark the corners of her eyes and length of her forehead.

"Hi, I'm Clement, and this is Yves." He waves. "We're here on behalf of New Orleans International Magnet High's band program—" I pause to point at my shirt and wriggle my brows at her, which makes her grin. "We'd like to talk to you about our upcoming performance year and the possibility of becoming an angel sponsor."

Her shoulders droop, and her smile fades. She's about to turn us away—fuck.

And my mind blanks.

Shit, shit, shit . . .

"Every little bit counts," Yves says, surprising me. "School programs like band, special-interest clubs, and sports have been statistically proven to improve teenage confidence and self-awareness and have also been linked to higher success rates at secondary institutions and beyond. I promise it won't be a waste of your time if you'll only let us explain how you can help."

She sighs. "Oh, all right. Get in here but make it quick."

We trade looks of relief and file inside.

The Dupres' home is pristine. Not a single thing seems out of place. The front room smells of lemon furniture polish and fresh banana bread cooking in the oven. But I can't help but feel a lingering sadness heavy in the air. I wonder if Mrs. Dupre thinks she can clean and bake the pain of her son's sudden death away. I know from experience that won't work. No matter how much you try to distract yourself, painful memories will always find a way to crop back up.

Adeline gestures for us to take a seat on her hideous floral-print couch, which looks like it doesn't see very many butts. We sit down, and she perches in another chair across from us.

She rubs her hands along the length of her thighs, her eyes flitting between Yves and me. "Well," she says. "Are you going to tell me about this angel program, or no?"

I steal a glance at Yves, who nods for me to get on with it. I grip both ends of the clipboard until the metal clip digs painfully into my palm. "I, uh, wanted to talk to you about something else."

Her whole body goes rigid. "Okay . . ."

"I want to know about your son, Auguste." I say it in one quick breath, as if getting it out faster will help it land better. It does not.

Her mouth thins so much, I'm afraid she's going to choke on her lips. "You boys should be ashamed, tricking your way into my house for gossip. My son's been dead almost three years now. Let him rest in peace. You need to leave now."

"I'm sorry," I say. "But we were afraid you'd slam the door on us if we'd asked outside."

"And you were absolutely right." She stands up and puts her hands on her hips, glaring like an angry sentry. "I'm not sure what part of 'leave' you're not understanding, but I want you off my couch and out the door."

"Please," I say, standing up, too, along with Yves. "I really need your help."

"Well, this was a piss-poor way to ask."

"Last night, I overheard one of my family members talking in secret with someone who used to be friends with Auguste." I throw a Hail Mary and cross my fingers behind my back. "You may know him—Jean-Louise Petit."

Adeline's hands slip off her hips. She blinks and shakes her head, as if trying to unhear Jean-Louise's name.

"Their conversation worried me," I add. "That's why I wanted to talk to you about what happened to Auguste, because I know he and Jean-Louise were friends once. Please, will you help me?"

Her eyes chill. "Whoever in your family is mixed up with that demon, tell them to keep away from him. It turns my stomach to think of all the evil he did with my son."

"What do you mean?"

She folds her arms and scoffs. "Jean-Louise infected Auguste with all sorts of demonic spirits—the same evil that took my baby's life in the end."

Yves, who'd already made it to the front door, retreats to tug on my arm.

Unable to break gazes with Adeline, I hold up one finger to him. "What did he do?"

She wrinkles her nose. "Jean-Louise turned my boy gay."

I want to scream. The only secret we've uncovered is that Auguste's mother is a raging homophobe. Her words remind me just how hard it is to find happiness in a world that refuses to accept me. I've been luckier than most in that I have a safe and loving home, but the problem is I have to exist in the larger world outside my house, under the scrutiny of people who think and behave like Adeline Dupre.

"Let's go," I tell Yves. "This was a dumb idea anyway."

Relieved, he pulls the door open and hurries out. I follow close behind.

"You'll listen to me if you're smart," she calls after us. "We couldn't even give our son a proper funeral because of that man."

I stop and whirl around. "What?"

"Auguste's body disappeared from the morgue the same night he died," she says. "The police never recovered it. But I know that man had something to do with it. There's no end to his perversion."

I say, "Sorry to bother you," and Yves and I hurry to the car.

But why in the infinite realms would Adeline Dupre think Jean-Louise stole her son's corpse?

FOURTEEN

CRISTINA

The Sun heats my skin, despite the feeling of ice in my stomach.

The protesters are still going strong when I exit the gangway of the *Montaigne Majestic* and wade back through the crowd. Luckily, they let me pass without incident, but unease still compresses my chest as they continue to shout with angry vigor.

A text message from Oz draws my attention, and I check it as I walk down the pier toward the parking lot. **Good morning, beautiful. I'm down at the pier shops, grabbing some of your favorite sour belts. Can I come by so we can stuff our faces and I can apologize?** He sends another. **Pretty please.**

I grin and begin typing a reply, but the shadow of someone standing in my path stops me.

Valentina Savant removes her sunglasses to glare full force. She's clinging to a bag of candied butterscotch, the same color as her skin. Those disgusting candies are her granny's favorite. Back when we were friends, we could never leave the pier shops without stopping so she could pick up a quarter pound of them for Lenora. Valentina treats that frightful old woman as if she's her own heart walking around outside her body. It's always been creepy as fuck.

"Leave me alone, Valentina." I try to push past her, but she grabs my arm.

"Hey," she snaps. "I need to talk to you."

I yank my arm from her grip. "What you need to do is be careful where you put your hands."

She appraises me curiously. "Yeah?"

"This isn't school, and I'm not taking your shit anymore."

She takes a step closer, and I get a sickening whiff of the floral perfume she wears that I always thought made her smell like a depressed middle-aged woman. "I don't know what's gotten into you or your ratchet auntie, but if y'all aren't careful, someone's going to sit y'all down—permanently."

I stare into her brown eyes and narrow mine. "And who's going to do that? You?" I snicker under my breath. "You could try, but we both know you can't beat my ass—with or without magic."

"My granny should petition the Council to bind your entire family from gen magic indefinitely. It's what you all deserve for how you've disgraced the community." She jabs her thumb over her shoulder at the protesters outside the *Montaigne Majestic*. "That's on *you* and your trashy-ass family. My granny was the best thing to ever happen to the Gen Council."

"What do you want from me, Valentina?" I throw my hands up. "Do you want to fight? Drown me in the river? Huh? What is it going to take to get you to leave me alone?" I shove her, which catches her off guard, judging by the way her eyes widen. She stumbles backward, just catching herself from falling over. "I've already lost every *fucking* thing! What *more* do you want?"

My throat burns from screaming, and I stand rigid, chest heaving, fists clenched. I wish I knew why she hated me so much. I'm not sure I was ever a friend in her eyes. If we have to fight today, then so be it. But I'm done taking her abuse. I'm done letting people take from me without consequence.

Someone shouts my name. I turn to see Oz running over from the shops.

"Cris!" He steps between me and Valentina and guides me a few paces away. "I heard you yelling down the pier. What's going on?"

"Nothing," I say. "I just want to leave."

He frowns at Valentina and turns back to me. "Okay. Do you want me to drive you?"

"What is it?" asks Valentina.

Oz and I both look at her inquisitively.

"Why her?" She waves her hand over the length of me. "She's nothing. She comes from nothing. And she's not even that cute."

I lunge for her, but Oz pulls me back. She shakes her head, throws up a hand, and leaves.

"I'm sorry," he says. "Are you okay?"

I honestly don't know how to answer that, but I nod anyway. "Your parents home?"

"Nope. They're both at work and Benji's out being Benji. Wanna go back to my place?"

"Please," I say. "I'm gonna need those sour belts now, though."

Oz leads me into his bedroom and closes the door, even though no one else is home. Like so many times before, I tiptoe around clothes strewn across the floor on my way to his bed, which looks like it hasn't been made since it was bought. After spreading out the blue plaid comforter and sitting, I watch him dart around, picking up his things and sniffing clothes before tossing them into one of two baskets near the closet. I'm thankful his room doesn't smell like it looks, but that's owing to the cinnamon plug-in air freshener his mother keeps in service at the outlet nearest the door.

A massive pile of dirty laundry takes up one corner of the closet and looks only a couple of smelly socks away from becoming sentient. Next to it sits a small tray lined with candles that catches my eye, but the door slams shut before I can get a good look.

Oz leans his back against the closet door and looks me in the eye. "You know none of that stuff Valentina said about you is true."

I never wanted to believe the rumors, but then doubt started to seep in. Regardless, I can't unknow what I know about me and my grandmother. We've both done terrible things.

"Of course," I lie.

He sits on the bed and puts one arm around me. I take a deep breath in and exhale all the vexing thoughts of Valentina and Lenora and hex dolls and secrets and everything else I'm powerless to fix right now. Oz hugs me, and I rest my head in the crook of his neck. *This* is why I love him. I can always escape into his arms when the world wants to rip me apart.

When we part, he kisses me and presses his forehead against mine. "I'm sorry about yesterday," he says. "I don't mean to be insensitive. I—"

I shush him, and he sighs, then grins. "Apology accepted. No more drama today."

He presses his lips against mine and holds my lower back. His touch lights up my body like a torch. Arching my back, I lean into him and every inch of me tingles with anticipation. For a moment, my head goes completely clear and nothing else matters. I feel like I'm drifting, as if under a spell, and I acquiesce—gladly, hungrily. I take his face in my hands and kiss him harder, closing my eyes against the bursts of colorful sparks that play in front of them. His mouth is warm, and he tastes like vanilla lip balm. I gather the strength to part with him, but only long enough to climb onto his lap. His eyes close, and he moans, his stiff excitement goading the underside of my thigh. When our mouths part, he presses his face closer, searching for my lips, like he needs them to breathe.

I kiss him again, and he releases a deep note of satisfaction from the back of his throat. His hands rove beneath my shirt, starting at my stomach but stopping just shy of my bra and diverting to my back. Sparks follow the trail of his fingertips, making my back arch even more, which urges his fingers on in an endless cycle of pleasure.

I yank his shirt off and run my fingers along his slender frame and the beginnings of muscle definition set among the sparse wisps of ginger chest hair and freckles. My thighs quiver, sending shock waves through me that I can't control.

A steamy, magical feeling engulfs me. All I want is to be with him.

He stops and lets out a deep, longing exhale. "Are you sure you're okay?"

I bite the corner of my bottom lip and nod. "I'm fine, I promise."

Oz and I have done "stuff" loads of times, but we've never gone All the Way™ before. Not that I haven't wanted to at times, and definitely not for lack of trying on his part. But every time I thought I was ready, something in the pit of my stomach would roll and make me so uncomfortable, I had no choice but to pump the brakes. I always trust my gut—that's never up for compromise. Oz claimed to understand and settled for alternatives, but never gave up the pursuit of exchanging my virginity for his. I never subscribed to that purity bullshit, but I wasn't having sex until I was ready.

And today feels right.

Gently, Oz slides me off his lap and leaps to his feet. Excitement burns behind his eyes. "I'll be right back, I've gotta get a, uh . . . I'll just be back. Don't move." He rushes out, and sounds of him rummaging in Benji's room next door echo through the wall shortly after.

A small flicker of light off to the side catches my attention. It's quick, like sunlight glinting off a bit of jewelry, which is odd considering Oz's curtains are drawn and the lights are off. I look around, but don't find anything of interest—except the closed door of Oz's closet.

It's wrong to snoop, but I'm curious.

A loud bang resounds from Benji's room, and Oz curses.

Nothing wrong with a quick peek.

Quietly, I open the door and kneel in front of the small tray, which holds three candles—purple, red, and pink. The outside of each one feels gritty, like they've been coated in something. Sugar? Then my heart nearly stops. Three small items lie at the base of each candle.

I recognize them all at once.

A gold honor society pin, which looks surprisingly similar to the one I thought I misplaced. In Oz's wildest dreams, he wouldn't have the grades, so the pin isn't his.

A lock of curly, black hair tied with a small bit of red ribbon.

With trembling hands, I pull my hair down and hold the lock up to it.

Spears of ice stab through me. It's fucking *mine*.

A sapphire journal with the words "fly boldly in the pursuit of your dreams" on the cover. I pick it up, still in disbelief until I flip through the pages and confirm it's mine, too.

I pick up the tray with all its contents and set it on the bed at the same time Oz bursts through the door, red-faced and pinching a condom in the air between two fingers.

"I found . . . oh . . . *fuck*." His eyes jump from the tray to me, and he drops the condom. "It's not what it looks like, I swear."

I snatch the tray, spilling the candles and my belongings onto the bed, and fling it at Oz like a murder Frisbee. He ducks without a second to spare, and the tray clangs against the wall.

"You've been conjuring love spells on me?"

He stands up and runs a nervous hand through his hair. "Cris, calm down—"

"Don't you fucking tell me to calm down, answer my question right fucking now."

"Yes, but it's not what you think."

I shake my head and stare up at the ceiling. I'm so confused and furious and hurt and so many other things that the mixture of emotions leaves me rooted to the spot, too numb to cry or shout or fight or run or anything. I guess this is what massive betrayal feels like.

Oz clears the room and reaches for me, but I slap his hand away. "Don't touch me!"

Tears fill his eyes and his bottom lip quivers, which intensifies my rage. "Please don't do this."

I pick up my journal and hold it in front of him, and he flinches, probably thinking I'm going to hit him with it. I should, but I don't. "Did you steal this? And my pin? And did you cut my fucking hair? I ought to damn you to the never-realm for that alone."

He nods and drops his gaze.

"Did you take Clem's knife, too?" I step closer, and he shrinks back. "I want it back." He doesn't respond, and I yell, "Now!"

He winces and stammers, "I didn't, I swear. I don't know anything about a knife."

I snatch out the drawers of his bedside table and upend them, spilling his belongings onto the floor. I kick through papers, candy wrappers, pens, and other useless shit, but Clem's knife isn't there.

"Cris, please stop," he says. "I told you, I didn't take any knife."

"Well, you're a liar, so I don't believe you." I empty all the drawers of his desk, tear apart his closet, and check underneath his bed, all while he watches anxiously from across the room.

I find nothing. He might not have taken my brother's knife, but I still don't trust him.

"All this time," I say, shaking my head. "They tried to warn me, but I defended you. And you've made a complete fool of me. I was protecting a fucking rapist."

"Whoa!" He frowns and holds up his hands. "You said you were okay."

I did tell him that. I had wanted it—or at least, I thought I had before I discovered my boyfriend was conjuring fucking love spells on me. I feel like I've been blindfolded and spun around a hundred times. Nothing makes sense. But I know this feels wrong.

"I was under the influence of a love spell, Oz. That's no better than slipping something in my drink." I wrinkle my nose, completely disgusted with him. It's like I'm seeing him for the first time. Is this who Odessa and Clem had seen all along? "And this is why I don't agree with you conjuring. Your intentions aren't genuine— just like the gods, whoever they are, who allow you to conjure. Just because you can do something doesn't mean you should; and just because you can hold something in your hand doesn't mean it fucking belongs to you."

"Cris, come on," he whimpers. "I'm sorry. I was being stupid and playing around with different spells. I didn't even think it'd worked. I didn't mean to hurt you."

I scoff. "Y'all never do."

"Are you seriously trying to make this about race right now? Not all white people are evil, you know."

"No, they're not, but white people made it so I can never *not* think about race. I have to constantly wonder if the white people I encounter every day, people who can change my fate as fast as the Sun sets, are going to hate me simply because I'm a Black woman. You'll *never* know that feeling."

"Look, I already said I was sorry, okay? Can you at least accept my apology?"

I roll my eyes. I don't give a shit about his apolo-lie. "How long have you been conjuring love spells on me?"

"A week or so before we hung out the first time."

My knees weaken, and I stagger backward. Our relationship was a lie. All of it. Over a year.

"And when was the last time you lit these candles?"

He casts his gaze at the floor.

"*When?!*" I ball my hands into fists and close the distance between us.

He flinches and screeches, "This morning!"

This morning. I feel light-headed, but I shake it off. None of his spells worked. Did they?

This feels like coming home and finding my house ransacked. But I can't just pack up and move to a new mind and forget what happened. The person I was made to believe I loved violated the fuck out of me, and I'm going to have to live with that forever. Fuck Oz for doing that to me.

I tuck my journal under my arm and snatch up the candles, my honor society pin, and my hair. My skin crawls wherever the gritty surfaces of the candles touch me. I'm relieved I found out about the love spell before I actually had sex with him. Even the thought makes me want to throw up.

Oz crumples to the floor in a pitiful heap. "Please forgive me."

My chest feels like a massive cold void. I feel tears building, but I blink them away. He doesn't deserve my tears, and he will never see them again.

"You held me while I cried over my dad, while Valentina waged war against me, and while my mother lay on her deathbed. You were my *only* safe space. And that is why I will *never* trust you again."

"You're right, but please don't throw all that away because I messed up. Damn the spell and damn magic altogether. I love you, and I know you love me, and you did that all on your own."

I laugh, and hurt twists his wounded expression further. "You should be careful meddling in things you don't have the range or depth to understand. Not all my ancestors take kindly to the twisted shit you folks like to get up to, which is exactly what I mean when I say it's not for you."

His mood shifts from sad to slighted. "Oh, so you're saying I'm not good enough for gen magic?"

I stare into his eyes for what I hope is the last time. "Yes."

He stands up in silent rage, watching me leave, his candles and my stolen possessions in my arms.

He had better thank the gods I've given up magic.

FIFTEEN

CLEMENT

Adeline stands on the porch, watching Yves and me like a sneering gargoyle statue. We get in my car and drive away, and my heart pounds until I turn out of the neighborhood.

Yves grips both sides of his seat and stares straight ahead with wide eyes. "Holy shit, that escalated quickly."

I turn in to a gas station and park. Maybe I should just leave this alone and mind my business, like Ursula suggested. I feel like an idiot, sitting here, picking at the threads of the steering wheel with my fingernail. "Sorry to have dragged you into all of this," I say. "I don't know what I was thinking."

"Eh . . ." Yves waves a hand. "Spending time with you beats running errands for Fab all day or locking myself in my room to paint."

I feel myself blushing and rip my eyes from his hypnotizing stare. My head floats away on the wings of a breeze, lost in a daydream. The last time I felt like this, I'd let Lamar Givens talk me into eating a piece of a "special" cookie he'd swiped from his dad's stash.

"Do you believe Adeline?" I ask. "Do you think Jean-Louise stole Auguste's dead body?"

The thought creeps me out. I stare down at my arms and the goose bumps running the length of them. Maybe I don't want to believe Auguste's mother because I don't want to imagine why Jean-Louise would want to hang on to his dead friend's corpse.

Yves frowns at the floor for a silent moment. "What if we're going about this all wrong?"

"What do you mean?"

"Maybe we should've just gone straight to the source from the start. I know where Jean-Louise lives."

"How do you know that?"

"How many times do I have to explain to you who my sister is?" He points to the street next to the gas station that leads west of town. "Take that road."

I park my car along the curb outside Jean-Louise's narrow two-story house. Much smaller than the two towering structures on either side of it, the home looks as if it's been smashed into the narrow space between. Several windows are missing shutters, and dark drapes conceal what lies beyond the dusty panes. Paint has chipped off the periwinkle siding in large patches, and the sidewalk leading to the front porch is cracked and broken, at least the portions that aren't buried beneath overgrown grass and weeds. So far, this place doesn't seem very inviting.

We approach the front door, avoiding the jagged upturned pieces of concrete that jut up from the ground like it's been smashed with a sledgehammer. Yves rings the doorbell and raps on the glass pane of the door. I try to peek through a tiny crack between the panels covering the window, but the room beyond is grim and deserted.

Yves bangs on the door again and it swings open so fast that he almost knocks on the broad chest of a tall man.

Jean-Louise is far more handsome than I imagined. I feel silly for letting rumors warp my image of him into some *Phantom of the Opera* villain. He casts a pair of brown, heavy-lidded eyes onto us. His cocoa complexion appears extra dark in the shadows of his foyer. The orange glow of the sunset makes his tall, muscular frame slightly more imposing as he towers over us.

He grimaces. "Can I help you two with something, or would you prefer to stand there and gape at me all evening?"

"Are you Jean-Louise?" I ask.

A shadow darts across his face. "No."

He steps back and tries to slam the door, but I stick my foot out.

The door bangs against it and bounces back open, and I wince and bite my lip to keep from cursing.

"If you don't mind," I say, scrunching up my face due to the intense throbbing of my foot, "we'd like to talk to you for a moment."

He closes the door on my foot again, pushing hard, which makes me yelp. Yves lets out a muffled whimper behind me. But I don't move.

"I don't want to talk to you," Jean-Louise says. "Now remove your foot before I call the cops."

"Call them. But I'm not leaving until you tell me why you're having secret nighttime meetings with my aunt."

He blinks several times. "Ursula is your aunt?"

"Yeah. I'm Clem, and this is Yves." I point over my shoulder at Yves.

"What do you want?" asks Jean-Louise.

"For starters, can you please stop smashing my foot?"

He snatches the door open and ushers us inside. "Maybe next time try properly introducing yourself first."

To my surprise, the inside of his home is nothing like the exterior, though it is a bit dusty and stuffy. It reminds me of the ultimate bachelor pad, complete with worn black leather furniture, a big-screen television (which currently has an international soccer game on mute), and a fully stocked bar where the dining room should be. The air smells of burned sage and the place is dead silent.

Jean-Louise leads us to the kitchen, which looks like it's been teleported straight from the nineties, complete with wood paneling and tiled countertops. I hobble over to the breakfast table that sits on one side of the kitchen, my foot complaining the entire way.

He pulls out chairs for Yves and me, and we both sit down. "I'll be right back," he tells us.

I scan the area, though I'm not sure for what. All I uncover is that Jean-Louise cleans the kitchen better than Odessa judging by the way the chrome faucets of the sink shine from across the room.

"You all right?" whispers Yves.

I nod as Jean-Louise slow-shuffles back into the room like a leaden-footed giant. His face settles into a natural glower, deep lines trailing from the corners of his nose and disappearing beneath the salt-and-pepper scruff of his short beard. He fills a glass with water, then shoves it and a bottle of aspirin in my face.

"Thanks." I set the water on the table and take the bottle. I examine the label carefully, hesitant to swallow any of the small oval pills inside. When I feel eyes on me, I look up to find Jean-Louise staring like he wants to squeeze my head between his large hands until it pops like bubble wrap.

"It's aspirin," he says. "If you don't want it, kindly give it back and leave."

I shake two pills from the bottle and swallow them with some water. I've barely had enough to wash them down before he snatches the glass from my hand, sloshing water over the sides. He empties it in the sink and drops it with a loud clink.

"I heard you and Ursula talking about Auguste Dupre last night," I tell him. "I know my aunt thinks differently, but I don't believe Auguste's death was your fault. And we thought you'd tell us the truth . . . about what really happened to him."

He leans back against the sink, crosses his arms over his chest, and laughs. "Bored this summer, boys? Find something else to do besides meddling in my personal business."

"You and Auguste were boyfriends," I say.

He feigns surprise and makes an exaggerated show of slow clapping. "Thanks, Captain Obvious. Seriously, kids, please get out of my house before you piss me off even more than you already have."

I want to punch this guy right in his thick neck. "That's how I know you didn't kill him."

"Not that I care, but how would you know such a thing?"

"Because you were in love with him."

He scoffs. "I wasn't the only one, which was the problem."

The proclamation slaps me across the face—because how could I not have guessed?

"Aunt Ursula loved him, too," I say. "Is that why she's so angry with you?"

I'm almost sure now as my mind rifles through the memory of Aunt Ursula's late-night conversation with Jean-Louise. Something about the intensity of the way she spoke about Auguste suggested they might've been more than friends.

Jean-Louise's eyes fall. Some of his rude swagger wilts and his great figure contracts before my eyes. "We all used to hang together. But things went south the day Ursula finally built up the courage to tell Auguste she had feelings for him and he turned her down. He hadn't come out to anyone as gay then—except me. And she had no idea he and I had been dating in secret. That was the beginning of the end of our friendship."

Holy hell. Now it makes sense why Aunt Ursula blames Jean-Louise. She never got closure with her friend and is now trapped in an endless loop of grief.

Something thuds upstairs, nearly giving me a heart attack. My eyes shoot up to the ceiling. "What was that?"

"Not that it's any of your business, but I have a cat who gets his rocks off by knocking my stuff over," he says. "Because I'm down here having my nerves danced on by you two, the little shit is likely having a field day up there." He stands up, his muscular frame looming over us. "It's time for you both to go."

Yves and I leap to our feet and start toward the exit. The ache in my foot has subsided considerably, and I feel like a jerk for how I acted about the aspirin.

I stop just inside the door and turn back to Jean-Louise. "Were all those things written in the news about Auguste true? Was he really an addict?"

He shakes his head. "Go ask your filthy cousin what happened to *our* friend August Dupre, that is, if you can manage to pry the truth out of him."

"Justin?"

Jean-Louise nods. "My mercy is the only reason that coward still draws breath."

I hold mine. I had no idea their beef ran that deep.

He narrows his eyes at me, as if extending the warning to me as well, and a shiver ripples through me. "Now get out of my house." He pushes me and Yves through the door and slams it.

I have no idea what Justin did to Jean-Louise, but it must've been pretty bad. The more I try to untangle the threads of my aunt's life, the more knots I find.

"So, what now?" asks Yves.

"I'm not sure."

I've had my fill of getting kicked out of people's homes for one day, but there's still one nagging question left: What the hell happened to Auguste's body?

I open the car door and take one last look at Jean-Louise's house. He watches from the front door, his hulking shadow filling most of the window. My eyes wander up to the second level, and my heart skips several beats.

A silhouette appears in one of the upstairs windows. It stands between the parted curtains, staring down at us. I blink and wipe my eyes.

But when I look again, every window is empty.

Am I imagining things, or does Jean-Louise's cat look an awful lot like a person?

SIXTEEN

CRISTINA

I throw my stolen belongings and the candles in the trunk of my car and pull out of Oz's driveway so fast my tires squeal.

The moment I turn out of his neighborhood, I pull over and let out the scream that had been billowing in my chest since I opened that fucking closet. I scream until my throat burns. I'm not sure how long I sit there on the side of the road, but I have to expel all this emotion or I'm going to explode.

After I make it home, I head straight to the backyard and toss the candles and the lock of my hair into the firepit, douse them in lighter fluid, and set everything ablaze. I don't bother to stay and watch them burn. Oz calls me so many times I have to block his number. He can drown in misery for the rest of his life for all I care. The worst predators are the ones who prey on your sympathy, too.

I sit on the front porch alone with my grief and shock, watching the Sun disappear to the other side of the world and listening to two chickadees call to each other from willows on either side of our home. Fireflies grow their ranks, drifting carefree in the warm evening air. They're annoying at first, but after a few minutes, when I'm surrounded by dancing, blinking lights, a sense of calm unfurls somewhere inside me.

Oz used magic—the same magic I'd loved more than him—to break into my mind and steal my power. Now I don't feel safe in my own head. And what the fuck am I supposed to do with that?

Oz isn't the only person who betrayed me today. Magic struck again. And together, the two of them stole so much from me over the last year. Everything from not-so-innocent kisses to intense groping, and head on occasion. Now, the mere thought makes me want to vomit.

They didn't just steal my body. They pillaged my mind, my emotions, and my time. So much time. A year of Oz pulling my strings like an evil puppeteer while I wallowed in grief and guilt.

This is exactly why I don't fuck with magic anymore. And also how I know I made the best decision to walk away from that toxic relationship forever—both of them.

The front door creaks open and Mama's voice pulls me away from my depressing rumination.

"Hey, baby," she says. "I didn't know you were out here. Aunt Jackie said she was coming by and I thought I heard her car."

I turn and force a smile. "Hey, Mama."

Her expression sinks, and she comes outside and sits next to me. Fuck. She knows something's wrong. I don't feel like talking, but I don't have the strength to lie either.

Mama rubs my back with one hand. "Cristina, are you okay, baby?" Hearing her voice feels like slipping on a pair of socks fresh out the dryer on a winter night.

I shake my head, too afraid if I say the words, I'll burst into tears again. I don't want to give Oz any more emotion, any more of me, but it hurts so fucking bad that I feel like I'm going to rupture if I don't. But Mama hugs me and squeezes so tight that I can't hold it inside any longer.

She embraces me while I cry, rubbing my back, but not saying anything. She lets me erupt, and I do, nestled into the soft cotton of her T-shirt and the rich, amber-scented oils on her skin. And when I'm done, she tilts my chin up and wipes my cheeks with her thumbs.

"What's the matter, Cristina?" she says. "Please talk to me."

I sniff. "Is magic evil?"

Mama purses her lips and thinks a moment before answering. "Magic is neither evil nor good. It enhances who we are in our hearts. Some folks use it for evil, but others do a lot of good with it."

"What about love spells?"

"Love spells are the result of someone twisting magic for their own selfish ends." Mama leans closer to look into my eyes, but I'm too embarrassed to meet hers. "Why are you asking me this?" When I say nothing, she blows out a harsh breath and stares at the sky. "Did Oz conjure a love spell on you?"

I nod. I'm mortified to have to talk about this, but also glad she didn't make me say it aloud.

"Oh, Cristina . . ." Her voice trails and takes a little more of my dignity with it—what little Oz left me with. I'm not interested in lectures about trusting the wrong people or making foolish decisions. I already regret ever meeting Oz. But Mama does none of that.

Instead, she scoots closer and puts an arm around me. We sit like that a moment, listening to each other breathe and watching the lightning bugs flash in and out of sight all around us.

"I have to ask," she says, finally breaking the quiet, "have you two ever had—"

"Ma! No!" If the word "sex" comes out of her mouth, I'm going to hurl.

"I'm sorry," she says, "I'm just trying to understand."

She holds me close—any closer and I'll be on her lap—but I let her. "It's okay to be mad and anything else you're feeling right now—even if you're angry with me. I should've done more to protect you. I'm so sorry I let you down."

"It's not your fault, Mama," I tell her. "I'm the idiot who trusted him."

"Listen to me, Cristina." She lifts my chin, so I have no choice but to stare into her deep brown eyes that almost look black in the dwindling evening light. "You feel whatever it is you need to feel right now, be it rage, sadness, whatever—but what you cannot do is blame yourself. I will not let you carry that weight, baby girl. That doesn't belong to you."

I stare out into the sky over the grand willows on our estate. I'm not sure when the Sun left us, but only a thin strip of orange sky remains and the Moon shines bright among the Stars, as do the fireflies that float all around us, some circling Mama's head in a crown of light. I'm too angry to appreciate how beautiful she looks right now, because all I can think about is how much I hate Oz.

"How do you want me to respond to this," Mama says gently, "on a scale of 'do nothing' all the way to 'drag Oz's sorry ass to the never-realm myself'?"

I grin, imagining her doing just that. I don't know what to do myself, so I have no idea what to tell her, so I just shrug. "I'm not sure there is anything we can do, realistically. People have a hard time getting justice for assault when magic *isn't* involved; and even so, there are no laws against magic, so it's not like we can go report him to the police for being a creep."

And even if there were laws against what Oz has done, everyone knows those same laws wouldn't apply to affluent white boys like him. I think to take Mama up on her offer to rid this realm of him, but that might only create more drama that our family doesn't need right now.

"You're right," Mama says. "I'm here to help you through it however you need. You're never alone, baby."

"Thanks." A tear falls again, and I wipe my face with the back of my hand.

"Did you ever have a moment of clarity, even a brief one, where you questioned your feelings?" asks Mama.

I shake my head. "I thought I loved him, but I don't know anymore. All I feel right now is disgust and rage."

I'm not sure what's real anymore—and I hate Oz for shifting my reality like that. And I also hate him for giving me so many moments I cherished, and then stealing all that away from me. A year of my life obliterated in a matter of minutes. How come no one has to pay for that besides me?

As if Mama can read my mind, she says, "It's okay to hate him.

I hate him, too." I can't explain why, but it makes me feel a little better to hear her say that. "Did you thank Wise John?"

I raise an eyebrow at her. "For what?"

"You hadn't considered his protection might've been what led you to uncover the love spell?"

I recall the faint glimmer of light, which I'd completely forgotten about after what I discovered in Oz's closet. I frown, which is probably not the reaction Mama's expecting, because what she doesn't know is that now I have to deal with knowing the same magic that hurt me and my family so deeply also saved me. How the hell am I supposed to wrap my head around *that*?

"I guess." I shrug, because I don't know what else to say.

"I won't push you to do anything you're not up to, but I would like for you to see a therapist. Would you be okay with that?"

I nod. I'm not sure how I feel about therapy, but I trust Mama, so I'm willing to try.

Aunt Jacquelyn's car pulls up and parks at one end of the circular driveway. She gets out and retrieves baby Baptiste from his car seat. He's already fussing before she can close the door.

"Hey, y'all," she says, looking flustered as she walks up the steps. "I'm gonna hang out for a while and feed him if that's okay."

Mama scoffs. "Of course it's okay. This is your home, too, Jackie."

Jacquelyn smiles and disappears inside without replying.

Mama sighs and hangs her head. I almost ask, but I don't care to discuss family drama right now.

"You okay for now?" she asks.

"Yes," I tell her. "Thanks."

She rubs my back again and kisses my temple. "I'm here when you need to talk again." She stands up and goes inside to fuss over Aunt Jackie's baby.

I'm glad Mama's here. Not just to talk, but for everything.

So damn glad.

SEVENTEEN

CLEMENT

Across the street from Jean-Louise's home, Yves and I crouch into the cool late-evening shade behind a parked car, my own hidden a few houses down.

"Well, I can say without a doubt, my life has been significantly more exciting since I met you," says Yves.

"This may be crossing the line, but I've gotta do this," I say. "You can still back out."

He pats me heartily on the shoulder, which sends my pulse racing. "Stop trying to get rid of me. It's offensive."

I don't mind being stuck with him for any stretch of time. This actually feels quite nice—notwithstanding the looming threat of potential jail time for what we're about to do.

But I can't get the image of the figure standing in the window out of my head. It reminds me of my nightmare after the car accident—the one with the black-sand beach and that dark spirit man. My mind won't rest until I know who or what I saw in that window.

Much of the evening passes while we stake out Jean-Louise's house, waiting for him to leave. Our chances are slim, given he's somewhat of a recluse, but we have to try.

Then the moment we've been waiting for finally comes.

"Quiet," I hiss, and yank Yves down behind the car.

We both peep over the hood.

Jean-Louise, wearing gray joggers and a hooded denim jacket with the hood pulled onto his head, walks out of his house at a quick pace. He gets into a silver sedan parked out front, and we duck out of sight. The car's engine starts with a hesitant whine and idles for a moment before gravel crunches under the tires as the car pulls off.

I rise up just enough to see the red taillights crest the hill. "Let's go."

We race across the street into Jean-Louise's overgrown yard. A very high—and very locked—fence prevents us from accessing the back, so we hurry up to one of the front windows instead.

"Gimme." Yves wriggles his fingers, and I hand him the flathead screwdriver I brought in my pocket. "Don't pretend you know how to break into a house."

"I've really gotta meet your sister."

He chuckles and sets to work jimmying the windowpane from the frame. "Watch my back. Nosy neighbors and such."

"Right." I peer at the darkened windows of the homes across the street.

Streetlights beam warm orange cones onto the surrounding road, sidewalk, and cars, all of which are devoid of life. The majority of the houses in Jean-Louise's neighborhood are in similar states of disrepair, and the section of street in front of his home is deserted, with the exception of a single old car that trundles by and tops the hill, heading in the same direction Jean-Louise went minutes ago. It seems we're alone, but the skin on the back of my neck prickles like someone's watching.

"So, uh, what if Jean-Louise catches us and calls the police?" Yves asks between grunts while he works.

"Let's just not get caught."

Something snaps behind me and I turn to find Yves carefully removing a pane of glass, which he hands to me.

He sticks his arm through the hole, unlocks the window, and lifts it. "Voilà!" He pokes his head inside and looks around, then nods at me. "You first."

I climb into the dark front room, but my toe catches on the lip of the sill and I fall, knocking over a lamp with a crash and pop as the bulb explodes.

Something bumps upstairs.

I freeze on the floor below the window, digging my fingers into the soft pile of the carpet to help steady my pulse and ragged breaths.

After several brutal seconds of silence, I exhale and motion for Yves to climb through. Once he's safely inside, I shut the window.

"Why don't you just announce to the entire neighborhood that we're breaking and entering?" he whisper-shouts.

"Sorry!" Sweeping the flashlight from my phone in low arcs across the room, I try to recall what I can about the layout of the house from earlier. Near the kitchen, I spot the stairs leading up to the second level. At the bottom, I shine my light up the hardwood staircase.

We take the steps gingerly, stopping on a dime whenever one creaks, which in this old house is often. My heart thunders in my ears.

I push open the door of the first room at the top of the stairs and find what appears to be an office. It's dark, but I shine my light on the desk that sits toward the back of the room, the surface of which is splattered with books, papers, jars filled with all sorts of dark-colored liquids, and even a life-sized skull made out of solid black stone. The scent of sage hangs thick in this stuffy room, more than anywhere else in the house. Not far from the desk is a worn brown leather recliner beside a small side table, atop which sits a crystal decanter of brown liquor. Next to it is an ebony-colored smudge bowl that's shaped like a large, wrinkled hand, palm facing up with its gnarled, too-long fingers slightly curled. A half-burned bundle of sage lies over thick smudges of black and gray ash in the bowl's palm.

"Clem," calls Yves from where he hovers over the desk, "come look at this."

He shows me a notebook that's had the spine broken so it lies open to a page containing a recipe for what I guess is some sort of elixir. I assume it's Jean-Louise's handwriting, which is messy and difficult to read, but what catches my attention is a note scribbled toward the bottom of the page.

Are opiates the only way?

Opiates. That's how Auguste allegedly overdosed. What is Jean-Louise doing?

"That's not all," says Yves. He spreads out two thick stacks of paper held together by binder clips. Multicolored flags stick out on all four sides of both reports, the whole document is decorated with highlighted strips of text, and Jean-Louise's messy scribbles hang on the margins. One report is about "naturally occurring mind-enhancers," whatever the hell that is, and another is on the efficacy and dangers of opiates and narcotics.

A black journal on the corner of the desk grabs my eye, and I pick it up. A skull is carved on the cover like it'd been done with a knife. The artist sucks at drawing almost as much as me, because the skull reminds me of Grim from that Cartoon Network show, *Grim & Evil*—and I'm almost certain that wasn't their intent.

I open the book, and Yves leans close to get a better look. Heat radiates from him and makes my already overly anxious stomach churn, and I'm suddenly aware how close he is to me, his shoulder pressed against mine in the dark of Jean-Louise's office. He smells like sweat and spice, which fogs my brain for a moment. My heart pounds, but I'm not sure if it's because of Yves or the fear of getting caught snooping through all Jean-Louise's shit.

With the exception of a handful of blank pages in the back, the book is filled with all sorts of hand-drawn symbols, from simple to intricate, small to large—some even stretching across the spine onto the next page. There's no denying—these are talismans. We use them a lot in gen magic, but I don't recognize these particular ones. They're all elaborate with dark imagery that makes me a bit uncomfortable. Severed heads and limbs. Animal carcasses. Daggers imbedded in skulls and hearts. Tombstones. And it looks like more than a few are drawn in what I'm hoping is dark red ink and not blood. Below each talisman is a very brief description of its purpose. One in particular catches my eye. It's a series of symbols and daggers surrounding a skull with the blades all pointing inward, which is labeled "for entrapping threatening spirits."

Yves sucks in a shaky breath and steps back. "This is necromancy. Dark Moon magic."

A shock of realization thunders through my nervous stomach. "That would explain why he'd want to steal Auguste's corpse."

A bump somewhere out in the hallway makes us both jump. The book slips out of my hand and thumps loudly against the floor. I hold my breath and stoop to pick it up, my heart galloping.

"What was that?" hisses Yves.

I place the book back on the desk where I found it and press a finger to my lips. I creep to the door and look out into the hallway. It's deserted. I turn and flash Yves a thumbs-up, but he only stares at me with broadened, fearful eyes. I tiptoe to the top of the stairs and peer down them. All the lights are still off, which means Jean-Louise isn't back yet.

"It's okay," I tell Yves in a hushed voice. "No one's here."

Yves hugs himself. "I think we should go before we get caught."

I'm just as scared as him, but this is the only way back to my aunt. I can't walk away without giving it my all.

"There's only three more doors up here," I tell him. "I'll do a quick sweep and then we'll leave. Five more minutes, tops."

Yves sighs loudly and follows me to the room across the hall from the necromancy office.

I open the door to a bedroom, likely belonging to Jean-Louise. Yves creeps over to the closet on the other side of the room and peers inside, his phone lit up in his hand. Unlike mine, Jean-Louise's bedroom is immaculate. The bed is neatly made, and no clothes or shoes are strewn across the floor. Nothing else interesting catches my eye.

"I don't think there's anything here," I whisper, taking one last look around.

But a single framed picture on the bedside table snags my attention.

I pick it up. It's a photo of Jean-Louise and another man. I'm not sure when it was taken, but Jean-Louise has far fewer stress lines on his face and far less gray in his beard. The other guy's dusk-brown eyes shine through the image, through the dark of the room, and straight through my heart. I rub a single finger across his happy face. *Auguste?*

What happened to you?

The lights flash on, temporarily blinding me. Yves yelps from the other side of the room, and I shield my face, blinking the purple spots from my vision.

A tall, bulky figure stands in the doorway.

Fuck. We're caught.

When my vision returns to normal, my breath leaves me. I take a tentative step back and bump into the bedside table, jostling the items on top of it. My eyes jump back and forth between the dead man in the picture and the one standing in front of me.

They're the same. But not. It's Auguste Dupre.

His body is emaciated, judging by the way his oversized clothes hang loose on his frame. His eyes seem larger than a normal person's sitting in their sunken, dark sockets. They're black like the desolate void of space and take in every inch of me and then rake over Yves. Auguste doesn't say anything. He just stands there, silent and opposing, his face blank and expressionless.

"Auguste?"

Yves shoots me an *Are you serious right now?* look.

I take a step closer, but Auguste flinches back. "We're not going to hurt you." I hold my hands up in front of me, speaking slowly as I inch forward.

He doesn't move a muscle.

"Can you talk?"

"What the hell is going on?!" A voice thunders from the top of the stairs.

I swallow the urge to leap out the window. Jean-Louise appears in the doorway, his eyes several levels beyond murderous. And my stomach faints into my butt.

He pulls Auguste from the room by the hand. Once they disappear, Yves and I share frightened looks, but neither of us dares move.

Jean-Louise reappears a moment later with a frown even Ursula would envy. "GET THE HELL OUT OF MY HOUSE!" His voice booms, rattling my eyeballs in their sockets.

Yves shoots past him. My feet move seemingly on their own, much to my relief, since my brain seems to have fled the building some time ago. I dart into the hallway, but Jean-Louise clamps onto my arm and nearly jerks me off my feet.

His strong fingers dig into my skin with the force of industrial vise grips. "If you tell a single person what you saw here tonight or if I ever catch you in my house again, I'll drag your sorry ass to the never-realm and leave you there to rot for the rest of your miserable existence." He releases me with a shove, nearly sending me toppling down the stairs.

I trip over the first step, fumble down the rest, and run outside. Yves beats me to the car.

I nearly burn my tires to the tread peeling away from the curb. Once we're safely out of the neighborhood, I swerve to the side of the road and slam the brakes, nearly giving Yves whiplash.

My breaths are still heavy, like I just sprinted a mile. "What—the—fuck—was—that?"

Fear wavers behind Yves's eyes, and he still trembles. "I-I've never seen anything like that before. Was he alive or dead . . . ?"

"Jean-Louise stole Auguste's body from the morgue and brought him back to life."

I've never known anyone who practiced necromancy. As far as I knew it was one of those dark arts we never talked about.

But Jean-Louise has done it. He's brought Auguste back. But . . . uh, Auguste seemed more than a little "off." The emotionless face. The bleak eyes. Images of him linger on the backs of my lids when I close my eyes. Jean-Louise brought back his lover, but at what cost?

"I've seen some wild shit before, but this is definitely top of the list." Yves casts his gaze at the floor and shakes his head, still quivering.

I feel bad for dragging him into this. I don't know what to say, so I move his hand onto my lap and caress his fingers. I freeze at his sharp intake of breath. My heart beats so loudly in my ears that I want to yell at it to shut up so I can think straight.

"I'm glad you were here," I tell him. "I don't think I could've survived all that on my own."

He smiles, still looking down. "I do like you, but I may have to pass on another Fright Night date."

Date. The word karate-chops me in the throat. I hadn't thought of this as an official date, but every second of bad decision-making with him has felt like magic. Yves folds so easily into my life—where magic permeates nearly every aspect—that it feels foreign. But no less good.

"Maybe Jean-Louise has uncovered the meaning of life," I joke. "To prolong it."

Yves shakes his head. "I'm not sure what he's done to Auguste has anything to do with the meaning of life."

"Fair point. But at least now we know most of the truth—and had the best first date ever."

His head snaps up, and his lovely black eyes find mine. I take his hand and pull him closer. I lean in, and he shuts his eyes.

When our lips touch, I lose the feeling in my toes. I'd kiss this boy until my entire body went numb. He moves his mouth so deliberately, but with a delicacy that gives me the sensation of floating. I sweep my arm underneath his and around his back to tug him closer, wishing I could press my entire body against his, feel his heartbeat thump against mine.

Finally, we have to pull away for air, but we both do so with heavy reluctance. We grin, still holding hands.

Maybe something in this moment holds the elusive meaning of life.

However, I can't ignore the terror lurking at the boundary of my happiness. I don't know what's happening between me and Yves, but I can't help myself. This boy fell from the sky and fit perfectly into the gap in my life I've been trying so hard to fill.

But he's dangerous.

One more person I'll have to hang on to. One more person who might leave me.

I'm not sure if I'll survive Yves, but I'm already in too deep.

EIGHTEEN

CRISTINA

My entire day was a shit show.

I'm still sitting on the porch, alone with my fireflies and my torturous thoughts. All I managed to learn today was that Justin is Lenora's bitch, the stain my grandma left on this family is worse than I thought, and my ex-boyfriend is the creep I was too naive to believe he could be.

Clem pulls his car into the driveway and parks next to Jacquelyn's. He and Yves get out, smiling and talking in hushed but excited voices, glancing back over their shoulders as if expecting someone to run up on them. They seem quite close after only a day together, and it's hard to miss the way they stare at each other with growing intrigue and infatuation.

I hug my knees and turn back to my fireflies. I wish I could confide in my brother. Not just about Oz, but everything. All my safe spaces have been obliterated, and the weight of the world sitting on my chest grows heavier every day.

"Hey, why are you sitting outside?" asks Clem as he and Yves approach. "You okay?"

"I'm fine." I wave at Yves. "Nice to see you again."

"How you holdin' up?" he asks.

I force a smile. "Pretty good."

Clem points his thumb over his shoulder at Jacquelyn's car. "Aunt Jackie came back?"

"She forgot Baptiste's bottles," I say.

"Oh." He sits next to me, and Yves beside him.

Jacquelyn steps out the front door with Baptiste cradled in her arms and a tote bag slung over her shoulder. She smiles down at the three of us sitting on the steps and says, "Oh, hey there." But her expression darkens when Yves turns around. She gives a brisk nod of acknowledgment in his direction, brushes past us, and makes very short work of strapping Baptiste in and leaving. She doesn't give a second glance back or the annoying customary honk of the horn all Black people do when we leave a family member's house.

"That would be our aunt Jacquelyn," Clem tells Yves. "She's usually . . . less awkward."

But perplexing as usual. I purse my lips and keep my thoughts to myself. I'm beyond exhausted with trying to figure people out.

"Hmm . . ." Yves watches my fireflies, deep in thought. "She looks familiar."

"You know her?" I ask.

Yves shares his connection to the House of Vans, owned and operated by his older sister, Fabiana Bordeaux. Now I understand why he's aloof at school. I can personally attest to the sad fact that high school hasn't been a place of love and acceptance, largely thanks to Valentina and people like her.

"I might've only seen her once, but I'm pretty sure I remember her face," Yves says. "She was kept separate from the other employees. I'm not sure why."

"So that's why Aunt Ursula asked if Baptiste was a Van Kid," I say.

Yves flinches. "That's a really ugly name jerks made up to shame people like my sister and her employees. I don't agree with everything Fabiana does, but she's made a big difference in the sex-work community in this city. After that slimy guy threw her unknowingly into that world right after our parents died, she fought her way to the top of the food chain and created the House of Vans so sex workers could do their jobs safely and with respect."

"Yikes," I say, heat rushing my cheeks. "Sorry."

"It's okay," he says. "I can't be certain, but I doubt your aunt's baby had anything to do with her working for my sister—if she even did. Fabiana takes her business very serious; a little too serious sometimes if you ask me. But she's very strict about things like contraception and sexual health."

"I asked Aunt Jackie about Baptiste's father last night," I say. "She was real sketch about it and bolted before I could ask anything else."

Clem turns to Yves. "Do you think your sister might know who Baptiste's father is?"

Yves shrugs. "If she does, she won't tell. She holds only three things in this world sacred—her business, her secrets, and me."

Clem leans back on his elbows and blows out a frustrated breath. "Soo many secrets."

"Speaking of," I interject, "I went to see Justin today. Jean-Louise was right—Justin and Lenora do have a weird relationship." I share the details of my earlier encounter with Lenora. "Justin's definitely hiding something, but I don't know why he refuses to tell us anything."

"I have an idea how we might get him to talk," says Yves. Clem tosses him an anxious look, but Yves ignores it. "It's not ideal, but it could work." He turns to Clem. "We have to at least try."

"Okay, I'm listening." I'm willing to try almost anything if it'll move my investigation around the wall I hit today.

Clem holds up a finger, and Yves swallows the story he was about to tell. "You have to swear you won't say anything."

"Because you've done such a good job upholding my conditions?" I peer around him at Yves. "No offense."

He holds up a hand. "None taken."

"Cris!" Clem nudges me.

"Fine!" I exclaim. "Just tell me what's going on already."

Clem and Yves share the details of their visit with Auguste Dupre's mom and subsequent encounters with Jean-Louise and the *not-so-dead-after-all* Auguste.

I cover my mouth, but a gasp still escapes. "You're lying."

Clem crosses his heart with one finger, and Yves shakes his head.

"And apparently, Justin is terrified of Jean-Louise," says Yves. "Maybe we can get Jean-Louise to convince Justin to come clean."

"And how do you suggest we do that?" I ask.

"Leave that part to me," Clem says, though he doesn't sound very confident.

"That worries me," I say. "This is important, Clem. You can't go about this haphazard—"

"I got it!" He stands up and grins. "Stop worrying. We'll go see him first thing in the morning, and I'll convince him to talk to Justin for us. But right now, Yves and I are going to order some pizza and hang at the firepit in the back. Wanna join?"

I shake my head and get to my feet as well. "Nah, I'm tired."

"Are you sure you're good?" Clem asks.

I want to wrap my arms around him and dive into all the genuine love and concern and sympathy resonating from him, but I hold back.

"I'm sure," I tell him.

"Okay," he says. "I'll bring your bacon and pineapple special up to your room."

"Thank you. See you guys later. Have fun."

I go inside and trudge upstairs, but stop at Mama's bedroom door, which stands ajar. I peer inside and listen. It's quiet, except for the faint sounds of water moving in the tub from behind the cracked bathroom door. She's probably soaking in a bath.

I turn to leave, but a single, worn brown envelope lying on Mama's bedside table catches my eye. There's nothing special about it, but curiosity still lures me into the room.

I lower myself onto the bed and glance toward the bathroom once more before opening the envelope. Inside is a handwritten letter and a stapled report. I set the letter aside and read the report first.

It's an autopsy of Alexis Lancaster. Dated June 21, 1989. About ten pages long. Why does Mama have this?

Next, I unfold the letter and recognize the handwriting immediately.

It's from Dad, addressed to Mama.

Dear Marie,

We made a vow a long time ago that we wouldn't keep secrets from each other, but I'm afraid I've betrayed that sacred promise—and I hope you can find it in your heart to forgive me.

This summer, a girl came by the brewery asking for you, but you'd already left. It was coming up on the anniversary of your parents' deaths and understandably, a difficult time for you. She gave me an envelope and made me swear I wouldn't open it or breathe a word about it to another soul and would give it straight to you. I asked her name, but she said she was afraid giving too much information before speaking with you directly was dangerous. She said she'd come by the house later to talk to you in person and would clear everything up, but she never showed.

Curiosity got the best of me, so I opened the envelope, but all I found inside was a copy of an autopsy report for Alexis Lancaster. Given the subject of the report and the timing of its arrival, I thought it was some cruel prank, so I didn't mention it to you. But as days passed, I couldn't stop thinking about it—so I read the report in detail. If that document really is from Alexis Lancaster's official autopsy and not a forgery, it might prove your mother wasn't responsible for her death.

Again, my love, we reach the point in this story where I betray our vow a second time. I kept this secret, too, because I had to be <u>sure</u> before I brought this to you. Please know I only ever wanted to protect you and the kids.

I reached out to Micah Jones, an old school friend and detective for the local police, to ask about the autopsy. He confirmed its authenticity and agreed to help me do some digging to find out what really happened to that woman. But strangely, the next day he called and said he couldn't find anything and that I needed to drop it. I did some research on my own, but my resources were limited—and now my time might be, too.

Strange things have been happening ever since Micah turned

me away. I might be paranoid, but last night, I felt someone watching me when I left the brewery. Whenever I'm out in public, I feel eyes on me. Sometimes, even at home. Something's wrong. I don't feel safe anymore. My heart is dying, knowing I might've put our family in danger. I'm not sure what I've brought down on us, but I'm going to fix this somehow.

If anything happens to me, I want you to know the truth. I strongly believe someone's trying to cover up what happened to Alexis—and whoever it is, they're connected, powerful, and likely very dangerous. You must promise me you'll steer clear of all this—and keep Clem and Cris safe, no matter what. Please do not repeat my mistakes.

I'm so sorry I failed you—all of you.

Your love always,
David

I can't breathe.

My hands tremble so badly that I drop the letter and jump to my feet. But something else catches my attention. I scoop Dad's letter back up.

I'll never forget the day he died. His letter is dated the same day. I study the words and the thump of my heart grows stronger when I realize something's off. His handwriting appears frantic and rushed, as if he was trying to get everything out in a hurry. He must've been terrified.

I snap pictures on my phone of Dad's letter and every page of the autopsy report. I'm carefully sliding the papers back into the envelope when Mama's soft voice jerks me back to reality.

"Cristina." She stands in the bathroom doorway, tying her satin robe closed. "The things in that envelope are private." Her voice doesn't sound angry, but instead bears a tentative, almost nervous tone. "Did you read them?"

"Did someone murder Dad?" As angry as I am with Mama right now for keeping this from us, I have to choke the words out.

If someone did kill him, that might mean his death wasn't my fault. Why would she keep this from us? Mama felt like the *one* adult I could trust, but even she has her own trove of messy secrets.

She hesitates. "I don't know, baby. I have my suspicions, but that's all they are."

"Did you show all this to the police?"

"If you read your dad's letter, then you already know why that was not an option."

My mind feels like a piece of lawn furniture in a hurricane. "So, what did you do?"

She sits on the bench at the foot of her bed and motions for me to join her, which I do. She takes the envelope and clutches it in her lap, staring at it like she'd fling it into another dimension if doing so wouldn't mean losing another memory of my dad.

"I made the mistake of sharing all this with Ursula when I first received it. We pored over everything, and we both allowed rage and revenge to consume us." She shakes her head. "Your father's letter terrified me. If someone had indeed murdered him, none of us were safe. I couldn't live with myself if anything happened to you or Clem.

"I wanted to find the people who'd done this and rip them apart with my bare hands, but the day your daddy left this realm, he wrote this letter, pleading with me to protect y'all. I didn't think twice about swallowing all the feelings that autopsy report brought to life inside me if it meant keeping my babies safe—and alive."

I get it. But I don't agree with it.

Someone has to stand up for *us.*

"Is that why you and Aunt Ursula are fighting?"

Mama sighs and nods. "She swears Lenora's behind everything, but we can't prove any of it. Ursula wants blood for blood, and so does whoever murdered Alexis, be it Lenora or someone else. But I don't need justice if I have to trade anyone else I love for it."

My gut tells me Aunt Ursula's right, but suspicions mean nothing without solid proof. Now I'm also wondering if Lenora might've cursed Mama. If Lenora and Gabriela Savant combined their capabilities on their best days, they still wouldn't be a fraction of the Queen that Mama would on her worst. I bet I'm not the only person who realized that . . .

"Does the hex doll we found have anything to do with this?"

"Cris—"

"Mama, please tell me the truth."

"I went to see Eveline Beaumont, who runs the Gen Council's Temple of Innocent Blood." She looks me straight in the eye. "Without Ursula. She still doesn't know I went, and judging by how things turned out, it was for the best. Eveline always seemed logical and on the side of justice, so I thought she could be trusted. She listened to my concerns about Lenora and the implications pertaining to the Gen Council and appeared shocked. She told me Lenora had fallen somewhat out of her favor, and judging by Lenora's reputation, I could guess why. Eveline said she'd address it with the Council and would be in touch with me soon after.

"But I never heard from her and then I got so sick that nothing else mattered. I felt so ashamed for wasting so much time with all that when I might've had so little left to spend with you and Clem. Every bit of bad luck our family has faced recently has stemmed from that autopsy report. Dredging up all the pain and hatred from thirty years ago is no way to serve ourselves or the magical community right now—especially on the cusp of the election for mayor."

Mama gets up and chucks the envelope into the fireplace.

"What are you doing?" I ask, silently relieved I thought to take pictures of the documents.

She grabs the matchbox from the mantel, kneels, and strikes a match. She lights each corner of the envelope and doesn't stop working the flames until the whole thing is ablaze.

She stands and turns to me, a fire in her eyes hotter than the one burning behind her. "Forget what you read in that envelope. Let this alone, Cristina." When I say nothing, she raises her voice. "Swear it!"

"Okay," I lie.

She sweeps me up from my seat and into a hug. I try to put aside my feelings for the few seconds the embrace lasts, but I just can't. We've lost so much. How can she not even want to know why?

She stands back and looks into my eyes again; this time hers are pleading. "Don't share this with your brother, please."

I nod, but that's a lie, too. Clem deserves to know the truth about Dad as much as me.

"I love you," she says.

"Love you, too."

She kisses me on the temple, and we say good night.

Everything's changed. I don't care what Mama says, I can't go back now.

From the beginning, I had a suspicion the hex-doll business ran deeper than anyone could imagine. And I'm going to find out just how deep it goes.

I also have a hunch Lenora Savant framed my grandmother for Alexis Lancaster's murder thirty years ago so she could steal the throne, and she might've also murdered my dad, because he tried to uncover the truth. Now I have to know if all that's true, because if it is, I'll stop breathing before I let her get away with it—I don't care if her connections run all the way to the spiritual realm.

I'm going to show her who I am.

If I get this right, I might be able to clear my grandma's name *and* mine. And that would mean Mama would be the rightful Queen because her birthright was stolen from her.

But I'll have to prove it first.

Breathless and overwhelmed with visions of a grand new future and the hope of redemption for me and my grandmother, I brew a pot of dark roast and open my journal to a fresh page.

I've got a long night ahead of me.

NINETEEN

VALENTINA SAVANT

Valentina was a master of invisibility.

However, her skill relied not on magic but the simple fact that her parents were most often too entrenched in their own bullshit to give a damn about her.

She was invisible again, sitting at the dining table and pretending to pore over her summer reading assignments for AP English. A stack of books she had no desire to read and a notepad she'd been scribbling mindlessly in lay in front of her. But she was more interested in the meeting going on between Granny, Mom, and Eveline Beaumont in the next room. Quietly, she rose from her seat and perched beside the open archway leading into the living room to better hear their conversation.

"That white-witch bitch has been campaigning among the other members of the Magical and Spiritual Coalition to conspire against me because I won't make Ben drop out of the race," Eveline scoffs. "I'm even more insulted she actually thinks I have no idea what she's doing. Madeline DeLacorte is as entitled and insufferable as her mother, and I didn't think I could hate anyone more than Bethesda."

Valentina wondered if Mom and Granny were part of Madeline's slur campaign against the Gen Council. If so, then by extension this was her problem, too. And she already had more than enough of those.

"Well, as long as Gabriela is chair of the Magical and Spiritual Coalition, you'll always have our votes," said Granny. "And I have more than a few allies among the MASC board. Madeline is no threat."

Madeline had certainly seemed like a threat to Valentina, and it troubled her that Granny wasn't taking this more seriously.

"A nuisance at best, but she will not deter me," said Eveline. "I will make the swamps of Louisiana bleed before I let anyone derail my plans."

An icy chill slipped down Valentina's back, making her shudder. What was Eveline up to?

"Why does everything you two contrive have to end in violence?" The softness of Mom's voice betrayed the anger she'd wanted to convey, making Valentina roll her eyes.

There was a terse moment of silence in the room where Valentina heard nothing but the drum of her heart between her ears.

"Never mind all that." Eveline's voice was first to cut through the quiet. "Considering what happened at the pier the other night, I'm beginning to worry you two have a situation that is well on its way to being out of control. And that cannot happen right now—certainly not with Madeline DeLacorte circling."

"Perhaps you're right," Mom said. "Maybe Lenora's in over her head and should step down from the Council."

"Now, hold on—"

"I don't care what you do," Eveline said, cutting off Granny, "but handle it, and do it quickly. I meant what I said earlier. Nothing is going to get in my way. I will see you *both* removed before I allow you or those white witches to destroy what I've spent more than three decades building." Her car keys jingled, and the old springs in the armchair groaned as she rose to her feet. "For now, I need to go see Justin. He's making me something to help me with these damned Benson & Hedges cravings. That man is truly gifted when it comes to elixirs—bringing him onto the Council was, admittedly, one of your better decisions, Lenora. Do try and get back to that."

Valentina started at the sound of approaching footsteps. She dove back into her seat, opened *Lord of the Flies*, and pretended to read as the voices in the living room fell to an inaudible volume.

Valentina looked up as Eveline passed the doorway to the dining room and smiled on her way out. She looked like a business executive today in her black pumps, kaftan, and glasses—a sharp contrast from the glamorous fits she saved for the Council Chamber.

Once their visitor had left, Mom's and Granny's raised voices drew Valentina into the living room. Mom was on her feet, staring out the window into the backyard while Granny scowled at her back. Neither of them noticed Valentina standing there. Maybe she was still invisible.

"Gabriela, you don't even have what it takes to lead your own family, much less the Generational Council *or* MASC," said Granny. "Be a dear and leave this little roadblock to me."

The drama in her grandmother's voice called to her, and Valentina edged farther into the room, still unnoticed.

"You may be Queen Mother," Mom said, "but *I* am Queen, and you are going to have to stop undermining me or I'll be the one to requisition the Council to have you removed."

Like hell she would.

Granny chuckled softly. "My dear, sweet daughter-in-law, I adore that you've managed to find your voice, but you have never been more than a figurehead. *I'm* the bitch behind the curtain."

Mom shook with anger, but Valentina cut off her rebuttal.

"Granny, I have an idea."

Mom cut her eyes at Valentina. "This does not concern you, Val. Go to your room."

Valentina's brows pinched. "Y'all are discussing my birthright, so, yes, it does concern me."

"She's right," said Granny. "And she might also have better ideas than the foolishness I have to put up with from you and Jack."

Valentina bit back the grin fighting to break free. This was her chance.

"Lenora—"

Granny held up a finger, shushing Mom. "Gabriela, why don't you be a doll and bring us all some tea?"

Mom threw her hands up and rolled her eyes. "I need to invest in a fucking doorbell camera," she mumbled under her breath on her way to the kitchen.

Valentina watched her mother go, curious about what'd gotten into her as of late, but still no closer to renewing her love or faith in the woman.

"Sit with me, sweetheart," Granny told her, patting the spot on the couch next to her. She frowned down at the old, faded carpet Mom got from Restoration Hardware over ten years ago as if she had a personal vendetta against it. "I never quite understood your mother's taste," said Granny as Valentina sat down. "She decorates as if she's fresh out of college and living in a studio apartment."

"I love the rug in your tearoom," said Valentina. "I want one just like it one day."

"Then one day it will be yours." Granny tugged Valentina close and planted a kiss on her temple.

Valentina's chest felt full of something warm and soothing. It was an unfamiliar feeling, but good. Things would get better because she was going to make them better.

Mom returned with three mugs of tea and cream and sugar containers all on a silver tray. She set it down with a sharp clink, which drew a look of indignation from Granny. Mom picked up her cup and sat in the armchair with a frustrated sigh.

Granny made show of ignoring Mom as she dumped cream and sugar into her tea. "Now tell us all about this plan, my dear."

Valentina explained her idea in detail, and Granny grinned and coaxed out the details, while Mom sat quiet, shaking her head. She probably thought Valentina was becoming just like her grandmother. But if so, she'd be wrong. Valentina was becoming better.

And this was only the beginning.

She was a queen. And the Gen Council throne belonged to her. No one was going to keep her from what she deserved. She didn't give a damn if Papa Eshu himself got in her way.

Cris and Oz both had taught her one thing very well—how to be ruthless.

And now Valentina would show them all why she was better.

TWENTY

ZACHARY KINGSTON

Zac Kingston's situation at home with his mom had escalated to a choice between life or death.

So, shortly after 1:00 A.M., while she snored behind her closed bedroom door, Zac tossed a duffel of his things into the passenger seat of the old Ford pickup his dad had given him and left Huntsville.

And he wasn't coming back.

He blocked Mom's phone number before looking up directions to his dad's place on his phone. He'd be long gone by the time she rolled out of bed. And he'd be okay if he never talked to her again. The old truck sputtered and grumbled on the surface streets at first, but once they hit the highway, it settled into a steady growling rhythm. The Alabama roads were deserted that time of night, and thick masses of trees pressed in on either side of him, the dark, Starlit sky equally crushing from above.

Zac gripped the steering wheel and stared straight ahead into the dark—focused only on his destination. Nothing and no one was going to stop him.

He gnawed on the inside of his cheek, a habit he'd picked up to bring his mind back whenever it strayed into the dark room. That was the name he and Luke, his ex-therapist, had given to where the bad thoughts lived, the ones that caused him to explode sometimes. The somber road trip reminded Zac of the drive he had to make after Mom ripped him away from Dad and his life to drag him to Huntsville. He'd chewed his cheek raw then, the only thing keeping him from ramming her car off the road. It was what she deserved for how she'd ruined his and Dad's lives.

He wished he'd done it.

Because fuck Mom and fuck that judge. Huntsville was a prison and staying there meant death—his or someone else's. So, Zac chose life. He chose to be with Dad.

But most importantly, he was done letting people get away with screwing him over.

As the Sun broke the horizon, he passed the WELCOME TO NEW ORLEANS sign and breathed a sigh of relief, his mouth tasting full of pennies.

Yeah. He'd definitely made the right choice.

I'm coming, Dad.

PART II

I'm for truth, no matter who tells it. I'm for justice, no matter who it's for or against.

—MALCOLM X

TWENTY-ONE

CRISTINA

My grandmother might not have killed Alexis Lancaster.

And the Scales of Justice might not have taken Dad.

I have a hunch that the person who might've framed Grandma could also be the same person who might've murdered Dad for looking into Alexis's murder.

Dad had used a chunk of his final moments in this realm to pen a letter to Mama, pleading with her to not follow in his path, to let the past alone to keep what remained of our family safe. Mama thinks we should heed Dad's warning, but I can't. Whoever's behind this has done too much—and is still out for blood thirty whole years later.

If my suspicions turn out to be true, it will mean Mama is the rightful Queen of the Generational Magic Council.

And I'm going to prove it.

I scour the details of the letter and autopsy, zooming in on the pics and squinting to make out the finer details and decipher the fairly bad handwriting on the report. By the time I'm on my second coffee, I've read so many news articles and blogs that the words blur together on the screen.

As promised, Clem stops by to deliver my pizza and nag me about drinking too much coffee. He also tells me he found Dad's knife out by the firepit, which is a relief to know it wasn't stolen for nefarious purposes like my journal. He's curious about what I'm working on, but I tell him I'll explain everything once I've compiled more information.

I'm thrilled for the distraction of this investigation, so I don't spend the whole night marinating in grief and anger over my discovery that Oz had been conjuring love spells on me since before we first started dating.

I work until well after the Sun breaks the horizon, spilling hues of bold oranges and reds across the dark sky. It's not until then that I feel confident with the clues I've managed to scrape together, which we're going to need before we question Justin. After we sic Jean-Louise on him, I doubt he'll be willing to help anymore. So, we have to make sure we get everything we need the first time.

I also set up a fail-safe in case Clem fumbles convincing Jean-Louise to help us. Clem might be upset with me when he realizes what I've done, but there's no room for error with Mama's life at stake.

When I finish gathering my notes, I nap for a couple of hours, then drag myself out of bed to shower and dress. Once the initial fatigue wears off, I feel a jolt of excitement about the day.

I've carried so much guilt about Dad's death for so long that I'd gotten used to the weight of it, so much that happiness feels strange. Joyful sparks of electricity zip through my chest whenever I think of the possibility of Mama being Queen someday—of *me* being Queen someday.

But I can never ascend the throne, not so long as I've given up magic.

Mama claims magic isn't good or evil, but it hadn't felt quite so simple to me. Magic had always been like a complex, living, feeling person with their own motivations, desires, and flaws—capable of betrayal on a massive level. It's clear now I might've been wrong—about a lot of stuff. But I'm well on my way to making it all right.

I grab my journal and knock on Clem's bedroom door, and he calls for me to come inside.

He and Yves are already dressed, sitting on his bed and leaning against each other, both with books in their hands and smiles on their faces.

"Morning," I announce, and they greet me as well. "You slept over, Yves?"

Before Yves can answer, Clem says, "It wasn't like that, if that's

what you're thinking. We talked and watched YouTube videos until
we fell asleep."

I hold up my hands. "I didn't say anything."

"You were thinking it."

Yves laughs. "Hey, I'm right here."

"How do you deal with him?" I sit on the edge of the bed and
open my journal.

"I actually find him endearing," says Yves.

"Aww." Clem grins and stares down at his book.

"Before I gag, I want to tell you what I found out," I say.

"You were up all night," Clem says. "Did you dig up anything
good?"

I tell them about Dad's letter and Alexis's autopsy report and
give Clem my phone so he can see the pictures I took. He looks
up at me in disbelief. "This letter's from Dad?" Yves puts an arm
around him when I nod. Clem's expression gradually shifts from
solemn to furious as he reaches the end.

I can't lie, it's tough trusting Yves fresh on the heels of Oz's betrayal. But I got to see Yves's character long before he and my brother
shared a bed, so I'll settle for just keeping a quiet eye on him.

"Someone murdered Dad over this autopsy report?" he asks.

"I'm not sure, but I think so," I say. "Our grandma might be innocent, too. I believe Dad's death, the hex doll you found in Mama's
room, and Alexis Lancaster's murder are all connected somehow. I
also think Aunt Ursula might've been right all along about Lenora.
But to find proof, we need to know what really happened to Alexis."

He raises an eyebrow. "So, you want to solve a thirty-year-old
murder? Who do you think you are? Nancy Drew?"

Yves nudges Clem and gives him a warning glare. Yeah, I definitely like him.

I pass Clem a printout of an article from *The New Orleans Herald* headlined MAYOR'S DAUGHTER SLAIN BY BLACK WITCH QUEEN.
"There was no shortage of articles about Alexis's murder, but that
one was the most interesting. Apparently, Lenora was a key witness

in the case. She claimed in her testimony that our grandmother had gotten into public arguments with both the mayor and his daughter on separate occasions, though the article doesn't mention what they were fighting about."

"I find it kinda fishy Lenora gave testimony against our grandmother and then took over the throne she helped her lose," says Clem.

"Exactly," I say. "After witnessing how she talked to Aunt Ursula, it's not a stretch to say she's motivated by power."

"Ursula should've slapped her twice," mumbles Clem.

I direct their attention back to the pictures on my phone. "But pay close attention to the details of Alexis's autopsy report."

Clem scans the first few pages, then looks up at me, brow furrowed. "This says her right arm had been dismembered at the elbow due to an 'explosive force.' But didn't the police claim our grandmother murdered Alexis in some gen-magic ritual?"

"They did," I say. "But that's not how our magic works—explosions and such. There's not a single gen spell I can think of that could blow a person's limbs off on the spot."

"Surely, we're not the first people to notice something was off about Alexis's death," he says.

"Probably not," I say. "Maybe that was the reason the case was wrapped so quick—so people wouldn't have time to ask too many questions about the funky magic that killed Alexis Lancaster."

"That sounds like light magic, actually," says Yves. "White mages and warlocks draw their power from the Sun, like how gen get theirs from the Moon. Sometimes they store light energy in crystals for emergencies—like if they need to cast at night. But so much magical energy confined in such a small object can be extremely volatile and dangerous."

"How do you know so much about light magic?" asks Clem.

"A few years back, my sister bought a charged crystal off a white mage and set it into a necklace, which she gave to a woman who'd been threatening us *and* her employees," says Yves. "The woman put the necklace on and left, but by the time she pulled onto the highway, the crystal had absorbed so much sunlight that it exploded. Blew her head right off her shoulders."

"Fuck," whispers Clem. "I haven't even met your sister and she terrifies me."

"It was brutal, but my sister would raze the world to protect the people she loves—and that includes her employees," says Yves. "After losing my parents, it was nice to know that I still had someone who loved me enough to kill for me, literally. Fabiana's actually really nice as long as you don't cross her."

"Could it be possible a white mage or warlock killed Alexis?" Clem asks me.

"Either that or Lenora wants it to look that way," I say. "But there's more. The article I showed you claimed Alexis had been murdered after a Council meeting in the basement of St. John's Cathedral."

Yves picks up the article, and his eyes dart back and forth as he reads it quickly. "And she was found on June nineteenth, which would mean she died on June eighteenth."

"Right," I say. "But the autopsy report says her estimated date of death was June sixteenth; and there was also evidence of the body having been moved post-mortem. Alexis wasn't killed in the cathedral—I believe someone planted her body there."

"But if there's all this evidence our grandma didn't murder that woman, how'd she get the blame?" asks Clem.

"Everyone still talks about how influential your grandmother was in the community," Yves says. "Seems like the police took advantage of an opportunity to discredit a powerful Black person, which is not a new tactic for them."

Clem sighs and shakes his head. I can't help but feel a twinge of guilt for believing the lies Valentina and everyone else planted in my head about my own grandmother.

But maybe I can make it right.

"They also discovered traces of Mashahir fibers on her corpse," I say.

"What's that?" asks Clem and Yves at the same time. They grin at each other, and I fight the urge to roll my eyes.

I find the page in my journal where I summarized my research on high-priced rugs (something I never imagined I'd want to know so much about). "Mashahir are a type of epically high-quality Persian rugs. They're extremely rare and expensive as fuck—like Beyoncé-might-think-twice-about-buying-one expensive."

"Then our grandmother couldn't have killed her," Clem says. "Our family's not *that* rich."

My heart practically thrums. Clem's affirmation reassures me I was right to not let this go, but I'm proud of myself for not seeking anyone's validation to follow my gut. I bet Dad would be proud, too.

"What about the girl who gave the envelope to your dad?" asks Yves.

"A mystery," I say. "The only person who could remotely help is Dad, and . . ."

I don't have to finish. Everyone casts their gazes downward. I wonder if there'll ever come a day when I won't feel the sour pang of guilt in my stomach every time I'm entrapped in one of these depressing moments.

Clem's first to break the awkward silence. "Well, let's hope Justin can help us fill in some of the blanks. And I was wrong earlier; you're not like Nancy Drew, you're better."

I can't help but laugh. "Shut up, Clem." I take my phone back and check the time. "We should go see Jean-Louise before he gets too busy."

Clem's smile fades, and he swallows hard, which reminds me to send a quick text before I drive the three of us to Jean-Louise's house. I hope Clem will forgive me for this.

When we turn in to the sketchy neighborhood where Jean-Louise lives, I wonder if we made the wrong decision coming here. Grass grows up past knee height in most of the yards. A few of the houses have windows boarded up, one of which sports charred remains of a fire, giant black smears erupting from the windows like splatters of rage.

Jean-Louise's home, though unkempt, seems considerably more inviting than those of his neighbors—as inviting as a necromancer's house can be.

Yves, who's been aloof the entire ride, hangs behind me and Clem. My brother also appears uneasy, judging by the way he keeps fidgeting and looking over his shoulder, like he's on the verge of bolting, which reaffirms the decision I made last night.

Clem hesitates to ring the doorbell once we stand on Jean-Louise's porch, so I push him aside and do it for him. A tall, muscular man with sleepy eyes opens the door and frowns down at us.

"I thought I told you degenerates never to darken my doorstep again?" He stands front and center in the doorway, hands clutching the jambs on either side of him.

No wonder Clem and Yves were nervous coming back here. It would've been nice if they mentioned he was already pissed with them any time *before* I rang his doorbell.

"Yeah, about that," Clem says, grinning naively. "We, uh, kinda need your help."

Jean-Louise cuts his eyes at all of us and slams the door.

I glare at Clem. "What the hell?"

"He's, um . . . just not a morning person." He rings the doorbell again . . . and again . . . and again, until Jean-Louise yanks the door open so forcefully, Clem nearly leaps through the roof.

"You've got two seconds to get the hell off my porch before you make me do something your ancestors are gonna regret," Jean-Louise snarls.

"Please," Clem begs. "There's no one else we can ask."

"That's not my problem." He steps back to slam the door again but stops when I speak up.

"Then maybe we'll go see Adeline Dupre. I bet she'll be keen to know her son is alive." I smile triumphantly, but it melts as soon as I see the color drain from both Clem's and Yves's faces.

Jean-Louise draws himself up what seems three feet taller and steps out onto the porch. "You misfits have the nerve to come to my house and threaten to blackmail me?" He grabs Clem by his arms, and I shriek. "You realize I could end all three of you right here with no one the wiser?"

Clem doesn't struggle. He just squeezes his eyes shut, and his limp body trembles in Jean-Louise's clutches. Yves lets out a muffled moan like a puppy in distress. I freeze, unsure what to do—

"Jean-Louise Petit, take your grubby hands off my nephew!" Aunt Ursula storms up to the porch with a serious frown. "I won't tell you twice."

I breathe a sigh of relief at the same time Jean-Louise releases Clem. Yves wastes no time pulling him aside, as far away as he can without falling backward off the porch.

I hadn't noticed Ursula pull up, but I'm glad she made it in time. I called her late last night and filled her in on everything.

"Ursula." Jean-Louise's voice softens and his shoulders slump, which makes him appear far less intimidating. "What are you doing here?"

Clem makes a nasty face at me. "Dammit, Cris! You told her, too?"

Ursula pops him on the back of the head, and he curses under his breath. "Watch your mouth. And ask yourself where you'd be right now if she hadn't had the good sense to call me."

He grimaces and looks away.

"We need to talk," she says to Jean-Louise.

Grudgingly, he lets us all inside.

TWENTY-TWO

CRISTINA

The scent of freshly burned sage greets me the moment I step inside Jean-Louise's house.

His home is a bit dusty, but surprisingly, the inside is in far better shape than the outside. Seeing the personal comforts of his home, a half-full cup of black coffee next to an overturned book on the table, artwork featuring Black people on every wall, pictures of him and his family on a bookshelf in the front room—all transform him in my mind, from the frightening, angry brute who threatened us moments ago to someone more complex and human.

He leads us into the surgically clean kitchen and motions for us to sit at the breakfast table. Everyone does but Ursula.

"I'm making coffee," he announces. "You're welcome to have some." He sets up a fresh pot, and a few seconds later the coffee-maker hisses to life. He leans against the counter, crosses his arms, and stares at Ursula. "What's this all about?"

"I want to see him," she says.

My blood runs frigid. When Clem first told me about Auguste's resurrection, I hoped it was a joke. Even now, sitting in the middle of Jean-Louise's kitchen with *whatever the hell* Auguste is now lurking somewhere upstairs, I still hope it's not true.

"Gotdammit!" He slams his fist on the kitchen counter, rattling the dishes in the cabinets above, which makes me flinch. He points at Ursula, tears brimming in his eyes. "This is not what I wanted." He turns and jabs the same finger at Clem. "Not—what—I—wanted."

I feel a twinge of remorse for barging into Jean-Louise's life like this. I'm sure we've reopened a deep wound for him. I hope the outcome of everything we're doing will justify our means.

"He was my friend, too, Jean-Louise." Ursula steps up and stares into his eyes, her voice quavering. I've never seen her this vulnerable before. "You weren't the only one who loved him."

"I didn't take him from you," he murmurs.

She nods. "But you did. The thing is, Jean-Louise, when you invite darkness into your life, you can't control where it spreads. It's like trying to hold the night sky in your hands."

"I didn't start this!" His voice cracks and tears stream down his cheeks. "Nor did I want *that*." He points to the ceiling, then hugs himself. "I begged him to leave it alone. But his mind was already made up—he was either going to do it with me or on his own." He stops and pokes Ursula's shoulder. "It was *your* cousin who did this." His lips curl downward. "Fucking Justin Montaigne."

"Justin may be a screw-up, but this is on all of you," Ursula retorts. "There's a reason necromancy is no longer recognized as an official magical practice anymore."

"You are impossible." Jean-Louise huffs under his breath. "I know this may be hard for you to grasp, Ursula, but you don't know every damn thing. *Auguste* was the one obsessed—not me. He kept going on and on about this theory he claimed would change the world's perception of necromancy."

"What theory?" asks Clem.

Ursula cuts her eyes at Jean-Louise. "Don't you dare suck my nephew into your bullshit."

He ignores her, I guess out of spite, and asks Clem, "Ever heard of the Kahlungha?"

Clem shakes his head.

"I haven't either," I add.

There's not much written about the different realms other than the natural (the one we live in), the spiritual (the one our ancestors, the gods, and *the* God live in), and the never-realm (the one no one wants to end up in). The infinite realms of our universe have always been as much of a mystery for us as "heaven" and "hell" (and every interpretation of the two) have been for the rest of the world.

"The K'ah-lung-ah," Jean-Louise pronounces, "is a realm that exists between the living and spiritual realms. Think of it like a secret hallway connecting the two. Since our magic originates in the spiritual realm, Auguste thought if he could find a way to the Kahlungha, being in closer proximity to the spiritual world would enhance his necromancy abilities—like on some next-level shit. He believed he could only find the Kahlungha in a state of extended consciousness beyond what we can experience in our natural state—something outside the confines of our five senses."

Clem perks up in his seat. "Do you know what the Kahlungha looks like?"

Jean-Louise looks at him peculiarly. "No, I've never seen it. Why?"

Clem starts to say something, but pauses and looks around before saying, "Just curious."

I really hope he's not thinking of following in Jean-Louise's and Auguste's footsteps. That path doesn't appear to lead anywhere good. Ursula and I share a quick, concerned glance.

"Well," Jean-Louise continues, "Auguste needed something to unlock his mind as a means of breaking into that realm—"

"Opiates," Yves says.

Jean-Louise nods. "But his overdose wasn't his fault, or mine, for that matter." He side-eyes Ursula.

"And you blame Justin for that?" she replies, resting her hand on one hip.

"Justin had *one* job," Jean-Louise says. "He was supposed to make the elixir that would help Auguste access the Kahlungha. But like most things Justin puts his grimy hands on, he fucked it up. When Auguste overdosed, Justin fled." He shakes his head and wrinkles his nose. "I'd say I hope he burns for an eternity in the never-realm, but that'd be a fate far too good for him."

Justin and I are connected in blood only, so I'm nonchalant about Jean-Louise's threat to my cousin. Even though Justin and Clem were close once, I always chose to keep my distance from him. Justin had a shiftiness in his eyes that made him difficult to trust.

"Jean-Louise," Ursula pleads again. "If my friend is alive, I deserve to see him . . . please."

He wipes his hand hard down his face with a huff. "Fine."

We follow him upstairs, and my heart slams against my ribs a little harder with each stair I climb. I'm not sure a live dose of the darkest branch of magic in existence is going to bode well for any reconciliation between magic and me. If anything, it frightens me more.

Jean-Louise leads us to a bedroom at the end of a dark hallway. He knocks gently and calls out to Auguste before opening the door slowly.

Inside, teetering stacks of books stand randomly throughout the room and volumes are thrown across the floor or lie in messy piles. The curtains are drawn, and a soft breeze rides the light spilling through the open window, filling the space with the scent of fresh air that mixes with the smell of all the aging pages of what must be hundreds of books spread around the room. The afternoon glow settles in golden pools across the person who sits in a weathered recliner, an open book on his lap.

Auguste Dupre.

He looks up at us with cold, dead eyes that are black as space. He's gaunt, and his oversized clothes hang off his skeletal frame. It's like something's sucked him dry. I latch on to my brother, and the hair on the back of my neck rises. I want to leave, but my legs are like immovable tree trunks.

"Auguste!" Ursula darts over and kneels in front of him, her cheeks already sopping wet, and takes his hand in hers. "It's me. Ursula."

He pulls away and brushes his fingertips over the contours of her face. The entire time, not a single emotion stirs to life on his. Everything about this feels wrong.

Ursula turns to Jean-Louise with a look of frightened bewilderment. "What's wrong with him? Why won't he talk to me?"

Auguste gently pushes Ursula away and sweeps over to the window to peer outside. Jean-Louise bounds over and flings the curtains closed, frightening Auguste. Watching the grown man retreat to cower in the corner feels odd. It's been four years now. I wonder how much longer Jean-Louise thinks he can keep Auguste a secret.

He leads Auguste back to the recliner, returns the book to his lap, and kisses him softly on the cheek. He stands up abruptly and grumbles, "Back downstairs. All of you. Now."

Auguste has flustered Ursula into silence—a Herculean accomplishment. None of us could've adequately prepared for what we just saw. Jean-Louise really restored someone's life—though I'm not sure what kind of "life" Auguste has now or if that can even be considered living at all.

This is only one of the dark facets of magic that make me so uneasy. I wonder if Jean-Louise would've brought him back had he known Auguste would end up like this.

When we return to the kitchen, Ursula retrieves a mug and fills it with coffee. She takes a sip and grimaces. "I'm definitely going to need something stronger than this."

Jean-Louise fetches a bottle of whiskey and pours some of it into her coffee. She takes a drink and shuts her eyes.

"What's wrong with him?" I ask.

"There are two ways to bring someone back," Jean-Louise explains. "The easiest is to reanimate a corpse that's been dead any period of time. That person's soul is long gone, and their body becomes an empty vessel, reanimated by a wayward spirit who'll do your bidding only for the opportunity to walk the earth in a physical body once more.

"The other is similar to locking the doors of the body to prevent the soul from escaping. That ritual must be completed no later than the next sunrise following the person's death." His eyes fall. "But the moment a person dies, their soul starts the process of transitioning to the spiritual realm, which means whenever you bring them back, some of them has already moved on. I wasn't experienced with this type of resurrection. I struggled, and . . . I lost quite a bit of Auguste before I could restore him."

Ursula shakes her head. "Why would you do that to him?"

"I said I didn't have a choice," he grumbles through gritted teeth.

"You always have a fucking choice, Jean-Louise," she screams. "You could've stopped him—"

"*How?*" The echo of his deep voice vibrates in my chest.

"I don't know," she says. "But I'd rather you had left him dead than turn him into that thing upstairs."

He throws his hands up.

I touch Ursula's arm gingerly. "We don't need to fight with one another right now." I meet Jean-Louise's gaze. Though his eyes are dark and sad, there's a stark contrast between the life in them and the dead pools of Auguste's. "Please," I mutter to them both.

"What's done is done, Ursula." He wipes his wet eyes with the heel of his hand. "If I could take it back, I would."

"Take care meddling between worlds," she says. "If you're not careful, you're going to come back to this one with more darkness than you left with—if you come back at all."

Clem shrinks behind me, and I can't blame him. After seeing the resurrected Auguste, I don't want to think about what lies in the Kahlungha or even farther away in other realms.

"But help me now," she tells him, "and maybe we can sort out the rest later."

For a moment, his face lights at the prospect of reconciling with her, but then it darkens again. "What have y'all gotten yourselves into?"

"Someone tried to murder Marie," she says.

His back stiffens. "What?"

While he makes himself a hefty cup of coffee, I give Jean-Louise a quick rundown of the situation, including our suspicions of Lenora's involvement in everything from Alexis's murder to the curse conjured on Mama. "Justin knows something, but he won't talk."

Jean-Louise frowns like he caught a whiff of old garbage on a hot summer day. "Don't be surprised if you get bit depending on a snake for help. It'll serve you better to cut ties with him."

"We can't," I say. "I think he's working for a bigger snake, who might want our mama dead. Please, Jean-Louise. Will you help us?" I clasp my hands in front of me for added effect.

"Lenora Savant is not someone to be taken lightly," he says. "After Justin left me to take the fall for Auguste's death, he returned with the gall to ask me to help him out of some situation he'd gotten into with that devil woman."

"What kind of situation?" I ask.

He shrugs. "I don't know, and frankly, I don't give a damn. I told him I hoped Lenora dragged him to the never-realm with her. And I still do." He sets down his cup with a sigh. "I'll help y'all with this one thing, but only on one nonnegotiable condition."

"Anything," I say.

"After this is done, none of you will utter a single word to anyone else about Auguste."

"Done." I turn to the others, who all nod. Auguste's story isn't one I imagine myself wanting to share widely, not that anyone would believe it anyway.

"And one more," he adds. "Keep your drama the hell away from my house."

I lead the way onto the *Montaigne Majestic,* which is open for business again, and to the Firefly Supplies shop inside. The bell on the newly repaired glass door tinkles as we enter to find the place empty of customers. Clem flips the OPEN sign to CLOSED.

"Be with you in a sec!" calls Justin from the other side of a towering display chock-full of crystals and herb bundles.

"Take your time," I say.

Something slams on the other side of the shelf, and he darts around but stops short when he sees Clem, Yves, Ursula, and Jean-Louise standing with me. He stumbles back and his foot catches on the corner of the display, pitching him backward.

Jean-Louise surges forward and catches Justin by the collar. He lifts Justin upright and rams him against the shelf. Crystals rain down, clacking onto the floor like hail against pavement. Justin attempts to knee Jean-Louise in the groin but misses. Jean-Louise tightens his grip on Justin, swings him around, and tackles him up against the shop door.

The newly repaired glass cracks, and Justin whimpers. "Okay!" he cries. "What do you want?"

"You owe me a blood debt," snarls Jean-Louise. "And I'm here to collect. Those are the rules your little council operates by, right?"

I've never heard of a "blood debt" before, and I want to ask about it, but we need to stay on task. As long as it gets us the information we need, I'm with it.

Justin cuts a bitter glare at Jean-Louise. "I don't owe you sh—"

Jean-Louise shoves his forearm against Justin's throat. Justin's eyes turn bloodshot and his mouth opens and closes like a dying fish. Ursula taps Jean-Louise's arm, and he backs off some. Justin coughs, his eyes welling.

"Cut it, Justin." Ursula cracks her knuckles and leans in. "Jean-Louise and I have learned a lot of really dark shit since we all used to hang out. We can make your worst nightmares reality."

Jean-Louise presses Justin harder against the door and the cracked glass creaks under the strain. "You ready to talk now, or do you need more convincing?"

"All right, all right," Justin wheezes. "I'll tell you everything. Just let me go."

My heart does a somersault. *Please, let him know something that can help us.*

"Every breath you draw is a gift from me." Jean-Louise releases him. "You deserve to hurt like I do every damned day of my life."

Justin stares up at him with a pained expression. "You don't think I'm hurting? Auguste was my *best* friend."

"Which makes what you did even more spineless," says Jean-Louise.

I'm not sure if Jean-Louise will ever be able to forgive Justin, even though Justin claims Auguste's death was an accident. Another reminder why I can't mention to anyone that I might've been responsible for Dad's death. I can't imagine Clem hating me the way Jean-Louise hates Justin.

Justin lowers his head. "I hate myself for running out on you. I loved you, Jean-Louise."

Clem nudges me with his elbow and when I look at him, he raises an eyebrow. This is quite possibly the messiest love rectangle I've ever witnessed—in real life or on television.

"Two things you will never get from me are forgiveness and love." Jean-Louise unfolds his arms and clenches his fists, drawing Justin's gaze. "Answer the kids' questions so I can go, because if I have to look your sorry ass in the face a second longer, I might deliver your rotten soul to the devil myself."

Justin frowns and turns to me. "After Auguste died, I was terrified I'd end up in prison, seeing as how I was the one who procured the opiates and made the elixir, even though it was an honest *accident*." He casts a sidelong glance at Jean-Louise. "I asked Lenora for help, hoping she could use her extensive connections to protect me."

Aunt Ursula tuts and shakes her head. "Why would you go to that old crone instead of your own family?"

"Yeah, because y'all have such an outstanding track record when it comes to being understanding and supportive," he says.

Ursula rolls her eyes. Well, he has a point.

"Anyway, Lenora said she'd protect me, but she needed something from me first—she wanted me to help her get rid of the Council's Root Doctor, and by 'get rid of,' I mean 'murder.'"

"Why did she want them dead?" I ask, though a better question comes to mind: Why does she think she has the power to decide who lives or dies?

"He'd started whispering about her in the ears of other Council members, particularly Lorenzo Vincent, the Gen Priest, a man known around the world for his impeccable skill and indisputable reputation. If anyone had the power to stand up to her, it was him. He convinced the Council to make Lenora step aside into the role of Queen Mother. She was furious but had no choice but to accept the terms or have her family's sovereignty revoked. She wanted revenge against the Root Doctor for snitching and a replacement who could serve as her pawn until the end of her days. She chose me.

"I grew to resent her as much as my decision to confide in her. She's made me do unspeakable things." An involuntary shudder snatches the breath from his throat, but he shakes it off. "I wanted to be free of her. I still do. But if she goes down, she'll take me with her—if not worse."

"You could've walked away," I say. "You didn't have to let her use you."

Justin cuts his eyes at me. "It's easy to judge a shit situation when you're not the one up to your eyebrows in it. I tried to make things right. I went to the Gen Priest, Lorenzo, and told him everything. About what we'd done to the last Root Doctor and a few of Lenora's other unsavory deeds."

"And what did he do?" I ask.

"Lorenzo revealed he'd had his own doubts about Lenora, particularly how she came into power," says Justin. "He said he'd been somewhat close with your grandma Cristine and had never believed she was capable of murder. He swore he'd investigate further, but that was before he died."

"What happened to him?" I ask, hoping Lenora didn't kill this poor man, too.

"The family claimed it was cancer, but I was terrified Lenora had found out he was digging into her past and took him out. And if she discovered I had anything to do with it, mine would be the next skeleton jammed in her closet."

"Did Lorenzo find out anything before he died?" I ask, desperate for something concrete that doesn't lead to a hundred more questions.

"Not to my knowledge," says Justin. "After I put him on Lenora's trail, I kept my distance from him, for obvious reasons." I blow out an exasperated breath, and Justin says, "I'm sorry. After Lorenzo died, I gave up trying to take Lenora down. She's too dangerous, too connected, and too powerful."

There's no denying Lenora is a force of pure evil, and I'd be foolish not to admit she frightens me. But I'm even more afraid of what we stand to lose if we don't start fighting back.

"Maybe if you're patient, Lenora will self-destruct," says Justin, his eyes hopeful, as if he actually believes that. "A few days ago, the Cardinal of the white mages crashed a Council meeting."

"Madeline DeLacorte," utters Ursula, a bitter edge to her voice, as if they have history as well.

Justin nods. "She's pissed the Council is supporting Eveline Beaumont's husband's run for mayor. When Lenora spoke up for Eveline, Madeline said Lenora wouldn't want details of how she came to power to come out."

"What did she do?" I ask, reinvigorated.

He shrugs. "All I know is the contention between the Gen Council and the white mages began over thirty years ago with the feud between your grandmother and Madeline's mother, Bethesda. As Queen, your grandmother garnered more power and influence among the Black community than the mayor, who was pissed about it. Things got even worse when the mayor's daughter and Cristine had an epic public falling-out because Cristine refused to teach the girl gen magic. After that, the mayor started making noise about magical regulation, which rattled Bethesda's cage all the way in Baton Rouge. She was terrified of the world resurrecting witch hunts of the past." He pauses to appraise me. "Cristine wouldn't back down to anyone—not the mayor and certainly not Bethesda. You got that from her, you know."

Not long ago, that same observation would've made my stomach sink. But as I'm learning more about my grandmother, I'm realizing she was an incredible woman. I'm slightly ashamed I haven't tried to learn the truth about my ancestors before now.

"Are you sure you don't know anything about the hex doll we found in Mama's bedroom?" I ask. "Would you like to see the picture again?"

He shakes his head. "I wasn't lying when I said I didn't know anything before. It's no secret Lenora isn't fond of our family, but if she did plant the doll, she kept it hidden from me."

I narrow my eyes at him. "Are you telling the truth?"

Jean-Louise inches forward, and Justin winces. "Yes!"

"A girl delivered an envelope to our dad before he died," I say. "She was supposed to come talk to Mama later that night, but she disappeared. Do you know anything about that or who she could be?"

He pauses a beat too long, and his eyes flick nervously to Jean-Louise and back to me. "I, uh . . . no, I'm afraid I don't." He kneels and starts gathering up the spilled crystals from the floor. "That's all I know. Now, if you're done fucking up my store, I'd like you all to leave."

"But—"

"I said *leave*."

"Why—"

"GET THE FUCK OUT!" Justin slings a handful of crystals at us, and I leap back in surprise. "GO!"

A member of the boat's security opens the door and asks Justin if everything's all right.

Ursula grabs me and Clem and pulls us outside. Jean-Louise throws one final death glare at Justin and follows.

Justin's voice fades behind us. "I'm good, Sam. Everything's fine."

TWENTY-THREE

CLEMENT

Ursula's phone rings the moment we exit the gangway of the *Montaigne Majestic*. "I'm on my way, Melony," she says as soon as she picks up. "Sorry, my meeting ran long."

The Sun blazes above us, and I have to shield my eyes to see. A soft breeze delivers brief stints of cool air off the water—thank the gods, because I've already started sweating. The water's calm today, and somewhere not too far away another ship's horn bellows.

Jean-Louise stares downriver, likely to avoid small talk, leaving Cris, Yves, and me standing in uncomfortable silence while Ursula finishes her call. I still can't believe he's a real necromancer. After Yves fell asleep last night, I stayed up late, absorbing everything I could find out about necromancy.

That branch of magic became the black sheep of our world once Moon magic was split into generational magic and necromancy when the War of the Moons ended, in 1865. During the conflict, white mages fought against gen and necromancers over the necromancers' right to practice. The war took place primarily in the U.S., often in the vicinity of where the American Civil War was being fought, which I found ironic given that the majority of people who practice light and shadow magic are of European descent like their minor gods, while gen and necromancers are typically Black or people of color, like our gods.

But the war ended in a stalemate, and the two sides negotiated the Treaty of Moons, which disavowed necromancy as an officially recognized branch of magic and established the Magic and Spiritual Coalition (MASC), comprised of leaders from magical communities around the world (a magical UN of sorts) and led by the

Queen of the Generational Magic Council. MASC allowed necromancy to remain legal as long as it was not used to commit any crime under human or MASC law.

Ursula smacks one hand hard on her hip. "They did *what*?! I'll be there in a few minutes." She scoffs and hangs up. "I swear, if it's not one thing, it's another."

"Everything okay?" I ask.

"Some asshole from the Office of Alcohol and Tobacco Control stopped by first thing this morning to shut my bar down, slap me with a three-thousand-dollar fine, and suspend my liquor license. Says he got an anonymous complaint from a member of the Chamber of Commerce about the live band we showcased last night."

"Three guesses who the complaint was from," I say.

"I only need one. I'm convinced Jack Kingston and Lenora Savant are conspiring to shove me into an early grave." She pulls her car keys out of her purse and waves a finger between me, Yves, and Cris. "I have to go, but you all keep your heads down. You need to let the adults handle this."

"And what are y'all going to do?" Cris asks. The bite of her tone suggests she already knows (and disagrees with) the answer.

"I don't know yet," retorts Ursula. "But that's for me and your mama to figure out. Y'all need to listen to her. I won't be responsible for any of you getting hurt."

Cris scowls but doesn't respond. There's no way in the infinite realms she's letting this go.

"I'll take you home," Ursula informs Jean-Louise, who accepts with a silent but no less relieved nod. He's probably ready to get back to his solitude—and his zombie boyfriend. "Remember what I said," she warns us over her shoulder once more as she and Jean-Louise head for the parking lot.

"I have to run a quick errand for my sister," Yves announces, still staring at the text from her. "She wants me to grab something from the pier shops, so I'll just get a car back when I'm done."

"You sure?" I ask.

"Yeah, I'm good," he says. "Text me later."

He leaves, and it worries me that it feels as if he's taking a piece of my heart with him. I don't have very many pieces left to give away.

"Madeline's comment suggests Lenora did something under-handed to take the throne," Cris says, bringing my attention back from Yves's world.

"Do you think Lenora might've been involved in Alexis's murder?" I ask.

"It sure seems that way." She chews her bottom lip and thinks for a moment. "But how do the white mages factor into all this?"

I shrug. The pieces to this puzzle keep multiplying the more entrenched we become. "It might be helpful to know what Alexis was up to in the time leading up to her murder," I suggest.

Cris snaps her fingers. "That's it! Maybe Alexis had family or friends she was close with who are still alive and willing to answer some questions. I'm gonna head home and start researching."

"You need help?" I'm desperate for something to divert my mind from dark spirits, necromancy, and zombies.

"Not right now. I'll let you know what I find, though. But can you give me a lift home?"

"Sure," I say, not caring to hide the dejection in my voice.

Just like everyone else, whispers the devil inside my head.

After I drop Cris at home, I drive back to the Quarter and wander by myself, people-watching and blasting music in my headphones. For some reason, being alone in public doesn't feel as desolate as being alone at home.

While I'm out, Mama calls to ask if I need anything from the grocery store. I can't think of anything to ask for because I'm so caught off guard. The last time I got one of these calls was before she got sick. I never thought I'd get one again. Funny how something can seem insignificant until it's gone and you notice the giant hole it left behind. I have a lot of those. Holes. I'm getting really exhausted with trying to fill them, and sometimes I don't even know why I keep trying.

I stumble upon a bookstore, and the scent of fresh paper and ink draws me inside, where I lose myself and time among the shelves. I purchase a copy of *Aristotle and Dante Discover the Secrets of the Universe* and tuck into a balcony table of a nearby café to drink coffee and read. I make a good dent in the book before my body complains of the uncomfortable iron chair in which I'm sitting. I should head out anyway, because for the last few minutes, my mind's been wandering off the page, anxious to slip back into the inexplicable world of my aunt.

My frustration with all her secrets aside, I do wonder how she's doing after seeing Auguste—restored. It was a lot for me to take in and I don't even know him. I couldn't imagine how I'd react if I saw Yves or Isaiah like that.

I fold down the corner of my page before closing my book and finishing my coffee. I think I'll pay Aunt Ursula a visit.

The Wishing Well looks strange, sitting empty in the middle of the day with the glaring yellow paper proclaiming CLOSED UNTIL FURTHER NOTICE stuck to the door. So many people pack into Spirits of Nola that it looks as if there's barely standing room inside through the front windows.

Meanwhile, the Wishing Well is dim and depressing. Ursula stands behind the bar, and it looks like she's talking to someone, which is strange—because she's alone.

I knock on the glass front door and she glances up and frowns. She stares for a silent moment, then comes over to open the door.

"What are you doing here?" she asks, blocking the entrance.

"I came to see if you're all right," I say.

"I'm fine, but I'm in the middle of something."

I peer past her, but the bar's empty. "Who were you talking to?"

"Let the boy in, Ursula," comes a deep, velvety voice from somewhere inside. "I'm heading out anyway."

She heaves a deep breath and stands aside.

I step inside and look around, but there's no one. The door closes behind me and the lock clicks. I turn to Aunt Ursula with a puzzled look. "Is there someone else here with you?"

"My apologies," calls the voice from behind me. "Here I am."

I turn back with a start. A man sits backward on one of the stools, his back leaned against the bar and his arms propped on the counter on either side of him. An empty glass and an open bottle of Tru Reserve sit nearby. The low light darkens his olive-brown skin and a pair of red mirrored aviators mask his eyes. His auburn beard and locs are both immaculate, and he's dressed casually in a cream blazer on top of a white tee, jeans, and boots the color of walnut wood.

"Were you sitting there the whole time?" I ask, still confused.

"It doesn't matter," Ursula says. "He was just leaving." She returns to the other side of the bar and hands him the bottle of Tru Reserve.

"This bourbon is simply delectable," he says. "Don't ever change the recipe."

"Since Marie sold the business, I, unfortunately, don't have as much say in those things as I used to," she laments.

I vaguely remember that fight between them. Mama had controlling interest since she was eldest, so she sold it and maintained vested interests and advisory rights for her and Ursula, who were the only two of their siblings who were interested in the family businesses. Ursula didn't want to manage them alone, but Mama couldn't carry on in the same capacity after Dad died. His death rippled through all our lives.

The mysterious guy lowers his sunglasses, revealing hypnotic, honey-colored eyes that are shockingly bright in the dim room. "You want it back?"

Ursula shakes her head. "No, I have my hands full here, as I already explained." She stoops and grabs another bottle from behind the bar. "Here. Take another for the trip home."

He tucks the second bottle under one arm with a grin. "You treat me so well."

"Likewise," says Ursula.

The man turns and extends his free hand to me. A soft blue light in the image of a full Moon glowing on his wrist attracts my attention—and pulls a gasp from my throat.

The mark of a god. I'd heard that was how conjurers were able to tell if the people they encountered claiming to be gods were true. But I thought those were only stories. I never imagined I'd ever get to see the real thing.

"Black Wolf," says the man, hand still extended. "Pleased to make your acquaintance, Clement."

I give it a firm shake, still awestruck. "How do you know my name?"

He lifts his sunglasses, and his intense eyes study my face for several too-long seconds; then he drops the glasses back to his nose. "More of us know your name than you'd think." He lifts two fingers, and a black card appears out of nowhere, pinched between them. An image of a wolf head glows from one side in similar blue light as the mark on his wrist. But before I can reach for it, Ursula snatches it from his fingers.

I take a step back and watch nervously as she glowers at Black Wolf. But the god only guffaws in response. I let out the breath I'd been holding.

"He is a child." Ursula rips the card in half, and it disappears in a puff of black smoke.

He snickers. "Very well. Last chance before I leave—are you sure you don't want me to take care of that place?" He jabs his thumb over his shoulder at Spirits of Nola across the street.

The sight of that raggedy bar never fails to conjure a wicked scowl from me. The place where Dad departed this realm forever. The business owned by the man who harasses my aunt and who also happens to be the father of the boy who harasses me at school. Nothing but evil in that building.

"Do it," I tell Black Wolf, not sure exactly what *it* is, but I have a feeling whatever Black Wolf has planned will be exactly what that hellish place deserves.

Ursula sighs hard. "I don't think that's a good idea."

I frown at her. "Then why did you summon Black Wolf?"

"Because I was angry," she says. "But that was a mistake. Actions have consequences, and our family's already in enough shit—we don't need to pile more on. I'll handle Jack another way."

"I want that place gone, and so do you. So, let it happen. Damn the consequences for once."

"Clement—"

"No," I interrupt. "People like them don't get to be evil incarnate and prosper."

"Fine," she says with a tired breath. "But listen to me well, nephew—if you're going to make mature decisions like this, you'll need to be mature enough to deal with the repercussions if and when they come. It's very dangerous to make a habit of making big decisions flippantly."

I stare across the street. Two drunk guys stumble out the front door of Spirits of Nola and stagger off. Blaring country music spills out like exhaust from a tailpipe, and before the door closes, a group of four people pile in. Those inside laugh and dance and spill liquor over the spot where my dad closed his eyes for the last time. And someone at that bar might've killed him because he was trying to get justice for our family. But who gets justice for *us*?

"I meant what I said." I nod at Black Wolf.

Ursula purses her lips but doesn't argue.

Black Wolf inclines his head to us both, a wry smile on his lips. "Very well then. Good day."

I watch him leave, a bottle of bourbon under each arm. He saunters across the street and disappears inside Spirits of Nola. "What do you think he's going to do?" I ask Ursula.

Already back behind the bar, she clears Black Wolf's glass and wipes down the space where he sat and moves on to the rest of the counter, which already looks clean, but I mind my business.

"Sit," she says, and I do. "Be patient and we'll see." She puts one hand on her hip and smiles at me. "It was sweet of you to come check on me. I'd forgotten how it feels to be cared about."

That was definitely a choice, but I didn't come here to fight.

"Will you be able to open soon?" I ask.

She sighs, staring out the window at Jack's bar. "I called in a favor at City Hall, so hopefully, in a day or two."

I glance over my shoulder at the garish neon SPIRITS OF NOLA sign and revel in the realization that I might not have to ever look at that ugly thing again.

"Jean-Louise is kind of cool," I tell her. "Do you think you two will ever be friends again?"

"I'm not sure. I wish it were that easy."

"Why can't it be?"

She stops scrubbing to glare at me. "Did you not see what he did to Auguste?"

"Yeah, but I can understand why he did it."

"Can you now?" She tosses her cleaning rag aside and meets my gaze. "Don't let Jean-Louise's gentle eyes lull you into a false reality. The dark magic he dabbles in has left a mark on his life, and unfortunately, on mine as well. Believe me, Clement, you don't want those problems."

I wilt in my seat but keep my thoughts to myself. Jean-Louise is not a villain. He loved Auguste and didn't want to lose him. I can't say I wouldn't do the same in his position. I wonder if she thinks that makes me a bad person, too.

"Enough people have left permanent marks on my life, and I've had enough, which is why I stay to myself now," she grumbles.

"Like that Celeste woman?"

She heaves a deep sigh and frowns at the ceiling for several moments. "Yes, exactly like her."

"Can you please just tell me what happened?"

"I was seventeen and Celeste Richard was eighteen," she says in a solemn voice. "She was gen, too, and we were friends. But she fell in love with an older warlock, who was nothing more than a power-hungry white man with dwindling morals—and I hated him. I tried to warn Celeste about him, but she wouldn't hear it because he'd promised they would elope at the end of the summer after graduation. Well, Celeste graduated, and that night she and I went to a party. He was there, drunk and high out of his mind, and he tried to kiss me." Ursula shudders and stares down, shaking her head. "I should've hit him. I should've cursed him out. But I didn't do or say anything. I just walked away. I went to find my best friend and tell her what happened. By the time I caught up with her, he'd already told her that I came on to him, and, of course, she believed him.

"Celeste and I didn't talk for the rest of the summer. The day they were supposed to elope finally came, but he stood her up—and she blamed me for the whole thing. She flew over to my house and crossed me on my own porch. Before she left, she told me my womb would be as barren as she hoped the rest of my life would be."

"You don't think—"

"I don't know," she says, sounding frustrated already. "But I don't have a man, or a best friend anymore, or children of my own. I'll be thirty-five this year and I've never even had a single pregnancy scare. Based on the evidence, I'd say Celeste got what she wanted."

"I'm sorry," I say.

"Don't be." She steels her stare. "This is why I didn't want to tell you this stuff, Clem. My cross is mine to bear, not yours—and I don't need pity from you or anyone. I don't mean to sound rude; I'm just being real."

Yeah, real rude, *but go off, I guess.*

Ursula's head snaps up, and she stares past me at something outside the front window.

I swivel around on my stool and gasp.

Dark tufts of grayish-black smoke billow from the doors of Spirits of Nola, and people scramble over one another, gagging and screaming, as they flee into the street. Bright orange plumes of flames kick up behind the windows of the bar as the final customers escape.

Jack Kingston stumbles out last, his face and clothes covered with soot. He clutches both sides of his head and falls to his knees, watching his business burn.

The front windows burst, sending huge balls of fire and black smoke shooting into the street. The force of the explosion bowls Jack over and rattles the Wishing Well's windows in their frames, but the building holds firm. I get the impression Ursula knew it would.

The sound of two glasses thunking onto the counter behind me draws my attention. Ursula pours a shot of bourbon into each and slides one to me.

"I warned him more than once not to fuck with me." She nods at me and picks up her glass. "Don't tell your mother."

"I won't if you don't." I lift my glass in a toast.

We drink, and I twist my face and cough, letting her believe I've never had bourbon before.

I turn back around and lean against the bar, and my aunt and I watch Spirits of Nola burn.

TWENTY-FOUR
ZACHARY KINGSTON

Zac held the memory close of his father grinning with happy disbelief from the porch of the familiar yellow bungalow as Zac had pulled his pickup into the driveway.

It'd barely been a whole day since he'd been back home where he belonged, but it'd already been one of the best he'd ever had. Being near Dad allowed Zac to let his guard down, which felt like exhaling after holding his breath for a month.

As expected, Mom had called shortly after Zac arrived. While Dad argued with her on the phone, Zac had wandered the house, shocked at how it'd fallen into disrepair in the short time they'd been gone. The breakfast table where Dad used to read the newspaper every morning with a cup of coffee before he took Zac to school had become a dumping ground for old pizza boxes and empty beer bottles. The sink where his parents washed up together every night overflowed with dirty dishes that not only had spread onto the counters, but also had begun to grow mold. The kitchen had an acrid stench of neglect and grief that reminded him of an infected wound.

Zac had faked being tired all yesterday to avoid discussing Mom's phone call. She wasn't going to make him go back.

But early the next morning, his father plopping down on the edge of his bed jerked Zac awake. His stay of execution had expired.

"I have to head into work," Dad told him. "But before I leave, I'd like to know what's going on between you and your mother."

Zac sighed and bit down on his cheek before speaking. "I want to live with you. I told Mom that, and I told the fucking judge that, too. I hate them all for what they did to you." He sat up, invigorated by a sudden burst of adrenaline. "Mom acts like you're not a hero, like you haven't put your life on the line for this country so she can run to church every night with her sister and her fugly nieces."

"Zac!" Dad barked, giving Zac a start. "Don't say shit like that about your family. And I've told you before, I'm no hero. . . ." The ghosts in Dad's eyes chased away the rest of his words.

Dad never talked about Afghanistan or what had gotten him discharged early or the details of all the horrible things he'd done. They had to have been bad, because the memories still haunted Dad, and no one got that screwed up from doing good things. But sometimes people had to do terrible things to protect the natural order. That's how war and life went. And that's why Zac had to get away from his mom. She only cared about protecting the order of *her* world and her world alone—no matter what effect her shitty decisions had on the people forced to exist in her orbit.

"Mom's still a bitch for letting them say all those things about you in court. She knows you're sick, but she doesn't give a damn. Why do I have to stay with her? I'm old enough to decide."

"Because I'm a shitty dad." A flush of crimson bloomed on Dad's cheeks. "And I've had to live with that since y'all left."

"You're not a shitty dad," Zac muttered. "Mom doesn't even want me. She only took me to get back at you. Sometimes I wish she'd just fucking die."

Dad's back stiffened and he cut his eyes at Zac. "Hey, hey, hey. Don't say that about your mother. What's gotten into you?"

Zac shrugged. It was true.

"Has your mom found you a new therapist in Huntsville?"

Zac stared at the floor. He didn't want to talk about Huntsville. He hated everything about that city. New Orleans was his home— *his* natural order. He was born and raised here. Huntsville was the waiting room to hell.

Dad snapped his fingers in front of Zac's face, already losing patience. "I asked a question."

"Have you found one for yourself?"

Zac didn't see the slap coming, but his cheek burned for several moments too long afterward. Instinctively, he clutched his stinging face and apologized. Dad lost it like that sometimes. But the best way through was to defuse the situation immediately, before it escalated further.

Dad's chest puffed out angrily, but he blinked it away a moment later and nodded.

"Mom wanted me to talk with the church pastor, but that guy gives me cradle-jacker vibes. I told her I was fine. She dropped it."

Zac remembered lying awake in bed all night, biting his cuticles until they bled while her response replayed over and over in his head. *I knew this move would be good for you. Your crazy father was probably rubbing off on you.* His dad wasn't crazy—he was *sick*. And no one but Zac understood that.

Dad sighed and lay down next to Zac, pulling him close so Zac could lie on his chest.

Lying there, his ear over Dad's heartbeat, Zac felt a cool sense of peace. Dad's strong arm, clutching him close, made him feel protected and loved. If he had the choice, he would never leave that spot. But he'd never gotten to make his own choices before.

He wasn't even free to choose who he loved.

"Everything's gonna be okay, Zac," muttered Dad.

Zac woke alone.

He spent the day cleaning and organizing the house. By the time he finished and plopped onto the couch it was early evening. Before he could release the entirety of a long, exhausted sigh, the front door burst open, giving him a shock of surprise. He turned and squinted, confused.

Dad walked inside and slammed the door behind him. He was covered in black soot and gray ash from head to toe, his hair wild and sticking up in some places.

"Dad . . . what the hell happened to you?"

Dad turned his blue-green eyes to Zac, took a deep breath, and spiked his keys to the floor with a sound like a gunshot. Zac tensed, clinging to the fabric of the couch, watching Dad melt down in real time.

Dad shut his eyes and took a deep breath. "I need to lie down."

Zac nodded.

Dad went to his bedroom and slammed the door.

He didn't come out again. Not even for the Hamburger Helper Zac made for dinner and left outside Dad's bedroom door. The plate was still there, untouched, before Zac went to bed.

Not long after he got in bed, Zac got a text from his best friend, Oz, whom he hadn't spoken to since Mom dragged him to Huntsville. Zac hadn't even told Oz he was back.

The text read Dude! and had a link to an article from the *New Orleans Herald* dated today. It was headlined BAR EXPLODES IN THE FRENCH QUARTER.

Zac's heart thumped so hard it ached as he read about the destruction of his dad's bar this afternoon, which would explain why Dad had come home looking like *he'd* been blown up. But the article was vague about what caused the explosion, which frustrated Zac even more since Dad wasn't talking either. Even though he was physically back home, he still felt locked out.

Zac turned off his phone and slid it underneath his pillow. It was that or smash it against the wall over and over until it became a thousand tiny pieces in the palms of his hands. Anxiety needled him relentlessly, and he tossed and turned for hours. Dad's bar was his life, and if he lost that, what kind of life could Zac hope to have with him now?

This wasn't fair. Zac had chosen the life he deserved when he left Huntsville. And he was back home. The rules couldn't just change—not after all he'd done to get back here.

Just after 5:00 A.M., Zac's mind ran out of diesel, and he fell into restless sleep until late afternoon. When he woke, Zac wandered from his bedroom, wiping the crust from his eyes.

Something *thunked* from the kitchen. Dad was up.

Zac found Dad sitting at the kitchen table, humming to himself as he wiped down the parts of an AR with a dingy white cloth, every gun in his collection spread before him.

"What're you doing?" Zac asked, leaning on the back of Dad's chair.

Dad kept his gun collection in a locked chest in the basement. Treasures Zac hoped would pass down to him someday. But Mom had forbidden him from learning to shoot. She claimed it was because she hated guns, but Zac had grown to believe she just hated everything his dad liked, Zac included.

"Cleaning," Dad said, "and a little admiring. I've been meaning to do this for a while, but I haven't had the time or felt up to it. Maybe having you back gave me a little boost."

"I can stay," Zac said, hopeful. "It's only another year and a half before I turn eighteen. I was planning to move back then to help you run the bar anyway."

Zac picked up one of the handguns, and his pulse quickened. It felt heavy in his hands as he turned it over and brushed his finger over the trigger. If he'd had this kind of power in the courtroom that day, he could've taken control of his future and run away with Dad.

Dad's shoulders drooped. "There's no bar anymore, son."

Zac gripped the gun tighter. "Yeah, I saw in the news. But we can rebuild."

Dad shook his head and went back to cleaning his rifle, slamming each part on the table as he finished. "There won't be another bar. Insurance is already fighting my claim. They're saying the explosion was due to negligence and even went so far as to accuse me of arson since business hasn't been doing well. It's like this whole thing was set up to ruin me."

"What?" Zac exclaimed, his chest tightening. "Did you tell Granddad? Can't he do anything?"

Dad scoffed. "Irving Kingston threw me away as punishment for disobeying him and joining the military instead of going to college to be a professional brown-noser like him."

"Then we'll start over," Zac suggested. "We'll come up with another business altogether."

Dad shook his head again. His negativity was really starting to piss Zac off. It was like he'd already given up. "I've already defaulted on my loans and the bank won't extend me any more credit."

Zac hit both sides of his head, the gun still in his hand, the hard metal butt smacking painfully but satisfyingly into his left temple. "Fuck, fuck, *fuck*—"

"Hey, hey." Dad grabbed Zac's hands and took the gun.

Zac pressed his forehead into Dad's chest. He could barely breathe. But he couldn't cry. That wasn't what Dad needed from him right now. He pushed back and apologized.

"It's okay," Dad said, giving him another once-over before returning to his seat. "I'm a fuckup sometimes, I admit, but this—" He stabbed the table with one finger. "—*this* wasn't my fault."

Zac narrowed his eyes, surprised. "Then whose fault is it?" He hadn't considered someone else might've been responsible for further ruining his already fucked-up life.

"Ursula Dupart." Dad's mouth pruned like he wanted to spit. "I know she's been using magic to fuck with my business. I report her to the Office of Alcohol and Tobacco Control and the next day my bar mysteriously explodes. That's no coincidence. That bitch put some kind of jinx on me and my business. I hate the entire lot of them. Right down to those disrespectful Trudeau kids."

Zac's crush on Clement Trudeau was born in eighth-grade gym class. But he'd had to repress it at once, because he was afraid his dad, the hardened masculine marine, couldn't love a gay son like a straight one. And so, Zac made himself hate Clem. But that didn't work either, which put him in a tough spot—because Zac Kingston could never love Clem or any other guy.

But Mauro Rainer could.

Zac created Mauro's Instagram account and became a seventeen-year-old bisexual model. He followed Clem last fall so he could look and like freely on Clem's profile without judgment. But one day after he'd gotten drunk on Dad's beers, Zac let loneliness and alcohol spur him into messaging Clem. They chatted through the night and into the next morning. Not about anything special, owing to Zac sucking at making up lies on the spot, but Clem had made Zac feel at ease with himself, something no one else had ever done before. They'd even traded nudes (faceless, of course), which was also a first for Zac, but he loved the rush it gave him. He'd tried to hang on to that fake reality for as long as he could, but Zac felt Clem grow distant after Zac's repeated refusal to meet in person.

He'd debated for nearly a week until he convinced himself Clem might understand if he knew the truth. There was no way either of them could throw away the connection they'd both spent months forging. He'd been happy about the prospect of being able to finally stop pretending to hate Clem in public, even though he'd still only be able to love him in private.

But the meeting was a disaster. Clem was enraged and hurt and, worst of all, disappointed. Clem's reaction left Zac feeling pathetic and revolting. And the worst part was Clem had found out Zac's secret—the one Zac hadn't even told his best friend. The one he was terrified of Dad knowing.

Afterward, Zac had tried to steer clear of Clem at school, but it wasn't easy with Oz dating Clem's fucking twin sister, who was just as infuriating. It wasn't long before picking at Clem became as satisfying as all his other angry habits combined. But one day he'd made a joke like he'd done any other day, and Clem just attacked him out of nowhere like a wild animal. Zac barely had a chance to fight back. In a way, he was glad he'd left the cafeteria unconscious, because he couldn't have faced everyone who'd laughed and recorded while Clem thrashed him. And then, as if he hadn't been humiliated enough, the meme happened. He knew Clem had had something to do with it.

He hated Clem and his entire fucking family, the bunch of

spoiled rich brats. They didn't deserve all they had. Not while good people like him and his dad struggled. But now they were struggling because of what *Clem's* family had done. Rich, powerful people were always flaunting their money and magic and fucking with the lives of everyone else for their amusement. And what was worse, Zac was afraid his dad was irrevocably broken. But Dad couldn't give up—he was all Zac had.

Dad's chair slid back, scraping against the tile floor. "You want a beer?" he asked as he trudged over to the refrigerator and pulled out two Bud Lights.

Zac nodded glumly.

"Cheer up," Dad said. "Let's go watch some bad TV. No more sad talk tonight."

Zac forced a smile. "I'll be right there."

After Dad left, Zac picked up the gun he'd held earlier, feeling the energy pulsating from it once again. He wondered if people who wielded magic felt that same raw power; if they allowed themselves to be swept away on the high that comes from knowing nobody else can fuck with them.

He tucked the gun behind one of the cereal boxes in the pantry. Dad had so many; he wouldn't miss one.

Zac plopped onto the couch and took the beer his dad passed him. "You're right," he said, and took a sip. "Everything's going to be all right."

TWENTY-FIVE

CRISTINA

Elouise Lancaster loves Facebook.

She's one of those people who post often about the monotony of their mundane lives—and I spent most of the evening after we left the *Montaigne Majestic* digging through all those unnecessary details. She was born in 1966, exactly one year and six months after her sister, Alexis. Elouise isn't married, but she's dating an older white guy named Frank, who owns several Chick-fil-A's and has two Great Danes named Daisy and Blue. She's also heavily involved in her church, where she leads Bible study at their Christian academy. This should be quite an interesting meeting.

Her latest update was a picture of her standing on the porch of her childhood home—where she still lives—holding an old photo of her family to commemorate the thirtieth anniversary of their deaths, which happens to be this month. In another post, she mentioned frequenting a doughnut shop she claims is "walkable," which also helped me narrow down her neighborhood inside historic downtown New Orleans. Her house is on a corner lot, so it doesn't take too terribly long to find it the next morning, driving around with the picture from her recent post.

Hopefully, she can tell me details of what happened between her sister and my grandmother, and more specifically, what Alexis was up to in the time leading up to her death.

I grab my journal and a pen and make my way up the long sidewalk to her two-story white plantation home. Honeybees flit from flower to flower in the colorful gardens on either side of the walkway leading up to the endless wraparound porch. The green shutters bordering every window are chipped and peeling, revealing old, graying wood beneath. The overwhelming smell of pollen from all the flora in Elouise's front yard makes me sneeze twice before I ring her doorbell. This place overflows with sentiments of fake sweetness muddled with rot. I'd jet if this weren't so important.

Ancient floorboards creak underneath heavy footfalls as Elouise approaches. She opens the door and looks me up and down before her light eyes narrow and she says, "How can I help you?" Her skin is the color of oat milk, and her thin lips are as sharp as her precisely cut dirty-blond bob, which she's tucked behind both ears. She's wearing khaki shorts and a floral print blouse, unbuttoned at the top to reveal the splotched, leathery skin of her chest.

"Good afternoon, Ms. Lancaster." I smile warmly, clutching my journal in front of me. "My name is Diana Armstrong. I'm working on a summer research assignment for my school's newspaper about your sister and was wondering if you'd be up for a short interview?"

All the tension leaves Elouise's face, and she smiles. "Oh, how sweet. Of course." She steps outside and gestures for me to sit in one of the wooden rocking chairs on the porch. "Can I offer you a glass of tea or lemonade?"

"No, thanks." I take a seat and open my journal to a fresh page.

"You have excellent timing. I need to tend my flowers anyway."

She grabs a nearby watering can and begins seeing to the army of potted plants of all sizes and types that line the entire length of her front porch. The clay and ceramic pots are a mismatched collection of various designs that span the entire spectrum of plain red all the way to acid-trippy mosaic.

"I'm happy to help you, dear, but I have to tell you, someone might've already done your assignment."

I furrow my brow. "I'm sorry?"

Elouise pauses between plants and eyes my journal. "Around this time last year, another girl stopped by, asking about Alexis for a school newspaper assignment. She looked around your age, Latina, about your height, long black hair, quite pretty."

"Do you remember her name?" It might be only coincidence, but

I can't help wondering if this could be the same girl who delivered Alexis's autopsy to Dad.

Elouise shakes her head. "I'm sorry, I'm not very good with names. I do remember thinking it strange, like something from a movie."

I record the description of the girl in my journal. It's not much to go on, but it's more than I had. I need to figure out who she is, especially if she might have important information that could help my investigation.

"No offense to you, darling, but I'm upset I've *yet* to hear from anyone at Channel Eleven," adds Elouise. "I *am* my father's and sister's last living relative; and the . . ." Her voice fades, and I raise a curious brow as she sniffs and apologizes. I search her silvery eyes for tears that don't come. "The anniversary of their gruesome murder is coming up in only a couple weeks. I thought certainly once they heard I was planning to march on the mayor's office with the Redeemers that someone at the station would be interested in what I had to say, especially seeing as I'm the one who's been most affected by magical malpractice."

It doesn't surprise me that Elouise thinks she's the sole person impacted by what happened all those years ago. They even colonize our trauma. But I need to appease her ego a little longer, at least until I get what I came for.

"That's exactly why I wanted to talk to you," I say. "I'd like to know more about your sister, Alexis—get a better idea of who she was, especially in the days leading up to her death."

Elouise sighs and stares at the street and the cars that pass occasionally. "My sister was obsessed with generational magic. I think she might've read every book in print about conjuring. The employees at the magic shops downtown knew her by name. It was an incredible waste."

"Why's that?"

"It never worked for her. No matter what she tried, she couldn't conjure. I told her that stuff was just for your kind." When she says "your," she nods at me.

I raise an eyebrow. "My kind?"

"You know, African-Americans."

"You mean Black people?"

"I . . . um . . . anyway, I begged Alexis to leave it alone. I warned her that Daddy would be furious if he found out. He hated conjurers with the passion of Christ. Always said their witchcraft was of the Devil. But Alexis didn't listen. She befriended an unsavory girl close in age by the name of Lenora Savant, who happened to be best friends with the resident Queen, Cristine Dupart." She says my grandmother's name with a pronounced wrinkle of her nose. I clench my jaw and focus on taking notes. "Alexis thought if she cozied up to her, Cristine would teach her to conjure."

"And what happened?"

"Oh, they had a grand falling-out." Elouise whistles and fusses with the leaves of one particularly large and healthy plant. "Alexis was pissed. She even argued with Cristine in the middle of town about it. Alexis never handled rejection well." She shakes her head and plucks several dead leaves, clutching them in her fist. "Things got worse when Daddy found out she'd gone to Cristine, begging to learn magic like a common panhandler." I wince at her crass words, but she barrels on. "He confronted Cristine and told her to stay away from our family or else."

I look up from my notes. "Or else, what?"

She shrugs. "Daddy died before anyone found out. When the police told him Cristine had murdered Alexis, he was so grief-stricken that he and my mama and a few of their concerned friends went to confront Cristine about what she'd done."

"That's funny," I say without laughing, and Elouise eyes me curiously. "Because your parents showed up at Cristine's house in the middle of the night with an angry mob at their back. Your daddy pulled Cristine's husband off his own porch and had his 'concerned friends' beat that poor man to death in front of his family and then turned on his wife. I think the proper term for that is 'lynching.'"

Elouise's face goes as pink as the flower she stands in front of.

"Well, that witch used her devil magic to slaughter a whole bunch of people that night, including my mama and daddy. Call it what you will, but she and her husband got what they deserved."

"Okay," I say, far calmer than I feel. "We're getting off-track. What happened to Alexis after your father found out she'd gone to Cristine to ask about magic?"

"He forbade her from having anything further to do with witchcraft. He burned all her books and magical supplies, which I thought was a bit harsh, but I certainly understood why he'd done it."

"I bet she didn't take that well."

Elouise scoffs. "Not at all. That night, she packed a bag and left—didn't even bother saying anything to Daddy before she went."

"Where'd she go?"

"Baton Rouge to join up with the white witches. And that was the last I heard from her until Daddy told me she'd died. A few months after her funeral, I got a call from an impound lot in Baton Rouge. They'd towed her car, because it'd been reported abandoned in a Piggly Wiggly parking lot. I had no idea how it got there, and the police had already closed the investigation, so I thought it was just a strange circumstance."

"Interesting," I say. "If her body was found in the basement of St. John's, do you have any idea why her car would be in Baton Rouge?"

Elouise shakes her head. "I wish I knew."

"Had Alexis come back to New Orleans before she died?"

"Not to my knowledge." Elouise throws her hands up and shrugs. "To be honest, I've questioned if Cristine really was the one who killed her for some time now. The whole thing felt a bit fishy to me. But justice always seems to work itself out in the end."

"What do you mean?" Justice never seems to work that way for Black folks, and certainly hasn't for me or my family.

"Cristine was a devil of a woman who I'm sure had other crimes to answer for, if not this one. And just like she got what she deserved, eventually so will the person who killed my sister."

I slam my notebook shut and get to my feet. "I've had e—I mean, I think I have enough information for my story." I force a smile. "Thank you for your time, Ms. Lancaster."

Elouise sets down her watering can with a surprised look. "Is that it?"

"I have all I need." More like all I can stomach.

"Well, aren't you going to take my picture?" she asks, hands on her hips.

"Huh?"

"For the article. Don't you need my picture?"

"Girl, no." I tuck my journal under my arm and make a beeline to my car.

I spend all evening and night scouring the details I've managed to scrape together, and by morning, I decide a change of scenery and some caffeine might give my brain the jolt it needs to make some more headway in my investigation.

Besides, I need a break from watching (and hearing) Clem and Yves become hopelessly lovestruck. I'm happy for them but watching them fall in love in real time keeps reminding me of what happened with Oz, which is the *last* thing I want to think about right now.

A cloud of worry kicks up in my gut when my anxious mind wonders if maybe Yves is conjuring—like Oz. But I toss the thought out the moment I remember one of the reasons I relished the comfort of Yves's brief presence after Valentina alienated me was because he made it clear he didn't practice any form of magic and had no interest in it. When I asked why, he'd said he preferred dabbling in other forms of magic he'd found in the world. I still don't know what that meant, but I was too busy trying to hold my life together with duct tape and bubblegum to worry about it.

The Bean is just crowded enough for me to feel invisible where I sit at one of the small corner tables, far away from the front door.

The smell of fresh beans amid the grinding whirs of the espresso machines is heavenly white noise to me.

I open my journal to a blank page and summarize what I've uncovered thus far.

PRIME SUSPECT: LENORA SAVANT, Present Queen Mother of the Gen Council
MOTIVE: TO STEAL THE THRONE FROM CRISTINE DUPART, Former Queen, and my grandma
EVIDENCE: LENORA GAVE TESTIMONY THAT ESTABLISHED CRISTINE'S MOTIVE FOR THE POLICE.
ORDER OF EVENTS

- Alexis Lancaster was mad at Cristine because Cristine wouldn't teach her gen magic.
- Gerald Lancaster (mayor) hated Cristine, because of her local influence and position. Gerald threatened Cristine to stay away from Alexis.
- Alexis went to Baton Rouge to join the white mages >> When did Alexis come back to New Orleans? How did Alexis get to New Orleans if her car was in Baton Rouge??
- Alexis's arm was severed by an explosion >> Did someone kill her with light magic? White mages (or Bethesda DeLacorte, former Cardinal of the White Mages)??
- Alexis's body was moved post-mortem >> Who moved her? From where?? Did she die in Baton Rouge????
- Who delivered the envelope to Dad? Who visited Elouise Lancaster asking about Alexis? >> Same girl? Where is she now??
  - Around my age >> 15, 16, 17?
  - Name from a movie?
  - Latina??
- Lorenzo Vincent (former Gen Priest) died investigating Lenora >> How did he die? Did he find out anything??

MORE LOOSE ENDS (UGH)

- Mashahir carpet fibers $$$>> Whose carpet? White mages?? Bethesda DeLacorte???
- Did the white mages (or Bethesda DeLacorte) kill Alexis?
- How is Lenora connected to the white mages?
- Did someone (Lenora?) kill Dad because he was investigating Alexis's death?

I set my pen down and lean back in my seat. I'm almost certain Grandma Cristine didn't murder Alexis. I believe something happened to Alexis when she went to Baton Rouge with the white mages. I just need to find out what, and who's responsible. Lenora? Bethesda? Maybe both.

Unfortunately, Bethesda died a long time ago, and dead or not, I'm pretty sure Bethesda's daughter, Madeline, will be less than willing to implicate her mother in murder.

And there's still the mystery of the girl who also visited Elouise to ask about Alexis, who I assume delivered Alexis's autopsy report to Dad as well.

Hearing Elouise speak so recklessly about my family and my magical heritage gave life to a new fire inside me, one I never knew existed or could exist. I imagine that fire devouring the people who abuse magic as a tool to further their own selfish, evil ends. People like Oz. And Lenora Savant.

I take a sip of my white mocha, but someone's voice almost makes me choke on it.

"What the *hell* are you doing?"

I slam my journal closed at the same time the skin on the back of my neck crawls. Valentina steps up from behind me and swipes for my notebook, but I snatch it off the table.

"Leave me alone, Valentina." I get up and brush past her.

I step outside, and the humid summer rushes me at the same time Valentina grabs my shoulder and spins me around.

"Why are you writing about my granny in that journal?" she demands.

"That's none of your business."

"First, your aunt assaults my granny, and now, you're what? Investigating her? Why?"

I walk toward my car, which I parked in the small lot behind the Bean, but she blocks my path. Cars whizz by on the busy street, and the few people who pass on the sidewalk part around us, some looking back to catch tidbits of our argument. I turn to cross the street, but she darts in front of me, her back to the traffic.

"You truly believe Lenora is someone to look up to, which means either you're hopelessly jaded or just as rotted inside as she is," I tell her.

Valentina shoves me, and I push her back, sending her stumbling off the sidewalk into the street.

"I swear to the gods, you'd better leave my granny alone," she says. "You have no idea—"

Her back is turned, so she doesn't notice when the driver of the blue sedan that's heading straight for us loses control. Time slows as the sound of screeching tires mutes Valentina's threats.

I lunge for her. "Watch out!"

Valentina yanks out of my reach, staggering farther into the street. "Get off—"

The car slams into her. A shriek rips from my throat.

She rolls onto the hood, and the car lurches to a stop, sending her tumbling to the ground in a bloody, panting heap. Several onlookers scream from somewhere nearby.

The driver opens the door and stumbles out, one hand clutching the side of his head. Giant, red welts paint his face where the airbag slammed into him like he did Valentina.

"I-I don't know what happened," he stammers. "I just lost control. An-And I couldn't stop. I t-tried, I swear. I didn't even see her standing there."

I ignore him and take out my phone. My hands shake so violently, I can barely dial 911. After I tell the dispatcher what happened and our location, I hang up and kneel next to Valentina.

Tears squeeze through her tightly shut lids, and she moans with gruesome pain.

"It's gonna be okay, Valentina." I pull her phone from the pocket of her shorts. Her ankle is twisted, and her legs and arms are covered in scrapes. Blood stains the pavement behind her head from where she cracked it when she fell. "Stay with me. Don't go to sleep."

"Unnnhhh" is all she manages.

I hope against hope her phone's passcode hasn't changed since we were friends. That's how close we used to be before she decided she hated me. Oz never even had the passcode to my phone.

111264. Lenora's birthday.

It still works. I find the number for "Mom" and call.

Gabriela Savant answers immediately. "Hey, Val, are you okay?"

"Mrs. Savant, this is Cris. Valentina's been in an accident at the Bean. Please come quick."

Gabriela gasps. "Oh, my God. Is she okay?"

"I'm not sure, but the paramedics are on the way, just get here fast."

"Okay, I'm not far. I'm on my way."

I hang up and take Valentina's hand. She squeezes back weakly. "Your mom is on the way, Valentina. Hang on, please."

She falls unconscious just as sirens sound in the distance. People press their faces to the windows of the surrounding shops, and a crowd encircles us, including one of the baristas from the Bean, who pelts me with questions about what happened, but I don't answer a single one. Valentina's blood coats my hands and I'm too busy trying to get her to wake up while ignoring the nausea clutching my stomach thanks to the metallic smell of blood mixed with the oil and grime from the street.

The ambulance pulls up and two EMTs jump out and begin attending to Valentina. I step back, still in a shocked stupor, the chaos of the world around me reduced to a dull roar in my ears. Then a thought nearly draws me to my knees.

The fucking Scales of Justice. Did *I* do this to her?

We hated each other, but I never wanted this. I only wanted

her to leave me alone. Dear gods above, please don't let this be on me, too.

Valentina's mother's car swerves up at the edge of the scene, and she leaps out and runs straight up to the ambulance. Her hair's in a messy ponytail and she's dressed like she just dashed out of a gym class. Panic flushes the skin of her face as she takes her daughter's side.

I stand back, breathless and wordless, as this nightmare unfolds in front of me. When several cops approach, my heart sinks into my shoes. They talk to a blond woman in yoga pants and sunglasses first, who's very animated in retelling her version of events. At the end of her story, she points at me, and despite the sweat dripping down my back, it feels as if I've been dunked in a snowbank.

The cop, a tall, clean-shaven white man with unsettling sea-green eyes, approaches. "Good afternoon," he says. "You see what happened here?"

I nod. "She and I were talking when the car hit her."

He looks at me suspiciously. "Talking? That lady says you two were arguing."

"I mean, we were, but I don't see—"

"She also says she saw you push the girl in front of the car."

"What?!" My heart drums. "That's not true. I saw the car coming and I-I tried to pull her out of the street, but she stumbled b-back and . . ."

"Carter!" calls one of the other officers, who stands near the ambulance with the EMTs and Valentina's mother. "She's awake."

Officer Carter presses his lips into a thin, disapproving line. "Let's see what she has to say." He points at me. "You better hope she says the same, or you're in trouble. Don't move."

I want to melt into the nearest storm drain. But if this is my fault, maybe I deserve to answer for what I've done.

I wander closer to listen in on the conversation between Officer Carter and Valentina. He points to me and asks if I pushed her in front of the car.

Valentina lies on a stretcher, her head already bandaged, while one of the EMTs tends to her foot. All she has to do is say yes, and she could be rid of me for good. Her mother looks between the two of us in inquisitive silence.

Please don't let her choose this moment for vengeance. So many Black women die in police custody, I can't rationally think my experience will be any different.

After what feels like ages, Valentina shakes her head. "She was trying to help me."

Officer Carter sighs and throws me an annoyed scowl. "Get outta here."

I hand Valentina's phone to her mother and duck into the alley next to the Bean that leads to the back parking lot. I don't exhale until I'm safe in my car. Inside is a sauna, but I don't care. I start the engine and turn the AC on max.

Tears rip through the wall I put up. My body quivers so bad that all I can think to do is hug myself. I rock slowly, trying to steady my breathing. My lungs feel like someone's using them as punching bags. My phone rings, nearly startling me into a scream. It's an unsaved number.

I answer, and immediately regret it.

It's Oz. "Cris, you sound upset. Are you okay?"

"No! Valentina just got hit by a fucking car right in front of me!"

"Are you serious?"

"Yes! I-I can't believe that just happened. I can't stop shaking."

Oz laughs.

My stomach turns over. "What the fuck is funny about that?"

He quiets, except for his ragged breathing.

"Hello?" I say.

"Am I good enough now?"

TWENTY-SIX

CRISTINA

After I hang up on Oz, I throw open the door of my car and vomit until I dry-heave.

When I make it home, I stumble upstairs, undress, and stand in the shower with the water on the hottest setting I can stand. I scrub my entire body until my skin burns, while I stare at the water mixing with Valentina's blood, swirling into pink before disappearing down the drain.

I barely sleep that night, owing to the haunting visions that spring to life whenever I close my eyes. The car slams into Valentina over and over, her bloodied and broken body hitting the pavement with a nauseating crack.

Am I good enough now?

It turns my stomach to think I was with him so long, that I trusted him, loved him—that I almost had sex with him. Ugh, just thinking about it makes me queasy again.

The next morning, Mama takes me to my first appointment with my new therapist, Dr. Omar, which Mama said she arranged so quickly by calling in a favor from an old friend. Dr. Omar is a Black woman, about ten or fifteen years Mama's senior, with flawless umber skin and a colorful hijab that is more beautiful than a canvas painting. Things start off well with Dr. Omar, whom I tell about the love spell (although I keep Oz's assault on Valentina to myself—I'm still trying to process it and can hardly put it into words right now nor do I want another entanglement with the police).

She validates how I feel, even my anger, but I lose all trust in her when she brings up the concept of "radical acceptance of things outside of my control." She wants me to slowly whittle my fury down to nothing—and for what? To clear the way for the next person to slaughter me in the middle of my safe space? I'm furious, and I'm going to stay that way until people start reaping the consequences for the fucked-up things they've done to me. They don't get to keep making people feel unsafe in their own skin while they do whatever they please. Sorry, Dr. Omar, but I'll take rage over fear any day.

On the ride home, I tell Mama therapy went okay but I'd like to take a break for a while. I'm honest when I say I'm not quite where Dr. Omar wants me to be in terms of "radical acceptance," which Mama understands. But I don't think I'll ever be at that place.

When I get home, the first thing I do is shut myself in my bedroom and call Valentina. To my surprise, she answers.

"Hello?" Her voice sounds unsure, cautious. She deleted my number.

I almost hang up on her rude ass. "Hey, Valentina. It's Cris."

"Oh . . . um, hey."

"I was calling to see if you were okay . . . after yesterday."

"I'm fine," she says dryly, as if me checking on her is annoying. "Doctor said I was lucky. Just a fractured ankle, a couple stitches on the back of my head, and a few scrapes and bruises."

"I'm glad you're okay." I'm honestly relieved despite her attitude. "We've said and done a lot of shitty stuff to each other, but I don't want to see you hurt—or worse."

She's silent several beats before muttering, "Thanks."

I'm about to say goodbye, but another thought snags me. I don't want to have this conversation, but she deserves to know.

"Can I ask you something?"

"Uh . . . I guess." She sounds like she really wanted to say no.

"Are you still cool with Oz?"

Valentina sucks her teeth. "Look, Cris, I—"

"It's not like that," I tell her. "We aren't together anymore. I found out he'd been casting love spells on me, and I just wanted to warn you to be careful around him."

"Oh . . ." Her voice fades. "Thanks . . . I guess?"

"Yeah," I say. "Bye." I hang up.

After all she's done to me, I strongly considered letting her find out about Oz on her own, but I didn't feel right leaving her open for Oz to prey on next. Though part of me feels guilty for not telling her Oz conjured her accident, Valentina has a knack for creating chaos, and I can't be caught up in her drama right now—not when I'm so close to finding out who murdered Alexis Lancaster.

Mama knocks on my door and opens it when I tell her to come in. "You up to hang this afternoon? We can grab some food at the Golden Key or Henri's and catch an early movie, just us girls."

I wince up at her from where I lie in bed snug underneath my favorite purple comforter. "Sorry, I'm not up to it today. Therapy took a lot out of me. Rain check?" I feel awful saying no, but I can't pretend to be happy right now, nor do I want anyone tiptoeing around me or trying to fix me.

"It's okay, baby," she says, smiling. "Offer still stands whenever you're ready."

I smile back, and she leaves. Not even twenty minutes later, there's another knock at the door. I sit up and tell her to come in, preparing to just give in and let Mama hover over me for the afternoon.

But it's Clem, whom I'm not unhappy to see. My brother's warm face, his presence, the way he looks at me with genuine love and concern, is so calming. I want to leap out of bed and throw my arms around him, but I stay put.

"Morning," he says as he approaches my bedside. "You okay?"

I hate that I've somehow wandered into this place where I don't feel comfortable talking with my twin—the one person who knows me better than anyone—about any of the very serious shit going on with me right now. Maybe I should've trusted him from the beginning.

"Sit," I tell him. "There's something I need to tell you."

He lowers himself onto the bed, looking concerned. "Am I going to need coffee for this?"

I shake my head. If I let him leave, I'll probably never re-collect the courage to open up again. But if I don't talk to someone, I'm going to implode.

I tell him the truth about Oz—the love spell, our breakup, and Valentina's accident. He listens without interrupting, probably due to shock and disbelief. I'm even somewhat incredulous as I repeat the whole story aloud, and I was there for every sickening moment. But it feels so good to tell someone.

When I finish, Clem hugs me. I'm crying before I realize it. But he doesn't make me feel ashamed, or foolish, or anything other than loved.

We part and I wipe my eyes with a sniff. "I'm sorry I didn't tell you sooner."

"I gave you a lot of shit about him, but I always hoped I was wrong. I never wanted this."

"Thanks," I say. "I know."

"He's still a creep, but he's also an idiot—do you think his spell actually worked?"

I nod, though everything inside me screams that I'm wrong. But I know that's not true. "Yes and no," I say, and when Clem looks at me curiously, I add, "I was in love with him. He pressured me for sex more than once, but it never felt right—I never felt right about it, so it never went that far."

"What if the ancestors were looking out for you," Clem says. "Maybe it was Grandma keeping you safe from the spiritual realm."

Chills ripple across my skin. Clem meets my eyes—his say what he's too kind to right now. The ancestors are still protecting me even though I turned my back on them. On magic.

"Or maybe the spell didn't work that well because he just sucked at magic," I say.

He shrugs. "Could be both."

"I'm questioning so much of what I thought I knew about my life right now."

He sighs and stares down at the bed. "Trust me, I know the feeling."

"He could've killed Valentina yesterday, Clem. And just to prove to me that he was 'good enough' to conjure. I honestly hope I never see him again."

"That makes two of us."

But it's not only the unmasking of Oz's true character that feels like sulfur simmering in the pit of my stomach. The secret I've been harboring about Dad is there, too, festering the longer I let it sit untouched. I should let that go, too. I can trust my brother.

"There's something else I need to tell you," I say.

He looks at me tentatively. "Okay . . ."

"It's about Da—"

The doorbell rings.

"I'll get it." Clem leaps up from the bed. "Odessa's out back in the garden and Mama just left."

"Wait," I call after him, but he's already gone.

I throw on some shorts and a tee and head downstairs. By the time I reach the landing, I hear Clem shouting and . . . is he fighting someone?

I rip down the rest of the stairs, nearly tumbling headfirst several times before I reach the bottom and find Clem yelling in Oz's bright-red face.

He presses Oz against the wall in the foyer by the throat. "You tried to rape my sister and have the nerve to come back here?" Clem snarls.

I shove him, and he releases Oz, who crumples to the floor, coughing and gasping. "Stop it!"

Clem takes a few paces backward, rage flaring his nostrils.

Oz reaches for me to help him up, but I smack his hand away. He looks surprised but hauls himself to his feet on his own.

"What do you want?" I thought I'd be nervous to see him again, but I'm not. He's the one who should live in fear, because he has no idea what *I'm* capable of.

Oz rubs his throat, and his eyes shift between me and Clem. "I came to talk to you, but your brother wouldn't let me get a word out before he attacked me."

Clem starts forward, but I throw my arm out, blocking him. "And I still didn't give you what you deserve," he says.

Oz rakes a shaky hand through his hair. "You're right. I deserve to have my ass beat and a lot worse. And maybe I deserve to go to jail for what I did to Valentina."

"Go on." I cross my arms over my chest. This is the first intelligent thing he's said in a while.

"I want to apologize," he says. "I-I don't know what I was thinking. Of course, that doesn't excuse what I did, I'm just trying to explain how I got there." Clem sighs dramatically behind me, which I ignore. "I let magic suck me in and I lost control. You were right, Cris; I didn't respect it like I should, and because of that, I did things I'm ashamed of."

I unclench my fists. His relationship with magic sounds uncomfortably familiar.

He hangs his head. "Unlike Benji, my grades suck, I'm not athletic, and I have zero talent. I felt like a waste until I found magic. Finally, I had something that was special to me, that I didn't have to share with Benji. That's why what you said about me not being good enough hurt so much."

I cross my arms again. "I hope you didn't come here for an apology."

"Yeah, because all we have are ass-whoopings today," adds Clem. "Fresh outta everything else."

"No, no, no," Oz says, holding up a hand. "Magic isn't more important than you." He takes a step forward but pauses when he sees me flinch back. "Please, Cris. I'll give up magic for you, not just gen magic, but all of it. I'll never conjure or cast or anything ever again. I'd do that if you give me one more chance. Please, let me make this up to you."

Clem bristles. "Cris, you had better not—"

I lift a hand, silencing him. "I'm glad you see how you were wrong and want to change, but you will do that without me."

He reaches out with both hands but knows better than to touch me. "I'm literally begging—"

"I think you should leave," I tell him. "Now."

"Are you really going to be that stubborn and self-righteous?" he says.

I narrow my eyes at him. "Get the fuck out of my house."

"You know what?" He scoffs and shoves his hands in his pockets. "Maybe you deserve what's coming to you." He stares at us with a smug look that lurches my stomach.

"What are you talking about?" I ask.

"I was honestly trying to help you both." His hand bulges in his pocket, and he shakes his head. "She warned me that I couldn't fuck up this time, not like with the hex doll."

My head swims and my knees weaken. It was him. The whole *fucking* time.

But when did he plant the doll in Mama's room? A tornado of questions spins through my already ravaged mind.

"I was willing to risk it all for you," he says in a grave voice. "I would've nixed the plan if you'd only taken me back. Now I can't save you."

"You motherfu—" Clem lunges, but Oz pulls his hand from his pocket.

I grab Clem by the waist and tug him back at the same time Oz flings whatever's in the vial he holds in an arc. Black dust fills the air, and Clem and I stumble backward, tripping over each other.

A wall of thick mist the color of dark blood shoots up from the floor, blocking the conjuring dust. The black cloud of whatever the hell Oz threw at us hits the wall and rolls over like a wave, then crashes back into his startled face. The red wall of mist recedes, sinking into the floor and vanishing as quickly as it appeared. Oz's hands shoot up to his neck, and he lets out a hoarse, gagging cough.

He gasps and drops to the floor.

Lying on his back, he claws his throat with both hands, his fingers trailing angry red welts across his milky skin. His sneakers squeak and scuff the wooden floor as his feet flail.

"Oh, my god," mutters Clem. "What's happening to him?"

I stand over Oz, staring into his frightened, reddening eyes. "It's your spell," I tell Clem calmly. "Don't you know?" I tilt my head, watching Oz's pale skin go from pink to bloodred to nearly purple in a matter of seconds.

"Cris!" cries Clem. "You have to help him. I don't know how to reverse the spell!"

"Hmm . . ." is all I offer.

Clem bolts from the room, leaving me alone to watch my predator ex die. I hope it's painful as fuck.

Oz chokes on his own ragged breaths as he reaches for me, his fingers scraping against the black fur toe of my slipper. I slide my foot just out of his reach and kneel beside him.

"So, all along it was you," I say, still calm despite the silent storm raging inside me. "A rapist *and* an attempted murderer. Magic's a bitch when someone's using it against you, huh?"

Vindication tastes sweet on my tongue, and I swallow it, savoring every bit as I watch my abuser writhe at my feet. I grimace at the bitter aftertaste once I realize I have magic to thank for this moment.

"Who put you up to it?" I ask Oz even though he's in the middle of dying. "Tell me—was it Lenora?"

He gasps and sputters, then falls still and his eyes close.

I rear back and backhand him hard across the face. My hand stings like a bitch. He jerks back to life for a moment, then passes out again.

"Cris!" yells Clem from behind me. "What the hell are you doing? He's *dying*!"

I stand up and wave a hand over Oz's still body. "Then help him, since you care so much."

Clem parts Oz's lips and pours the contents of a vial, filled with what I imagine is peace water, into Oz's mouth. He uses the last bit of water to paint a cross on Oz's forehead and throat with his thumb and mutters a quick prayer. When he finishes, Oz's color returns and he lets out a long breath as his lungs refill with air he doesn't fucking deserve.

Clem checks Oz's pulse and falls back onto his bottom with a relieved huff. Once he's collected himself, he stares up at me, his face twisted, which annoys the heck out of me. "What the hell, Cris?"

I glare back at him. "My bad, did you miss the part where he said he tried to kill Mama?"

"And you just casually murder people in the parlor now?"

"Technically, it was *your* spell that almost killed him. You shouldn't conjure if you're not willing to accept the consequences." The irony of hurling that advice at my brother stings. But it's true.

"And what if I hadn't figured out how to help him? Would you have let him die?"

"But you did figure it out."

He frowns at me. "You had no way of knowing I would."

"That was clearly a defensive spell you conjured, which means Oz could've left unscathed if he hadn't attacked us." I sit beside him. "I don't have sympathy for him, and I won't apologize for that. I'm tired of apologizing for being human. He assaulted me and would've killed Mama if you hadn't found that hex doll when you did. I can't forgive him. He's done too much."

"But you don't get to decide who lives or dies, Cris."

"Says the person who conjured the spell in the first place."

"That spell might've saved our lives; but what about you?"

I look my brother in his judgmental eyes. "And what if we found out he had something to do with Dad's death, too?" I nod at Oz, still unconscious and sprawled on the floor. "Would you still think that piece of shit deserves saving?"

"I don't want to fight with you," says Clem. "But I also don't want you to do anything you're going to regret for the rest of your life." He gets up and goes into the kitchen.

I hug my knees tight against my chest. Oz might never get what he truly deserves. He's destroyed so much—and for what? He's scum, but I recognize a pawn when I see one. I'm not wasting any more of my time with the help. I'm saving the worst of my wrath for the Queen Mother.

The jarring sound of shattering glass comes from the kitchen, and Clem shouts, "Fuck!"

"Are you okay?"

When he doesn't answer, I get up to check on him.

He's stooped in front of the refrigerator, mopping up spilled water with a wad of paper towels and setting aside shards of a broken drinking glass with shaky hands.

"Here, let me help." I kneel beside him and take the towels.

He stands up with a sigh and pulls another glass down from the cabinet. "Thanks."

"Don't worry about it." When I finish cleaning up his spill, I wash my hands and watch him sip from his fresh glass of water. "You good?"

"I guess." He points his thumb over his shoulder in the direction of the foyer, where Oz is still out, spread-eagle. "What are we going to do about him?"

"When he wakes, I'm going to make him tell me who sent him here and for what purpose."

"And what if he won't talk?"

"Then I'll *make* him. Look, I said don't worry. I have this under control; besides, we still have the protection of Wise John's Moon plus whatever homicidal add-on you conjured."

"This is getting serious," he says. "We should tell Mama."

"Not yet. There's still one more thing I need to find out before I can trust her with this. Remember Justin said that Lorenzo Vincent was investigating Lenora before he died?" When Clem nods, I say, "What if he asked someone to continue his work after he was gone?"

"You think that might be who gave that envelope to Dad?"

I nod. "Not only that, but I think she might be Lorenzo's daughter.

I couldn't sleep last night, so I did some more digging. Lorenzo had two kids, a son and daughter. His daughter, Aurora Vincent, is about a year older than us and matches the description that Elouise Lancaster gave, albeit vague."

"I know Aurora," says Clem. "Well, not personally. We had Honors Calculus One together last year, but she didn't show up to part two last fall. Everyone thought she'd moved."

"Well, I intend to find her."

"And how do you plan to do that?"

"I have an idea," I say. "But first, we need to deal with Oz. He should be coming around soon."

Clem follows me to the foyer, and the moment I notice the empty floor, I curse aloud. I run to the front door and throw it open.

Oz got away.

TWENTY-SEVEN

CRISTINA

"What do we do now?"

Clem stands next to me on the front porch, and we both stare at the black tire marks Oz's car left at the end of the driveway. The hanging leaves of the willow shift in the cool breeze like floral curtains.

"I've got to find Aurora Vincent—and fast," I say. "If I'm right and she was also looking into Alexis's murder after her father died, she might know something that could help us."

He starts to say something, but his phone rings, and he answers it.

"Hey, Yves." I don't miss the slight upward twitch of his mouth when he hears Yves's voice. It's sickeningly cute. Clem looks at me and says, "I, uh, I'm kinda in the middle—"

I wave and mouth *Go, go, go* to him.

"Never mind." He sounds hesitant. "Yeah, I'll be right there." He hangs up. "That was strange. Yves says his sister wants to meet me and he also has something important to tell me."

"You should definitely go." I lead the way back inside. "Maybe she knows something about Aurora, too." I grab my car keys and trade my slippers for a pair of sandals.

"Okay, but where are you going?"

"To see Justin." Before he can argue, I add, "I'll call you as soon as I can."

I sit inside my car in the pier parking lot with Aurora Vincent's Instagram page up on my phone. She didn't post often, but when she did, it was stunning and spellbinding. My favorite is a video she uploaded back in October last year, which I watch for what must be the hundredth time. It's late evening in the video, the sky half dark, half light. Aurora stands on a deserted white-sand beach and walks into the water up to where the gentle waves sliding in only bump gracefully against the backs of her knees and brush the hem of her gorgeously simple linen dress. Her long dark hair is swept back in loose curls. She looks like a goddess standing there with the evening light reflecting off the water all around her. She smiles at the camera before turning to the sky and lifting one hand toward the Moon, which shines bright and full despite the setting Sun. The camera zooms in on her hand as she cups and twists it, the angle of the shot making it look as if she's unscrewing the Moon where it sits in the sky.

Raw moonlight pours from the sky in wispy spirals that wind toward Aurora. She guides it so it pools on the water's surface, then sweeps her hand through it, and the light churns in response. The camera zooms in to show the moonbeams transforming into tiny dolphins, each no bigger than a cell phone, swimming in front of Aurora and leaping in and out of the water. Then she holds both hands in front of her and works them as if molding a lump of clay into a globe on a potter's wheel. The moonbeams collect into a sphere the size of a basketball, and when Aurora flicks one finger toward the sky, the ball of light rockets upward with a *whoosh* that jostles the camera's mic.

The camera zooms in on Aurora's face, and she grins at the cameraperson. "Don't worry, Remi." Her voice is smooth and confident, as are her eyes, which are bold and unafraid. She points toward the sky, and Remi shifts the camera upward.

The ball of light sails high into the air and explodes into a million tiny twigs of blue light that rain down all around Aurora like icy blue sparks. She throws her arms out and tilts her head back, like she's standing in the middle of a summer rain, letting the moondrops (a word I just made up, because I've never seen anything like this before) hit her skin, where they glow brighter before disappearing. When it's over, she smiles at the camera again and curtsies in the water.

The way Aurora controls magic sends chills up and down my body. I've never seen anyone harvest raw moonlight without a mark or spell, and the task is still incredibly hard even with them. Aurora might even be more powerful than Mama and Ursula.

Where'd you go, Aurora?

Her last post was a tribute to her late father, Lorenzo Vincent, who'd served as the Gen Priest of the Council. Mama had explained once that a Gen Priest is like a master of magic, and their job is to know everything about it, which makes them very powerful (and sometimes dangerous) people. In the picture, Aurora looks to be four or five years old, with the same captivating smile and gallant eyes from her recent video. The photo captured her father in mid-laugh, showing all his teeth. But when I look closer, I notice something I hadn't before. I have to zoom in, and even then it's not easy to make out, but another kid, a slightly older boy, stands in the background, arms stiff at his sides, glowering at Lorenzo and Aurora. That must be her brother, Xavier, who became the Gen Priest after Lorenzo died.

Lorenzo Vincent appears to have been well liked. The post got over five thousand hearts and 120 comments. The caption under the picture reads, "I will do my best to carry your legacy forward and make you proud."

I open the comments and browse through them quickly, but there's nothing but condolences, well-wishes, and a few randos advertising diet tea. I'm about to give up when one comment catches my attention.

Zay Vince: delete this.

Both the comment and the original post are from days before someone, likely Aurora, delivered the envelope to Dad. "Zay Vince," I mutter. That sounds a lot like Xavier Vincent. I click on the profile, but it's private. He doesn't have many followers either.

The profile picture is just a stock photo of a full Moon. I wonder if Aurora's brother, Xavier, had anything to do with her disappearance.

I open my journal and make a few quick notes.

Where's Aurora Vincent? And what does she know?
- Order of Events:
  - Justin snitches to Lorenzo (Gen Priest) that he and Lenora murdered the Root Doctor
  - Lorenzo investigates Lenora but dies before he can find anything. >> How?
  - Lorenzo passes the investigation on to Aurora before dying
  - Aurora goes to see Elouise Lancaster about Alexis Lancaster's death
  - Xavier Vincent (Aurora's brother, new Gen Priest) comments on her tribute post >> Is he mad at her? Why??
- There are two people who might know where Aurora is:
  - *Justin*: He was acting weird when I first brought up "the girl who delivered the envelope to Dad"; he's still keeping secrets!!
  - Remi: The camera person from Aurora's 16 video. They're not tagged, they aren't in any posts with her, nor is she friends with anyone named Remi on 16. >> Who is Remi?
- Aurora disappeared sometime between dropping off the envelope with Dad (June) and the start of school, which she missed (August); She's been gone nearly a year, but there's no news about her disappearance >> Where is Aurora?
- Is she alive?????

I'll go see Justin, as planned. If he doesn't know anything, I'll have no choice but to track down this Remi person. It's a blind shot, but it's imperative I find out what Aurora knows. If I can find her.

The *Montaigne Majestic* is open and already buzzing with business by the time I arrive. I visit the Firefly Supplies shop to talk to Justin, but the woman working tells me he took the day off. Luckily, he lives on the boat, and one of his employees is more than happy to show me to his suite once I explain I'm family.

I ring the doorbell and wait.

No one answers. I ring it again and knock hard.

Justin opens the door and sighs when he sees me. His eyes are red, and judging from the pillow lines creasing one side of his face, I must've woken him up.

"Come for another pound of flesh?" he grumbles.

"No," I say. "I need your help again."

"I already told you, I've helped all I can," he says. "Lenora's already digging my ass nonstop about her ridiculous tribute play on top of the million other things I have—"

"Please, Justin." I clasp my hands in front of me. "Someone, likely Lenora, sent my ex, Oz Strayer, to our home this morning to conjure a spell on me and Clem."

Justin straightens up. "Are you two okay?"

"Yes, we're fine. Oz admitted to planting the hex doll in Mama's bedroom, and Clem conjured a spell that knocked him out, but he got away before we could interrogate him. I'm so close to figuring everything out, but we could all be in danger. I really need your help. Please, I don't have anyone else."

He sighs. "What do you want?"

"I think the girl who gave Dad the envelope was Lorenzo Vincent's daughter, Aurora. I need to find her, but it seems she's disappeared. Do you know where she might be?"

Justin shuffles his feet before leaning out to look up and down the deserted hallway. "See what you can find at Château des Saints Assisted Living Center," he whispers. "You didn't hear that from me." I start to say thank you, but he interrupts me. "Do not come back here again. I've already explained why I can't be part of this." He stands back and says, "Have a good day, Cristina." He shuts the door in my face.

I stand silent and confused in the empty hallway.

Why the hell is Aurora Vincent in an assisted-living center?

Chateau des Saints appears harmless enough from the outside. The facility is a collection of one-story brick buildings spread over a campus with sparse greenery and the occasional flower bed. As soon as I step through the sliding glass doors and the cold, stale air hits me square in the face, I want to turn around. A woman dressed in canary-yellow scrubs enters after me and scans her badge on the reader next to a set of glass doors off to the left, which I assume lead into the facility.

The receptionist stands up from behind the front desk and smiles. "How may I help you?"

"I'd like to see Aurora Vincent, please."

She sighs. "Ms. Vincent sure is popular today; but unfortunately, her family has strictly forbidden visitors."

"Why can't Aurora decide who visits her? And who was here earlier?"

"I can't reveal private information about the patient," she says. "Again, I'm sorry."

I start to complain, but an idea strikes me, and I smile and shrug instead. "It's okay, miss. I'll just call her brother this afternoon about visitation. My great-aunt Shirley, from St. Petersburg, had an accident a few years back and had to come to a facility like this one. Same deal. My grams had to approve anyone who came to visit."

"So, you're familiar with protocols?"

I nod, feeling only slightly bad about my lie. "May I use your restroom before I go?"

The receptionist leads me around the corner from the waiting area to a single-person bathroom not much larger than a broom closet, which is next to the glass doors leading to the patient halls. I thank her and duck inside the restroom. It smells of lavender-scented air freshener, and the Pepto-pink floral wallpaper has to be the ugliest I've ever seen. I press my ear to the door until I hear her footsteps retreating to her desk. I tear off some paper towels, stuff them into the toilet, and flush and repeat until the bowl overflows and water splatters onto the floor.

I throw the door open and call for help, and within moments, the receptionist rounds the corner. Her eyes widen when she sees the growing pool of water inching across the bathroom floor and into the hallway.

"I'm so sorry," I say. "I don't know what happened."

She exhales deeply and her shoulders slump. "This is supposed to be my lunch break."

I wince and begin inching back toward the waiting area. "I'll, uh, just be on my way."

She turns her back and waves me away. I head back to the waiting room and peer around the corner just in time to see the receptionist scan her badge and hurry through the door. I dart from my hiding place, catch it just before it closes, and slip inside.

The receptionist stands outside an office marked MAINTENANCE, talking with someone who I assume is the maintenance tech, and the nurses' station is empty. I duck behind it. A notebook filled with patient charts sits on the desktop in front of one of the computer monitors. I slide it off carefully and flip through the pages until I find Aurora's name and room number.

After I return the charts, I dip around the corner just as the receptionist and the maintenance tech exit through the glass doors back to the lobby.

I navigate through the sterile hallways of the living center until I pass underneath an archway labeled D WING. I sneak glances into the open doors as I pass. I can't imagine having to spend the rest of my days here. My only knowledge of mental institutions comes solely from the exaggerated television versions that are nothing like Chateau des Saints, which has an unsettling calmness in the atmosphere, underscored by every distant eye or incoherent murmur of the residents.

I stop in front of room D-09 and knock once, but no one answers. I push the door open and go inside.

Aurora's room is stark and depressing. There are no decorations, no flowers, not a single hint or clue of who this girl really is. Only a twin bed, an armoire, a chest of drawers, and an uncomfortable-looking armchair furnish the room, which is dark, except for a sliver of light that slips through the narrow opening between the drawn curtains.

Aurora sits in the armchair beside the bed and doesn't say anything when I come in. She doesn't even crane her head in my direction. Instead, she stares blankly at an empty corner of the room.

"Hi, Aurora." My voice trembles. "You don't know me, but my name is Cris."

She doesn't move.

I throw open the drapes, and brilliant light floods the room, illuminating Aurora's face, though she doesn't flinch or even squint against the sunlight. She's dressed in gray sweats, and her long, jet-black hair has been brushed into a single braid that drapes over one shoulder. Despite her somewhat sunken eyes and cheeks, she has a beautifully intense face with sharp angles and prominent cheekbones. Her skin has taken on a pale, tan hue, even in the afternoon light.

I kneel and wave my hand in front of her face. Nothing. It's like I'm not even here. I grab her shoulders and give her a gentle shake, but her eyes remain distant. "What happened to you?"

I wonder if the staff just rotate her around the room throughout the day like some sort of eerie life-sized doll. "Can you at least hear me? Can you blink if you understand?"

I stare into her eyes, waiting for her to answer. They're black, speckled with gray and silver. I look closer and clap my hand over my mouth to stifle a shriek.

The colored specks in her eyes swirl together to form the ghostly figure of a woman, who bangs on the inside of her eye—like a prisoner.

I leap to my feet, stumbling backward.

Something is *very* wrong with Aurora Vincent.

I sneak out of her room and down the hallway, in the opposite direction from the way I came, to a door with a glowing, red exit sign above it. I slip through and, thank the gods, no alarms sound. I snatch one of the large leaves from a shrub near the door, fold it up, and wedge it inside the metal plate in the jamb.

I hurry back to my car, but even once I'm safe inside, doors locked, my heart still races.

Someone's crossed Aurora into silence.

And the only way to figure out the truth now is to uncross her.

TWENTY-EIGHT

CLEMENT

I'm not too comfortable leaving Cris alone after whatever that was that Oz just tried, especially considering that jerk is still on the loose. But I bet he'll think twice before trying anything else after what my reflection spell did to him.

I'm not as concerned with Cris's safety as I am with who she's becoming. What I saw in her today terrified me. I honestly think she might've let Oz die. I hate him, too, but I don't know if he deserves to *die*. But then again, I could be biased. I've seen enough death.

I disliked Oz before he and Cris started dating (which only magnified my feelings), because he was best friends with Zac Kingston. I'll never trust anyone close to that homophobic closet case. Even after he catfished me, I didn't out him, but he *still* wouldn't leave me alone. The day we fought, he'd been relentless. He'd said my dad died because he couldn't stand having a fag for a son. By the time I realized what I was doing, Zac was out cold on the cafeteria floor. Someone (not me) got ahold of the video and turned it into a fake ad for Ambien and uploaded it to YouTube. He was a meme by dinner.

Despite my feelings about Oz and my sister's new bloodthirsty transformation, it still hurts that she's effectively sidelined me in her investigation. This was supposed to bring us closer, but it seems the gap between us is widening, and she's filling it with the responsibility for solving Alexis's murder.

I get it. I just don't get *her* right now.

I'm actually kind of glad for Yves's distraction.

Yves and Fabiana's home happens to be a swanky penthouse above the House of Vans. I'm relieved they have a separate entrance—the last thing I need is someone like "part-of-the-family" Roger seeing me walking into this place and blabbing about it to everyone at the Golden Key.

I'm anxious as fuck about meeting Fabiana. The way Yves describes his sister makes her seem super intimidating. I just pray she doesn't hate me and forbid Yves from seeing me again.

I ride the elevator up to the top floor, and the doors slide open to reveal a narrow hallway with white marble floors and polished concrete walls and ceiling. Scantily clad women and men stare out at me with smug, seductive expressions from the paintings on display on both sides of the corridor. It's mesmerizing and a little creepy at the same time. At the end stands a single dark-stained door with an oversized iron knocker, which I find surprisingly heavy as I lift it to knock.

Yves answers, smiling wide in a pair of sweats and a T-shirt, his fingers stained with dark blue and white paint. He draws me to him, and we stand in the doorway, entangled as if this is our last embrace before the world ends. He smells like spice and cedar, which I close my eyes to relish, emblazoning it onto my memory banks.

When we part, a flirtatious voice floats over from across the room. "Are you two going to come inside or do you prefer cuddling in the foyer?"

A woman who looks to be in her late twenties sits cross-legged on a stool in front of a large, ornate bar with a glass of wine in one hand. She seems a tad overdressed for someone just lounging at home, with the long pearl-colored dress she wears and her bone-straight dark cherry-colored hair. The oiled bronze skin of her bare shoulders gleams in the natural light flooding the wide-open space.

"This is my sister," Yves says, leading me inside. "Fabiana, this is Clem."

Fabiana slides gracefully off her seat, and her high heels tap delicately as she sweeps across the room like a goddess. She extends her hand, nails anointed with black gel like oily teardrops attached to the ends of her fingers. Everything about her is artisanal, from her flawless smile to her regal poise and the way her yellowish-brown eyes, which also bear a fatal sweetness, seem to never miss a single detail of her surroundings. "Fabiana Bordeaux," she says. "Very nice to finally meet you." She appraises me from head to toe, which makes me feel terribly awkward. "Interesting."

"Fab," grumbles Yves. "Stop being weird."

She giggles. "Am I embarrassing you, little brother?" She taps a nail against his cheek, and he swats her hand away. "Few boys have managed to garner such attention from you, I just wondered what was so special about this one."

His face flushes. I can't blame him. Mine heats, too. I'm just relieved she doesn't hate me.

I catch a big whiff of a hypnotic, sweet scent wafting from her, like ripe cherries and rain, and immediately feel light-headed. I shake my head and try to blink it away.

"Pardon," she says. "I don't mean to bewitch you, but I'm glad to see my new recipe works." When my confused look registers, she explains, "Ho-Van Oil. I'm wearing a new signature blend. It entraps every sense, uproots the desires of even the strongest-willed person, and, most importantly, loosens the purse flaps."

Before I can respond, a familiar voice sounds behind me, almost making me jump. "Clem! What are you doing here?"

I turn to find . . . Aunt Rosalie???

"What are *you* doing here?" I ask, frowning in surprise.

Yves sidles closer to me and whispers, "That's what I wanted to talk to you about."

I'm so confused right now.

Rosalie's dressed in an all-white sleeveless pantsuit, her hair in loose, extravagant curls. She glides over to Fabiana, who turns to meet her. The two women kiss on the lips, which pushes this situation into peak awkward territory for me—because what are the freaking chances Aunt Rosalie would be romantically involved with Yves's sister? New Orleans ain't *that* small.

Anxiety rolls the log in my stomach and slithers out. I can only pray my family's drama doesn't ruin my friendship with Yves.

"I didn't know you had a girlfriend, Aunt Rose."

"We're not girlfriends," Rosalie says.

"Neither of us enjoys being tied down," adds Fabiana.

"Oh . . ." is all I can say.

But I'm not sure if I have less to worry about with that admission. Once you break the anxiety seal, it's hard to close it back up.

"By the way," says Rosalie, "you know I don't care what anyone thinks about me, but I'm not up for unnecessary drama, so can you please not tell your mother about this?"

"Um . . . okay." I don't care enough to tell Mama, but I'm damn sure gonna tell Cris.

"We need to get going or we'll be late," Rosalie tells Fabiana.

Fabiana checks her appearance in an expensive-looking mirror leaning against the wall, before grabbing her purse. "We're off to attend to some important matters. You boys have fun and be safe."

Yves and I both nod and wave as Rosalie and Fabiana leave, Fabiana's sweet scent lingering in her wake. Once they're gone, we both let out a sigh of relief.

"Well, that was sufficiently embarrassing," he says.

I can't help but laugh. "Just a normal day in my family. I love that you can relate to my unconventional life more than you know."

Yves chuckles. "Yeah, me, too."

"So, uh, how long's that been going on?"

He shrugs. "Honestly, I just found out this morning. Fabiana dates, but she never invites anyone back home. I imagine either she really trusts Rosalie or really likes her or both. But I wanted to tell you, because I don't want there to be any secrets between us. I appreciate that we can be honest with each other, and I'd like to keep doing that."

Yves's admission catches me off guard, but I feel the same. Everything about him screams that he can be a safe space for me, but my internal frenemy screams just as loud that that makes Yves even more dangerous. Fuck anxiety.

"I'd like that, too," I tell him, ignoring the unease building in my gut.

I lie on my back at the foot of Yves's bed, staring up at the ceiling behind a maze of ductwork, pipes, and thick wood beams. He sits up at the head with his back against a giant mound of pillows, his knees pushed up to his chest and held in place by his paint-stained fingers. An empty easel perches nearby, alongside a narrow table lined with small containers of paint and used brushes.

"Are you sure me hanging out isn't interrupting your plans?"

He shakes his head. "You're fine. Always fine."

I grin. "Were you working on something earlier today? Can I see?"

"Um . . . It's nothing. I was just playing around with some color mixes." He hugs his legs tighter and rests his chin on top of them. "If you're worried about your sister, you should talk to her."

I shake my head. "I've tried. Honestly, I'm sick of having to pry information out of everybody. Maybe I'm supposed to be alone and should just stop fighting it." I sigh and drop my head, but a pillow slams into me, knocking me off the bed. I pull myself back up and find Yves scowling at me.

"Really?" he says.

I throw the pillow back at him. He dodges and reaches for another, but I leap onto the bed and grapple him. He howls with laughter and tries to squirm out of my grasp.

I lie on top of him and he reaches up to snuggle me, our bodies flat against each other. I burrow my nose in the nape of his neck and he yips with excitement, shrugging his shoulder in an attempt to make me stop. Eventually, he acquiesces, and I trail the tip of my nose gently across the tender skin of his neck. I feel him relax underneath me as I press my lips against the spot where his neck and shoulder meet. I suck gently, until he shudders.

I straddle him, yank off my shirt, and fling it aside. His hands explore my chest and stomach before he tugs me back down, positioning my nipple over his mouth. I try to keep my breathing steady as the hot wetness of his tongue makes my entire body quake. His teeth gently bite and a rush of blood and adrenaline surges to my groin. It doesn't take much more before I'm fully hard and pressed against his stomach. I want to know if he is, too. I shift my thigh, and it bumps against his stiff dick. I grin, and so does he.

My heartbeat picks up and I pull him into a sitting position, take his shirt off, and push him back down onto the bed so I can snake my tongue over every delicious inch of the taut bronze skin of his chest and stomach. I plant gentle kisses a few inches below his navel, along the thin patch of curly hair that spreads beyond the waistband of his underwear. He throbs with desire, I can feel it. A steady pulse against my chest. My heart beats so hard now, I worry it might give out. I slide his sweats down, and he wriggles out of them. I manage to tug my pants off, too.

I've never experienced this level of nerves with anyone before. I've also never been with a guy I've wanted completely. My mind races with images of Yves inside me, and me inside him, the closest two humans can ever physically be. But I also want him emotionally, spiritually, intellectually—every single part of him. Even the parts he's embarrassed about.

He props up on his elbows with a sultry smile. "You good?"

"Are you kidding me?" I raise an eyebrow, but it trembles.

"It's okay if you're not ready."

"I'm fine if you are."

He pulls me back on top of him. We kiss as our seminaked bodies mash together, our legs intertwined, and our hips grinding against each other.

With a deep shuddering breath, I pull off my briefs with a snap of the elastic waistband. I ball them up and toss them as far as I can, to make it harder for me to chicken out. I slip Yves's trunks off and throw them, too.

He rolls over and pulls a bottle of lube and two condoms out of a drawer in the bedside table. He hands one to me, and I set to work putting it on. My hands tremble so bad that I have to concentrate extra hard not to look like an amateur. Even though I am.

Please, please, please *don't do anything stupid.*

To my relief, I get it on without incident. Yves and I kiss some more, our tongues raiding each other's mouths. He takes advantage of the moment and reaches down to guide me inside him.

I've often imagined what sex is really like, but I never came close. It's definitely the most amazing thing I've ever felt—maybe because I care about the person I'm doing it with—but it's a lot tighter and warmer than I imagined. Also, a bit messy, courtesy of the lube.

I have no idea what the hell I'm doing. I just move like the guys did on some of the porn I've seen before. But Yves is patient, and guides my hips gently with his hands, until I reach a rhythm that makes him moan, and we both work up a sweat.

I never want this to end. I want more of this, more of him, as much as I can have. We roll around the bed, taking turns letting the other in, truly in, and nothing else matters. I allow myself to become entwined in him even more than I already was.

I lose count how many times both of us have the toe-curling, speaking-in-tongues experience of orgasming, but we go at it until we're both so tired we can barely speak between heavy breaths.

Afterward, we lie in each other's arms, our sweaty, sticky bodies melded together.

"Can I ask a question?" The bass of his voice rattles my chest.

I hold him a little tighter. "You can ask me anything."

"Was I your first?"

"Except that."

He laughs. "Come on, I want to know."

"Yes," I answer, feeling slightly embarrassed. "Was I yours?"

"No," he says. "But you were my favorite."

My heart swells. Yves makes me feel like everything might turn out okay for once.

He dozes off, and I lie beside him, ignoring the murmuring voice that wants to tell me how naive I am for falling for this boy who's destined to hurt me, too. I scoot away from him, wondering if I've made a mistake as familiar fear begins to encroach.

In his sleep, Yves feels the space where I'd lain. His eyes part just enough for him to find me, and he slides closer and buries his face in my neck again.

The voice vanishes.

Maybe Yves needs me just as much as I need him.

TWENTY-NINE
VALENTINA SAVANT

Oz Strayer had always been a creep, and Cristina Trudeau was naive as fuck.

Valentina had found Cris's "warning" about Oz laughable. She intentionally overlooked Oz's many, *many* faults, because having a morally challenged person in her pocket was like saving that Draw 4 for the last turn in Uno. At the time, it'd seemed logical to include him because he was already so entrenched in the situation. But as soon as his name had left her lips while explaining her plan to Granny, she'd regretted trusting him to handle something so critical.

And that was why her stomach sank when Oz texted her.

Val. U there?

> What?

I fucked up.
Pls don't be mad.

> WHAT?!
> Omg.
> WTF did you do?

The spell u gave me backfired.
I dunno what happened.

> Are you kidding me rn?

I almost died, but I'm OK.
U know. If u care.

> What happened?
> Did you tell them anything?

Valentina wanted to murder Oz, but she couldn't. At least not until she assessed the damage. Granny had trusted her, and she'd fucked up in a major way by relying on him. How was she going to explain this?

And what was worse, Cris had been researching Granny for some reason. Valentina hadn't been able to see anything beyond Lenora's name written in the notebook, but she had a feeling Cris was up to no good. The last thing Valentina needed was Oz snitching to Cris about what she'd put him up to—with her granny's blessing. She wanted to scream until her throat caught fire.

> **HELLO?!**
>
> **You better not fucking leave me on read Oz or I stg . . .**

U still haven't asked if I'm okay.

Typical.

> **Clearly your fingers and your ego are fine.**

U know what?

I'm done being u and ur grandma's do-boy.

Figure ur shit out on ur own. I'm out.

Valentina blocked Oz's number.

She'd made a royal mess of everything. She wasn't better than her parents.

She was much worse.

THIRTY

CLEMENT

"It's family." Yves holds my hand up and stares at our interlaced fingers. "Look at what you're going through with yours."

We're both still in bed, naked and embracing underneath the sheets—where we've been all afternoon. We didn't even bother turning on the television. Conversations and naps dominated our time instead—when we weren't doing other, more interesting things with, and to, each other.

"There's more to life than family," I say. "What about the people who go through it alone?"

He doesn't have an answer, but it's cute the way his forehead wrinkles and his mouth twists to one side whenever he's thinking hard.

"Maybe it's related to the moment we die," I say.

"Okay . . ."

"That's all I got." I shrug. "I don't know if we'll ever figure it out."

"Eh, don't be so pessimistic." He plants a kiss on my neck before climbing out of bed and pulling on a pair of shorts. "Bathroom. Be right back."

"Wanna grab some food? I'm starving."

"Sure." Then he leaves.

While my stomach grumbles, I collect my clothes from where we threw them earlier and dress—except for one stubborn sock that eludes me. I get down on my hands and knees to check for it under the bed. It's draped across a canvas, which I pull out. I study the painting and my face heats. It's me.

I'm nude, poised in midleap from what looks like a ball of chaotic, angry energy. Yves, also naked, lies on a fluffy white cloud above me, arms outstretched, pulling me up with him. The heavens are our backdrop, just the two of us set against the universe.

It's the most breathtaking thing I've ever laid eyes on. I've never felt so seen by anyone. I want to run my fingers along the surface, feel the raw emotion of every brushstroke, but I'm afraid I'll ruin it.

"Oh, God." Yves's voice startles me.

I jump up, still clinging to the canvas. "Um . . . sorry. I wasn't snooping. I was just looking for my sock and found this."

He trudges over to the bed and plops down with a heavy sigh. "Well, this is embarrassing."

I sit next to him and rest the canvas on both our knees. "Are you kidding me?"

He throws me a confused look.

"This is fucking amazing! I don't even have words for how awesome this is, for how awesome you are. I love you." *Shit.* I nearly choke.

I meant to say "it"—I love *it*, the fucking painting.

I want to melt into a puddle and evaporate into nothing.

Yves lays his head on my shoulder, and I let out a quiet sigh of relief. "When I can't find proper words to express my feelings, I paint them."

I remember all the artwork hanging along the walls of the corridor leading up to their apartment door. "Did you do the ones in the hallway outside, too?"

He nods.

"Incredible." I put one arm around him. "That's what you are."

With the worst possible timing, my stomach roars. Yves laughs, but my heart is too full to be embarrassed. I'd walk between worlds for him.

I'm never letting him go.

We decide to grab dinner at Henri's, a Creole restaurant tucked away on a side street in the Quarter, which is, most importantly, close to Yves's place, since my stomach likely won't wait for us to drive anywhere.

The hostess leads us along a winding path through a collection of tables arranged in the center of the dining room. The curtained doors of a private room stand ajar near the booth that the hostess directs us to. She sets down our menus and leaves swiftly. Inside the room, several people speak loud enough that I can just make out what they're saying.

"I'm already working on that, Jack," says a raised—and vaguely familiar—voice.

I move closer and sneak a glance. My heart skips a beat.

Lenora and Gabriela Savant, Jack Kingston, and Eveline Beaumont sit together, discussing a folder that lies open amid a collection of papers spread out on the table between them. Eveline studies a document closely, her glasses low on her nose.

Jack taps the paper in front of him with his finger. "All due respect, Lenora, but fuck your plan—that's just a temporary distraction. Nedric Whittier is the key."

Eveline tightens her lips and sets the paper back onto the pile. "I'm struggling to see how this helps us, Jack. Besides, didn't you say the guy's dead?"

"He died in '92," he says. "At Chateau des Saints—the place where Lorenzo's kid is now. Nedric's wife admitted him soon as he got sick, then she up and moved to Baton Rouge. Don't you find it odd she'd leave her husband and practically give away their business? And to *them* of all people. It's obvious, isn't it?"

"Is Eileen Whittier still in Baton Rouge?" asks Gabriela. "Do you think she would talk—"

"Oh, please," interrupts Lenora. "This is asinine, even for you, Jack."

Jack scoffs. "Or maybe I trick that idiot kid into doing my dirty work, too? Because that worked so great for you, right?"

Eveline waves a hand over the table, shushing them.

When she looks toward the open door, I duck into our booth,

ramming my thigh against the corner of the table and rattling the glasses and silverware. I shrink into the far corner, my heart ready to burst. Yves turns to look back, but I reach across the table to stop him. "No, don't."

The doors of the room behind us close with a soft click.

Yves whispers, "What happened?" When I tell him what I overheard, he asks, "Were they talking about your family?"

"I think so. Jack argued with my aunt last week at her bar, not long before his burned down. I think he might be plotting with Lenora against my family—Ursula, specifically."

The door to the private room opens.

I wave Yves quiet.

Eveline Beaumont emerges. She's wearing a pair of black slacks and a silk blouse with plenty of long frills to spare, and the large-framed glasses on her thin face make her look like an evil scientist. She takes a few steps and fakes interest in something across the room, then pretends to notice us.

I hold my breath as she smiles and walks over.

"Good evening, boys," she says. "I trust you're having a good one."

"Splendid," replies Yves, returning her smirk.

I nudge him with my foot under the table. We don't need trouble with this woman. She scares me more than Lenora.

Eveline's venomous smile remains firmly in place. "Ah, my favorite little spawn of vice."

Yves's lips turn downward and his nose wrinkles. It'd be cute if he hadn't just poked a grizzly in the eye.

"I hope your sister's been making sound investments," she continues. "Business is such a finicky creature. One minute you're on top of the world, and the next"—she shrugs one shoulder—"it's on top of you."

He clenches his jaw and averts his eyes.

Eveline presses her fingertips delicately on the edge of the table and leans in. "Fabiana and I have had our differences in the past, but please let her know my temple is always open for her." She turns to me, and my skin crawls, but I meet her eyes anyway. "Wandering ears can bring home far more dangerous tidings than news." Her smile twitches. "You two take care." She takes a few steps away and doubles back. "Oh! And do try the gumbo. It's exquisite." She tips her head at both of us and leaves.

I lose my appetite immediately.

Existential dread happens to be quite filling.

THIRTY-ONE
CRISTINA

After leaving Chateau des Saints, thoroughly shaken, I shut myself in my bedroom and fly through every website, blog, and journal I can find about anything related to Aurora's magical affliction or her family.

After several hours, the Sun and I retire at the same time. I sit back with a huff, having accomplished nothing aside from frustrating myself. I have no idea what's happened to Aurora or how to fix it. I've never even heard of a spell that could incapacitate someone like that. The thought of being imprisoned inside my own mind, forced to watch the world carry on outside the body I've lost nearly all control of, makes me shudder.

I have to help her, if for nothing more than to free her from that hell.

Who crossed Aurora?
- Someone (Xavier Vincent? Lenora Savant?) crossed Aurora into silence. >> What spell?
- Xavier doesn't want her to have visitors. >> Why? Does she know something??
- The receptionist mentioned others have been trying to see Aurora. >> Remi?
- DID Xavier cross Aurora? >> Probably. Assuming he had easier access than Lenora.
- Did Lenora find out Aurora was investigating Alexis's murder and silence her?
- Is Xavier working with / for Lenora?
- Xavier was already the Gen Priest heir, so what did he gain from

incapacitating his younger sister? And why would Xavier have been
upset about Aurora's tribute post to their father?
- WHY would Xavier hide Aurora away in Chateau des Saints?
- HOW AM I GOING TO BRING HER BACK????? 😡

Clem knocks on my door, a welcome distraction. I call for him
to come in.

"You'll never guess what just happened," he says the moment he
opens the door.

"Seems I'm not the only one who had an interesting day." I set
my computer aside. "What's going on?"

He sits down and recounts his meeting Fabiana and the news
that apparently she and Rosalie are seeing each other, which comes
as a bit of a shock at first, but the more I consider it, the less surprised I am. Rosalie lives her life as she damn well pleases, which
must be pretty great when not sullied with other people's bullshit.

"But that wasn't even the most interesting part of the day," Clem
says, reclaiming my attention before detailing his encounter with
Eveline Beaumont at Henri's. "Jack kept talking about some guy
named Nedric Whittier being the 'key,' whatever that means. Have
you ever heard of him?"

"Yeah—you have, too," I tell him. "He's the guy who started
Whittier Brewing, our brewery that Mama sold after Dad died."

Clem smacks his hand on his forehead. "Duh! *That's* where I
know his name from."

I grab my laptop and navigate to Nedric Whittier's Wikipedia
page. "It says here, 'Nedric developed an unknown debilitating illness in 1985, and his wife, Eileen, sold Whittier Brewing to her
housekeeper and longtime family friend, Cristine Glapion Dupart,
for the sum of twenty dollars.'"

Clem chuckles. "What? That has to be a typo. Why would she
do that?"

I shrug. "Maybe she wanted to get rid of it?" I keep reading. "Nedric died seven years later . . ." A small gasp escapes me.

"What?" asks Clem.

". . . at Chateau des Saints Assisted Living Center in New Orleans."

"What's so special about that place?"

"That's where Aurora Vincent is right now."

Clem listens with ardent interest as I share the details of sneaking into Chateau des Saints to find that Aurora had been crossed into what appears to be semipermanent silence.

"Cris, don't you think it's time to tell Mama what's going on? I'd even feel more comfortable if we told Aunt Ursula, at least."

I shake my head. "If Mama finds out what we're doing, she'll shut the whole thing down and will *never* let us out of her sight again. And I can't trust Aunt Ursula won't go full tilt if she were to find out what we know. I'm *so* close, Clem. Please trust me. I promise, we'll tell them everything once we have evidence to prove Lenora framed our grandmother. We still have a few weeks left of Wise John's protection—no one can touch us right now, at least not with magic."

He sighs as if he doesn't want to believe me but doesn't want to fight either. "So, what do we do now?"

The idea of more internet searching makes my head hurt. I check my phone. It's already past nine, which means all the shops have closed for the night.

"We need to make a field trip to some magic shops in the morning," I say. "Hopefully, we can find something that can help."

"Have you tried Great-Grandma's spell book?"

My stomach retreats behind my spine. "I, uh . . . want to check some other stuff first."

"Riiiight." He rolls his eyes and gets up. "Okay, well, I'm going to shower. Shout if you find anything. I'll look up some shops we can visit."

"Thanks," I murmur, but he's already gone.

Ignoring that spell book feels foolish right now, especially because it won't leave the brink of my consciousness. When I first set out to find out who crossed Mama, I vowed to do it without magic. Although I'm not sure I'll have that choice much longer, not if I want to help Aurora.

But I'm terrified of getting into another entanglement with magic. I don't know if I was really responsible for what happened to Dad, but either way, I can't endanger another innocent person. What if the spell goes wrong and I end up hurting her, too?

I can only hope tomorrow we find a book that will release me from the overwhelming burden of having to crawl back to the one that might've ruined my life.

I wake Clem midmorning and rush him to get dressed so we can head out.

We spend through the early afternoon wandering the streets of the French Quarter and plundering local magic shops. The longer our little adventure takes, the more agitated Clem becomes, eventually resigning himself to frowning into the book he brought along instead of arguing.

He disagrees with how I'm handling this, not consulting Great-Grandma's spell book, but it's only because he doesn't understand. He and I haven't exactly shared the same world outlook since Oz almost died in our living room and I was going to let it happen. Maybe it's for the best I didn't get the chance to come clean about Dad and the Scales of Justice. I don't need anything to derail me right now.

I'm so freaking *close*. But the only way forward is to uncross Aurora to find out what she knows about who really murdered Alexis Lancaster.

I purchase two books, *The Ins and Outs of Magical Incapacitation: Spells to Mystify (or De-Mystify) the Mind* by François Montcler, and *Conjuring Consciousness: A Journey into Magically Induced Afflictions* by Dr. Cheryl Hauser. These hefty volumes will probably be as exciting to slog through as watching a snail sunbathe, but I'm hopeful they'll provide some insight into what happened to Aurora and maybe even how to reverse it. I pay cash.

After we leave the last store, we stop to get beignets and lemonade from a street vendor. Clem devours his before we get to the car and sips his lemonade quietly while I drive home. His phone chimes, and he smiles when he reads the text.

"Yves?" I guess.

He nods. "He says he has a surprise for me later. He dropped a pin and told me to meet him there at seven tonight." He squints at the map on his phone. "It's at the New Orleans International Museum of Magical History." He hammers out a quick reply, grinning long after he sets his phone down again.

"Y'all are so annoying," I say with a smile.

Still beaming, he averts his gaze. Something about him seems different today; in fact, he's practically glowing. I've never seen my brother act like this about a boy. Ever . . .

I punch him in the arm. "You two did it, didn't you?"

He flinches, blushing. "Can I tell you something?"

"Duh."

"He, um . . . was my first." He sounds unsure if I'll be happy or disappointed.

And now I feel like an epic jerk. I assumed that he lost his virginity a long time ago and that once he'd gotten a taste, he'd been sampling as much of the local flavor as possible—which I wouldn't care about if it weren't an unhealthy coping mechanism for his grief over Dad's death and Mama's illness.

"I know, I know." He rolls his eyes. "You thought your brother was a rainbowed whore."

I wince. "Why'd you never say anything?"

"You made your own assumptions without talking to me, so I just let you run with them."

"Wow. And the Worst Sister Ever award goes to—" I point at myself, and he laughs. "I'm really sorry. I shouldn't have judged you."

"It's okay," he says. "I'm actually judging you right now."

"About what?" I chuckle nervously as I turn onto our street. The j-word is a little triggering for me at the moment.

He faces me, now looking painfully serious. "Cris, even you have to admit today was a major waste of time. The answer you're look-ing for is probably in the spell book at home. Why do you act like that book is going to murder you in your sleep? If you've conjured something evil from that book, you can tell me—no matter what it is. I won't think differently of you. I swear."

I want to believe him, but I can't risk losing him, too.

I pull into the garage and turn off the car's engine. "What if I told you I conjured a spell that killed someone? Would you feel the same then?"

"Was it an accident?"

"Does it matter?" I'm sure any dead person in any scenario couldn't care less about the nuance of their murderer's intent. I get out of the car and slam the door.

He gets out and looks at me with unease in his eyes, like he doesn't recognize me all of a sudden, which feels like an ice pick through the chest. "Wait," he calls after me as I brush past him and head upstairs, and he follows. "Did you do something—"

I turn in my bedroom doorway and steel my gaze. "No, Clem. And I don't have time for this." I hold up my shopping bag with the books I know damn well I don't want to read. "I have a lot of work to do, and you have a date to prepare for." I upend the bag, dumping the thick tomes onto my bed.

He sighs and leans on the jamb. "Do you need help? I can cancel with Yves or ask him to come over. Six eyes are better than two."

"No," I say. "I got it."

"You sure everything's okay?"

"Yes, Clem! For the love of the ancestors, go on your date!"

He opens his mouth and shuts it before disappearing. Moments later, he reappears—with Great-Grandma Angeline's spell book. He tosses it like a Frisbee, and it smacks into the other books on my bed. "Thought I'd help you out, you know, for when you're ready to grow the fuck up."

He's gone before I can say anything back. I knock the book onto the floor, launch myself up from where I'm sitting, and slam my bedroom door. On the way back, I kick the damned spell book underneath the bed.

A fog of dread plumes in my stomach and its icy tendrils wind through my chest. Clem's right.

THIRTY-TWO

CLEMENT

I really wish my sister would get over herself.

Yet, here I am, pulling up to Jean-Louise's house to see if he knows of a spell that could help uncross Aurora, because I can't stop helping Cris even though I don't feel she appreciates it. Since this whole ordeal began it seems I've been more of her dopey side-kick than her partner.

The Sun's color has deepened in preparation for nightfall in about an hour. The sounds of children playing football echo down the street in one direction, but the neighborhood appears to be deserted in the other, with the exception of a pale white pickup parked at the top of the hill several houses down. I imagine it's in need of a new muffler, the way the engine rumbles like the snores of a sleeping dragon. I start across the street, but when I glance back at the truck, it makes a U-turn and disappears over the hill, the roar of its engine fading soon after.

Jean-Louise answers his door and meets me with an exasperated expression. "I'm going to have to move to know peace again, aren't I?"

"You only pretend to like being alone," I tell him. "Can we talk? I won't be long, I promise."

He sighs and lets me in.

We go to the kitchen, where he'd been sitting at the table with a mug of coffee and the sports section of the newspaper. "You want something to drink?" he asks.

"No, thank you." I drag a chair from the table and sit across from him. "Would you happen to know of any spells that could uncross someone who's been magically incapacitated?"

His brows knit together. "I'm afraid not. I've only ever practiced necromancy—what are you kids up to now?" I tell him the abridged version of the situation with Aurora, and when I finish, he asks, "Why don't you ask Ursula? Surely, she can help with this."

"She doesn't know," I say. "She thinks we should leave it alone and let her and Mama handle it, but they're not doing anything."

"You should listen to her."

"She says I need to leave you alone, too."

"Then you should *definitely* listen to her."

I hang my head, unsure what to say. I hate how everyone misjudges Jean-Louise. He may be the grumpiest person I've ever met, but I find comfort in him. I'm not sure why.

"Look," he says, "I don't mean to hurt your feelings. Your aunt is only looking out for your safety. You shouldn't be poking around dangerous people like Lenora Savant and you shouldn't be hanging around people like me either."

"There's nothing wrong with you. I admire you, actually."

"I'm flattered, Clement, but I'm no role model. I've made some awful decisions in my past."

"So." I shrug. "We all fuck up. You still deserve a chance to make things right."

Jean-Louise chuckles. "I miss the innocence of my youth so much."

Only because I don't want to spoil our conversation, I'm going to assume that comment wasn't meant as a dig. "Is there nothing you can do for Auguste? Is he stuck like that until he dies . . . again?"

"Part of Auguste's soul is lost in the spiritual realm. Even if I were to somehow find a way to recover the missing piece and put his soul back together, it would bear the cracks forever." The look on his face reminds me of when I'm fighting not to cry about something that's made me cry far too much already. "I should've let him go—let his soul transcend to the spiritual realm whole, so he could be at peace."

"Maybe," I tell him. "Maybe not. You loved Auguste and you did what you thought was best."

"It was selfish."

"Was it? Auguste didn't want to die."

He sits back and heaves a sigh. "You don't know that."

"No one wants to leave the people they love most behind," I say, my voice bold and even. "And Auguste also wouldn't want you to give up on him. If there's even a small chance you could bring him back, you owe it to him to at least try—or let him go."

"I—" Jean-Louise cuts himself off and clenches his jaw, staring hard at the table.

My phone goes off with a text from Yves. *Shit, I'm going to be late.*

"I have to get going." I stand up, startling Jean-Louise from captivity of whatever he was pondering. "It was nice talking with you."

"Yeah," he mutters distractedly, following me out.

His hulking silhouette stands in the doorway, watching my car until I disappear over the hill.

Yves found free parking only a block away from the museum. It's dark by the time I pull into the small lot tucked behind an old building off the main street. He waits for me, leaning against the wall next to an open parking space and scrolling on his phone.

He smiles when I step out of the car. "Hey there." He throws his arms around me and kisses my neck, which sends electricity pulsing through me. "I thought you'd like this, plus it'll be good for you to take your mind off things for a couple hours."

"I appreciate that a lot," I tell him.

I love that he knows what I need before I know I need it. Tonight, I only want to focus on Yves and being fucking happy for once.

A blue sedan pulls into the parking lot and five people climb out. The trunk pops open and they grab hand-painted signs from inside. I catch sight of one that reads, GUNS KILL PEOPLE AND SO DOES MAGIC. IF GUNS MUST BE REGULATED SO SHOULD MAGIC.

Redeemers. They must be protesting tonight.

"There might be one tiny problem," Yves says, wincing inno-cently. "Since this is the first week of the exhibit and the museum is open late for the showcase, the Redeemers are posted out front. Counterprotesters have shown up, too, so we might have to wade through a bit of a zoo to get inside. If it makes you uncomfortable, we don't have to go."

I shrug. "It's fine." I have far scarier things to worry about than a few angry protesters.

A single wide stone path leads to the museum's front entrance, splitting the grassy front lawn in two. Masses of Redeemers and counterprotesters gather on either side, shouting across the walk-way and pressing angrily against the waist-high barricades keeping both sides at bay.

It's there, as we walk down the center aisle between the opposing crowds that pulse with raw energy, that I finally think I might've fig-ured out the meaning of life. The sea of people, entangled in body and thought, two sides of the same coin, screaming for change—this is the epicenter of social disruption. Yet, they're but a small part of a much larger world, comprising a vast collection of people whose lives crash into one another in peace, love, or anger—like me, like everyone around me.

The words pirouette inside my head, and I struggle to corral them into something meaningful to share with Yves.

But I have to leave those thoughts behind, because after the host scans our tickets on Yves's phone, we're whisked inside and ushered to a corner of the main atrium where a few other people form a small tour group. Above the arched entrance to the main exhibit hangs a banner that reads MILLENNIA OF MAGIC alongside a picture of the artist, Ayden Holloway. His locs are pulled back into a ponytail and the dark brown skin of his face is adorned with colorful swipes of paint from a brush, like the same one between his bared teeth. He stares straight into the camera with wise, dis-arming eyes. Below his picture is his Instagram username. I take out my phone and follow him. I'm scrolling through his feed, which is primarily his art, most dealing with the three branches of magic, with a few selfies sprinkled in, when Yves draws my attention to the atrium exhibit.

An immense sculpture of the Sun and the Moon hangs in the center of the room. The main lights have been dimmed so the primary source of light comes from within the giant sun, which is made from what must be thousands of precisely cut panes of plexiglass brought together by thin, shiny metal seams. Next to it is a sculpture of the Moon, made with powdery blue dimpled paper that reminds me of an enormous celestial paper lantern. The moon's exterior glows a soft blue against the bright yellow of the sun beside it.

Yves pulls me to one side, so when I look at the exhibit from another angle, the moon perfectly aligns with the sun. I gasp at the eclipse effect that happens when we walk from one side of the display to the other. We stand in the center of the eclipse, and Yves pulls out his phone to take a picture of us. He smells of sandalwood with a subtle, warm spice I can't get enough of. Before he snaps the picture, he grabs my hand and interlaces his fingers with mine. I squeeze back, and we both smile. My phone buzzes in my pocket when he sends the pic to me. For some reason, my heart refuses to slow down.

"I, uh, wanted to tell you something before the tour started," Yves says as we return to our group and linger toward the back.

The ever-present knot in my stomach tightens. "Sure, what is it?"

He moves closer to me, so our shoulders touch and he doesn't have to speak as loud for me to hear him. "I never addressed your comment the other day . . . when you said you loved me."

I feel my hands immediately start sweating and I want to fucking disappear. "I—I didn't mean, um, that was an accident—" His brows lift, and I stammer on, "Not that it couldn't be true or anything . . . I just don't want things to be weird between us now, because I really like you, and—"

He chuckles, and the rest of the words die on my lips. When he notices me frowning at him, he says, "I'm sorry, I just can't get over how unbelievably cute you are."

"Heh." I run a hand across the back of my head and grin. "Thanks, I guess?"

"When you first said it, I admit, it scared me. I'm not used to getting close to people, and meeting you was an unexpected change of pace for me. I'm still a bit off-balance from it all, but that's not a bad thing. I've never been in love before, so I have no idea how it's supposed to feel. But I do know that I love the way you accept me and my weird-ass sister. I love that you're so passionate and spontaneous and smart and funny. I love that despite all the shit life has thrown at you, you still love so innocently and purely. I love everything about you, Clem. So maybe that means I love you, too. But what if we stopped worrying about all that and just allowed ourselves to be free to feel whatever we feel whenever we feel it? Would you be okay with that?"

"Yeah, that's great," I say. "But I have to be honest, an I-love-you-too would've sufficed."

He nudges me with his shoulder, and we both share a laugh before our guide starts the tour.

A seed of happiness sprouts in my chest, but a storm of anxiety rips it from the root. My mind latches on to the danger of things developing too fast between Yves and me. But I can't help it.

This feels like I'm on a runaway train that I can't stop, so I might as well hang off the side and enjoy the wind on my face before we crash.

But Yves doesn't make me feel like I'm in danger. He feels safe. And I love that about him.

Our first stop is a stunning collection of four murals painted across eggshell-colored tapestries that resemble thick bedsheets hanging on the wall. It's nighttime in all the paintings and the Moon sits in a different phase and place in the sky of each. Yves and I both mumble "Wow" at the same time.

Our guide, a short, plump Black man with sharp eyes, a naturally projecting voice, and a gentle face, steps to the front of the group and introduces himself as Jacob.

The first painting shows a young male slave standing at the edge of a cotton field alongside a black-cloaked god. The god cradles the man's head in both hands while he whispers something into the man's ear. His wrist faces outward, showing the glowing mark of the gods.

The image of the god, with skin like onyx and eyes bright as stars, makes the hair on my neck and arms stand up. He looks familiar—like that scary-ass man-spirit thingy who chased me in that dream I had after the car accident. Maybe it's just a coincidence. But the tingle in my shoulder, a flair of memory from the icy touch of his hand on me, tells me otherwise.

"Mr. Holloway calls this collection *Baba*, for it tells the story of Papa Eshu's rise to godhood in four acts," Jacob announces. "The first depicts the gods whispering the secrets of Moon magic to a slave by the name of Henri Eshu. Henri was born the child of slaves on a Louisiana plantation in the early seventeen hundreds; the exact date is unknown, as are most intimate details surrounding his upbringing."

Jacob points to me when I raise my hand. "Yes?"

"Who is the god speaking with Henri?"

"Unfortunately, we don't know the name of the deity who first contacted Henri Eshu. Some have even speculated they might've been God themself."

How strange. I make a mental note to check out Ayden's IG again later. Maybe if I send him a DM, he'd be willing to tell me more about this painting. Or perhaps I'm just paranoid. Too much espresso and anxiety. People in paintings often look familiar. Last year, Isaiah swore our English teacher, Mrs. Betts, had somehow photobombed every European painting we studied in art history.

Jacob moves to the second piece, which shows a young female slave running hand in hand with a white woman, who clutches a baby in one arm. They're heading for a small one-room cabin where Henri stands in the open doorway, holding a lantern in one hand and what our guide tells us is his medicine satchel in the other.

"Henri became well known among the people on his plantation for conjuring concoctions that could heal any ailment—some even referred to him as a god in the flesh," says Jacob. "When the plantation owner's grandson fell ill with scarlet fever and doctors advised them to begin making funeral preparations, a slave woman who'd grown fond of the child brought the baby and his mother to Henri late one night, desperate for help. Well aware of the implications, Henri healed the baby. However, the next day, despite the child's life having been saved, the plantation owner was livid to find out Henri had practiced magic on his grandchild."

Jacob herds us over to the third painting, which shows Eshu at the head of a group of Black men and women whose bodies are smeared with dirt as if it were some kind of war paint. They stand bold and unyielding in front of a white man who's fallen to his knees with a look of agony on his face, a rifle cradled in his arms. Beside him lies the bloodied body of a smaller white man.

"The plantation owner dragged Henri to the crossroads of the estate where he often punished or killed those who disobeyed him and threw Henri facedown into the dirt. He'd planned to execute Henri in front of everyone to make an example of him. But when he pulled the trigger, the shot ricocheted off Henri and blasted through the skull of his son instead.

"You see, Henri had been working on conjuring a magical dust that could render someone coated with it invulnerable to physical attack. Not only had he spread it over the crossroads that morning, but he'd given it to the rest of his people to protect themselves. A bloody massacre followed that spread to the surrounding plantations."

The final painting shows Henri leaning against an old, majestic-looking willow at a crossroads, staring up at the full Moon. It's lonely, and haunting, and fucking gorgeous.

"Henri and his followers went on to free hundreds of slaves, who all traveled north, but there's no record of Henri ever making it there himself or of his death," recites Jacob. "But for his valiant efforts while alive, he was granted godhood and became the Father of the Moon, or as some like to call him, the Guardian of the Crossroads. It's a well-known fact today that the best place to call on one of the generational gods is at a crossroads."

Next, we see a painting of a white woman tied to a stake in the center of a burning pyre. The bottom of the billowing dress she wears has already caught fire and the flames stretch toward her face like dozens of hands of greedy children reaching for candy. A single rolled cigarette hangs loosely off her lips, which she leans forward to light in the flames of her own bonfire. Her arms, which are tied down to her sides, bend at the elbow, and she gives all of us the finger with both hands. Jacob tells us that one's titled *Agnes Sampson, the First White Mage.*

We also view a very unsettling painting that's just the dark silhouette of a person against a similarly dark background. I have to squint to make out the faint outline of hands cupped around a bustling flame in the center of their chest. Yves shudders beside me, still rapt by the strange picture when I read the name aloud. *"Divine Spark; Portrait of a Vamp."*

We wander with the group for about an hour, marveling at Ayden Holloway's work. I drink up every bit of my magical culture, which fills me with so much pride. Our family was part of this history. Our own grandmother. Now I understand why Cris is fighting so hard to clear her name.

The tour ends, and as we enter the main atrium on our way out, Yves exclaims, "I've got it!"

"You've got what exactly?"

"Magic. That's the meaning of life. I mean, God created us and eventually the minor gods from us. And the minor gods created the different branches of magic and grant those who practice their abilities."

I don't get to answer before we're swept up in a rush of people who push through the doors to slip by the protesters and to the safety of their cars as fast as possible. Several police cruisers have pulled up out front, strobing the crowd outside with bright blue lights.

Neither Yves nor I try to talk over the chants on both sides of us, which cobble together into indecipherable raucousness that begins to fade as we walk back to my car.

"I don't think that's it." I lead us down the alley to the parking lot.

"You know the rules. If you disagree, you have to explain why."

Yves and I are alone in the lot, with the exception of whoever sits inside the loud, idling white pickup backed into a spot near the exit. I'm wondering where I remember that truck from when Yves taps me, snapping me back to our conversation.

"So . . . are you gonna tell me why magic isn't the meaning of life?"

"The gods don't bless everyone with magic, nor is everyone's life touched by it." He rolls his eyes and I stick my tongue out at him.

We make it to my car, but Yves leaps in front of me with a grin, blocking my door. "Okay, then you have to give an answer, too, or you can't leave."

"Oh, yeah?" I step closer and he licks his lips as his eyes trace over my face. "What if I don't want to leave?" I grab his waist and pull him flush against me. Our lips meet and it feels like our souls crash into each other while we kiss. When we finally part, Yves smiles again.

But he gasps, and his eyes widen at something behind me.

"What's—?" I turn, but he shoves me aside.

A gun fires.

The sound is deafening. My ears ring. I flinch and cover them.

Yves slumps against my car and slides to his knees. I scramble to catch him.

Across the aisle stands a guy dressed in a Redeemers tee, black jeans, and a ski mask. His light eyes are feral behind the mask, and his trembling white hand still grips the gun that's now pointed at me.

I'm frozen through to the bone.

"Please," I cry, clutching to Yves, who's gasping in my arms. "Don't—"

He jabs the gun toward me, and I flinch. "It was supposed to be *you*," he snarls.

The sound of approaching voices startles him, and he tucks the gun into the back of his pants and takes off. He jumps into the idling pickup and barrels out of the parking lot, nearly hitting another car on the way.

I move to chase him, at least see which way he went, but Yves grabs my arm.

"No," he mutters. "Please—don't—leave."

Warm blood from the gunshot wound to Yves's chest spills onto my arms. He coughs, blood splattering down his face.

The life in his eyes begins to fade. The portal to the other world I once saw in them is closing in real time. I sit on the ground beside my car and cling to him.

This doesn't seem real, but the pain in my chest feels tangible— and I want to dig it out with my bare hands. Why the fuck is this happening to us? To me?

I grit my teeth and shake my head.

I struggle to unlock my phone to call for help. I don't know if anyone else has yet. "Yves! Please . . . don't die on me."

He tries to say something, but a wet cough interrupts him.

"I swear to the gods, I won't leave you," I say. "But you gotta stay with me, too."

It's too late. He's as good as gone. Just like the others. When will you learn?

By the time the dispatcher answers my 911 call, one final breath limps across Yves's lips, and his eyes close.

"Noo! Please!" I cry, but he doesn't wake.

I throw my phone and it shatters against the brick façade of the building beside us.

I shake Yves, but he doesn't wake up.

Fuck, fuck, fuck! Please, God. No.

"Wake up . . . please, Yves. I'm so sorry. I love you. Remember?" Tears turn my vision into wavy splotches of color. "You can't leave me. Not now. Not like this."

Not a damn thing else in the world matters right now.

"We have to go," I whisper to him. "We're already running out of time."

I swerve so fast that my car hops the curb and kicks up grass and dirt onto the sidewalk. I throw open the back door and lift Yves out. His head lolls from my staggered gait, and blood rushes in my ears as I stumble up the steps of the front porch and ring the doorbell.

Please, for the love of the gods, be home.

Yves grows heavier by the second, and the muscles in my back and arms sear. Swaying warily, I ring the bell over and over until the porch light blazes on and Jean-Louise snatches open the front door.

He stands mouth agape, staring at Yves and then me. "Dear gods," he mutters.

"I-I figured it out," I tell him. "He d-deserves to know."

He tilts his head. "What happened, Clem?"

"M-Meaning of life. I know wh-what it is." Warm rivers of tears run down both sides of my face as I stare into Jean-Louise's heavy-lidded eyes. "Please . . . help me?"

He stands back, shaking his head. "No. I can't. I want nothing to do with this."

"I don't have anyone else. *Please.*" I push the words out with what little strength I have left, and my legs quiver. They finally give way and I collapse on Jean-Louise's threshold in a pitiful heap, with my bloodied boyfriend still in my arms. "I can't lose him, too. I can't. I ca—"

Jean-Louise tries to take him from me, but I shake my head and grip Yves tighter. "No! I promised I wouldn't leave him." A quiet moment passes, and I say, "Help me now, and we can save them both. Together. I'll do whatever it takes. I swear it."

He stares down at me, a gentle, silent giant cloaked in shadow. Forever passes in the dark of his doorstep before Jean-Louise releases a heavy sigh and stands aside.

I scramble to my feet. My muscles are on fire and screaming at me, but I won't let him go.

Still cradling my boyfriend, I stagger inside.

THIRTY-THREE

CRISTINA

Just as I'd suspected, the books I wasted my money on are useless.

The longer I delay that realization, the angrier I become at Clem for not only being right but also calling me out and dragging my fear and insecurity back to the forefront of my mind.

Great-Grandma Angeline's spell book lies beneath my bed all night, like a ghoul waiting to wrap its claws around my ankle the moment I let my guard down. Truth is—it scares me. I'm terrified I'm going to fuck up again and someone else might suffer for it—again.

Gen magic used to feel like an extension of myself, an innate part of who I was, but now even thinking of conjuring feels awkward; especially after how Oz used magic to take advantage of me. Even if I wanted to conjure again, gen magic doesn't work without confidence. My ancestors didn't mutter and stumble their way into positions of grace and power, and I certainly can't expect to either. I'm just not ready to untangle that ball of trauma yet. There must be another, less nerve-racking way.

I comb through both research books until my eyes are tired and red and the Sun starts its slow crawl over the horizon. I drift off, facedown in *Conjuring Consciousness,* and sleep peacefully, until I find myself in a dream where I'm trying to uncross Aurora with magic but end up throwing her into a very bloody, excruciatingly painful death. Her screams echo and I jerk myself awake, feeling spent from the entire ordeal. When my head stops swimming, I check my phone and realize it's one in the afternoon.

I drag myself out of bed and wash my face and throw on some clothes. In the mirror, I stare at my shoulder-length curls, which are screaming for moisture and attention. I've been taking short-cuts with my hair-care routine ever since we found the hex doll in Mama's room. I just don't have time to spend the bulk of an entire day washing and deep-conditioning and drying and moisturizing and oiling and twisting my hair when someone's trying to kill me and my family. With a sigh, I put my hair into another ponytail and trudge to Clem's room so I can apologize, yet again, for being a jerk.

I knock on his door a few times, and when he doesn't answer, I crack it and call his name. Nothing. I push the door open and peek inside. His bed's made, but Clem *never* makes his bed after waking up. My heart plunges. He must not have come home last night.

I call him, but it goes straight to voicemail. I text him and stare at the screen, waiting for the three bubbles to appear to let me know he's typing, and most importantly, *alive*, but they don't come.

Panic slithers out of hiding somewhere deep inside me. Should I tell Mama? Clem could be in danger, or worse. And this could be my fault, too. He asked me to get help, but I refused.

I turn to go find Mama, but yelp when I almost crash into him.

He sidesteps me, throws open his closet door, and slings an empty duffel from inside onto his bed. He's changed out of what he was wearing when I last saw him. He's in a white tee and some old, ratty basketball shorts now. "What are you doing in my room?"

I throw my arms around him, but his response is cold. He barely pats my back before pushing away.

"I called, but your phone was off. I was afraid something happened to you," I tell him. "You didn't come home last night. Where were you?"

"My phone broke," he says. "I need to shower, can I have some privacy, please?"

His nonchalance stings, but I guess I deserve it for how I treated him when we last talked. "I'm sorry about yesterday."

"Don't sweat it," he says. "Please, Cris. I have to go."

"Where?"

"To a friend's. No one you know, so don't ask."

"Is that where you were last night?"

"Yes," he says, sounding irritated.

"Why?"

He takes a deep breath in and out. "Cris, you've been different so long I've almost forgotten what the old you is like. I begged you to confide in me for so long, but you refused every single time—yet you have the audacity to demand to know every detail of my life. How is that fair?"

"Seriously?" I throw my hands up in disbelief. "I'm worried about you! Now you're just being petty."

He shrugs. "Then call me Petty Betty." He grabs hold of the door and waves his hand toward the hallway. "Please. I have things to do—one being getting my phone fixed."

Pressure builds behind my eyes, but I bite my tongue until that pain distracts from the one in my heart. I leave without another word, and he closes the door behind me.

Standing in the hallway, I listen to him moving around the room for a few moments before the shower turns on and the bathroom door slams. I wait a little longer, then crack his bedroom door. Steam billows from underneath the closed bathroom door. I tiptoe inside his room.

Clothes are strewn across his bed, like he ripped them from the closet in a hurry. A copy of *Challenger Deep* sticks out of the overnight bag on his desk. I peek inside the bag.

Underclothes. Hairbrush. Deodorant. Toothbrush. Nothing special . . . except the prescription bottle. It's the narcotic the doctor prescribed Clem after the car accident.

By the time I hear him open the bathroom door, it's too late. I drop the bottle into the bag before he reaches around me and yanks it away. The shower's still running, and he stands in front of me (still fully clothed, thank goodness) with a frightening scowl. Maybe it's a good thing I gave up my childhood ambition of becoming an international spy.

"Why the hell are you going through my stuff?" He tosses the bag to the far end of the bed.

"Because I'm worried about you." I cross my arms and glower back at him.

"Well, don't. I'm fine." He throws the rest of his clothes into his bag and zips it up. "I'll shower later." He darts into the bathroom, turns off the water, and comes back to snatch his bag from the bed.

I block the door so he can't leave. "Did something happen yesterday?"

"Cris, please move."

"Are you and Yves okay?" When he doesn't answer, I ask, "Did you guys break up or something?"

My heart writhes. Something's going on with my brother, but he won't tell me. This must've been how he felt about me for an entire year. No wonder he's so angry with me.

He searches my face for a moment before muttering, "Yes." His puffy, bloodshot eyes well, but he tilts his head up farther and blinks the tears away.

I can feel him falling apart. This is what I feared about him getting too close to Yves too soon. And even worse, I'm worried he's self-medicating with those pills. I should tell Mama, but I quickly snuff out that idea. If I snitch, he'll never trust me again. I have no choice but to trust him, even though everything in me is screaming not to.

"I'm sorry," I tell him. "Look, sit down and let's talk—about everything. I'll tell you why I'm afraid of magic and anything else you want to know."

He scoffs. "I don't care anymore, Cris." He steps past me, knocking my arm aside like in an angry game of Red Rover.

I follow him and grab his shoulder at the top of the stairs, and he whirls around. "Clem, please! I understand you're pissed at me and you have every right to be. I should've told you the truth a long time ago, I just couldn't."

"Then you should understand why I wish to do the same."

"Why are you being so dramatic about a breakup? Just talk to me and let me help you through this." I hug myself instead of him, because I don't want to feel the stab of his rejection. "I can't watch you spiral again."

His nostrils flare, and I fear that, again, I've said the wrong thing. "I'm not spiraling, and I'm not some helpless kid you need to protect. I can handle myself—just like you."

"What about Aurora?" I ask in a last-ditch effort to stop him from walking out on me. "Are you just going to leave me to figure this out on my own?"

He hefts his bag higher up on his shoulder and shoots me a glare that makes me take a step back. "I've been trying to help you since you started your little investigation and you always say you've got it; so, handle it now, Cris. I don't have time to pick up your slack because you're too prideful to deal with your shit. I have my own, more important, shit to worry about now."

He turns and leaves, but this time I don't chase after him.

I go back to my room and slump to the floor beside my bed. Clem's words cut away at the thick shell protecting my pride. He's right. I'm the only one who can get myself out of this mess.

But I'm going to need help from my ancestors.

With a sigh, I kneel and fish Great-Grandma Angeline's spell book from underneath my bed. It feels cold and foreign in my hands, but it's all I've got right now.

Despite all my efforts to the contrary, I've pushed my brother and only confidant away. I won't let all this be for naught.

I drag my fingers across the rough, weathered surface of the old book's cover and mutter, "Hello, old friend."

THIRTY-FOUR

CRISTINA

> Hey. I'm so sorry. I miss you so much. Are you okay?

It's okay. I'm fine. I miss you too.

> Where are you?

Still at my friend's place. He's been really nice.

> It's been two days.
> Who are you with?

I just need some space.

I don't feel like talking to anyone right now.

> I love you.

I love you too.

I'm fine.

I swear.

> I'm worried about you.
> What were you doing with those pills?

I'm not abusing painkillers. You know me better than that.

> Then why did you have them?

The moment I send the last message, I know he won't respond.

A chasm has opened between us and I can't stop it from spreading, no matter how hard I try.

I wish he would confide in me.

I miss him so much.

THIRTY-FIVE

CRISTINA

When it came to conjuring, Great-Grandma Angeline Glapion was the GOAT.

She personally crafted most of the spells in her book, like the one I found almost immediately labeled "Cleansing Ritual for Powerful Crossings," which I pray, to every god listening, can uncross Aurora. The irony is not lost on me that the spell I need is also the most complex I've ever seen. A year ago, I would've welcomed the challenge, but now it only makes me anxious. What if this goes as wrong as the Scales of Justice? What if I screw up and lose the only living person who can help us?

I am descended from a long line of incredible Queens. Magic is in my blood. I can do this.

I arrange the items I've collected for the spell on my desk.

Two white and two black candles.

A small jar filled with a solution of Epsom salt and thirteen drops of peace water.

A larger jar of moonlight, which I harvested late last night.

A concoction called "Clearing Oil" that I had to mix from equal parts patchouli, sandalwood, and aloe oils. Luckily, I was able to scrounge all the items from Mama's conjuring cabinet.

But the final ingredient listed on the weathered page of the spell book has been tripping me up since I first read it. *A part of the conjurer's heart.* There's a brief, albeit not very helpful, note beneath.

Magic of the Moon, passed down through generations of conjurers, dwells in the blood of those the gods deem true, yet still sometimes sacrifice is required to bring about great works.

When a true conjurer is willing to give of themselves, they can gain the power to unravel even the most powerful of crossings.

I'm almost certain she couldn't have meant a literal piece of my heart, but what could I sacrifice to fulfill the spell's request? The longer I ponder this riddle, the angrier and more frustrated I become. My grandmother was taken from us, as well as decades of knowledge and tradition along with her. She should've had the opportunity to pass all that on to Mama, and eventually to Clem and me. But thanks to Lenora, I'm on my own.

I lean back in my seat with a huff and my eyes land on my journal. I trace my finger along the indentations of the cover quote: "Fly boldly in the pursuit of your dreams."

I wish Dad were here to help me find my way through this. I've been so lost since he died. He always had a way of gently nudging me in the right direction whenever my life seemed to veer off course. Like when I was ten years old and he carved my initials on the trunk of the willow tree at the crossroads after I fell out of it and broke my arm. He'd told me it was to help me remember—that I fell but survived. He hadn't wanted me to fear climbing trees because of my accident.

I clutch my journal close and shut my eyes. This notebook is like a talisman representing my connection with Dad, who's a large part of my heart—even though he's gone now. A warm sense of calmness radiates from the center of my chest, beneath where I hold the book.

I know what I have to do now.

I swipe a metal mixing bowl from the kitchen, along with some matches, and go outside to the back patio. I set the bowl on the ground and place my journal inside. This book, the last gift from my dad, represents a portion of my heart. The cover quote perfectly illustrates how Dad taught me and Clem to approach life. I'm sure burning my journal classifies as a "bold" move toward my dream of proving my and my grandmother's innocence. If Dad were here, he'd chuckle at the irony.

I strike the match and toss it in, the smell of burnt sulfur dioxide tingling my nose. The book is slow to catch, but the fire soon swallows it hungrily. I hold my head high and watch it burn until the flames shrink to smoldering embers and eventually die, leaving only ashes behind.

I take the ashes back up to my room and dump them carefully into the jar of moonlight. I swirl the contents briskly, as instructed by the spell book, and after a few moments, it transforms into azure-colored flakes that resemble ethereal blue rose petals. Magic is so beautiful.

I snap a picture of the spell's instructions and load all the ingredients into my backpack. Now all that's left to do is wait until almost sunset; then I'll go see Aurora and perform the ritual that will hopefully uncross her.

Dear gods, please let this work.

It's been an entire day since Clem left me on read. I wish I could do this with him, but I've pushed him too far away. I'm on my own now.

I take a long, deep breath as I pull into the lot of Chateau des Saints and park at the end closest to Aurora's room and the exit door I escaped from the other day. I give the lot a quick once-over, but no one's around, only a few cars I imagine belong to the nurses who staff the evening shift. The Sun has begun its retreat toward the horizon, and the pale Moon hovers in the sky to the east. A soft breeze bends the stalks of the flowers in the gardens as I pass through them to the side entrance.

The leaf I stuck in the jamb is still there, so I'm able to pull the door open easily. I peek in and find the dim hallway deserted. I duck inside and ease the door shut behind me. Most residents have already retired to their rooms for the evening, based on the snores and muffled sounds of televisions that come from behind doors. The drum of my heart intensifies the closer I draw to Aurora's room. Once there, I push inside.

The room is eerily dark, with the exception of the soft glow from the lamp on Aurora's bedside table, which illuminates the side of her face—and haunting eyes that are transfixed on me.

I hurry to the bathroom and fill the tub half full of warm water and unpack the ingredients for the spell. I pray this works. The only way to find out what Aurora knows about Alexis Lancaster's murder is to uncross her.

First, I add the Epsom-salt solution and the Clearing Oil to the water. My fingers tremble so hard that I can barely put the lids back on the containers.

I add the flakes of moonlight, which float atop the water like lily pads dipped in pale blue bioluminescence. The water splashes softly as I fan my hand back and forth to mix everything together and pray, "Papa Eshu, I beseech you, please open the gateway for the gods and ancestors of goodwill to bless this bath and uncrossing ritual."

It feels strange, praying to Eshu after all this time. I wonder if he'll answer, if my ancestors will deliver my message. Though I could understand if they're upset about how I turned my back on them.

I set up the candles at the end of the tub and light them before checking my phone. Only fifteen minutes before sunset. *Shit.* I have to hurry.

I go back out to the room and draw back Aurora's bedsheets. "We're going to take a quick bath, and hopefully you'll feel much better afterward."

I shoulder the brunt of her weight, which isn't much. She cooperates, though moving slower than I'd like. I slip off her nightgown, leaving her undergarments on, and help her into the water. The moment she sits down, she tilts her head back and releases a deep, shuddering sigh.

When she lifts her head again, her eyes flit among the pulsing flames of the candles at the end of the tub, but the candlelight doesn't reflect in them. I look away, not wanting to meet her eyes again. Instead, mine stray across the thinner portions of her chest, stomach, and thighs. It looks as if something has been siphoning the life out of her.

What did they do to you?

I rinse her thoroughly and help her to her feet. With a small pitcher I nabbed from the kitchen at home, I collect bathwater and pour it over her head. She flinches, but I rub her back to soothe her as the warm water dribbles down the length of her shadowy hair and slender body. I rinse her this way thirteen times, while reciting Psalms 7:1–10, which I read from my phone.

With each recitation, my discomfort fades, making way for the formidable energy that surges through me, all the way to my fingertips. By the time I finish, I feel powerful enough to hold the Moon in my bare hands. This sensation is familiar and rich and incredible. Like getting a hug from Mama or Odessa or Clem at the moment when I need it most, and stepping back, feeling invincible—and loved. Magic wraps its arms around me, like I'm reuniting with a dear friend I've been apart from for ages.

I don't want to ever lose this feeling again.

I help Aurora out of the tub and wrap her in a bathrobe I pull from a hook on the back of the door. I direct her out to her room and lower her into an armchair. There's still one more thing left to do.

Aurora stares blankly out the window, and I go back to the bathroom and fill the pitcher with some of her bathwater.

Five minutes until sunset.

I drain the tub, clean it with a sprinkle of blessed salt and water, and mumble a quick "Be right back" to Aurora on my way outside.

I dip through the exit at the end of the hallway and dart back out to the parking lot, where I have a clear view of the setting Sun.

I face in the direction of the sunset, mumble one final prayer to Papa Eshu, and fling the water from the pitcher. It turns to mist and evaporates inches above the pavement right as the last sliver of Sun disappears.

I head back to the building feeling like a superhero—and my heart crashes into my gut the moment I step inside. Someone screams with what sounds like all the force of their lungs.

It's coming from Aurora's room.

I rip down the hall and throw the door open to find Aurora sprawled on the floor, writhing and shrieking as if she's being burned alive.

Dear gods. I've screwed up. My nightmare has become reality. Magic fucked me over—again.

Just like the damned Scales of Justice.

I cover my mouth with both hands, trapping the gasp waiting to escape. The door jerks open, knocking into my back. I whirl around and throw my weight against it, slamming it closed. I lock it.

Aurora continues to shriek as the person on the other side pounds on the door. "Ms. Vincent?" they yell from the hallway. "What's going on in there? Open this door!" They bang again, the vibrations rattling my back and my brain.

Aurora's back arches, and she gasps as if all the air's vacating her lungs. I lunge for the armchair and grunt and strain as I slide it in front of the door. I drop to my knees beside Aurora, who's still thrashing, and try to hold on to her, but her body jerks into the air, knocking me back.

I watch in shock as Aurora's body, suspended in midair above me, convulses and rolls like a log in water. She moans, sounding just at the edge of another screaming fit. But she falls silent at the same time she stops spinning, facedown. Then she drops to the floor with an *oompf* that startles me.

I roll her onto her back and call her name. Her eyelids flutter and her head lolls, but at least she's breathing and doesn't appear to be hurt. I take her cool, slender hand in mine, and her eyes pop open, revealing beautiful streaks of mahogany, chestnut, and ocher that look very much alive—quite the opposite of the horror I saw in them before.

She stares into my eyes, her own spilling over. "Thank you," she murmurs.

I smile, blinking back my own tears. My breath—and gravity—both leave me for a second.

The spell worked. Magic hasn't forsaken me after all. I did it.

Oz used magic to strip me of my power—just as someone else had done to Aurora. But tonight, Aurora and I both snatched our autonomy back. I saved her life. The mere thought fills my chest with the warmth of the Sun.

Magic and I have collided yet again, not like scorned lovers or sworn enemies but as dear friends. A friend I'd lost for a while but somehow found again. I know so much more now than I did when we first parted ways. I gave magic too much power, surrendered too much of my control. I've learned that magic can consume you if you allow yourself to become lost in it.

But I'm seizing every fucking bit of my power back.

I am the granddaughter of a legendary Queen.

Magic exists in me, but it is not me. I've finally reset the balance, relit my spark.

But we don't have time to celebrate, because the sounds of multiple voices and a heavy set of keys jingling comes from the hallway outside the room.

"We need to get out of here," I tell her, but she's too groggy to respond beyond a nod.

I bolt to the bathroom, blow out the candles, tip the wet wax into a compostable container that I intend on burying later, and shove them into my bag along with the rest of my belongings. When I come back out, Aurora's sitting up, one hand to her head, straining to pull herself together.

Leaving the way I came is no longer an option. I check the window for a latch, but there's none. I search for something to break the glass but find nothing. We're trapped.

The lock clicks, and the door jerks open and slams into the armchair. "Aurora! Please open the door, it's Dr. Jones. We only want to make sure you're okay."

I clench my jaw and stare around the room for an idea or something, but I'm stuck. Whoever put Aurora here intended for her to stay here, so there's no way I'm trusting the center's staff. My hands tremble and I hug myself. *Dammit.* I've come too far for everything to fall apart now.

Icy fingers take hold of my leg, and I look down to see Aurora clinging to me. I help her to her feet, and she staggers a bit, but grabs on to my shoulder.

She takes a slow, deep breath in and blows it out. "I can help," she mutters as she turns to the window and places both hands on the pane.

"What are you doing?" I ask.

She shuts her eyes and mumbles something inaudible under her breath, which seems to be doing nothing until I notice the moonbeams twisting down from the sky to pool on the window. She's harvesting raw moonlight, just like in her Instagram video. But how can she do this with no mark? Once the entire pane is covered in light, she stands back and raps her knuckles against it once.

The moonlight vibrates like the diaphragm of a speaker, filling the room with a dull hum and drowning out the shouts of the staff still fighting to get inside. The vibrations intensify, and so does the hum, until the glass shatters outward, blasting the grass outside her window with shards.

Aurora throws on her sweat suit and tosses her bathrobe over the windowsill. I help her out and climb after her. Broken glass crunches underfoot, and I dip out of sight right before the door slams open, flinging the armchair backward. The voices of the people who flood into her room turn to distant echoes as we tear across the flower beds and back to the parking lot.

We dive into my car, and I peel out of my sparking spot.

Once we're a safe distance away from Chateau des Saints, I make a fist, press the edge of it to my lips, and hold it up to the glowing Moon lording over the dark sky.

"Thank you," I whisper to my ancestors.

THIRTY-SIX

CRISTINA

I drive us far away from Chateau des Saints and hide my car in a crowded Target parking lot. Night has fallen, and despite the store closing soon, people still pour inside.

Aurora Vincent sits in my passenger seat, peering out the windows as if she expects someone to break in and snatch her away any moment. Reminds me of how Oz made me feel, which hollows my chest.

"It's okay," I tell her. "You're safe with me." And I feel the same with her.

"I know," Aurora says, finally relaxing, but only slightly. Her confident, sultry voice hews through the nervous air between us now that the rush of adrenaline has begun to ebb. "You're Marie's daughter." When I nod, she asks, "How'd you find me?"

I tell her the whole story, beginning with finding the hex doll in Mama's bedroom and ending with uncrossing her. Once I'm done, she takes my hand, which startles me at first, and gives it a long, loving squeeze. I smile and place my other hand on top of hers.

"It was me who delivered the envelope to your father," she confirms.

"Why didn't you just tell him what you'd found right then?"

She looks down, but I catch a glimpse of the terror in her eyes. "I was waiting on one final piece of evidence that would tie everything together before I delivered it all to your mother. But shortly after I uncovered the lead, everything changed. I believed I was in danger, but it was always only a feeling. Like how your neck prickles when you feel someone's following you to your car, but you turn and no one's there." She heaves a deep sigh that sends a chill rippling across my chest.

"My dad mentioned someone was following him, too, in the days before he died," I say. "Do you have any idea who it might've been?"

Aurora's eyes widen. "Your father died?" She hangs her head when I nod. "I'm so sorry. None of this would've happened had it not been for my brother's idiocy." She grimaces like she just got a taste of something truly foul.

"What do you mean?"

"I wanted to wait until I had everything I needed before I went to your mother, but I was afraid I wouldn't have time. So, I gathered what I had and went to the brewery, but your father said she'd already left and promised to give her the envelope. My plan was to retrieve the final bit of evidence and come by your home later that night to explain everything. But my brother intercepted me first."

"Was Xavier the one who crossed you?"

"Yes." Her jaw clenches. "My own fucking brother."

"Was it because he found out about your investigation?"

She shakes her head. "Before he died, our father asked me not only to continue his investigation into Lenora, but also to carry forward his legacy on the Gen Council." She glances out the window again and drops her gaze. "But I made a grave mistake in letting my guard down around Xavier.

"My brother had been at odds with our father for some time. It was no secret that Xavier lusted for power, much like Lenora Savant, who'd become his business partner and mentor." She frowns as if Lenora's name sours in her mouth. "Our father didn't want the Gen Priest's seat to pass to Xavier after he died, lest my brother abuse the power that came along with it. So, he wrote a final decree that his succession would skip Xavier and pass to me." She huffs a deep sigh—I know that particular brand of tired very well. "I only wish he hadn't revealed his wishes to Xavier before he died."

Aurora's story enrages me all over again. So many people have suffered because of others' lust for power and control. Lenora Savant. Xavier Vincent. Oz.

"The night I was supposed to meet with your mother," continues Aurora, "my brother insisted we sit for a discussion about the future of our family. I should've known by how adamant he was that he was up to something. In toast, he poured two glasses of wine, from the same bottle, and drank with me. I lost consciousness shortly after and woke up in Chateau des Saints, helpless to do anything. Imprisoned within the confines of my own mind." A tear streams down her cheek. "I thought I was going to die in that awful place. I would have, had it not been for you."

I take her hand again. "We have each other now, and we're going to fix this together."

She wipes her tears and smiles.

"I believe Lenora framed my grandmother for Alexis's murder to steal her throne and also might've had help from the white mages," I tell her.

"You're correct."

Aurora's words crash into the cliffs of my mind. I *fucking* knew it.

"What did you find out?" I ask.

"I'll show you," she says. "But first, we have to go back to my home."

I throw her a tentative look. "Umm . . . where your brother, the person who crossed you and stuck you in a sanatorium, lives?"

Aurora nods.

"Well . . . I guess we don't have another choice," I say. "Just tell me how to get there."

"I've been wanting to ask," I say after Aurora directs me to turn in to her neighborhood, which is a secluded subdivision of mammoth homes with plenty of tree-lined acreage to go along with each. "How were you able to harvest raw moonlight with no mark?"

"My father taught me magic not long after I learned to walk. I've known magic as long as I've known language, but my connection to my father also plays a significant part in it."

"But magic isn't genetic."

"Well, it is in a way, isn't it?" She points for me to make a right at a stop sign. "We draw power from our ancestors who became gods at the end of their mortal lives, which they spent calling upon their ancestors to aid them in magic. The stronger your family's connection to magic, the stronger you are."

I'm speechless for a moment. "I hadn't thought about it like that."

This girl is brilliant. Maybe she can teach me some of those cool moonlight techniques I saw on her Instagram. I'm even angrier that her own brother would violate her in such a cold and brutal way. Guys like Oz and Xavier need to be taught a lesson, and karma isn't working fast enough for me.

We drive by Aurora's home, a large two-story brick colonial with a blanket of leafy green vines draped over the entire front face. Most of the windows in the front are dark, but the porch light draws an army of moths to its yellow glow. Xavier's SUV sits in front of the house in the circular driveway that's bordered by precisely man-icured hedges. I park on the street at the neighbors' house and we get out.

Aurora leads me among the shadows, through the gate of a tall wooden fence, and into the backyard. Lights illuminate the surface of a pool, which reflects wavy patterns onto the back of the house. The blinds and curtains are open to the dim kitchen and sitting room just beyond the patio. The lights in the kitchen come on and Aurora yanks me back into the shadows, where we crouch behind the wide trunk of a tree near the fence.

Xavier Vincent, with his midnight-black hair and full, thick beard, passes in front of the window on his way to the cupboard. He pulls down a glass and fills it from a decanter. Aurora's skin tone is much fairer than his, which I guess is the result of being holed up inside Chateau des Saints for a year.

Aurora taps my shoulder and points to an old shed toward the back of the yard, which sits near a small garden overtaken by weeds. Once Xavier sits at the counter with his drink, we head for the shed in a low crouch. The moment we step in front of the double doors, blinding floodlights snap on, wrenching away our cover of darkness. Aurora throws the door open and we dart inside.

A thick layer of dust and cobwebs coats almost everything in the old garden shed, and I have to cover my nose and mouth to stifle a sneeze. The air inside this place also reeks of gas and oil, which come from the red containers gathered in one corner. In the center of the shed sits a large workbench, whose surface is completely hidden by weathered boxes, faded containers, hand tools, and other random things.

"I forgot about those damn lights," she says. "And the switch is inside the house, so we'll have to hurry."

"Did Xavier see us?" I ask.

"I don't think so. Can you keep watch?"

I nod and slide into her place to peek through the cracked doors.

Aurora kneels at the back of the bench to plunder the bottom shelf, which is likewise a chaotic mess of Lorenzo's forgotten belongings. She drags out a metal tackle box and opens it. Inside are small gardening tools and a variety of seed packets labeled and separated in a manner quite contrary to the mess of the rest of the shed. She lifts the bottom tray and pulls out a folded brown envelope.

"This is everything we need," she says.

I choke back another sneeze. "Okay, let's get out of here."

A slender black cat with frighteningly bright eyes slips through the crack in the door, winds through my legs, and slinks straight up to Aurora. She kneels to scratch the cat's head, and it purrs. "Hello, Phillippe. How I've missed you."

Movement outside draws my attention, and when I look again, my heartbeat skips. "Shit," I cry. "Xavier's coming."

I duck behind the workbench. "Quick, back here," I whisper-shout to Aurora.

She crouches beside me with Phillippe in her arms, both of us watching the doors and praying Xavier doesn't come in here.

"Hello?" he calls from right outside. "Is someone there?"

The door's hinges creak as he pulls it open. He stands in the entrance and squints against the dark, and I hold my breath. "Who's there?"

Phillippe leaps out of Aurora's arms and darts around the bench. His back arches and he hisses at Xavier, who scowls in return. "Fucking cat," he snarls.

His phone rings, and he answers immediately.

"Dr. Jones," he says. "It's late—is everything okay?" He pauses a moment, and in the quiet, I hear the muffled sound of someone's frantic voice on the other end. "She did *what*?! Okay, I'll be right there." He hangs up and bolts back inside the house.

Aurora and I let out a collective sigh of relief.

She scoops up Phillippe again, and we hurry back to the fence just in time to see Xavier's SUV speed off into the night.

Once we're back inside my car, Aurora opens the envelope, Phillippe curled up and purring softly in her lap. The paper crinkles as loud as my heart beating in my ears as she pulls it out.

"What is it?" I ask, my heart still jackhammering.

She opens a folded sheet of paper, revealing a handwritten letter signed by Lorenzo. "My father's decree for my succession to his seat on the Gen Council." She sets it aside and hands me two documents.

The moment I realize what these are, I want to shout to the spirit realm. "Insurance policies," I say. "How'd you get these?"

"My best friend Remi Prince's dad happens to be running for mayor, and the private investigator his dad has on staff doesn't mind doing favors for the right price."

I wonder how much a private investigator costs and if that's something a teenager can normally afford, but I realize I'd be nowhere without this information, so I don't question it.

"Alexis's autopsy report said that blue Mashahir fibers were found on her body. And Mashahir are the extremely rare and expensive kind of rugs someone would definitely want to insure." I tap the dates on the policies and smile to myself at Aurora's sheer genius, also wondering why I hadn't thought of this. "Bethesda DeLacorte had an insurance policy for a blue Mashahir rug that was transferred to Lenora Savant on the day Alexis's body was found at St. John's Cathedral."

"Have you figured it all out yet?" Aurora's eyes shine despite the dark inside my car, and I hear nothing aside from our excited breaths in the silence following her question.

"I think so," I say. "Alexis was pissed that my grandmother refused to teach her gen magic, so she joined the white mages, who I assume weren't very fond of her either, given her connection to the mayor and their firm stance on not mixing magic and politics. This was the same reason Bethesda also hated my grandmother— because of my grandmother's ongoing beef with Alexis's dad. Now this is where I have to make some assumptions—" I glance at Aurora. "Please correct me if you disagree."

She nods.

"Both Bethesda and Lenora benefited by murdering Alexis and framing my grandmother. Bethesda effectively squashed any potential threat to the magical community from the local government, and Lenora got to steal my grandmother's throne. And just in case her plan backfired, Bethesda must've 'gifted' the rug to Lenora to rid her home of the most damning piece of evidence in Alexis's murder."

Aurora sits back, a satisfied look on her face. "All facts."

I've done it.

I've finally gotten what I need to take Lenora down.

THIRTY-SEVEN

CRISTINA

It's only late morning and the Sun has already turned the pavement into the Scorch.

I'm relieved to dip inside the Bean before I start broiling. The comforting smell and rumble of grinding coffee beans meets me before I notice Clem waving from one of the booths toward the back.

His eyes are puffy, and the rest of his face is heavy with grief, a stark contrast from the usual playful smile he wears. I feel bad for being happy when my brother is visibly hurting.

"Hey," I say as I slide into the booth, and gesture at the coffee. "Is this for me?"

He nods. "Oat milk white mocha, one pump of peppermint, extra shot of espresso, no whip."

I smile, and he forces one to match. "Thank you."

He dips his head. "What was this urgent development you had to tell me about right away?"

"We'll get to that, but I want to know how you're doing first."

He hugs himself and thinks for a moment before saying, "I'm okay."

"You don't look okay—"

"Cris—"

"At least tell me where you've been."

He sighs and slides to the end of the booth. "I'm not doing this today."

"Wait." I grab his hand, and he sits back down. "I'm sorry. I'm worried about you."

"I'm fine," he says. "I'm dealing with a lot right now."

"Did you at least take your anxiety meds with you?"

He nods. "I appreciate that you care, but I need time. I promise I'm safe and I'm coming back soon. Please, just trust me."

I sigh and slump in my seat. I'm watching life chip away at my brother, but I'm powerless to help him. This isn't my problem to solve, but how do I sit here and watch him suffer and do nothing?

"I'm always here for you," I say. "I'm not going anywhere. Ever."

"I know." He flicks the edge of the cardboard sleeve on his cup. "I love him, Cris."

"I could tell." I want to ask so many questions, but I know he won't open up until he's ready—we have that in common. "It's not fair, and you don't deserve any more pain. I hope you know that."

He nods again.

"I'm sorry for being such a shitty sister. I shouldn't have gone through your stuff. I was so worried and wanted to know what was going on, but I should've waited until you were ready to talk."

"It's okay. My brain felt like someone had turned the room upside down. I couldn't make sense of anything and didn't want to talk about it."

I move to his side of the booth and put my arms around him. He doesn't complain like usual; he just sits there and lets me hug him. If only I could off-load some of his burden through hugs alone.

"I'm sorry I left you to deal with Aurora by yourself," he says when I finally release him.

I shake my head. "You were right. I needed to do it on my own." I grin at him. "And I did."

His eyes widen. "You conjured?"

I nod, and he high-fives me.

"You better werk," he says. "You really did it."

I share the story of breaking into Chateau des Saints to see Aurora, uncrossing her, going to her home to find the evidence she'd hidden in her father's old gardening shed, and that now she's waiting for me in the old Montaigne house, which has been un-inhabited since Justin moved onto his riverboat. Clem sits back in shocked silence when I tell him about the evidence Aurora collected and my theory behind Alexis's death and Lenora's and Bethesda's motives. Now that magic is back in my life, it feels right again. Magic makes me feel powerful. I can understand why Lenora wants it all to herself. But I won't let her have it.

"It's like history repeating," Clem says. "Grandma Cristine and Lenora. You and Valentina. Intergenerational bestie drama."

I smile despite myself, but it fades fast. "I still can't believe all this mess started thirty years ago because a white lady couldn't deal with someone telling her no."

"Oh, I can believe it."

"Please come home," I say. "You don't have to stay, but I want you there with me, to help finish this."

"Maybe," he says, "but only if you do one thing for me."

"What is it?"

He leans closer and raises a brow. "Admit you're the Black Nancy Drew."

We both laugh.

Lenora Savant has taken so much from us, played god with all our lives for decades, and that is a trespass I'm not willing to easily forgive. But before we can do anything, we have to reveal what we've uncovered to Mama and Aunt Ursula. It's late evening by the time Clem and I assemble them both at home in the dining room. They seem nervous about the occasion. Odessa joins us as well, though she doesn't wear as much of her emotion on her face.

When I bring Aurora into the dining room and introduce her, everyone falls silent. Both Mama and Ursula stare at me and Clem with expressions of bewilderment and concern.

I explain everything that's happened over the past few weeks, right up until last night, when I uncrossed Aurora and helped her escape Chateau des Saints. Mama scowls at me for disobeying her order to not meddle right up until that point in the story; then she and Aunt Ursula both sit up a little taller, prideful smiles playing on their lips.

Aurora holds every ear captive with her part of the tale—the details of her father's initial investigation and dying request, her encounter with Dad, and Xavier's grand betrayal that prevented her from ever speaking to Mama.

"One thing I have not been able to figure out through all of this is, how come the hex doll didn't work?" Mama asks. "Lenora's no novice and I hadn't conjured any protection at the time. If she wanted me dead, how am I still alive?"

"Not even I have an answer for that," says Ursula. "It's times like this I wish our mama was here."

Mama takes a deep breath. "When I was thirteen, I went to see the most powerful medium in all of New Orleans. She claimed to have a direct line to the spiritual realm, but not even she could contact Mama's spirit."

Ursula looks surprised. "You never told me that."

"Truth be told, I was ashamed," Mama says. "You all depended on me so much. I couldn't let you find out how scared I was." She hangs her head and sighs. "I just wanted to hear Mama's voice one last time. For her to tell me everything was gonna be okay."

Ursula sniffs and looks away, and the room falls silent. Odessa pulls a handkerchief from her pocket to wipe her eyes. But my rage intensifies. I almost lost my mama, too—because Lenora keeps spinning the cycle of trauma for my family. Death is a consequence too decent for someone like her.

"What should we do now?" I ask, breaking apart the depressing silence.

"I'm not sure," Mama says. "We certainly can't trust the police, not after what happened to your dad. Nor can we trust anyone on the Gen Council. That's what got me in this mess to begin with."

Ursula glowers at Mama. "What are you talking about?" Her eyes widen as Mama reveals how she'd gone to Eveline to try to appeal to her to remove Lenora from the throne. "Now it all makes sense." She stares at Mama in disappointment. "Why didn't you let me help you?"

Mama narrows her eyes at Ursula. "I'd just lost my husband and I wasn't going to lose my sister, too—or anyone else I cared about."

"Arguing about the past isn't going to help us," I interject. I've worked too hard to let them squander everything with their drama. "We should pray to Papa Eshu for guidance."

Clem beams at me, and I ignore him. I'm still not absolutely certain I had nothing to do with Dad's death, but it's clear to me now that magic and the gods aren't my enemy.

"It never hurts to ask the gods for help," says Ursula. "And should we need, Black Wolf is always one summons away."

Mama cuts her eyes at Ursula. "We will call upon Eshu." She opens the conjuring cabinet and removes the jar of crossroads dirt and four peace candles, then raises a brow at me. "I expect you'll replenish my candles and other supplies you've borrowed."

"Yes, ma'am," I say, my cheeks heating.

She spreads the crossroads dirt in the shape of a cross on the table and sets the four white candles at each end. Clem tosses her a box of matches from inside the cabinet, and she lights the candles.

Ursula fishes several small sample bottles of Tru Reserve from her purse and sets them on the table, and Clem dashes to his room and returns with a cigar to add to the offering. Mama fixes him with a stern look, until he assures her that he only had it for offering purposes.

Odessa removes a small hemp sack filled with coffee beans from the pocket of her dress. "I made this to offer in prayer this evening." She chuckles to herself and sets it on the table next to the other items. "Guess the gods must've blessed me with the gift of foresight today."

We all hold hands, Clem on one side of me and Mama on the other, in a semicircle around the table.

I speak up before Mama can begin the prayer. "May I lead us?"

She smiles. "Of course."

I clear my throat so I can project my voice with the same bold confidence as her, as I imagine Grandma Cristine also did so many years ago. "Papa Eshu! I beseech ye! The souls gathered around this offering call upon you and our ancestors for spiritual guidance regarding those who seek to destroy us."

As I stand with my family, a warm feeling flows through my hands that are connected with Mama's and Clem's, which reminds me of the rush that follows after guzzling an energy drink.

"Please heed our call and guide us on the proper path toward reclaiming all that has been stolen from us," I intone, then make a fist with my left hand and kiss the end closest to me. "Thank you," I tell Eshu and the rest of my ancestors as I raise my fist. Everyone does the same.

I pull Mama and Aurora aside, while Aunt Ursula and Clem slip into their own conversation. "Until all this is done, is it okay if Aurora and her cat, Phillippe, stay with us?"

Mama turns to Aurora. "Is that what you want?"

"Our father left the house equally between my brother and me, but until all this is sorted, I think I'll be safer here"—she glances at me—"with friends."

My heart swims. I hadn't considered I'd gain a new friend in Aurora through this. Admittedly, it feels scary to start a new friendship right now, but I get the impression Aurora's nothing like Valentina.

"Okay, then I'll ask Odessa to prepare the guest room for you." Mama squeezes Aurora's hand. "I'm sure Lorenzo's watching you with the rest of the ancestors, all with big smiles on their faces."

"Thank you, Ms. Trudeau," says Aurora.

Odessa takes Aurora upstairs to the guest room, leaving me, Clem, Mama, and Aunt Ursula in the dining room.

"Anyone besides me have a taste for bread pudding?" asks Mama.

"It's a little late for baking, no?" says Clem.

Mama tuts under her breath. "It's never too late for baking."

"Now you know I can't turn down your bread pudding," adds Ursula, "no matter what it does to my thighs."

Mama laughs. "You have our mother to thank for those ballistics, darling, not me."

We gather in the kitchen to help Mama cook, and for the first time in what seems like forever, our house feels like the home it was so many years ago before everything went to shit. Mama and Aunt Ursula are talking and laughing with each other again, and even Clem maintains a smile for longer than a few fleeting seconds, something I was afraid I'd never see from him again.

Once the bread pudding is in the oven, Ursula and Clem disappear to the patio together, leaving me and Mama alone in the kitchen. She leans on the other side of the island, reading something on her phone. I spread my fingers on the counter in front of me and stare at the brown skin of my hands. I never thought these hands would ever conjure again—

"You okay?"

"Yes," I say, snapping back to reality, "just thinking."

She sets her phone facedown. "About what?"

"I, um . . ." Something prods me to tell the truth about the Scales of Justice and release myself from that final burden, but I'm not able to push the words to the forefront. I might've nearly cleared Grandma's name, but my "innocence" is still in question. I wish there was a way I could know once and for all—was Dad's death my fault or not?

"How is it you're always able to be calm when the world is burning down around us?" I ask Mama, slightly jealous and over this constant feeling of unease that's been hovering far too long.

She chuckles under her breath. "I'm glad you think I'm calm, because I actually feel like I'm losing my mind. You don't often wear your feelings on the outside either."

I sit up and pull my hands into my lap. Maybe she's right.

"My entire life, I've felt stuck in the wrong place," she tells me. "I dragged myself through college and tried miserably at making a career of running our family businesses, but none of that made me happy. When I was a little girl, my mama told me that as Queen, she wanted to build a legacy based on empathy and respect and community. And my dream of taking up your grandmother's work died along with her, and nothing can replace that. When I think that not only did someone take away my future, but also my husband—your father—I am filled with unfathomable rage."

Even at her angriest, I've never seen Mama in a state of rage—and something tells me I don't ever want to.

"But no matter how furious I may be," she continues, "I will not trade one life for another, nor will I do anything to put my children or sisters in danger. I want to take Mama's throne from those despicable twats more than anything in this realm and the next, but we must be smart about how we go about it—far too much is at stake."

I understand her caution, but that's where we differ. I don't want anyone else to die either, but I refuse to stand by while Lenora knocks us down like chess pieces.

The doorbell rings and someone pounds hard on the door, nearly startling me off my stool.

Mama looks at me curiously. "You expecting someone?"

"No . . ."

She and I go to the foyer, and I stand behind her as she opens the front door. A tall man with rich, dark brown skin dressed in a crisp black suit with a black hat low on his head, covering his eyes, stands on the porch. He removes his hat, revealing a friendly enough face, though he doesn't smile. He taps his onyx cane with worried impatience.

"May I help you?" asks Mama.

"It's so good to see you alive and well, Marie."

Mama looks surprised. "I'm sorry, but who are you?"

I step beside Mama to get a better look, and his dark eyes fall on me and linger for an eerie moment. "It's quite rude to summon someone, especially the Guardian of the Crossroads and Father of

Moon Magic, and then make him stand on the front porch like a misplaced garden gnome."

Mama stands aside and clutches her hands over her heart, and I take an incredulous step back. I must've heard him wrong.

The man steps inside and his eyes rove over the interior of our home. "I do like what you've done with the place."

"Oh, now who's this?" asks Ursula as she steps into the foyer, Clem on her heels.

"Papa Eshu?" I murmur as I close the door behind him.

"In the flesh, or so to speak," he says.

Ursula and Clem don matching looks of disbelief, and Papa Eshu stares into each of our faces with a firm expression. He lifts his right hand to show us the image of the full Moon emblazoned on the underside of his wrist, which resembles a birthmark that glows with a faint blue light.

The mark of the gods. It's really him.

"You know, most conjurers are more excited for a visit from me so soon after an offering," he adds. "If you summoned me by accident or you no longer require my assistance—" He points his thumb at the door. "—I can be on my way as I do have many pressing matters to attend to."

"No! Please!" I cry, drawing everyone's attention. "I led the prayer. I'm sorry. It's just—"

He waves away my explanation, then makes an exaggerated show of sniffing the air. "What *is* that divine aroma?"

"Homemade bread pudding with a Tru Reserve glaze," answers Mama, still blinking with disbelief that she's talking with a real god right now. "Can I tempt you?"

Papa Eshu grins, clutching his opulent cane in both hands. "Now, *that* is what I call an offering!" He makes his way to the kitchen despite a strong limp.

"I'll show you the way," Mama says, hurrying ahead of him.

He chuckles. "No need. I remember, though this place does look quite different now. I like it."

Gooseflesh rises on my arms. He's been here before. Did he visit our grandmother when she was Queen? Have any other gods been to our home?

On the way to the kitchen, Papa Eshu detours into the dining room. He doesn't touch the switch, but the lights pop on the moment he enters. Clem nudges me and gives an incredulous look that I return. I know. I can't believe it either.

Eshu takes each of his gifts, pausing to inhale the scents of the coffee beans and cigar before pocketing them. When he's done, he limps to the kitchen and takes a seat at one end of the island.

Mama removes the bread pudding from the oven, beaming with confidence because she knows it's fire. She'd found the recipe in one of Odessa's old cookbooks and tweaked it a bit, and Dad had come up with the bourbon glaze, which is best when made with Tru Reserve. Her bread pudding is definitely a dessert fit for the gods.

I stand off to the side between Aunt Ursula and Clem, who are both uncharacteristically silent. I guess an impromptu visit from Papa Eshu can be slightly disorienting.

"Would you care for something to drink while the bread pudding cools a bit?" asks Mama.

"I'd love to have some of that bourbon Black Wolf can't stop raving about." He throws Ursula a knowing smile, to which she responds with a nervous cough. His smile fades and when he speaks again, it's with a grave tone. "Take care, dear Ursula. Black Wolf is not one you should find yourself spending an inordinate amount of time with. Eventually, he takes more than bourbon."

Clem sucks in a sharp breath that I don't miss. Both he and Ursula look uncomfortable, which makes me wonder if they've had dealings with Black Wolf, and more importantly—about what.

All minor gods were once people, just like us. Even in godhood, they each maintain their own desires and motives. Eshu's warning is a frightening reminder that not every ancestor wants the best for us, so we must be careful what energies we invite into our lives.

Ursula looks rattled, her mouth opening and closing while she tries to find the appropriate response, which means she understands, too. She simply nods and stands quiet like a kid in time-out.

Mama pours Eshu a double of Tru Reserve, neat—per his request—and sets the glass in front of him.

He sniffs the liquor and raises his brows, impressed. He takes a sip, rolls it across his tongue, and swallows. He grins, then drains the glass. "This is by far the most exquisite bourbon I have ever tasted," he says as she pours him another. "It is truly magnificent!" He looks at Mama, who's moved on to cutting servings of bread pudding, and then Ursula. "Why would you ever sell this business?"

Ursula frowns at Mama. "I don't know. Why would we do that, Marie?"

"I . . . well . . ." Mama starts but doesn't find the words to finish.

"It's okay. I think I understand." Eshu's voice is forward, yet soothing, and I wonder if this is how he always sounds or if this is just the voice that goes with this particular skin suit.

Clem approaches tentatively. "Papa Eshu, I pray to you—"

"—every day," finishes Eshu. "I heard every single one."

Clem frowns, which makes my skin tingle with dread. "Then why'd you never answer?"

Eshu sighs and contemplates his response for a long while. "My silence didn't mean I'd forsaken you. I couldn't help until you *both* were on board." His eyes shift to me, and I narrow mine.

"What?" asks Clem.

"He was waiting for me . . . to come back to magic," I announce, burying my anger.

God or no, I don't appreciate Eshu invalidating my brother like that—and also giving Clem yet another reason to be mad with me.

"But what about me?" Clem pokes his chest with his thumb. "I never turned away. Don't I matter?"

My mouth tastes like ash, because here's yet another thing I've taken from him. I wish now more than ever that I'd trusted him from the beginning. Maybe I would've never turned my back on magic, and we could've both avoided a lot of pain.

"Of course you matter!" Eshu has the gall to sound offended. "You *and* your sister. You're different, yet similar—like the Sun and the Moon, working in unison, pushing and pulling all the intricate moving parts of our vast magical world. You two shared a womb, the closest connection you'll ever share with another person. This is just as much Cristina's story as it is yours, Clement."

Clem's expression softens, but I'm still skeptical. Something about choosing when to answer prayers seems a bit self-serving, even for a god, but I keep my mouth shut.

Eshu gestures for us to come closer, and we do, though my heart beats harder with each step. Even being so near to him in his human form feels overwhelming. He practically emanates divine energy, as if he was born from the magical core of the Moon. There's probably no limit to his power, which is as frightening as it is fascinating.

He lifts Clem's chin and stares into his eyes. Clem's breath hitches at Eshu's touch. "Hmm . . . You are on a dark road, my boy. But it is no less the right one, yeah?"

Clem's voice trembles slightly. "Sometimes I don't know."

Eshu nods once, still focused on Clem. "In time you will."

"When?" asks Clem.

"I'm afraid my concept of time and yours are vastly different as I've dispensed with far more of it than you. Do not fret, my boy. Kings are not born overnight. They take time, if they're to be made just right—like your mother's fantastic-smelling bread pudding."

Clem smiles weakly. "Okay."

But Papa Eshu is wrong. My brother doesn't want to be a king. He just wants to be whole again, to not feel like he deserves to be deserted by everyone he loves.

Eshu turns to me, and when he stares into my eyes, I'm flooded with the sensation of falling upside down into a bottomless pit. I'm surprised I manage to keep my balance.

"Something's weighing quite heavily on you." His eyes are haunting and black, but the whites are bright and splotchy, reminding me of the surface of the Moon.

"I, umm . . ." The tears come before I can get another word out. Heat rushes to my cheeks, and I swipe away my sudden, unwanted rush of emotion.

I'm pissed at Papa Eshu for evoking these feelings in me, but I also realize he's the only person who can give me the answer I've been seeking since the start of my journey. And it's going to eat me from the inside out if I don't address it.

I take a deep breath in and out. "Was it my fault? The spell?"

Clem eyes me curiously, but I focus on only Papa Eshu. Now is my time to find out the truth.

He sighs and puts a gentle hand on my shoulder. "There is no blood on your hands, Cristina."

My body sags with the weight of the breath I release, and I have to grab hold of the counter's edge to steady myself. The elephant that's been sitting on my chest for a year finally stands up, and I can breathe again. Even the first bit of air I take in after feels fresher, different. I want to scream with relief, but I settle for hugging myself instead. More tears come, but I'm okay with it this time.

Because I'm free.

I'd subconsciously prepared to carry this guilt with me to the next realm . . . but Eshu says it was never mine to carry. All that time. But I'm free now. The Scales of Justice didn't take Dad. His death wasn't my fault. Magic never betrayed me.

I'm free.

But wait . . . if Dad's death wasn't my fault, that must mean . . .

"So, did it work? The Scales of Justice?" I feel every eye in the room boring into me.

Eshu lifts one of his thick brows. "That's one answer you'll have to find on your own."

I wish magic wasn't so damn frustrating. Though I am glad to have my friend back.

He smiles and takes my and Clem's hands. "My children, my remarkable, tenacious, beautiful Black children, you both have an inconceivable journey ahead of you, which is going to strip you down to the worst parts of yourselves; but by the end of it, you stand to come out far better than either of you could've ever dreamed you'd be. But it is imperative that you get—and remain—on one accord. So much is depending on you two."

Mama sets a bowl of bread pudding with a healthy scoop of vanilla ice cream drizzled with bourbon glaze in front of Papa Eshu and wrings her hands. "Are my children in danger?"

What happened over the last year was bad enough, and I've already been stripped down to nothing but muscle and sinew. How could things possibly get worse? I can't sign up for more pain, and certainly neither can my brother.

Eshu takes a big whiff of the dessert and closes his eyes. "Oh, this is cut straight from the heavens."

"Please," Mama pleads, leaning in to get his attention.

"Danger has attached itself to your family like your own shadows." He rears back and looks around the room. "Now's probably the time you'll want to keep your family close."

Ursula and Mama swap one of the same worried looks as Clem and me. Our family can't peacefully coexist in the same room for five minutes. We're all going to die.

Papa Eshu tastes the bread pudding and coos with pleasure. He eats fast, showering Mama with muffled compliments all the while, but she barely smiles.

When he finishes, he rubs his bulging stomach and checks his watch. "Oh! It's nearly midnight." He looks at Clem. "See what I mean? I lost track of time and now I'm afraid there's not much left." He gets down from the stool and points to the dishes. "Would you like me to clear these?"

"I'll take care of it," Mama says. "What exactly do we not have much time for?"

"You'll see." He picks up his cane and grabs his hat. "Come with me."

Mama and Ursula follow him out the front door, and Clem and I trail behind them.

"What the fuck is going on?" Clem whispers to me.

My heart races. "No idea."

We walk at a steady pace to the large willow at the crossroads. Thick, blue-gray clouds dominate the sky, hiding the Moon and making it hard to see where I step.

Papa Eshu stops in front of the tree and turns to face us. Mama, Ursula, Clem, and I stand shoulder-to-shoulder, and I hold my breath.

He looks at his watch again and sighs. "Eleven fifty-two already. My sincerest apologies. I hadn't realized I'd taken up so much time enjoying that wonderful bourbon and bread pudding. I'm afraid I can only open a rip between realms for another seven minutes. All rips must close by midnight for reasons I'd rather not get into right now."

"What's going on?" asks Mama.

"You can come out now," Eshu calls over his shoulder.

A woman . . . no . . . a spirit, judging by the way her form wavers softly around the edges, steps from behind the tree. Her hair ends in long black curls, tossed over her shoulders onto the front of her plain white dress. The skin of her round face is tawny and warm, just like mine and Mama's. She's older, but no less gorgeous.

When she passes Eshu, he leans close and mutters, "Remember our deal."

She nods, and her eyes glisten in the gentle light of her form as she stares longingly at each of our faces. I glance at the others, but no one seems to have noticed the exchange between her and Eshu.

Ursula's mouth falls open and her tears stream.

Mama takes a shaky step forward and reaches out. "Mama?"

My grandmother nods, and her face splits into a teary smile. Mama grabs her hand, but it passes through. She looks back up at Grandma, disappointment dragging the smile from her face.

"I'm so sorry," Grandma says, and turns to Ursula.

"I can't believe it's you," Ursula mumbles, her cheeks sopping wet.

"It's me, my love," says Grandma with a smile. She moves to me and Clem and clasps her hands in front of her, deep longing welling in her eyes. "My precious grandbabies. Oh, how I wish I could put my arms around you both."

Clem practically clings to my arm. This all feels like a fever dream.

"Me, too," I say, my voice trembling.

That's my grandmother. Cristine Dupart, no, *Queen* Cristine Dupart. My ancestor.

I never imagined I'd get the chance to see or speak to her, not until my time to cross over to the spiritual realm (which I hope is a long way away). But now she's here, I can't find a single word of appropriate value to say to her. Instead, Clem and I, both ensnared with awe, just stare at her ghostly figure.

Grandma looks around and then turns a confused face to Mama. "Where are the others? Where's my Rosalie, and Desiree, and Jackie?"

"They left," says Mama.

Grandma puts her hands on her hips and glowers at Mama and Ursula. "I am very disappointed in you both. I gave my life to protect you girls, and you will not let it be for nothing. You must not let our family fall apart—it is paramount to your protection. Do you understand?"

"I do, but we haven't—" Mama starts, but Grandma cuts her off.

It's weird watching Mama and Aunt Ursula get scolded by *their* mother.

"We don't have time for excuses," she says. "I expect you to make it right, but that's not why I'm here. There's something of dire importance I must tell you." She looks at me and it feels like being pricked by a million icy needles. "I know what you've been doing, Cristina." I tense, anticipating the sting of her disapproval, but she smiles. "You've made me so proud."

I feel like I'm floating. I never considered that I'd ever get to hear my grandmother, former Queen, say those words to me. I had no idea how much they would mean to me until now.

"It was Lenora all along," I tell her. "She framed you for Alexis Lancaster's murder so she could steal your throne."

Grandma's mouth prunes and her jaw clenches at the news of her best friend's betrayal. "Thirty years in the spiritual realm, and I didn't want to believe what I knew deep down in my heart was true."

"Lenora tried to kill Mama and might've also killed Dad because they were looking into what really happened to Alexis Lancaster," I say. "But Lenora controls the Council and has spies in the police department. Everything I've uncovered might've been for nothing, because I'm not sure how, or if, we can stop her."

Grandma sighs and shakes her head. "This is all my fault."

Her words feel like chilly fingers wrapped around my heart. I know what it's like to carry that kind of guilt and pain. I want to reach out to my grandmother, but I remember it's no use. She's gone.

"Lenora and I had been friends ever since we were little girls, when my mama was Queen," says Grandma. "Lenora had always shown an intense interest in magic, so I taught her everything I knew. Not long after my mama passed and I took the throne, I noticed Lenora's interest in magic warped into a terrifying obsession with power.

"But my focus shifted from Lenora to caring for my family, helping Baptiste run our family's businesses, and leading the Council while the Cardinal of the white mages, Bethesda DeLacorte, grew more and more comfortable threatening me and other members of my community. My main priority became clearly communicating to any magical person, not just the white witches, that any attack on a member of the gen community would bear severe consequences. And that was how Lenora Savant helped me develop the Council's policy regarding blood debts—and that was also when I saw her at her most vicious. I should've never given that woman access to that kind of power. But I'm giving you my blessing to make it right, to recoup our family's blood debt."

"What's a blood debt?" asks Clem.

"Blood for blood," I reply, drawing every eye to me.

Grandma nods. "The only way to put an end to Lenora's wickedness once and for all is to call in the rather large debt she owes us."

Clem and I exchange glances, but I don't share the trepidation I see on his face. It's time people started paying for fucking with our lives—and it's okay if my brother's not quite up to it.

I'll be the reaper for all of us if I have to.

"I knew it all along!" exclaims Ursula, hands on her hips. "And y'all thought I was ridiculous!"

"No one thought that, Ursula," says Mama. "This situation isn't as simple as you make it out to be. Did you forget Lenora might've killed David and almost killed me, too?"

Lenora is extremely dangerous. But that's no reason to let her off the hook and give her more license to keep raining hell down on us.

"She could not harm you—at least, not with magic." Grandma reclaims everyone's attention. "The night Gerald and his mob came to murder me and your grandfather, I left my babies with Odessa and went outside to help Baptiste, but someone knocked me over the head, and when I fell to the ground, they beat me until I lay still then promised they'd take their time with me once they were done tearing my husband apart. While Baptiste fought for his life, I dragged my broken body to the crossroads to call on Papa Eshu, to ask him to open the floodgates of the spiritual realm and protect my family, no matter the price. With my final breath, I finished my prayer, and Papa Eshu answered.

"Fog thick as my mama's favorite winter quilt unrolled across the lawn. La Uroboros grabbed hold of the earth and gave it a great shake, releasing her snake army. They rose from the ground like pus from a wound, and every bastard that'd trespassed onto my estate died, writhing in the fog like the miserable dogs they were. And when I lifted my head again, I was no longer in the natural realm."

Grandma's story gives me goose bumps, along with a myriad of emotions in direct conflict with one another. I'm filled with immeasurable rage at the injustice that's been flung upon us. Sadness from the pain in Grandma's eyes as she tells the story of her and my grandfather's deaths. Pride that I've proven Grandma was not only an incredible conjurer and leader in the magical community, but also fiercely protective of her family—just like me.

And Lenora Savant took her from me.

"That night at the crossroads, I made a deal with Papa Eshu to protect my children," says Grandma. "That protection is strongest when you're all together, but it has been weakened by your petty infighting. That is why Lenora's hex doll only made you ill. At its worst, it would've still taken years to kill you."

A familiar sensation surges through me. I thought I'd felt strange the night all our family came together to conjure Wise John's Moon. I wonder if that was Grandma's magic. I'm awed that the power of her magic held strong for thirty years.

She turns to Ursula. "The same goes for whatever crossing Celeste Richard might've *thought* she put on you."

Ursula presses a hand to her stomach and heaves a shaky breath out. "Are you saying . . . ?"

Grandma nods. "I died so my babies could live. So, live, Ursula."

Her words are like a flame, igniting the adrenaline in my veins. I would give anything to hug her right now. What would it have been like to see her when she was Queen?

"I suggest letting the children be your guide," interjects Eshu. "They've gotten you all this far. Trust that I will come to your aid when you need." He turns back to Mama. "And you have my full support in your bid for the throne, Queen Marie Trudeau."

I grab hold of Clem's hand, which feels clammy inside mine.

Mama could be Queen. Not Gabriela Savant.

Which means that I'm heiress to the throne—not Valentina.

Lenora stole Mama's and my birthrights. That's the only reason

Valentina has the station in life that she loves to lord over anyone unfortunate enough to wander beneath her shadow. But the throne she worships no longer belongs to her family. It's mine. And I'm taking it back.

The sharpened, grave tone of Grandma's voice slices through my reverie. "But there's something else I must warn you about," she says. Eshu cuts his eyes at her, but she continues anyway. "The Moon King is coming for this realm—"

"Cristine," warns Eshu, his eyes narrowed.

She reaches for Clem, but her hands pass through him. "He's touched you already. Clem, baby, you need—"

Eshu snaps his fingers and Grandma disappears in a wisp of otherworldly mist.

My heart drops, and Clem's hands fall to his sides.

"What'd you do?" I cry.

Eshu taps his watch. "I warned you we were limited on time, which is not negotiable. And now I must be off as well." He tips his hat to us. "Good evening." Then he steps around the tree.

I run to the other side, but he's already gone.

Mama frowns at Clem. "Who's touched you?"

He presses a hand to his head and his eyes search the ground as he thinks. "Nobody. I-I don't know what she's talking about."

But I remember.

And it fills me with a dense sense of unease.

"Let's go back inside," says Aunt Ursula. "We clearly have a *lot* to talk about. Cris, can you make us a pot of coffee?"

I nod. Aunt Ursula tugs Mama back up the road to the house, and I hang back with Clem.

"I was scared to tell them," he says, breathless. "I still don't know if I believe it myself."

"I'm sorry I didn't believe you when you first told me about what happened after the car accident," I say. "Who the fuck is the Moon King?"

His eyes darken and he trembles. "I hope you never find out."

I hug him and he lets out a deep breath. "I swear, I'm not going to let anything happen to you. We're done hurting."

He stands back and grins. "So, now you're Wonder Woman?"

I laugh and start the trek back to the house. "Come on. I have to tell you about this wild idea I have."

We ask Mama and Aunt Ursula to convince Justin and Jean-Louise to meet us at the house the next morning, which they do. When the guys arrive, we introduce them to Aurora, and Justin is shocked into a stupor when he sees she's alive and well.

It takes a lot of storytelling and question-answering to get everyone caught up to all that's happened, but as soon as we reach the end, Jean-Louise, who's been quiet and patient the entire time, raises one polite finger. "I don't mean to be rude," he says, "but as enthralling as all this is, why am I here?"

"We have a plan to take back the Gen Council," I tell him. "But if it's going to work, we'll need your help." I nod to Justin. "And your boat."

"What?" His eyes widen. "Why do you need my boat?"

"You're going to absolutely love what we've come up with," Clem interjects, grinning.

Justin hangs his head. "Why does this worry me?"

I share the details of my plan and the roles everyone will play. If we can pull this off, Mama and Aurora will all take their rightful positions on the Council and Justin will be free of Lenora's stranglehold on his life.

After hours of what often devolves into vicious debate, everyone finally agrees on a plan. Night falls by the time we all go our separate ways, each with a long to-do list and sworn to secrecy. I would've preferred to use magic to keep everyone honest, but Mama seems to think we can trust them.

I just hope I don't regret trusting her on this.

The true depth of the risk we're taking is unfathomable. It unsettles my stomach whenever I think about it. We won't be able to come back from this.

Regardless of the outcome, a lot of lives are going to change forever.

With Grandma's and Papa Eshu's blessings, I'm finally calling in Lenora Savant's blood debts.

And in three days, I intend to collect.

PART III

A riot is the language of the unheard.

—DR. MARTIN LUTHER KING, JR.

THIRTY-EIGHT

CLEMENT

THREE DAYS LATER

❧

Tension thick as the storm clouds in the sky above takes up every inch of space between me and Jean-Louise in the backseat of our Uber. My involvement in all this makes him uneasy, but it's too late. We're in this shit together now. And tonight, we're going to get justice for our family and our ancestors.

Cris did it. She cleared Grandma's name and made all this possible. And because of her, I got to talk to Papa Eshu. But now I'm not so sure how I feel about him after he admitted to ignoring my prayers while he waited for Cris to come back to magic.

Our Uber pulls up outside the warehouse, which looks like it's been abandoned for decades. Weeds have grown up through the cracked pavement of the lot like miniature trees, and the only other vehicles there are a black panel van and an old charter bus. A vinyl banner hangs on the side of the bus that reads NOLA ACTORS GUILD.

The driver peers at us curiously in the rearview mirror. "You sure this is the right place?"

Jean-Louise grumbles, "Thank you," grabs his bag, and gets out.

I shoulder my backpack and climb out after him. The car pulls off as thunder rumbles in the distance, and the scent of rain clings to the breeze that tumbles through the deserted lot.

"You should try to be nicer," I tell Jean-Louise. "Your Uber rating matters, dude."

Jean-Louise looks up from his phone with a scowl so deep-set, it looks like the lines on the side of his mouth have been chiseled in stone. "Don't make light of all this, Clem. Against my better judgment, you're balls deep in this shit, so it's time you grew up."

I scowl at the deep crack in the section of pavement between my feet. I may be deep in some shit, but I don't need my face rubbed in it, too.

I follow him around the side of the building to the loading bay, where we take a set of stone steps onto the dock and through the door that's been left open for us.

The inside of the tiny warehouse must've been gutted for quite some time, judging by the thick layers of dust and grime that cover the walls and floor. The space is bare, except for fifty cadavers, lined up in rows of ten and covered in white sheets in the center of the room. A hefty black duffel bag sits at the edge of the row closest to the door.

Jean-Louise kneels and pulls a small propane torch and a branding iron from inside the bag. I recognize the talisman on the end of the iron. A set of concentric circles with other symbols fitted between. It's used for control.

He fires up the torch and holds the brand in the flame until it glows molten red. As we walk down the rows, I flip up the edge of each sheet so he can brand the bottoms of the cadavers' feet with the magical symbol. I turn my nose up at the putrid, sulfurous smell that rises from the sizzling decayed flesh.

When we're done, he fishes a small scroll of parchment tied with a garnet ribbon out of his pocket and slips it into mine. "A protection talisman. Whenever we use necromancy, we open a door between our world and the spiritual realm. What I've given you will ensure nothing slips through that crack and latches on to you."

I nod, even though I almost piss myself. I shiver at the thought of some seductive spirit running its icy fingers along the edges of my soul.

I shrug off my backpack and take out nine ceramic bowls and a cloth sack containing the conjuring powders Jean-Louise mixed before we left home. He draws a series of chalk circles and symbols around the bodies, while I space the bowls along the outside of the circle, pour a little powder in each, and light them. Like a fat cat rising from a midday nap, a turquoise flame unfurls in each bowl.

Jean-Louise lowers to his knees and I do the same next to him. He shuts his eyes and mutters a prayer under his breath, so fast it sounds like he's speaking another language. Outside, dark clouds, filled to bursting, blot out the Sun. A bold wind kicks up, whipping through the interior of the warehouse, and blows out the fires in the bowls.

I grab Jean-Louise's hand to keep from screaming. The interior of the warehouse lights up electric white as lightning streaks across the sky. A crack of thunder follows that rumbles the building. The feet of the body closest to me twitch beneath the blanket. I try to yank away, but Jean-Louise's strong, callused hand grips mine tighter.

"Do not run," he says. "You'll never control something you fear."

I take a deep breath and nod. Jean-Louise doesn't let go of my hand, and I'm glad. He makes me feel safe in the midst of all this dark, scary shit.

Lightning strikes again. Thunder claps at the same time the first body sits bolt upright. The sheet falls away, revealing a brown-skinned man dressed in an old Lakers jersey and cargo shorts. Normal, orange fire springs to life in the bowls, and every other cadaver folds upright at once.

Jean-Louise gets to his feet and I follow suit. One by one at first, then all at once, the reanimated cadavers shuffle to their feet. Their dark eyes stick to me and Jean-Louise, snatching all the air from my chest.

"Do you control them now?" I whisper to him.

He grimaces. "Let's see." He points at one of the larger ones and calls him forward.

The undead shambles for a few seconds like a toddler still getting the hang of walking. Once he's acclimated to being reanimated, he stands up tall and rigid. His bulky frame looks even scarier in the low light with the thunderstorm raging outside. He's dressed in a dusty, wrinkled black suit, like a secret agent who's been through some serious shit.

Jean-Louise holds out his hand to me. I open my backpack and dig out a small, blessed loaf of bread wrapped in cloth. It was easier to make than I thought it'd be. The bread must be prepared under the light of the Moon to anoint it, but we had to improvise since Jean-Louise doesn't have a good view of the sky from his kitchen. I harvested a little raw moonlight and dipped his kitchen lightbulbs in it, which, technically, allowed us to bake the loaf of bread under the "light of the Moon."

I unwrap the blessed bread and hand it to him.

He breaks it in half, pinches off a tiny morsel, and holds it out to the undead man. "If you eat from my hand, you shall abide by it as well."

The undead man's eyes shift to the bit of bread pinched between Jean-Louise's fingers. He lifts a graying hand but stops short of taking the offering. With lightning speed, his hand whips to my neck, and his fingers squeeze my throat so hard my ears ring.

I claw at his arm, but it's like trying to punch through cement. My muscles whine and the bones of my neck creak under the pressure. My hands drop. For a second, I give in.

Because maybe I deserve to die.

But I can't. Not yet. There are still promises I must honor. Things I need to set right. So, I cling to the fading light of my life.

Jean-Louise whips a knife from the inside pocket of his jacket. The blade barely has time to glint in the flash of the string of lightning strikes outside before he buries it in the man's skull.

The fingers fall away from my throat and I tumble to the floor, sucking down precious air. The man crumples with a dusty thud.

Jean-Louise crouches beside me and puts one hand on my back. "You okay?"

I throw my arms around him, and he hugs me back. I can still feel the undead vise grip crushing my throat. It squeezes out all the emotion I've been holding at bay since the day I carried Yves to Jean-Louise's door. As I sit slumped on the warehouse floor, I hate the tears that stream down my face, because freeing them is like letting the pain win.

I wipe one side of my face with the heel of my hand. "I'm sorry."

Jean-Louise lifts my chin and wipes the rest of my tears. "I said 'grow up' earlier, but I didn't mean stop being human."

"Thank you," I tell him. "Not just for saving me . . . but everything."

Something about Jean-Louise makes me feel like I can count on him—when it really matters. He's solid, like a mountain of granite.

"Yeah," he says with a gruff sigh as he stares at the—now forty-nine—undead bodies watching us silently, waiting for their command. "Do you think this is actually going to work?"

I shrug. "Only one thing's certain."

He stares at me curiously. "And what's that?"

"We're going to put on a show tonight the likes of which the *Montaigne Majestic* has never seen before—and will never see again." I check my watch. "And it starts in just a couple hours."

THIRTY-NINE

CLEMENT

The Sun sets while my sister and I soak up the warmth of its final rays of the evening. I take a deep breath, inhaling the scents of impending rain. People file onto the *Montaigne Majestic*, dressed in their finest cocktail attire, chatting and laughing with one another, excited for an evening of decadent debauchery. It's a special night for us, too. Fortunately for them, they won't be attending our special show.

I haven't mentioned it to anyone, but what we're about to do makes me a tad queasy. I'm not quite as tenacious as my sister when it comes to delivering blood justice.

Cris isn't dressed yet, and neither am I. I'm still in a white tee, shorts, and sandals.

She wears a silver satin robe over a tank and shorts, and her hair is styled in an opulent bun with a few curly strands framing both sides of her face. Rosalie did her hair and makeup, which makes her look older and regal.

Ursula and Mama met with Rosalie, Desiree, and Jacquelyn a few hours ago and told them everything, including Grandma's warning that we all needed to find some way to get along, because our lives literally depended on it. Without question, Rosalie wanted to be part of reclaiming our family's birthright—she'd even donated some of the money she'd made from investing with Fabiana to purchase the cadavers, uh, *actors and actresses*. Although she gave her blessing (gee, *thanks*), Desiree wanted no part in what she'd called "superfluous criminal activity." Jacquelyn pleaded with everyone to find another way or to leave it alone, but Mama and Ursula insisted there was no stopping what we'd already set in motion. Everyone was sworn to secrecy, whether they were involved with the plan or not.

"Only two weeks ago, we thought Mama was going to die," Cris says. "But tonight, we're going to take back everything that was stolen from us."

"I'm so nervous, my hands won't stop shaking."

Cris leans over and takes my hands in hers. My sister's always there to take my hand and calm my anxiety. I wish she had let me do the same for her.

"I still can't believe you didn't tell me about the Scales of Justice," I say. "Enough people have turned their backs on me. How could you ever think I would do that to you?" I pause, but she doesn't answer. "I would've helped you, y'know. We all fuck up, Cris. One day soon, I'll need that same grace from you, too." Perhaps sooner rather than later.

"I realize that now," she says with a deep breath, and leans into me. "The same goes for you. When you're ready to talk, I'm here."

"Soon. I promise."

I want to tell her everything, but I haven't processed it all yet. I don't even know how to put it into words. How can I tell her—

The *Montaigne Majestic*'s horn sounds, rumbling the deck below our feet and startling me from my thoughts. The smoke-stacks beside us bellow cloudy tufts into the purpling sky. The hosts attending the gangway rope off the entrance and disappear onto the boat just as the first drops of rain fall. We're about to get underway.

"It's time," Cris says.

I sigh. "It's time."

Everyone gathers backstage to make final preparations for what's about to be one hell of a show. Lenora Savant thinks tonight is a dress rehearsal of the show she commissioned to celebrate thirty long years of her tyranny ruling the Generational Magic Council of New Orleans.

She's in for quite the surprise.

I dress in a super snazzy black tuxedo with a black shirt and black top hat. Aunt Rosalie lines my eyes in black kohl for added effect. Rosalie, Ursula, and Mama all wear elegant gowns with hair and makeup that makes them look like Black royalty. Justin's dressed in a gray suit and white-speckled shirt underneath, unbuttoned at the top in his signature style.

Even Jean-Louise wears a black tux similar to mine. I've never seen him dressed so nice—now he resembles a classy sleepy giant. I manage to pull half a grin out of him when I tell him that he looks good in a tux, but not as good as me.

However, there's no denying Cris is the star of the show tonight—and technically, she is. She's wearing a midnight-blue long-sleeved gown that cinches at her waist and explodes over a nest of tulle. Her skirts glitter when they catch the light, as if they were sewn from the fabric of space. Mama ties a black silk scarf in a seven-pointed tignon on Cris's head and smiles at her when she finishes.

"You look like a queen," I say when I walk up.

Cris grins. "And Mama *is* one."

Mama smiles and pulls us both into a hug. "I love y'all so much."

I step back and give a slow model spin. "How do I look?"

"Like a young Papa Eshu," Cris says, which warms my cheeks.

Mama sneak-kisses me on the forehead, and I swipe it off.

"Maaa," I groan.

She just laughs and squeezes my shoulder.

Rosalie joins us, having changed into a black satin dress that resembles a shadowed lake flowing across the curves of her body. Her makeup is so elaborate and fantastical that I wonder if maybe she changed her mind about being in the show. She gently lifts Cris's hand and puts on a thin bracelet made of a string of dark, small blue gemstones the color of the nighttime sky.

Cris turns her wrist, admiring the bracelet. When it catches the light, deep blue hues glow inside. "It's beautiful," she says.

"You can have it," Rosalie tells her. "There's just the tiniest bit of sunlight contained inside—" My and Cris's eyes widen at the same time. "It's perfectly safe. It won't blow your hand off or anything. At its worst, it's only a bougie glow-in-the-dark bracelet."

Cris smiles at Rosalie. "Thanks."

I bet only I notice the uncertainty peeking at the edges of my sister's smile. And I wonder if it has anything to do with the light magic, however innocuous, trapped in that bracelet.

Justin and Aunt Ursula approach, each with their own unique expression of worry, redirecting all our attentions.

Justin is the first to speak. "We have a problem."

"What kind of problem?" asks Mama. "We can't have problems right now."

"Gabriela is missing," he says. "Lenora has been trying to contact her all evening."

"Where the hell is she?" asks Ursula.

Justin shrugs. "Look, this can still work. Getting rid of Lenora is like cutting the head off a serpent. Gabriela only took the throne to appease her. She might even be happy that woman is gone."

"We don't have a choice but to keep going," Cris says. "We can deal with Gabriela later."

The thought of Gabriela as a loose (and potentially dangerous) end prowling about reignites the torch of anxiety in the pit of my stomach. Tonight's performance will send that family an undeniably strong message about fucking with us. I'm just worried they might not take it so well.

"Lenora and Felix are set up in their private booth," Justin tells us. "And your other special guest is in another." He turns to Jean-Louise and asks, "Are your, uh, folks in place?"

"Unlike you, I'm capable of doing my part—completely and accurately," says Jean-Louise with an undeniably sharp edge to his voice that makes even me nervous.

Though he seems uneasy, Justin ignores that and says, "You ready to start the show?"

Cris nods. "Let's do this."

FORTY

LENORA SAVANT

By the time Lenora and her husband arrived at the *Montaigne Majestic*, she'd called her daughter-in-law no less than six times.

Felix sat in the passenger seat of their sedan, his long legs bent like a grasshopper's. "Still no word from Gabriela?"

Lenora shook her head. "She didn't tell me she wasn't coming."

He grunted and stared out the window.

They'd parked in the lot near the dock, close enough to see the glow radiating from the windows of the riverboat through the heavy downpour of rain.

"Something feels off," she said. "Maybe we shouldn't go tonight."

"Gabriela is a grown woman." Felix's voice was low and steady, as usual. His calmness in times of crisis made her blood boil. "Besides, it'd be rude not to make an appearance—especially after all the fuss you put up for this show in the first place."

She pursed her lips and tried Gabriela one more time. That woman had grown even *more* insufferable once she'd found out that Valentina's plan—which Gabriela had made very clear from the start that she never agreed with—had failed miserably. Lenora would never admit out loud she'd fucked up—something that rarely happened. She'd gotten too comfortable. Now she was afraid she was trundling straight into a shitstorm. She didn't have time to deal with an uppity daughter-in-law with dreams of wielding the power it'd taken her *decades* to amass.

Lenora and Felix tucked underneath a large umbrella and hurried through the rain to the boat, which was already bustling despite the horrid weather. Justin met them inside the entrance, grinning like a Cheshire cat. He took the dripping umbrella from Felix and led them to a bar near the theater.

"We're still setting up your VIP booth, so feel free to have a drink on the house," Justin explained as he pulled out two stools. "I'll escort you personally once your room is ready."

She shot him a curt look as she settled onto her seat. "I hope it's private this time."

He nodded. "I apologize for your previous lackluster experience, and I assure you, we'll more than make up for it tonight."

She waved him away with an annoyed flick of her wrist, then raised two fingers at the bartender, who hurried over. She ordered a double gin and tonic with lemon instead of lime, and Felix asked for a bourbon straight up.

"We only have Tru Reserve tonight, sir," said the bartender, a very tall, young boy with bright eyes and naturally flushed cheeks.

"That's fine," Felix grumbled.

Lenora resisted the urge to backhand him off the stool. "He'll have a scotch neat."

The bartender glanced at Felix, who nodded.

Lenora glowered at her husband.

"It's just bourbon," he said, spreading his hands.

"I'm trying to get those dreadful people out of our lives, not line their pockets," she growled.

The bartender set their drinks in front of them. Felix thanked the boy and sipped his scotch.

Instead of pressing him further, Lenora sent Gabriela a text, smacked her phone down, and picked up her glass—but stopped suddenly, the rim inches from her lips.

A lime floated at the top of her drink.

She slammed the glass down and shouted for the bartender, who was lollygagging with another customer at the opposite end of the bar.

He spun on his heels, his entire face pale as an eggshell, and rushed over, tripping on the edge of a floor mat along the way. "I'm sorry, what's wrong, ma'am?"

"Unless my lemon is having an identity crisis, I believe this is a lime—and also not what I asked for." She nudged the glass toward him, and he swept it up in a shaky hand.

"My apologies," he said. "I'll remake it."

Felix leaned over and said in a quiet voice, "Calm down, Lenora. The boy made a mistake."

"I am plagued by morons," she said. "And don't fucking tell me to calm down."

The bartender set a new cocktail in front of her—with a lemon this time. She took it and waved him away, her mind already redirected to her myriad of problems.

After Eveline had told her about Marie's impromptu visit and allegations, Lenora had begged Gabriela for *months* to take care of the meddlesome woman. But by the time Gabriela had finally gotten the nerve to act, they'd have stolen the entire Council from underneath them. Lenora had had no choice but to take charge before Marie unraveled her entire world. Lenora often wondered if Gabriela was more trouble than she was worth, but she was stuck with her. For now.

And then there was Oz.

She'd been disappointed Valentina hadn't set her sights higher when she discovered they were dating. The boy had an obsessive curiosity about magic—which Lenora had enjoyed nurturing. She'd watched it grow like a pet tapeworm. She'd had reservations about looping Oz into the plot from the start, but he was the only person who had access to that family.

It was past time she handled this issue personally—exterminate that whole family, rip them from this realm by the root, and be rid of them for good.

"Mr. and Mrs. Savant, your booth is ready," announced Justin from behind them. "I have fresh drinks and charcuterie waiting for you there."

"About time," she said as she slid off the stool and tucked her purse underneath one arm.

He escorted them to a room center to the stage. The theater lights had already dimmed for the show. The spacious booth had a single table in the center, butted against the balcony, and two velvet couches on either side. A centerpiece of lavender and black candles burned softly on the table alongside the food and drinks Justin had promised.

She stepped inside and rounded on him. "I've never been in *this* booth before."

"Because it's newly renovated," he said. "You're the first to enjoy it, which I hope you will. The show's starting, so I'll leave you to it." He left swiftly, closing the door after him.

Felix pulled out her chair, and she lowered herself into it. He sat across from her and didn't delay taking up his fresh scotch. She glanced over the assortment of meats, cheeses, and fruits, but her appetite had abandoned her right around the second time Gabriela had sent her to voicemail earlier this evening.

She cursed the woman for soiling her special night. At least this was only the dress rehearsal. But even as the curtain slowly rose and applause thundered below, Lenora wondered what Gabriela was up to. For her sake, it'd better be something innocuous.

Sipping her gin and tonic, she peered over the balcony at the sea of shadowy figures below. She'd been hesitant when Justin first suggested allowing a limited group of people to view the dress rehearsal, but then he assured her they would carry the news of how great this production was to every corner of the city, so on debut night the theater would be packed with people eager to celebrate her. Everyone sat still, heads facing the stage. She couldn't see the VIP booths on either side of her, but she assumed they were empty like the others. She grinned behind her glass.

Present issues aside, she thoroughly enjoyed the ambience at the top of the food chain.

FORTY-ONE

CLEMENT

The stage curtains open slowly, revealing a backdrop painted like the nighttime sky with a bright full Moon. Yves would've loved that. My chest clenches.

The theater is moderately sized, and intimate. Clothed tables with high-backed chairs below, grandiose booths high above the main floor at the back of the room. This is the sort of place where history happens. A raised, circular platform sits center stage, just large enough for one person to stand on comfortably. My sister looks over to me, and I nod at her. She takes a deep breath and walks onto the stage.

The spotlights bathe her in blazing warm light, stark against the dark auditorium and the silhouettes of all the people seated at tables throughout, who are cloaked in shadow—and have been since Jean-Louise and I seated them. The light follows her as her heels click against the wooden floor in a powerful rhythm that lulls everyone in the room into silent awe. She lifts the front of her gown and steps onto the platform, facing the audience.

From the corner of the stage, I peer around the curtain at the central VIP booth where Lenora Savant—the woman responsible for my grandmother's death—waits for the show to begin alongside her husband and accomplice, Felix. And in the booth beside theirs sits Eveline Beaumont, Reverend Mother of the Temple of Innocent Blood, who allowed it all to happen.

They're all in for quite an evening. I take my place near the corner of the backdrop and grab hold of a hanging rope attached to an overhead lever.

Several silent moments pass before Cris lifts her hands, palms facing upward. I pull the rope, and a track in the rafters overhead that we preassembled with twenty jars of raw moonlight tips. Viscous beams rain from above like twenty miniature waterfalls and pool onstage, filling it entirely, save for the small platform on which Cris stands, giving the illusion she's floating.

The jars empty, and Cris's voice booms from her small but powerful frame. "Stories have existed since our first ancestor walked this realm. Great tales of triumph and love and courage passed down through generations, like the magic our people have drawn from the power of the Moon for centuries. Tonight, you will hear a new tale, one of passion, betrayal, heartbreak, and ultimately— justice."

Her speech chills me, and I run my hands along the gooseflesh on my arms. Lenora and Felix must be moved, too, judging by how their silhouettes fidget up in the balcony.

She kneels and dips her hand in the moonlight. When she rises, so does a glittering image of our grandmother, as grand and ethereal as she'd been the night we met her at the same crossroads where she'd died.

"Cristine Dupart, Queen of the Generational Magic Council of New Orleans and Chair of the Magical and Spiritual Coalition of the entire magical world." Cris pauses and lifts her chin a bit higher, and so do I.

A few members of the audience clap, which makes me wonder if any of them knew our grandmother when they were alive. It wouldn't surprise me if they did. Maybe they're all from around here.

"Cristine had a lasting effect on the magical community of New Orleans and conjurers around the world." Cris drags her hand in a dramatic arc through the moonlight, and throngs of people spring up from the pool and approach the projection of our grandmother, who embraces them with kindness. "Cristine led with grace, by example, and with a level of integrity that has not been witnessed in a queen since her untimely demise."

I glance up to the central booth to see Lenora get to her feet and head for the door, but it swings open before she gets there, projecting a rectangle of light into the darkened room. The shadow of a person twice her size appears, directs her back to her seat, and forces her into it. Another person enters the booth and hovers behind Felix. They fall still.

Someone steps up behind me and puts both hands on my shoulders. I think it's Mama at first until Ursula whispers, "I'd always prayed that the day she got hers I'd be in the front row."

I want to reach up and grab my aunt's hands, but I don't. I'm afraid she'll pull away. But I hold my breath, take both her hands in mine, and lean into her. I hold tight to her. I'm not living in fear anymore. I'm not letting anyone else go.

Aunt Ursula kisses the crown of my head. I can't help but grin.

Onstage, Cris continues her captivating tale. "Cristine Dupart was a light for us in an otherwise dark world, but the greatest lights also create the darkest shadows." She kneels and taps the moonlight.

Images of humanoid forms shrouded in darkness arise, chasing the bystanders to the rear of the stage, where they melt back into the pool. Cristine stands boldly against the dark forms, but Cris sweeps her hand through the pool again and everyone disappears.

I've never seen Cris like this before. Her magic is powerful and graceful and gorgeous and complex—just like her. I've watched my sister grow and change a lot over the last two weeks. She's been through so much shit, but she's not better *because* of it, she's better *in spite* of it.

And I'm so fucking proud of her.

But I can't help but wonder, what am *I* in spite of everything I've been through?

Especially after what I did. I swallow the lump in my throat and try to focus on the show.

"Cristine had a best friend with whom she'd shared a childhood, to whom she'd exposed her most intimate dreams and revealed her darkest fears, and whom she loved like those of her own blood."

Cris palms the pool three separate times, each time conjuring an image of Grandma and Lenora, projecting the two of them at different stages of their lives.

Small children playing and laughing.

Teenagers huddled together in trust and solidarity.

And finally, adults, standing hand in hand.

Cris throws her arms out on either side of her and each image explodes into droplets of light that rain back to the pool. I make a mental note to ask her to teach me some of this shit.

"Our Queen touched many hearts in the magical community," she says. "However, some sought to silence her, others to use her, and one to rip out her legacy from the root and seed her own.

"Enter Gerald Lancaster, mayor of New Orleans, and his daughter, Alexis Lancaster, who wished to appropriate the very magic that had been born from the suffering of Cristine's ancestors at the hands of Alexis's." Moonlight images of Grandma arguing with Gerald and Alexis appear. "When denied access to our sacred heritage, Alexis sought apprenticeship with the white mages; but little did she know, they wouldn't accept her either." The images of Grandma and Gerald disappear, and Alexis runs to the other side of the stage, where she meets the moonlight form of a severe-looking, older woman. "And the white mages under leadership of their Cardinal, Bethesda DeLacorte, launched a sinister plot to murder Alexis and frame Cristine, thus bringing a premature end to Cristine's legacy."

Alexis clasps her hands in front of Bethesda, silently pleading, and Bethesda smiles, then pulls a blade from her pocket and slits Alexis's throat. Pure, blue light pours from the open wound, and Alexis melts back into the pool from which she came. An image of Lenora appears and huddles with Bethesda, conspiratorial grins on both their faces, as they whisper over Alexis's corpse.

"Lenora Savant, with the help of Bethesda, framed her best friend, Cristine, for the murder of Alexis Lancaster, leaving the Queen to reap the consequences, which came in the form of an angry mob set upon her home by none other than Gerald Lancaster, who would not rest until he got misplaced revenge."

On one side of the stage, the terrifying image of Grandma and Grandpa standing in front of Mama and her sisters, all small children, appears—the lynch mob led by Gerald on the other. The two sets of moonlit projections glide across the stage and crash into each other, erupting in a bright flash of blue light.

An image of Grandma appears. She crawls toward a willow that springs from the pool. Once she's underneath it, she collapses and melts back into the moonlight. The scene clamps my heart like a vise grip. When Cris came up with it, I was the first person she showed it to, and it hit me hard then, too.

Cris's voice takes a melancholy tone. "Cristine and her husband Baptiste would perish that night, while the friend who orchestrated her downfall would inherit the throne she coveted above all else."

A moonlight Lenora swirls up from the pool beside a throne that also materializes. She wears a long gown and a tignon crown and sits on the throne with a devilish grin. Cris snaps her fingers and the image of Lenora throws her head back and shrieks before melting dramatically back into the pool.

Cris looks up at Lenora in the central booth and narrows her eyes. I glance up as Lenora's silhouette rises and clings to the railing. I can't see her face, but I imagine she's glowering something fierce right now. Good.

Cris gathers her gown and steps off the platform into the moonlight. She strides to the front of the stage, rippling the moonbeams like water and turning them into dense red fog that resembles a bloody mist in her wake. She lifts one hand toward the central booth, and the spotlights swivel to illuminate Lenora's enraged scowl and the affronted bewilderment on Felix's gaunt face.

"What is the meaning of this?" Lenora shouts, still gripping the railing and leaning so far over, it's a wonder she doesn't slip and plummet to the floor below.

"Justice," announces Cris. "You orchestrated the ruination of my grandmother's legacy. You had my father, David Trudeau, assassinated for trying to uncover the truth of your misdeeds, and you attempted the same with my mother, Marie Trudeau, rightful Queen of the Gen Council. Lenora Savant, you owe my family a tremendous blood debt, and tonight, we're collecting."

Lenora cackles from the booth. "Little girl, I've been a force in this town since your mother was in diapers. I've never taken anything I didn't deserve."

Aunt Ursula taps my shoulders and urges me out from where we've been watching off to one side of the stage. She doesn't have to tell me twice.

I walk out and stand tall next to Cris, who takes my hand. Mama, Ursula, Rosalie, Aurora, Justin, and Jean-Louise all assemble behind us. We stand together in the spent moonbeam fog lingering onstage.

Cris and I kneel together and drag our free hands through the red moonlight, which feels eerily tepid against my skin, not warm and soothing like the raw stuff. It flows off the stage and onto the floor where the rest of the guests sit.

The lights click on, temporarily blinding everyone. When the spots in my vision fade, Lenora glances at the faces of the people seated below her, who've all turned to face her. She presses a hand to her chest, taking in the small army of undead patrons glowering up at her. Felix perches beside her, likewise shocked.

Eveline stands, a puzzled look on her face, though she remains silent, not alerting Lenora to her presence, which I find interesting, considering she had no idea what tonight was about beforehand. If Eveline had any part in Lenora's deception, she seems perfectly okay with letting Lenora take the fall.

"You-all think you've done something with all this?" Lenora sneers and waves her hand over the heads of all the reanimated cadavers sitting calmly below. "Well, let me tell *you* riffraff something—Cristine Dupart was a subpar queen on her best day. She didn't deserve to have so much power only to squander it seeing to the petty ailments of the dusty nobodies of this city. I didn't deserve to be beneath the thumb of someone as weak as her—so I cut off that thumb.

"But I made a grave mistake that night thirty years ago." She clutches the rail tighter and leans forward. "I should've never left your family's lives in the hands of that woefully inept lynch mob." She scoffs and shakes her head. "I should've come in after them and squashed every single one of you roaches. But instead, I gave you the gift of mercy, and now you've multiplied and infested my world with your delusion.

"And for the record, I regret nothing—not even getting rid of that nosy bastard David." She wrinkles her nose with distaste that sours my stomach.

Cris and I both squeeze each other's hands angrily at the same time. I didn't think she'd ever confess to killing Dad. The blunt pain of it strikes me, cracking my façade so fury can seep out.

That woman took Dad away from me, and I can never forgive her for that.

"Had the Strayer boy not messed up, I would've gotten the rest of you, too." She points a shaky finger at the stage. "And Justin, you filthy, duplicitous rat—I should've never trusted you.

"I don't know what you imbeciles have planned, but let me remind you that using necromancy for criminal acts is strictly forbidden by the laws of MASC and the Treaty of Moons. If any harm comes to me at the hands of these undead barbarians, you'll all face charges of treason."

"A minute obstacle at best," announces Papa Eshu, who simply appears onstage and limps over to stand beside me.

His presence is electric, crackling with sheer power. I jolt and stand a bit taller, and I notice Cris rise an inch or two as well.

He holds up his right wrist, and his Moon mark glows with intense blue light. Lenora drops her stranglehold on the railing, and her mouth falls open.

"As Guardian of the Crossroads and Father of Moon Magic, I grant the family of Cristine Dupart the right to invoke blood justice tonight by a means of their choosing. And let it be known that I fully endorse the ascension of the true Queen, Marie Dupart Trudeau." He nods at me and Cris and takes a step back, relinquishing the floor.

The heads of all the undead people seated at the tables below turn with a shuffling roar, looking to me for instruction. I glance at Mama, and she nods.

"Bring me her head," I order my undead army.

Four of the closest approach the stage, hands held aloft to help me and Cris down. They lower us gently to the ground, just as the two in the booth with Lenora and Felix pitch them over the railing.

Lenora and Felix hit the floor with one and then two sickening crunches, but I'm the only one who flinches. Cris watches steel-faced, the mist casting a frightening red glow onto her face. Felix's neck cracks the moment he lands, killing him instantly. Lenora's not so fortunate.

Sharp, bloodied bones protrude from both her legs, which twist at odd angles below the skirt of her green dress. One of her shoes hangs off her feet; she must've lost the other on the way down. Her hair has come loose and sits like a ransacked nest on her head, and her makeup has smudged and run.

She sobs and pants as she drags herself away from the slowly encroaching undead, leaving a bloody trail behind. They let her slither into a corner, where she cowers with frantic eyes. The crowd parts to let us pass through. Anxiety trembles my hands, but Cris takes one in hers and interlaces her fingers with mine.

"P-Please . . ." Lenora begs. "Have mercy."

The undead take both her arms and lift her up, then look to me.

"No," Cris and I say in unison.

They descend upon Lenora Savant like a swarm of bees suffocating a murder hornet.

They rip her apart, limb from bloody fucking limb.

And she shrieks right up until the very end.

FORTY-TWO

VALENTINA SAVANT

An anxious feeling had taken residence in Valentina's gut and stayed all evening, but she couldn't figure out why. She'd tried everything to distract her mind, but nothing had worked, not even video games.

After she'd come clean about her and Oz's major fuckup, Granny had given her that same disappointed look she often reserved for Daddy or worse—Mom.

And that hurt Valentina more than if her granny had slapped her instead.

Valentina had also developed a nagging worry that Granny thought she was weak for not turning Cris over to the police after the accident. It frightened her to think what her granny might've done if she'd been in that situation instead. In some ways she was comfortable not being like her granny.

But that was only the tip of Valentina's stressberg. Her parents had argued again that morning, but this one had been their worst yet. All the shouting woke her, and she emerged from her room in time to see her mother hit her father hard across the face before hefting an overnight bag onto her shoulder and leaving. Valentina had no idea where Mom was going or when (and *if*) she'd be back.

Mom hadn't even bothered to say goodbye.

Valentina got back in bed and stayed there until late in the evening, when the slam of the front door and the sound of a feminine voice pulled her out again. She snuck down the hallway, as quietly as she could, considering the clumsy boot she had to wear until her ankle healed, and stood out of sight at the top of the stairs.

But the woman standing in the foyer talking to her father wasn't

Gabriela. She was a short, curvy woman with light eyes. The kind of pretty that turns all sorts of heads. And Daddy's head stayed on a swivel, so Valentina had an idea what this was. The woman cradled a sleeping baby in her arms, who stirred occasionally whenever she or Daddy raised their voices.

"You need to leave," he said in a low, forceful tone. "What the hell were you thinking showing up here like this? And you need to stop fucking calling and texting me, too."

The woman held the baby closer. "You don't really mean that, Arturo."

He crossed his arms, shadows dulling his bright brown skin. "I signed an agreement with Fabiana. *This* wasn't supposed to happen. Damn y'all both for putting me in this predicament."

A tear streamed down Jacquelyn's cheek. "Remember when you told me you loved me and wanted to spend the rest of your life with me?"

"I don't know *half* the shit I said when I was with you in the House of Vans. That place does something to people. That Ho-Van shit Fabiana pumps through the air ducts fucks with your mind. It was all like one big hallucination."

Jacquelyn held out the baby. "Well, your son is real."

Daddy shrank back, shaking his head.

A fucking *baby*? Daddy had a Van Kid. Valentina's half brother.

Jacquelyn readjusted the child in her arms with a sigh. "But the reason I came is I'd hoped . . . if I helped your family, your wife, you'd eventually realize I'm good—and we're good for each other. And you might also remember how much you loved me once."

Daddy pinched the bridge of his nose and heaved a sigh. "Jacquelyn, what the fuck are you talking about? Please leave. My daughter's upstairs, and Gabriela could be home any moment."

No wonder Valentina's parents were so edgy all the time. All the secrets, lies, and betrayal were getting out of hand.

Jacquelyn's eyes widened. "Where is she?"

"I don't know," he snapped. "Why do you want to know so much about my wife?"

Jacquelyn shook her head. "You don't understand—"

"I'm not kidding," Daddy said in a severe voice. "Stay away from my family."

"I'm trying to *help*. There's a plan—" Jacquelyn glanced up to where Valentina was hiding at the top of the stairs.

Valentina cursed under her breath and ducked back into the shadows.

"Never mind," Jacquelyn said, sounding anxious. "You're right. I shouldn't have come here."

Valentina peeked again.

Jacquelyn reached for the door, but Daddy grabbed her and spun her back around. "What's going on?" he demanded.

She pulled away from him. "Nothing. You wanted me gone, so I'm leaving. Forget I came."

Before he could protest, she threw open the door and disappeared into the rain. Daddy slammed the door and mumbled to himself, clutching both sides of his head.

Valentina stood up at the top of the stairs and held on to the banister as she glared down at him.

Her father looked up at her and sighed. "I guess you heard everything."

"Yup."

He tossed his hands up on either side of him. "Is it worth asking you not to tell your mother?"

"If you're so miserable here, why won't you just go?"

"Is that what you want? For me to leave?"

"I want you and Mom to be fucking adults. I'm tired of being an accessory to y'all's bullshit, and I'm tired of feeling like I don't matter in this house. I'm out."

"Valentina—"

She turned and hobbled back to her room, where she pulled

down her carry-on suitcase from the closet and packed it with enough belongings to get her through the next couple of days.

She'd just zipped it closed when her father appeared in the doorway. "What are you doing?" he asked.

She pulled on her shoe. "I'm going to stay with Granny until you and Mom get your shit together, but I'll be honest, I'm not hopeful."

"Don't be ridiculous, Valentina," he chided, sending more heat exploding through her. "Put that bag away. What are you? Ten?"

"Old enough to know when something's messed up enough to get the hell out, unlike you and Mom."

"You're not being fair."

"Fair? You've got a whole secret love baby, and you tell me *I'm* not being fair? What's not fair is spending day after day sitting in your shit, and you expecting us to just keep sitting here while you pile more of it on." She threw up the handle of the suitcase, which made a sharp click, and nearly rolled over her father's toes on the way out. "I'm leaving, and you can't stop me."

She got to the stairs and had to slow down, her boot landing on each stair with a resounding thump, followed by the bump of her suitcase right after. She didn't care if it took all night to get down the damned stairs. She was getting the fuck out of that house, and she was doing it on her own.

"It's storming out," Daddy said, dejection weighing on his voice. "At least let me drive you."

"I'm fine ordering a car. No worries, I'm used to figuring shit out on my own."

The rain had died down to a soft drizzle by the time Valentina sat on top of her suitcase on the front porch to wait for the car to arrive to take her to Granny's—and away from her hell-home.

She pretended not to notice her father watching her from the front window.

She didn't turn to look back at him after the lights of the car swung into their driveway, nor when the driver loaded her bag into the trunk and helped her into the backseat.

All she felt as the car pulled away was numb rage at the gaping hole in her life—courtesy of her parents—that she didn't deserve. She had to believe her granny could help make her whole again.

That feeling was all she had left.

But one day, she'd be Queen—and then she'd make Granny look at her again with the love and admiration she deserved.

FORTY-THREE
CRISTINA

I watch every bloody moment of Lenora Savant's end.

I imagine my grandmother standing behind me, both hands on my shoulders, smiling pridefully at how I redeemed her legacy, how I snatched the justice that had been denied to our family for thirty years. I whisper, "Thank you," to her and the rest of my ancestors.

One of the undead places Lenora's head in a burlap sack and hands it to Clem, who passes it to me. Clem and I walk back to the stage, and two others move at my side to lift us up to join Mama, Ursula, Rosalie, Aurora, Justin, Jean-Louise, and Papa Eshu.

The throng of undead part, clearing a path for Eveline, who approaches the stage with her head held high and eyes narrowed, though I see the slight tremble in her knees and hands. She'll never show it outright, but she's terrified. Perfect. I consider asking Clem to order our army to tear her apart, too, but I'll let her live—today.

Eveline glowers up at us once she's reached the edge of the stage. "You all certainly got your message across, but I find your theatrics quite crass and barbaric."

"If you recall, Eveline, I tried the civilized approach when I first came to you for help," Mama says, her voice bold and unapologetic, which electrifies the energy coursing within me. "I'd already lost my husband and I could've burned the entire Council to the ground, but I didn't. And staying my hand almost cost me dearly."

"I'm sure we can all admit, there was a less messy way," says Eveline.

"Well, sometimes you have to speak the language of your oppressor to make your point clear . . . and we needed ours to be *crystal*," I tell Eveline, my eyes never leaving hers.

"I am truly sorry for everything y'all have experienced," Eveline says.

For me, her apology rings hollow. Mama stands statuesque, one hand on her hip, clearly not buying the bullshit either.

"Lenora was out of control, and eventually I would've had to deal with her one way or another," Eveline says. "But I simply cannot be involved in scandals of this nature while Benjamin is in office."

"You speak as if he's already won the election," says Ursula.

Eveline inclines her head toward Papa Eshu. "Gods willing."

He leans on his onyx cane and presses his lips firmly together but doesn't respond. I wonder what business those two have together. Can we trust *any* of these bitches?

Eveline softens her expression and steps closer to the stage. "I'm only trying to build a better world for the entire magical community, and Ben wants to help me do that. I'm no stranger to people like Lenora and folks with a capacity for evil a hundred times hers. So, I can empathize with your call for justice, more than you know." She expels a heavy sigh, and I can feel her defenses lowering. "How do you suggest we move forward?"

"Call an emergency meeting of the Gen Council," says Mama. "Tonight, we will revoke Lenora's and Gabriela's sovereignty and I will officially become Queen and Chair of MASC."

"And what about Gabriela?" asks Eveline.

"Gabriela is missing," Mama replies. "Besides, she doesn't get a say in this. She was weak and fit only to be Lenora's pawn." After Eveline nods her agreement, Mama adds, "And Aurora Vincent will replace Xavier as our new Gen Priestess."

Eveline looks at Aurora curiously. "Xavier is Lorenzo's eldest and has a higher claim than you."

Aurora hands her Lorenzo's decree, calling for Aurora to succeed his position on the Council. Then she shares the story of how Xavier crossed her and left her in Chateau des Saints to die so he could steal her seat.

"Well . . ." says Eveline, almost breathless.

I'm not buying that she had no idea of all the deception going on right under her nose. But we need to cooperate with her—for now.

"Xavier appears to be just as iniquitous as Lenora," continues Eveline. "I'll actually be relieved to see him removed. I found him to be as simple and myopic as Lenora's entire family." She nods to Mama. "I will do what you ask—"

"We're not asking," I say, hardening my glare at Eveline.

There's no way I'm going to lay my head on my pillow tonight without taking back everything that belongs to me. Mama can be diplomatic if she chooses, but Eveline will not intimidate me.

"I understand," Eveline replies, though I do not miss the subtle bite in the way she says it. "I will call Xavier to meet immediately in the chamber at St. John's."

"Thank you," Mama says.

Although Eveline has finally joined the right side of history in all this, I will never trust her. As satisfied as I am with Lenora's end, I still can't help but wander along the remaining threads of the spider's web of conspiracy that ensnared so many people for so long.

Dr. Thomas.

Gabriela Savant.

Xavier Vincent.

Oz.

They should all face repercussions for their parts in this.

"Perfect timing, too," Justin cuts in, glancing at his phone. "The boat just docked. We need to move."

"What's going on?" asks Eveline, looking confused and exhausted.

Before anyone can answer, the fire alarm sounds, and Clem runs from backstage. I hadn't even noticed he'd left. A great fire crackles behind us as the curtains catch and flames dance across the length of the backdrop.

Jean-Louise steps to the edge of the stage and stares down upon the army of undead, who've been silently awaiting their next command. "May your return journey to the spirit realm be swift and true." He kisses his fist and raises it above his head.

The undead all crumple to the floor at once with one tremendous, rolling thump.

I turn back, and the fire lapping at the untouched portions of the tall stage curtains catches my attention. Something about the flames dancing up the fabric to brush against the ceiling draws me closer and drowns out the sounds of the others huddled at the front of the stage. Even time seems to slow.

The stone bracelet Rosalie gave me grows cold on my wrist—and chills until it burns my skin with what feels like frigid fire that sears down to my bones. I try to rip the bracelet off, but the latch holds like iron links. But when I let go, creamy honey-colored light sticks to my fingers as if I've just stuck them in a honeycomb. The light feels shockingly cold, but my skin adapts quickly. The bracelet doesn't burn my wrist anymore. I think this stuff is the trapped sunlight, but . . . this doesn't make sense.

I don't know a single thing about light magic.

I pull my free hand back from the bracelet, drawing the rest of the sunlight with it, which oozes out in a lazy arc like magic baby drool. Yuck. My heart skips when the light moves on its own, snaking down my fingers to pool in a sphere. It hovers just above my palm, spinning and pulsing with magical energy. Strangely, the flames on the curtains have ceased licking the ceiling to reach fiery tendrils toward the miniature disco ball of light in my palm.

I give it to the fire.

The magic explodes, sending glowing sparks across the floor and curtain like shrapnel. But the magic's not gone yet. I still feel it calling to me, sending vibrations along an invisible tether attached to my gut. Tugging at me. Begging me to take control.

The magical flames burn white-hot and stand out from the others working on the farther parts of the stage. I lift my hand, the same one that held the magic a moment ago, and sweep it across the length of the curtains. The fire obeys.

Flames gallop across the massive folds like a herd of wild horses, dragging destruction behind.

"How'd you do that?"

Clem's voice gives me a start, and I turn to find him staring at me curiously.

"I-I don't know," I say, but he looks like he doesn't believe me.

I reach for the bracelet, but it turns to ashes and falls away.

"Cristina! Clem!" Justin shouts. "What are you doing? Let's move!"

Clem grabs my hand, and we follow the group as Justin ushers everyone from the theater.

Guests are already rushing for the exit, gossiping among themselves about what could've possibly happened as crew members usher them to safety. It stormed while we were under way, but the only evidence is the heavy scent of rain hanging in the air and the dark, wet wooden planks of the pier.

By the time we get a safe distance away, an enormous ball of fire erupts from one of the smokestacks, and several windows burst, pulling screams and gasps from people in the crowd migrating down the pier and away from the gangway. The boat rocks on the water, engulfed in walls of orange flame and black smoke. At the rear of the group, Justin falls to his knees and watches his life's work burn, his hands crossed over his heart. Sadness clips mine.

He fought hard against destroying it, but it was the only way to get rid of all the evidence, including the bodies of forty-nine people who were supposed to already be dead.

The boat becomes a gigantic bonfire over the water, releasing thick plumes of smoke into the night as it sinks. I remove my tignon, undo the knots, and tie the flowing satin fabric around my waist as sirens sound in the distance. When I finish, I stare up at the Moon and the Stars beyond, ignoring the acrid smell of smoke as I walk side by side with my family.

The towering steeples of St. John's Cathedral are ominous set against the dark hues of the late-night sky. Shadows and crickets fill the manicured gardens on either side of the main sidewalk that our group marches up toward the church, Eveline Beaumont leading the way. The adults walk in a tight group, Aurora with them, talking quietly with Ursula. To no surprise at all, Jean-Louise lags alone at the rear.

I hang back and fall in step with Clem. "You okay?" I ask him.

He nods. "Watching Jean-Louise raise so many of the dead was a spiritual experience."

"Yeah, it was something all right." The memory of Jean-Louise and my brother at the head of the small army of walking dead, disguised as a troupe of actors and actresses for the dress rehearsal, marching onto the *Montaigne Majestic* will probably haunt my dreams for a long time.

"So . . . you a white mage now?" he asks.

"That depends," I say. "You a necromancer?" I scoff when he doesn't answer. "We're gen, Clem. And for the first time in a long time, I feel like I'm right where I belong. And please stop me if you ever see me about to accept another weird piece of jewelry from Aunt Rosalie."

Clem chuckles, then falls silent.

Hint received. I squeeze his hand, and hurry to catch up with Mama.

We step through the front doors of the church and enter the dark sanctuary. Tall stained-glass windows filter moonlight into pale colors that paint the stone surfaces of carved pillars and arches throughout. The ceiling stretches straight to the underbelly of the heavens and is adorned with beautiful artwork like I've only ever seen in history books. Our footsteps echo overhead, and Mama glances at me as we make our way to a hidden doorway at the end of the room.

"I'm proud of you," she says. "I don't like you disobeying me and putting yourself in danger, but you helped save our family."

"Thanks." I glance over my shoulder at Clem, who stalks silently beside Jean-Louise, both of whom are captivated by the stories trapped in the intricate stained glass.

We file through the door that leads into a dim hallway. Shadows lap at the meek fires of the sconces on the wall, barely revealing stairs that descend into darkness. Scents of dusk and dank stone ride the chilly air up from below. We take the winding staircase down into the bowels of St. John's.

"You shouldn't worry about your brother so much," says Mama. "I know you want to protect your family, but you can't wear everyone's burdens and your own. Clem's going to be fine."

"But how do you know?" I'm not certain she remembers him at his lowest after everything with Aunt Ursula, Dad, and Yves. If she did, she'd be just as worried as I am right now.

"Because we talk."

"He talks to you?" That's news to me. I'm happy he's talking to someone—though I wish that someone were me.

"Not as much as I'd like, but we're getting there. I just let him know I'm here for him and I love him." She slows and lowers her voice as we navigate the maze of underground corridors. "Everyone has their own way of dealing with things, though we may not always agree with them. Our job is to love them through it."

As we walk through the depths of St. John's, I wonder how different my life would've been over the last year if I'd confided in Clem or Mama or both. And what secret is Clem holding on to now that seems to be eating him alive?

When we arrive at the Council hall, Eveline pushes the doors open and leads us through. The Council Chamber is cavernous and twice as grand. Thick stone columns with golden collars and stately candelabra are abundant throughout the room, and a gleaming bloodred stone aisle leads to a dais toward the back. The candlelight throws an ominous blend of shadows and light across the face of Xavier Vincent, who sits in a small, intricately carved seat on the lower platform.

He rises when we enter, looking annoyed and bewildered, until he sees his sister. His eyes widen and his mouth hangs open for a moment before he claps his hands together and says, "Oh! Thank the gods, it's a miracle! I was so worried when I got the call that you'd disappeared from Chateau—"

"Cut the shit, Xavier," says Aurora coldly. "Everyone knows what you did."

He opens his mouth to retort, but Eveline holds up a hand, quieting him. She steps onto the dais, and the rest of us line up in front, Mama at the helm.

"Marie has invoked blood justice with the blessing of Papa Eshu," says Eveline.

Xavier wrinkles his nose at Mama and Aurora. "What is this?"

"Lenora's and Gabriela's sovereignties have been revoked and Marie shall ascend the throne immediately," Eveline announces.

Xavier laughs. "Nonsense. You don't have the authority. Where are Lenora and Gabriela?"

"Lenora is dead," Aurora says. "And if I had my way, you'd join her for what you did to me."

Xavier pounds the table and curses in Spanish, but Aurora doesn't flinch. Neither do I. We're both done being messed over by fuckboys like Xavier Vincent and Oswald Strayer.

"And that's not all." Eveline unfolds Lorenzo's decree and brandishes it in front of Xavier. "Aurora will be taking over as Gen Priestess, also effective immediately."

Xavier stands back and narrows his eyes. "That is a forgery! I am the eldest; my father's seat belongs to me!"

Eveline sighs, unmoved by his tantrum. "You know how this works. You can leave on your own or with help." She signals a robed man who stands guard by a door at the back of the room.

He disappears through it and returns a moment later with three others. They march up to the side of the platform beside Xavier and wait like sentinels.

Holy shit. The Gen Council has its own private army.

Xavier spits on the floor next to his empty seat. "You lie with jackals," he utters to Aurora. "You will pay for this."

Xavier shrieks when a guard grabs him from behind and slams

him to the ground. His head lolls and his eyes roll back as another guard assists the first in dragging his limp body from the room by one leg.

Aurora watches them go, frowning and reticent, then takes her seat and closes her eyes while she runs her hands over the surface of the ancient wooden table before her, where her father once sat. She looks at me and mouths, *Thank you.*

I smile and nod. Aurora's finally where she belongs. And one day I'll be there with her—my friend.

Mama ascends to the top of the dais before a grandiose throne made of wood and stone, with images of snakes and moons carved onto it. Pride swells in my chest. She settles onto her seat with a smile, in her rightful place as Queen.

I follow after her and remove the silk scarf I'd tied around my wrist. I drape it across my forearms and present it to her. She nods.

I tie a perfect seven-knot tignon on her head and stand back to marvel at my beautiful Black mother on her throne, wearing her crown, the embodiment of Grandma Cristine.

She turns to Justin and says, "You shall remain in your position as Root Doctor. But no more secrets. And no more lies."

He agrees and takes his seat between Aurora and Eveline.

"Now, let's get down to business," Mama says, addressing the new Gen Council. "I want to know everything you've been up to the last thirty years." She folds her hands in her lap and smiles like the queen she is. "Spare me no details."

The rest of us exit the room.

Before the doors shut behind us, Ursula pulls me and Clem back from the group and grapples us both in a hug. Tears glimmer in her eyes when she lets us go.

"I love y'all so much."

"Thank you, Aunt Ursula," I say. "For everything."

She nods and turns to Clem. They hug again and stand, swaying in the dim light of the tunnel. He needs all the love he can get, considering the hell he's been through. The sight warms my heart.

I can't recall if I've ever felt this full before. After Dad's death, I never thought I'd be happy again, but this is a start. Even though it wasn't my fault (thank the gods), I'll still bear the pain of his absence forever. But I know he's somewhere in the spiritual realm, watching over us with Grandma Cristine and Grandpa Baptiste. And then my breath hitches.

When the dead rise to claim the living . . . The undead killed Lenora.

When fire dances over water . . . The *Montaigne Majestic* burning before it sank.

Silence will devour your enemy's pleas . . . I have no clue about Valentina's pleas going unheard, but justice was definitely served.

My and my grandma's names have been cleared, and Mama is Queen.

I've reclaimed my birthright.

I had to fight for that justice, but dammit, I got it.

My knees weaken and I have to lean on the wall to steady myself. I rest one hand over my racing heart and grin to myself. I want to scream, but I don't want to frighten anyone. So, I settle for giggling to myself, one hand cupped over my mouth.

Valentina is not going to take the death of her granny well. After my own experiences with grief, I wouldn't wish that on her despite all the foul shit she's done to me. When I first cast the Scales of Justice, I had no idea Lenora's death would be the outcome. Valentina may be wicked, but this was bigger than her, and I never wanted her to experience that kind of pain.

I'd be unwise not to consider the cost of my justice. Valentina and I will never be friends again, and I don't regret casting the Scales of Justice, but I sincerely hope she can find a way to heal.

Besides, I have much bigger mountains to topple than Valentina Savant.

The moment we emerge from the underground tunnels, Ursula's phone rings. She hangs back to take the call, which sounds urgent.

"She asked to meet you? What does she want?" She turns her

back when she sees me watching. "I'm wrapping up something right now, but I can be there by morning." Her voice fades as she steps away to speak in private.

I'm too high off what just happened to get sucked into any more drama. Instead, I float on clouds all the way out of the cathedral, across the dark grounds, and to the car.

Magic has sparked to life inside me again, and I can feel its pulse in sync with mine, like a second heartbeat. It's powerful. And amazing.

My family has taken back our legacy.

My mother, Marie Trudeau, is Queen.

And I'm next.

FORTY-FOUR
VALENTINA SAVANT

GRANNY

Hi Granny! Are you home? I'm on my way over.

I need to talk. If that's okay.

U there?

Hey. I'm at your house. I forgot my spare key at home, so I'm sitting on the porch.

Sorry! I don't mind though.

I just needed to get out of that house.

Will you be back soon?

I tried calling, but your phone went straight to voicemail.

I'm getting worried.

Is everything okay?

Granny.

Please answer me.

GRANDPA FELIX

Hey Grandpa. Is Granny with you?

And are you home?

I've been texting and calling but she won't answer.

Can one of you please just call or text back?
I'm getting really worried.

GRANNY

Please answer me.
I know I messed up big time and you're probably still mad at me but I'm really sorry.

It's midnight and I'm still sitting on your porch. Where are you?

Hello???

FORTY-FIVE
CLEMENT

This summer was one I'll never forget.

I met and lost the love of my life.

I helped a necromancer raise a small army from the dead.

My sister and I snatched Mama from death's grip, and she clawed her way back to her throne.

And our aunts have all moved back home, with the exception of Desiree, who's now engaged to Michael Prince. But at least they've all begun to heal—something I thought could never happen. Things are almost like before.

Except I'm not really there.

Thanksgiving is coming up soon. But I'm still not ready to go back. Jean-Louise said I can spend as much time here as I need, as long as Mama agreed, which she did, though she made it clear she preferred me home. Despite that, she and Cris are both giving me much-needed space.

I do miss my sister. I want to tell her the truth about why I'm spending so much time here, but I can't. For now, this will have to be my secret. Mine and Jean-Louise's.

I sit on the old couch in the living room, which has begun to contour to the shape of my ass. A copy of *Invisible Man* sits on one side of me, but I haven't been in the mood to read for a while now. I haven't felt up to doing much of anything lately. I've cried myself to sleep so much that my body has come to expect that release in order to shut off at night.

Dad's knife presses against my thigh from inside my pocket. I'm forever glad to have his memories close to me, but like my books, it also provides little comfort these days. I take the knife out of my pocket, set it on top of the book, and turn on the television.

I switch the channel to the news, just in time to watch the mayoral election results. A banner scrolls across the bottom of the screen, congratulating Benjamin Beaumont, our newly elected mayor. He's a giant of a white man with beady brown eyes, a stubby nose, and curly ash-brown hair.

He stands behind a podium outside City Hall with his wife, Eveline, by his side. Her face beams with excitement and her eyes flit from side to side as she smiles and waves. Ben raises his hands and leans in to the mic to give his acceptance speech.

"I am humbled and honored to represent my beloved city of New Orleans as the fifty-first mayor. I'm greatly looking forward to working with each and every one of you to preserve the history and integrity of this wonderful city. A summer marked by political unrest has inspired my foremost order of business as mayor. Starting my first day in office, I will work to draft a bill to regulate special-interest groups, with distinct focus on magical cultures, which will be governed by the Magical Regulation Bureau. The bureau will operate out of my office and will be led by none other than my wife, Eveline Beaumont." He turns with a wide grin, and steps aside for his wife to take his place at the podium.

The crowd cheers, but quiets as Eveline leans toward the mic. "It is more than an honor for me to accept the position as chief of the Magical Regulation Bureau. I am excited and ready for the challenge of regulating magical sectors of society and keeping New Orleans safe for all our citizens and visitors for the foreseeable future."

My stomach flips upside down, and I turn off the television to head off the nausea that's surely coming if I listen to another word. I don't know what Eveline Beaumont is up to, but I have more important shit to worry about.

"I still can't believe I figured it out," I say. "I've been thinking about it for a while, but now I'm sure. The meaning of life is human connection. Everything about our lives, what we do, what we say, how we think—all of it is linked to the actions, words, and thoughts of others. It's what drives us.

"We're here to interact with one another, across the broad spectrum of all the different, innumerable ways living beings can. We're born through interaction and sometimes die because of it. It all fits. . . . I know, because of what I did . . . to you. I just hope one day you'll be able to forgive me for it."

A single tear streams down Yves's face. His eyes are no longer portals to another world; instead they've become dead and empty, like pure darkness.

He lays his head on my shoulder, and I take his cool hand in mine. I'm not letting anyone leave me ever again.

"I'm going to fix this," I whisper. "I'll bring you back. I swear."

He squeezes my hand.

EPILOGUE

JEAN-LOUISE PETIT

Jean-Louise had never felt power like what he'd experienced a few months ago aboard the *Montaigne Majestic*. It had surged through him with the force of a hundred lightning bolts. He needed to feel that rush of magic again, to float on that cloud of euphoria, to reach levels he'd never achieved before.

Perhaps if he enhanced his abilities, he could bring Auguste all the way back. Maybe Yves, too.

The boy was right. He needed to help Auguste or let him go, and he wasn't ready to let go yet. Clem had reminded Jean-Louise why he'd fought so hard to hold on to Auguste in the first place. That kid could be more annoying than a swarm of gnats on a muggy summer day, but all things considered, he wasn't that bad to have around sometimes. Without him, Jean-Louise might've spent the rest of his days imprisoned in the house with his guilt and a fraction of his former lover to torment him until fate flushed his poor, damned soul to the never-realm. But there was still a chance he could help them both.

It was settled, then. Jean-Louise had to go to the Kahlungha.

He sat on the edge of his bed with a mortar and pestle, grinding up four white pills. Oxycodone. The wonderful thing about prowling the darker streets of a magical underground world was he got to connect with people who could get him anything.

Even fifty cadavers.

Once he produced a fine white powder, he set it aside and went to the bedroom door, which stood ajar. He listened for a moment. The sound of the television floated up the stairs. Clem was still there . . . with Yves. His heart felt like a lead weight in his chest. He'd regretted bringing the boy back as soon as he'd done it, but he couldn't have turned Clem away, not after seeing the look in his eyes.

It was too familiar.

Clem reminded Jean-Louise so much of himself when he was younger. A pure soul tarnished by the shit life kept spewing up. Trauma has a way of transforming kids, hardening them from the inside out. Something drove him to want to protect Clem, to polish him back to the brilliance he deserved. Maybe it was love. He wasn't sure. He hadn't felt anything close to that since before Auguste died.

He shut the door and sat back on the bed. He popped open a vial, which held a deep purple concoction he'd whipped up that morning. It was a creation of Auguste's that he'd improved upon in the past couple of weeks. He transferred the crushed pills into the potion, shook it up, and drank it.

After a few minutes, his head swam, and his vision sparkled and blurred. His eyes closed, and he fell back onto the bed, but his soul kept falling, separate from his body. Through the floor, the ground, hurtling through the dark of space.

The soft sound of low waves hitting the shore woke him.

He stood up in a bleak world with inky black sand beneath his feet. Something resembling the Moon hung in the blank sky, bathing the beach in subtle light.

He looked around but paused with a start.

He wasn't alone.

A dark figure sat a few hundred feet away, just at the edge of the water. Jean-Louise called out, but the person didn't turn around. He jogged closer and stopped nearby. The abnormally large man's skin was dark as the sand beneath their feet, and he sat naked in front of a pile of sticks, like he'd given up halfway through building a fire.

"Hello," Jean-Louise said tentatively.

"Not you." Without turning, the man spoke in a deep, rumbling voice, barely above a whisper.

"I'm sorry?"

"Where is the boy? He is who I want. Not—you."

"Who are you?" asked Jean-Louise.

With his back still turned, the man flashed the underside of his right wrist. A mess of splotchy, glowing white scar tissue shone there against his shadowy skin; long, deep gashes, as if some animal had clawed the flesh from his arm. Jean-Louise's eyes widened, and panic ran amok inside him.

A god. He shouldn't have come here.

The man stood slowly and turned around. His blank face stared, from a towering height, down at Jean-Louise, who froze, trembling from head to toe.

"Hmm . . . you reek of his scent." The man's dark tongue snaked out of his mouth to lick his dark lips, and his face split into a grin so wide it looked as if his jaw separated from the rest of his head. His haunting smile revealed several rows of jagged teeth that reminded Jean-Louise of diamonds dipped in the Stars that had been stolen from the blank sky above them. "You shall take me to him."

A coldness gripped Jean-Louise in the center of his chest.

He turned and ran.

Sand shifted underfoot as he sprinted. He panted and pushed harder, faster.

But he wasn't fast enough.

He slowed. Stopped.

And fell to his knees, caught.

It was foolish to think he could outrun a god.

ACKNOWLEDGMENTS

While the magic system of *Blood Debts* was inspired by Voodoo, the names, spells, histories, etc. are all fictional and meant for entertainment purposes only. The real-life practices of Afro and Afro-Latinx rituals are sacred within our communities and should always be treated as such. I'm deeply appreciative of the ancestors who've paved the way for me to have the privilege of telling this story.

To my husband, Kevin, it's incredible that you supported, uplifted, and encouraged me consistently throughout my eight-year, seven-manuscript journey to finding an agent and then the long (and incredibly busy) road to publication and never once doubted me. Thanks for being a great husband and father. This one's for us!

To my son, Aiden—you're probably wondering why your name is here since you rarely let me work on *Blood Debts* in peace; however, I want to thank you for giving me a reason to put work down and live in the moment—with you. Daddy loves you.

To my agent, Patrice Caldwell—thank you for changing my life. You were the first person to give me a chance. And then the first person to genuinely fight for me. You are the Olivia Pope of publishing and the perfect example of why having the right agent makes all the difference. I'm eternally grateful to you. We did it!

To my absolutely brilliant, rock-star editor, Ali Fisher—after we talked for the first time, I got off the phone and called Patrice and said, "Oh, my god! I love Ali so much!" And since that day, that feeling has only grown stronger. I had the time of my life making magic with you. It meant so much to me how much care and thought you put into this project and these characters and staying true to the heart of the story I wanted to tell more than anything. Thank you so much for believing in me and always pushing me to be my best self. I appreciate that (and you) more than you'll ever know.

To Lesley Worrell, cover designer extraordinaire, thank you so much for your patience and thoughtfulness and dedication to my vision and this project. To my cover artist, Khadijah Khatib, I will forever be grateful to you for the beautiful way you brought Cris and Clem to life, which was so very important to me. I couldn't have dreamed of a better cover team—I appreciate you both.

To Trinica Sampson, Kristin Temple, Dianna Vega, Ashley Spruill, Saraciea Fennell, and Eileen Lawrence—thank you all for your genuine love and support, hard work, and patience with my many, many questions and emails.

To Veronica Vega, thank you so much for your thoughtful and detailed sensitivity read of *Blood Debts*.

Many, many thanks to the best film team ever: Pouya Shahbazian and Katherine Curtis. I'm honored to partner with you two on this incredible journey. I'm looking forward to seeing where we go from here!

My agent might have been the first person to give me a chance, but my mentor, Bree Barton, was one of the first people to believe in me. After so many years of fighting for my life in the query trenches, I never imagined that I'd be chosen for anything. But the day I met you through Author Mentor Match, I not only got a kick-ass mentor, but also a very good friend—the best part. Thank you for always believing in me and guiding me with honesty and love and care. I love you!

To my informal mentor, Anica Rissi—I don't know where I'd be without your thoughtful and patient guidance, especially when you so often intercepted me mid-crisis, lol. Your love and support have meant the world to me; the only thing dearer is your friendship.

Jamnia! We made it, bitch! Naseem, you've read so many different versions and drafts and scenes and snippets of *Blood Debts* that I think I might owe you reparations, lol. The world is so much better with you and your words in it, and I'm so happy to call you one of my best friends.

To my bunny, the Tankette, Adam Sass, thank you for always believing in me and giving me the gift of belly laughs every single day—they're always appreciated. This journey to publication has been so much more pleasant with one of my best friends by my side.

To my friend and work wife, Nic Stone, I'll forever be grateful for how you've loved and shown up for me genuinely since day one. You're a real one. I love you now and always.

Liesa Abrams, your words of advice on everything from sex positivity in YA lit to the horrors of parenting a tiny screaming human will always remain with me. Your work and influence in publishing is legendary, and my life has been forever impacted by your presence in it. Thank you for being you.

To my mom, Shirley—all those trips to the library every summer and helping me tote armfuls of books back to the car for Summer Reading Club seems to have paid off, huh? Thank you for your guidance and instilling in me the importance of education and reading at a young age. I love you.

To my mother-in-law, Joan, your love and belief in me helped light my way on many a dark path on this publishing journey, and this author can hardly string together the words to express how much that (and you) has meant to me.

To Domonique Bouldrick, we walked through hell and back together, and I'd do it again if it'll end with us as friends. Thank you for always showing up for me and believing in me and celebrating me and with me.

To Le'Marus Young—remember when we were sitting on the couch in that AirBnB in Rosemary Beach, Florida, and I pitched the first season of this show called *Queen*, about a group of Black witches fighting to control a magical throne? At that time, neither of us had any idea that would turn into *Blood Debts*, but I did it! And I cherish every happy hour conversation we had at Alma Cocina after work, where for so many years, you listened to my dreams about finally breaking into publishing. Turns out it was time well spent. Thank you for always believing in and loving me.

To Ashton Tuggle, you've been on this road with me for a very long time, my friend. Thank you for not jumping out the window, even when the road got really rough. I love you, friend.

Thank you to all my Critique Avengers and everyone who read an early version of *Queen* and/or *Blood Debts* and offered feedback or love, particularly: Faridah A., Ashley A., Alex H., Ashanti I., Adiba J., Amalie J., Jo L., Caitlin L., Tara L., Myk M., Amanda M., Sarah N., Mark O., Kathy P., Jamar P., Alex S., Morgan R., Pamela W., Emily W., and Brendon Z.

To the entire team at Tor Teen and Macmillan, from our very first interaction, everyone has always made me feel supported and appreciated, and it has truly been a dream come true to work with each of you. I hope we get to make plenty more magic together!

* President of TPG & Tor Teen Publisher: Devi Pillai
* Chairman/Founder of TPG: Tom Doherty
* Marketing lead: Anthony Parisi
* VP, Director of Marketing: Eileen Lawrence
* Publicists: Saraciea Fennell and Ashley Spruill
* VP, Exec. Director of Publicity: Sarah Reidy
* SVP, Associate Publisher: Lucille Rettino
* Production Editor: Megan Kiddoo
* Production Manager: Steven Bucsok
* Interior Designer: Heather Saunders
* Jacket Designer: Lesley Worrell
* Publishing Operations: Michelle Foytek
* Copy Editor: Terry McGarry
* Proofreaders: Melissa Frain and Laura Apperson

Thank you to everyone who blurbed, reviewed, or shared *Blood Debts*. And thank you to the readers, without whom I would have no purpose.